BOOK ONE OF THE

HOW TO
BREAK
A
PARADOX

RUTHANNA WITTER

Carpenter's Son Publishing

To my parents, Aunt Debbie, "Uncle" Dave, and Elizabeth C.
You believed in me from the very start.
And to God, the Author.

How to Break a Paradox

©2018 by Ruthanna Witter

Published by Carpenter's Son Publishing, Franklin, Tennessee

Published in association with Larry Carpenter of Christian Book Services, LLC
www.christianbookservices.com

Cover and Interior Design by Suzanne Lawing

Edited by Robert Irvin

Printed in the United States of America

978-1-946889-09-6

PROLOGUE

Flat Top Mountains, Colorado. Bear's Claw Lodge.
Thursday, July 12, 3:28 A.M.

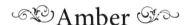Amber

They'd found me. Again. But this time, they were here, actually here! I should have run at the first sign. Letting the curtains fall back, I stumbled away from the window. The deep darkness of the room closed in, threatening to crush me. My hands were trembling uncontrollably. I couldn't catch my breath. *No. No, no, no! This can't be happening. It's only been two months. How did they find me?* I shook my head, scattering the frantic thoughts before they could cripple me. *I'll figure that out later.*

Focusing on calming my panicked breathing, I tried to get ahold of myself; an anxiety attack would seal my doom. I had to look at this logically. Plan A: hide. A quick scan of the room revealed what I already knew. There was hardly any furniture and the closet would be the first place they'd look. Alright, then. Plan B: escape. There appeared to only be two options: the door and the window.

A glance through the glass told me they had left the cover of the trees. They were probably already inside the building. I was trapped. If I went out the door, I'd walk right into them. The window was high. I wasn't sure I could make the jump unscathed. But it was my only chance.

I had to leave everything. There was no time. But I would still have my life, my freedom, and my laptop: the three things my midnight visitors would do anything to take from me. Grabbing my computer bag, I turned toward the window and froze. I didn't know where to go. Confident that I was safe here, I'd never settled on a plan. My brain churned. *I'll continue my path west. No more rural hideaways. I need to disappear in the crowds …* California. *Yes, California. They won't easily find me among the masses. And if they do, I can escape along the coast.*

Unlatching the window, I flung it open, leapt out, and hit the ground—stumbling and falling hard. The moonlight cast a ghostly glow over the landscape, covering me in dangerously bright, silver light. As fast as I could, I was up and running. Running away from mountains, away from Colorado, and toward the Golden State, I melted into the night like a living shadow.

The intruders rushed up the stairs, broke down the door, and searched the room. When they discovered their prey was missing …

An armed young man approached his superior.

"قفز وا من النافذة" Sir, Laelaps is not here. "يا سيدي، العلبس ليس هنا" They jumped out of the window. "ال يوجد أي للكمبيوتر علامة" There is no sign of the computer. "ما هي أوامرك لنا؟" What are your orders for us?

There was a pause. Without a hint of emotion, the superior spoke.

"وسنحاصرهم مرة أخرى، ولكن هذه" We will track them down. "سنعقبهم" We shall corner them again, but this time, we المرة سوف نقبض عليهم" We shall corner them again, but this time, we will catch them. "وعندما نمسكهم، سوف نحمي هذا العلبس" And when we catch them, we will obliterate this Laelaps.

CHAPTER 1

Santa Barbara, California. The Salt Breeze
Apartment Complex, Apt. 1307
Saturday, July 14, 7:45 A.M.

Jordan

BEEP! BEEP! BEEP! BEEP! BEEP!

Groaning, I rolled over and blindly smacked my alarm clock for the fourth time. It was getting truly annoying, yet it didn't occur to me to simply turn it off; I had an inexplicable sense that I didn't need to get up today. Just as I drifted off again, it alarmed for the fifth and last time. *That does it.* Its dreadful screeching was cut short as I pulled its plug from the wall.

Two hours later, I was awakened by the sun shining through the glass balcony doors at the other side of my room. *Come on Jordan,* I scolded myself. *You can't sleep forever. People will start to worry.* This, at last, forced me out of bed. I sat on the edge for a minute, wondering what day of the week it was, mentally groping for my brain's "on switch." It was going to take some work to jump start my memory. So, I started with what I could find.

Let's see, yesterday—no, the day before that—I went to the library. I think I checked out twelve books. Yes, that was the day. And after that I came back here to meet up with Matt, Dylan, and Chloe. (My social circle, and closest friends.) *We meet on Thursdays after work ... OK, so yesterday was Friday, and that means today's ...* I smiled, and my mind whirred to life. *Saturday.*

Suddenly, getting up and facing the day didn't seem so bad. The weather reports had been saying there would be high winds all weekend. Wind means waves, and waves mean great surfing. Eagerness helped boot me out of bed. I darted around, getting ready for the day. Pulling on a T-shirt with the slogan "I'm So Board, Let's Go Surfing," orange swim trunks, and the floppiest pair of flip-flops I owned, I hurried on, already feeling the distant pull of the tide.

Surfing is the best thing in the world. Nothing compares to being swept up to the top of a glittering, bright blue wave and then peeking over the edge at the water far below. Better yet is the exhilarating feeling of crashing down at the speed of light and skimming over the surface of the water like a well-thrown skipping stone.

A lively, happy tune sprouted in my head, pacing my steps. My surfboard already stood propped by the door; I had waxed it the night before. Only one last task before I hit the beach: breakfast. Humming, I strode into the kitchenette in the corner of my apartment and pulled open the fridge. *Decisions, decisions: Toast or bagel?*

Soon I was racing—more like tripping—down the hall with a bagel stuffed in my mouth and a giant surfboard over my shoulder. Typically, it's not too hard to get my board in the elevator, as long as the car is empty. It wasn't. The ride down was awkward and silent; there was hardly enough room to sneeze.

Eventually, the elevator opened at the ground floor. The tiles reflected the sunlight wafting in from the doors, throwing a warm morning glow over everything. The hum of voices and movement filled the lobby. Summer was in full swing and everyone was out and about; it was a little more crowded than usual. Thankfully, I didn't whack anyone in the face with my board. After some careful navigation and a few apologies—"I'm sorry, sir," "Excuse me, ma'am"—I finally made it out the door.

I love my home, and one of the things I love most is its name: The Salt Breeze Apartments. I could actually smell the salt in the air and hear the waves crashing on the shore. Smiling, I sighed. Life was good. I didn't want anything to change; I couldn't imagine things any better. *Enough dreaming. The beach is calling!* Tearing across the street toward the beach, I followed the path over the golden sand dunes. As I caught sight of the huge waves and endless shining sea, I knew it was going to be a fantastic day. All seemed perfectly picturesque.

Little did I know, my life was about to change, for better or for worse. There would be no going back.

CHAPTER 2

Santa Barbara, California. Somewhere
near The Salt Breeze Apartment Complex
Saturday, July 14, 7:00 A.M.

⸎Amber⸎

When I was a teen, I decided that driving was terrible. My skills were borderline bad and I was easily frightened; the highway was my enemy. These days, I drove only when I was fleeing for my life. Therefore, I was a little rusty. Being behind the wheel automatically filled me with stress. And I had been behind the wheel for almost two days straight. My disappearing act left me with horribly sore legs, exhaustion from the adrenaline drop, and, in my haste, I even strayed off course. My phone was not only dead, but rendered useless by the rental car's shorted-out charging port. Until I charged my mobile, I didn't have a navigation system. So I ended up fighting with an actual, physical, folding paper map—which was another weak point for me.

When I lost my way for the fourth time, I pulled off the road to finish planning my route. After scrutinizing the vague map, I soon had a general idea of where I was. *OK, I'm not totally lost.* I tapped on the paper, absentmindedly humming to myself. *I'm here. The web page said the apartment is on Driftwood Avenue, which is …* I traced my finger across the roads marked on the page. When I found it, I sighed miserably and let my head fall to the steering wheel. *Driftwood Avenue is nowhere near here.*

It took a discouragingly long time to find the place. Gathering my frayed nerves, I parked and walked to the lobby to check in. Thankfully, the reservation had held, and the apartment was mine.

"Welcome to The Salt Breeze Apartments, sweetie!" the lady behind the front desk exclaimed as she handed me my room key card. "My name is Beatrice, but everyone calls me Betty. What's your name, Sugah?"

I could hear a hint of the South in her voice. How one could hold on to their southern accent while living in western California, I had no idea. Betty seemed to be in her mid-thirties. With a sandy blonde braid falling over her shoulder and a trail of freckles across her cheeks, I could imagine her sipping sweet tea while relaxing on a sun-soaked oakwood porch.

"Amber. Amber Gibson," I replied. I forced a tired smile. "Thanks."

Usually I notice a few warning signals before I have to flee Teumessian, the terrorist organization my midnight visitors were from. But they took me by surprise in Colorado and there was no time to get the papers for a false identity. So, here I am. Amber Marie Gibson. The real me. At least I had a fake death certificate in Maryland. I decided that was enough cover for now. After all, terrorists don't hunt dead people. As I turned to leave, Betty called after me.

"And welcome to California, darlin'!" I stopped in my tracks and slowly turned around, making sure my face showed confusion and not fear.

"How did you know that I'm new to California?" I asked carefully. Betty chuckled.

"Well, for starters, honey, you must be baking in that sweatshirt. Cold is practically nonexistent here during July. I'm guessing you only just arrived. Also, people usually look at an apartment before they rent it long term. You reserved yours online without having seen it and paid three months' rent." She paused to size me up. "Then there's the fact that you aren't sunburned in the least. You're not even tan." Seeing the blank look on my face, she said, "It's summer, sweetheart, and it's like eighty-five degrees outside. Everyone's either waist deep in the ocean or loafing in front of the television."

I stared at her for a moment, a look of shock on my face. Slowly, I nodded, feeling foolish. After a pause, I turned and walked away, making a mental note to work on my invisibility skills. I secretly nicknamed Betty "Sherlock."

I trudged back to my car to grab my things. Since I made sure to get a place that was already partly furnished, I didn't have to worry about buying anything big. I did, though, pick up some secondhand necessities along the way; it would be conspicuous to arrive at a new place with no luggage whatsoever. With a suitcase in each hand, a computer bag over my shoulder, and a backpack on my back, I waited for the elevator to reach the fourteenth floor. It opened to an empty hall with pale yellow and green wallpaper, the walls lined with doors. Looking to the odd-numbered side, I searched for my new home. *1401, 1403, 1405 … 1407.* I came to a stop. *Well, this is it.*

When the door opened, I came to a stunned halt. It was beautiful! Letting the door swing closed behind me, I kicked off my shoes and walked in a daze to the main bedroom. Dumping my luggage on the bed, I noted everything seemed to be aglow. Turning, I discovered why. The sun shone through the crystal clear balcony doors, and the light was bouncing off the bright turquoise walls. Pulling on the handle, I slid open the glass and stepped out onto the worn, wooden platform. There was a rope hammock swaying in the breeze, a singing wind chime, and a lovely ocean view peeking over the tops of neighboring buildings. Reluctantly, I returned to the air-conditioned room and began to explore.

Everything appeared to be made of driftwood, shells, or granite, a rustic but charming look. Built into the wall beside the door was a TV with a green, three-seat couch in front of it. Beyond the couch, in the far corner, was a kitchenette, complete with a refrigerator, microwave, and stove hemmed in by a little counter. I couldn't cook to save my life, but in the unlikely event that I learned, the kitchen would prove to be useful.

Down a short hall was a spare bedroom that resembled the main one. Further still was a study room. There was an oak desk, a chest of drawers, and a tall, empty bookshelf begging to be filled with novels, atlases, and sketchbooks brimming with art. Lastly, there was a small bathroom. An oval mirror adorned with seashells, hanging above the sink, caught my eye. I stared at its surface, then beyond at the girl behind the glass. *I am such a mess. And Betty is right: this heat is unbearable. Yes, this sweatshirt has to go.* Pulling it over my head certainly didn't improve the untamable mess I call my hair, but I couldn't have cared less. Wandering back to the main room and flopping on the couch, I finally allowed the exhaustion to catch up with me. I fell into a shallow, dreamless sleep . . .

I woke up famished. My last meal was yesterday morning, and according to the clock, I had been asleep for a little less than an hour. With no chance of continuing my nap on an empty stomach, I started toward the fridge. But before I was halfway there, I stopped and groaned. There wasn't any food. I hadn't bought any yet.

After a moment of brutal inner scolding, I headed for the bedroom, feeling frustrated yet undaunted. Grabbing my keycard from the dresser, I turned to my computer bag, which had all my "irreplaceables." After digging past my laptop, a timeworn USB stick, tangles of wires and circuit boards, my sketchbook/journal, and driver's license, I pulled my credit card from the bottom of the bag, stuffed it in my pocket, and slid into my shoes. *I think that's everything. I hope this doesn't take long. There must be a grocery store around here somewhere.* When the elevator reached the lobby, I strode to the front desk.

"Betty, do you know of any grocery stores around here?" I asked hopefully.

Her face lit up. "Well, there's a shop within walking distance. Down the road a bit and to the right. About half a block away," she said. I nodded and started to turn, but then she began to digress. "I know the owners, real nice folk. They run a good business, you know? Unlike most shops, they don't mark the prices way up because of all the tourists. Come to think of it, I haven't spoken with them in a while. Tell 'em I said hello, would ya? Oh, you shoulda seen it. It was last year when there was this … "

I suffered silently for at least eight minutes, then finally managed to get a word in edgewise.

"OK, thanks Betty! I'll be back later. Bye!" I turned decisively and headed for the door. I didn't mean to be rude; I just needed some peace and quiet in the midst of this tiring day.

I strolled down the sidewalk and gazed up at the bright baby blue afternoon sky. The wind was warm; it was a pleasant day to say the least. It didn't take long to find the little store, and I was done in no time. *Alright, that wasn't so bad.* Four large bags of food dragged me down, though, and what was originally a short walk became an arduous trek. By this time, the sun was glaring down from high in the sky and the warm wind had turned hot. Sighing, I frowned at the shimmering pavement. *I miss cold, sleety, snowy Colorado.* Despite myself, I let out a pathetic chuckle at this. *That's just sad. Cold? I really am sleep deprived.*

CHAPTER 3

*Santa Barbara, California, the beach across the road
from The Salt Breeze Apartment Complex
Saturday, July 14, 1:14 P.M.*

Jordan

I was bored. There hadn't been any good waves for about ten minutes. The stillness was dragging on far too long. I gave up watching the water, and with my back to my surfboard and my surfboard to the sea, I stared up at the sky, trying to imagine creatures in the few shapeless clouds floating overhead. *This is pointless,* I eventually admitted to myself. *If there isn't a wave in one minute, I'm heading in.* Sighing, I started counting in my head. *One, two, three …*

Then, with thirteen seconds to spare, it finally happened. "Outside! Outside!" I heard the other surfers shouting as a few began paddling toward the shore. I smiled. The warning. Whenever a larger-than-normal wave forms, surfers yell "Outside!" to alert others it's about to break.

Sitting up and swinging my board around, I glanced behind me; my mind balked. This was the kind of wave that formed in the midst of a hurricane. And I was right in its path. For a moment, I simply gawked at it, the way a deer stares enchanted at the blinding light from oncoming headlights. By the time I snapped out of my daze, it was almost too late. I would be crushed … There were only two choices: bail and still risk getting crumpled like a can, or, be crazy and try to surf this monster. I chose the latter. Just as the wall of water yanked me up to throw me over the edge, I shot forward and took the drop.

In an instant, I was on my feet, fighting for balance while weaving across the face of the wave. Gathering speed, I headed for the peak. Breaking the crest, I flicked my board under my feet. It flipped like a coin along its length, and I landed back on top. A kickflip! I quickly regained my balance. *Alright. Let's try something harder.* Aiming the nose of my board up the wave again, I spun it, turning it like a Frisbee—a full 360 degrees—and landed safely once more. A "shove it." Suddenly, intense concentration gave way to elation, and a huge grin spread across my face. *That was, undoubtedly, the best wave of the day.* As I rode to the shore, I noticed a little kid watching me. His eyes tracked my every movement, and the moment I stepped onto the sand, he came running, a tiny surfboard trailing behind him.

"Mister, how did you do that?! That was so cool … even my big brother can't surf like that! I mean, he can do some tricks, but not like yours. If I could surf like that, maybe I could surf the big waves with him!" I smiled.

"Do you think you could surf like that?" I asked.

He shook his head. "No, I don't think so. I'm not very good. But I want to! I really do!"

I knelt to his level. Looking straight into his huge eyes, I simply said: "Well, I think you could. Don't give up. You'll be surfing waves bigger than that like a pro in no time." A smile spread across his face. Nodding enthusiastically, he turned and scampered toward the sea. I watched him go, then headed my way. It was lunchtime, and I was starving.

The encounter with the kid made my day. I tucked away the mental image of his wide-eyed, serious face and bright smile. Since my brain was fully awake, I was feeling pretty on top of things. All of yesterday's memories were coming back, important or trivial: the time it took to microwave my breakfast, the vague comment Betty made about the weather, the last sentence in my book, and the colors and numbers of umbrellas on the beach. Everything of the slightest importance is permanently etched in my mental library. Forever. I won't lie: my mind is practically my only gift. I might be oblivious and socially awkward at times, but everything about people—their smile, their favorite color, their personality—always stays with me, even if they leave. *Oh, speaking of remembering things—I am soaked, and Betty is going to be less than pleased.* I tried not to be all wet and sandy by the time I reached the lobby.

"Jordan! You better not be … " Betty was always on my case. If I leave a trail of sand behind me, well, guess who gets to clean it up?

"Not this time, Betty. Don't worry about the floor. It's still spotless," I promised.

That seemed to pacify her. I hurried on before that changed. Thankfully, it was no longer rush hour in the lobby, so getting my surfboard into the elevator didn't prove to be as much of a problem this time around. I lugged it back to my room and put it on the balcony to dry off.

Since there wasn't anything particularly appealing in the fridge or cupboards, I decided to hit the stores. There were plenty of choices lining the streets, mostly seafood. There were, of course, typical fast food restaurants, Chinese buffets, and pizza places. But in my mind, the decision had already been made: The Flying Turtle.

Apart from the name, The Flying Turtle was a perfectly normal coffee shop. It was the best one in town and I went there often. It was conveniently close by, reasonably priced, and had the finest coffee in the world. Well, that I knew of. Despite the many times I'd been there, I had yet to learn how it ended up with such a ridiculous name.

There was no point in taking a shower. The ocean hadn't seen the last of me for the day; waves this good didn't come around very often. A dry T-shirt, shorts, and flip-flops later, I was ready to go. For some reason, I was feeling almost excited. *What's gotten into me? I'm just going for lunch. Nothing special is happening today.* With a sense of adventure, I nudged the lobby button on the elevator.

I can see the front doors! Come on, Amber, you're almost there. Just a bit more ... It felt like the grocery bags were filled with bricks instead of food. But I had to lift them, because if they dragged on the ground, the plastic would wear thin and break; if I let them hang by my sides, my legs knocked them around. So I ended up holding the bags in my arms like the precious cargo they were. There had to be a better way of doing this. I just couldn't think of it.

There was a brief fight between the front doors and me, but eventually I won. Surprisingly, Betty hardly looked up when I came in. She seemed preoccupied, and there was no reason to disturb her. Keeping my head down, I made my way to the elevator. After a short struggle, I managed to elbow the up button.

I was anxious to get back to my room, have lunch, and sleep for a week. Or perhaps I would only sleep for a day, and then be motivated and do some sketches. The whirring of the elevator quietly sliding down to earth was a lovely sound. When it stopped, without lifting my head, I strode forward … and ran smack into someone.

Down went the grocery bags, and out came all the popsicles, oranges, water bottles, and frozen dinners. Something inside me snapped. I looked up and gave a withering glare to the offender, but then stopped. I saw a look of surprise and remorse in the deep emerald eyes that met mine. He looked genuinely sorry, and my conscience pinched me with a twinge of guilt, urging me to hold back my temper. I decided not to tear him to shreds. At least, not yet …

Good job, Jordan. You just messed up big time. I peeked up. Behind the curtains of sandy brown, reddish hair, two fiery, tawny eyes were glaring at me with enough malice to kill. Despite her petite stature, I still got the sense she could knock me flat. *Oh no. She's mad. I'm not good at this kind of thing.* I took a deep breath. *OK, here goes.*

"I … I am so sorry. I am so sorry, I wasn't looking—I should have—oh, I'm sorry." I blundered through an apology as I tried to help scoop up the oranges strewn across the floor. Her glare seemed to soften a little as she helped gather the remaining items.

I looked up. From my position, I could see Betty's raised eyebrows and amused grin. Evidently, this was quite entertaining for her. I wasn't going to hear the end of this one for a while. I turned my attention back to the dilemma at hand.

"I'm sor—" She cut me off.

"You can stop saying sorry now," she said quickly, a slight bite in her voice, as if trying to make me shut up. At this, I felt rather exasperated. *She doesn't have to be so sour about it. It's just as much her fault as it is mine! It's not as if …* This time, I cut myself off. It was the look in her eyes, the tone in her voice; this wasn't the first bad thing to happen to her today. I exhaled the stinging retort that was festering in my lungs and replaced it with something better.

"OK. I won't say it. Though I mean it." With that, I picked up two of the bags from the ground, walked to the elevator, and held the door open with my foot. The look on her face … I thought she would either cry or punch me in the nose.

"What are you going to do with those?" she asked slowly. My answer came with a slight grin.

"I'm going to prove my sorry-ness. Anyway, you shouldn't have to carry so much." After some contemplation, she followed me into the elevator. "Floor?" I asked.

"Fourteen," she squeaked. *She lives on the floor above me. Why haven't I seen her before?*

We rode the elevator in an awkward silence. If someone held a match to my cheeks, it would have ignited; the embarrassment was unreal. *Amber, you know better,* I scolded myself. *He's being really nice; don't be such a jerk.* By now, we were walking down the hallway toward my apartment. Coming to a stop in front of my door, I began to fumble with the key card, desperate to disappear.

"You live directly above me," he said, sounding curious. "But I don't think I've seen you before ... " Without warning, my thoughts froze. All the excuses I'd saved up over the years went right out of my mind. *Does he suspect something? What do I say?* I shrugged:

"I don't know. Guess I don't go out that much." My hands were trembling. *I'm so scared ... Oh, Ashley, I wish you were here.* Pushing the door open, I turned to see him gazing at me curiously. There was a heartbeat in time, then he extended his hand toward me and smiled.

"The name's Jordan." I shook his hand.

"My name's Amber, and thanks for helping me carry my things." Jordan handed back my groceries and gave a little nod.

"Nice to meet you, and don't mention it. Anyone would have done that. I suppose I'll see you around?" At this, I almost frowned. *Why does he genuinely seem to care? Doesn't he have anything better to do?*

"Guess so," I replied, trying to sound nonchalant.

"Great! Well, see ya." With that, he was gone.

The elevator carried Jordan away and I was left alone. It was too easy. He didn't question my excuse, though he probably saw right through my bluff. I knew I couldn't stay invisible forever, but I thought it would last longer than a few hours.

A tiny seed of suspicion was beginning to grow in my mind. For all I knew, this "Jordan" might not be all that he seemed. There were many people who wanted me dead, and he might be one of them. I had to be careful.

Slowly nodding to myself, I considered my course of action. *I'll keep an eye on him. Once I look into his background, I'll know what kind of person I'm dealing with. I have to make sure people won't remember me. That way, when I disappear, no one notices.*

I don't remember her. Could I have forgotten? I frowned. No, no one could forget eyes like hers: *amber* eyes. I'd never seen anything like them. Yet, somehow, I had no memory of her. *No, I didn't forget. There must be something …*

Recalling the faces of all the people who had crossed my path over the years, I tried again and again to find any trace of Amber. Nothing. After reviewing our brief interaction, it hit me. *No wonder I haven't seen her before. She must be new! How strange. Why didn't she just say so?* Curiosity edged into my mind, and I kept pondering why this strange new girl seemed so distant, so mysterious, so … scared.

Surprisingly, most of my food was intact. Apart from a few bruised oranges and broken popsicles, all was well. Soon the perishables were in the fridge and the rest had been shoved into the cupboards. Dumping some pretzels sticks and a water bottle onto the speckled counter, I dropped onto one of the stools and started my lunch.

Before long I remembered my sketchbook and decided to grab it. After messing around with some abstract designs, some intricate patterns of random shapes and lines, I clicked my pen for a minute, bored, trying to think of a title for my little array. Nothing came to mind, so I closed my journal and went back to my snack. Just as I began to make a flower of pretzels, there was a knock at the door. Cautiously, I tiptoed to the door and looked out the peephole. *Jordan? Hasn't he caused enough trouble for one day?* After a second of internal debate, I decided to open it.

"Hey, Amber!" he said, smiling. I regarded him skeptically for a moment.

"What are you doing here, Jordan?" Thankfully, the confused, curious look was gone. He seemed happy. Carefree.

"I was thinking, seeing as I've wrecked your lunch—I was wondering if you would join me for mine."

My brain went blank and words failed me. Finally, I came up with a partial excuse. "I don't know, Jordan. Maybe some other time." Now he looked disappointed.

"Please? I'll buy." Over my shoulder, he caught sight of my snack. "You can't live off pretzels and water."

"It's OK. I like pretzels," I started to explain. All of a sudden, disappointment changed to determination, and he held up a hand to cut me off.

"Before you decide, let me just say: I didn't make a very good first impression, so this is take two. Also, based on your amount of groceries, I guess you don't eat out that much. You basically said so yourself. But that's not why I've never seen you before. You're new here, right?"

I had to work hard to keep from visibly cringing. "Yeah. Arrived in California today," I admitted. Jordan grinned.

"Well then, in that case, you should have a good first day! I can tell it's been a rough one so far, and I only made it worse. So, this is my chance to make it a little better."

A soundless sigh escaped my lips. I didn't have the energy to deal with this. But, there was no gracious way out. I didn't have a reason not to go; he was just trying to be nice, right? Sighing slightly, this time audibly, I nodded.

"OK."

CHAPTER 4

The Salt Breeze Apartment Complex
Saturday, 1:48 P.M.

ᴄᴀ᷎Amber ᴄ᷎ᴀ

It amazes me how the smallest thing can make the biggest difference. The moment "OK" was out of my mouth, Jordan was all smiles. And that's when the endless jabbering began.

"So what brings you to California?" he asked. "Where do you call home?" All of my defenses and walls shot up. Even though these were probably innocent, honest questions, answering might give him too many puzzle pieces as to who I really was. I was tired and off my game; who knew what might slip?

"Guess I just needed a change of scenery. And I believe home is where the heart is, so home is many places for me," I answered cryptically, hoping he would take the hint.

"Well, what are some of your favorites?" Jordan asked, totally missing the cue.

"I don't know. Never thought about it," I mumbled. There was a pause, during which Jordan seemed to be trying to suppress his curiosity. Thankfully, he changed the topic. Well, somewhat.

"What about your family? Do you have any siblings? Or, maybe just a pet. A dog? Cat? Maybe a fish, or a lizard or something?" For a moment, I hesitated. Should I answer? How? This was dangerous information. But, I didn't want to lie. I decided to tell a little.

"I have five sisters and seven brothers. Most of them were adopted, but they're my siblings nonetheless." *Ashley's my only true sister.* "And no, I don't have a pet."

"Oh. OK."

"Do you always ask this many questions?"

"Yes." More silence. "So, what do you do for a living? Do you like it?" Jordan said, seemingly honest in his intrigue. I had to work hard to hide my exasperated sigh, and swore to myself that if I ever got back to my room, I would never leave it again.

"I'm a graphics designer." *Not totally false.* "Some of it's digital, some of it's physical, as in paint and pencils. I wouldn't say 'like.' Love, maybe." *True.* Jordan grinned.

"That must be loads of fun. I don't have an artistic drop of blood in my body, but I wish I did," he said, shaking his head. "Once in sixth grade I drew a picture of my dog for art class. It took hours. I was really proud of it. But when I showed everyone my masterpiece, they all said it was a wonderful hippo, or a pig … I think I shredded it." He chuckled.

"Well, everyone's artistic, just in their own way. You just have to find the right medium." I surprised myself. *Why did I say something so lame?* I wished I could have erased my words—until I noticed Jordan's smile.

"That's a relief. So, does this mean there's still hope for me? Should I try again, or let a dead dog lie and pursue finger painting?" My composure broke within seconds. I couldn't help it. An unexpected giggle escaped from behind my hands, which I had clamped over my mouth. I bit my lip and waited to see how he would react. It seemed to me as though he let out a short, silent sigh of relief. "There we go! So, she smiles! Good, I was beginning to think I broke you."

By now, we had come quite a way. Running to beat the light, we crossed the street, and I saw where we were headed. It seemed to be a coffee shop of some kind. Painted to look like it was built from warm red bricks, it appeared welcoming. (Very little in California is built from real bricks due to the many earthquakes.) The dark cyan umbrella tables complemented the red perfectly; beside the entry were large flowerpots bursting with pink and yellow blossoms. Then there was the name.

"The Flying Turtle? What kind of name is that?" I asked, bewildered. Holding the door open for me, Jordan shrugged.

"I legitimately haven't got a clue."

The inside was just as charming as the outside, with its striped wallpaper, circular tables, chairs made from intricate patterns of iron, and glowing sphere bulbs hanging from the ceiling. Overall, the mood was like a seaside fairytale. After giving some thought to the menu, I made my decision. Jordan kept his promise, though, and intervened before I could pay. We sat down, I sipped my coffee, and he talked.

And talked. And talked. He was happy, like a child at the end of a wonderful day, ready to tell his tales and stories to anyone who would listen.

I don't know how he found time to eat his sandwich, but it disappeared before long. Also, I noticed he paused and closed his eyes for a couple of seconds before digging in. Strange. I brushed it off, chalking it up to the possibility of him being religious or something. Instead of sitting idly, I decided to be productive.

What do I know about him? OK, observe. His name is Jordan, white male, about ... five-foot-eleven, dark green eyes, rather messy dark brown hair, my guess is ... about 27. I don't think he's in the files. At least, not in the ones I've memorized. So, he's not a Level 8 criminal or worse. Seems nice, noticeably polite, happy, considerate ... I don't trust him.

She didn't seem keen on chatting, so I did most of it. It was nice to have someone to talk to, though, to retell the best stories and jokes that everyone else had tired of. I gave up asking loads of questions, though I was dying to. Sometimes I would get a half smile, a stifled laugh, a comment, or the occasional question. But for the most part she simply sat and listened, watching me over the top of her muffin or coffee. It was as if she was trying to stare into my soul, see into my mind. She didn't seem annoyed, amused, bored, unhappy, or pleased. Just ... there. I couldn't read her expression. It was unnerving. So I kept on talking. " ... the Endangered Species Act apparently made it illegal to whack a shark on the nose with a ... "

I couldn't take it anymore. Leaning forward and putting my elbows on the table, I asked, "Where are you right now?"

That caught her off guard.

"What? What's that supposed to mean?" she asked.

"I mean, what are you thinking about? Where's your mind? I'm pretty sure it's not here, so where is it? You've done nothing but observe me from over the rim of your cup for about ... " I glanced at my watch. "Twenty-eight minutes. And you've hardly said a word." She lowered her coffee mug and leaned back a bit. It took a while, but I finally got an answer.

"I can't figure you out," she stated. "You hardly know me, yet you have been quite considerate, despite the fact I'm not the most agreeable person. You helped me carry my things. You not only invited me to lunch, you paid for it. You seem to truly care about me and my interests. I certainly didn't ask for any of this. And you have talked with me for the past twenty-eight minutes. Why?"

"Because it's the right thing to do," I said simply.

For a moment, Amber froze. Her eyes went a tad bigger and she stared at me in shock. Apparently, she wasn't expecting me to say something like that, and was unsure how to respond. And yes, it was the right thing to do. But if I was totally honest, the second reason was that the curiosity was going to kill me. I couldn't figure her out, either. With every minute, the mystery grew. Most of the questions I shot her way came back, stamped "return to sender." The best I got was a vague answer that just made me want to know more. This didn't seem to be going anywhere. Maybe it was time to call it a day.

"Is there actually any coffee left in there?" I asked.

"No," Amber admitted sheepishly. I shook my head and chuckled.

"I take it you're ready to head back?" I offered.

"Yeah."

The afternoon heat met us at the door. I must confess, it was nice listening to someone other than myself or the weather man. But silence would be a welcome change; my energy was at an all-time low. Surprisingly, Jordan kept the conversation level to a bare minimum. Perhaps he sensed my mood. We parted ways at the thirteenth floor. Jordan now seemed especially quiet. As the doors opened, this time I spoke first.

"Thanks," I said quietly. Jordan gave a polite little nod.

"Anytime you want to go again, let me know." Then he grinned. "Does this mean take two was a success?"

I allowed a small smile. "Yes, take two was a success." A grin lit his face.

"Good to hear. See you later."

Before long, the gray silence crept back into my head. It was comforting, yet lonely. The pretzels were forgotten as I booted up my computer and clicked on one of my playlists. Retrieving my sketchbook from the counter, I stepped out onto my "back porch" and started fighting with the hammock. After detangling myself from the ropes a couple times, I eventually won, deciding it qualified as a health hazard.

About half an hour had passed in peace, when all of a sudden, there was a screeching-sliding sound beneath me. I almost jumped out of my skin. Peeking over the edge of my death trap, I could see Jordan's balcony through the cracks between the warped boards below. I watched him grab what appeared to be a surfboard, then scamper back to the door. There was another *screech*, then silence.

Carefully, I sat up and leaned forward to watch the ground far below. Sure enough, within minutes, I saw Jordan running across the street to the beach. I watched him go and absentmindedly flipped my sketchbook open.

If I wasn't watching Jordan pull off marvelous tricks on the water, I was watching my pencil fly across the paper. I finished my drawing, and this time the title came easily. "The Flying Turtle." Turning to the journal part of my notebook, I wrote: "He's actually quite good. Will elaborate more later." Closing the sketchbook, I went back to watching the daredevil. Yet, before long, the annoyingly responsible side of my conscience spoke up. *Time to get to work, Amber. You're not on vacation. You still have a job to do.*

Sighing, I flopped out of the execution net and walked back inside. Sending my music program into the background, I pulled up my secure chat.

Compose > To: Edge > Subject: Moved Again.

Laelaps
Close call in CO. I had to make a break for it. My identity is still safe, though. My new location is Santa Barbara, CA, the Salt Breeze Apartment Complex on Driftwood Avenue, Apt. 1407. Found it?

Edge
OK, got it. By the way, how "close" is close?

Laelaps
Very. Hitmen on site. Could have shot one with a rubber band through the window, that's how close. Can you get me a list of the names of all the people staying in these apartments? If you can, include what room they are in.

Edge
view.attachment.docx[SaltBreezeApartmentComplexResidentList]

Laelaps
Thanks. When you do the general check on my surroundings, be especially thorough on the rooms near mine and let me know what you find. Also, see what you can find about "Jordan Tyler West."

Edge
Jordan Tyler West, the one in Apt. 1307?
What has he done to raise your suspicion?

Laelaps
He's friendly, no threatening air about him; the fact that he's interested at all is a little strange. He might suspect something is amiss. Not yet convinced he's all that he seems, just need to clarify.

Edge
Alright, will see what I can find. Remember, though, I'm only at your beck and call until we get you sorted out. My turn to give orders: you need to lay low until you're cleared. You may set up base, but you may not launch any of your programs or make any attempts to enter Teumessian's database until further notice. Until then, do try and blend in, but keep a low profile. You do realize Jordan is probably just curious, right? Even so, be careful. You're no use to us dead.

Laelaps
Fine. But don't put me on probation for long. We need to find out why Teumessian is interested in *Project Plutonium*. Their intentions are unclear, might be trouble. It's a ticking time bomb, I can feel it. I'll consent for now, though.

CHAPTER 5

The beach across the road from The Salt Breeze Apartment Complex
Saturday, 7:17 P.M.

Jordan

I'm rarely the one to call it a day. Usually it's the lack of waves, food, or time that compels me to return home. But today, it was a lack of energy. Between swimming back and forth from shore to sea and carrying my board all over the place for hours, I was thoroughly exhausted. My board left a stardust trail through the golden-white sand behind me as I towed it along, heading for my little heap of belongings. One step after another, until, suddenly—I almost fell on my face.

"PUFFERFISH—Ow!" For a moment, I hopped about, trying to regain my balance, wondering what cruelly shaped object I had stepped on.

I don't usually take shells home, especially when they almost cripple me, but I could forgive this one. Picking it up, the words murex shell came to mind: they're like conch shells, except with more painful spikes. But they are beautiful. Basically, a blessing gift-wrapped in a cactus. I decided to take it. This was the second look-where-you're-going lesson I'd had today, and once again, my mind returned to the unusual events and the quirky girl I had run into.

Reviewing my conversation with Amber, I turned the few things I knew over in my mind: she had twelve siblings, it sounded like she'd been to a lot of places, she was artsy, new, and living above me. That was about it. *She doesn't seem very keen on talking to me. If she were a book, it would be on the mystery shelf,* I thought, feeling a mixture of slight frustration, determination, and curiosity.

People and books are fantastic. They both have so much in common and so much to tell: epic adventures, loveable people who grow up and change the world, mind-blowingly beautiful places, and stories with happy endings.

My cheerful thoughts were interrupted, though, as I sauntered into the lobby and heard Betty call my name.

"Jordan." I turned to see her regarding me with an unimpressed look on her face, like a teacher expectantly waiting for a guilty student to come forward and receive punishment. Well, I couldn't say I hadn't seen this one coming. Destination: trouble. I made my way over. I didn't stand a chance. "Jordan, I can't believe you! You should be ashamed of yourself, slamming into Miss Gibson like that, not paying attention in the least. As always." Thus began the tongue-lashing. "And that apology of yours was less than adequate. I dearly hope you're gonna think of a better one. Poor girl, she only just arrived. You really need to be more conscientious."

"Miss Gibson?" I asked, but understood the moment the words left my mouth. *So that's her full name. Amber Gibson.* Betty looked exasperated.

"Miss Amber! Goodness, Jordan, it's not like you to be so ignorant. You usually know a person's whole life story within an hour or so," she exclaimed.

"She was really quiet," I started. "I tried to talk with her, but she shut me out. I did my best, Betty, honestly. Cut me some slack, please. I do feel awful." Betty pursed her lips and looked somewhat displeased.

"OK. I believe you." She gave a little laugh. "You're easy to trust. I can tell you're being sincere. Do try to endear yourself to her, though. She needs a friend, and you seem just the kind she needs." I started to agree, but stopped when I noticed her mischievous grin. *Wha …? Hey!* Giving Betty a sideways glance, I ordered her to stay out of it and not to worry, because I intended on doing just that.

Betty means well, always has. She's been like an aunt to me ever since my family left … when they moved up in the world and left me behind. When success calls, people tend to drop everything to follow, even if it's very far away. When I heard we were going to Vegas, I simply refused. Westmont College had just accepted me. Ocean Front Rescue had offered me a job. To leave the sea, my home, my friends, my life and future … how could I? It stung when my parents didn't try to dissuade me. They decided I was old enough to stand on my own two feet without them, but I think the real reason is that they disapproved of me. I've always been a bit of an oddball.

I pretended to be fine, but there was a vast hole in my heart. Dad, Mom, Hunter … Lexie. My angel. My little sis … my wish-come-true. She made me a big brother. Oh, I missed them so much. But I refused to let my insecurity show. I thought my carefree, hurt-free act was seamless—but Betty has some kind of ridiculous radar. The moment I walked up to claim my new home, she was on me like a panther—just with claws retracted and motherly instincts out. She looked out for me, reminded me to not stay up too late, and encouraged me to do my mountain of homework; college wouldn't last forever, she said. She talked with me and listened to me ramble about my day. Still does. *But her attempts at matchmaking are getting annoying. Seriously, this has to stop.* I shook my head. *And think happy thoughts. The past is in the past, and today is sweet but short. Live it while you can.*

Unscrewing the electrical outlet cover usually isn't a good idea. Unless, that is, I'm the one doing it. The phrase "don't try this at home" doesn't apply to me. I spent the rest of my afternoon reassembling my Internet router/generator, and now it was time to power up.

I gazed at the seemingly endless clumps of wires swinging behind the wall. As far as I could see, there were about fifteen power-related cords. Problem was, they were all from different dates and manufacturers. If I chose the wrong one, bad things could happen: death by electrocution, massive explosion, destruction of the electrical grid, fire, maybe more. Occupational hazards. I could cope. After some close scrutiny, I managed to narrow my options to three. Frowning, I brought them forward and pondered. *Alright … which wire should I choose?*

I had just finished getting the salt and sand out of my hair and was shaking it around until it reached an acceptable point of dryness … when I heard something. Standing stock-still and listening intently, I tried to pinpoint where the sound was coming from. It was very faint, but eventually I followed it into the book cave.

I call my study room the book cave. There are maps, documents, calendars, pictures, notes-to-self, my computer, and a library-worthy collection of books. Tape and papers cover the walls, some hidden by stacks of books. Nothing is where it should be. It's a mess.

Something behind the wall was moving. *Swish, scratch, clack, swish, scratch, pause, clack ... repeat.* It's always fun living under someone, to hear the sounds they make and try to figure out what they are doing. But this was something I had never heard before. *It kinda sounds like ... wires?*

Then, two things happened almost simultaneously. First, the power went out with a loud *PZZSTT*, and then I heard the most amusing thing. It sounded like a squealing piglet mixed with a yowling puppy. I don't know how else to describe it. There was a muffled sizzling, then silence. *Well ... that was a cute noise.*

My alligator clip was in flames. The protective coating was melting rapidly, dripping molten plastic on the carpet. For a split-second, my humanity got in the way and I freaked out, shrieking in surprise. I quickly regained control. Yanking the glove off my shaking hand, I started whacking the cord. It hissed and went out. Shoving myself backward, I stared in horror at the smoking wire lying in front of me. Then, adding insult to injury, I realized the power was out. *Oh no.*

Aiming my flashlight at the hole in the wall, I could see the frayed copper strands sticking out of the wires in every direction. *This could take hours to fix! If the maintenance crew traces this to me, I'm done for.*

Countless desperate questions for the Internet later, I managed to bring the power back. Duct tape really can fix anything. Sighing in relief, I sat back. *Glad that's over. Now, only two more choices ... left wire or right wire?*

After about half an hour, the power came back as if nothing had happened. *Strange, what could have caused the outage? And did Amber make that funny little sound?* Just as these thoughts entered my mind, the lights flickered, went off again—and then blazed back to life. I was done asking questions. There didn't seem to be enough answers to go around.

The right wire was not the right wire. In other words, the left wire was the correct one. At least there hadn't been any more fire. Once I was sure there would be no more surprises, I carefully hooked the charred alligator clips to my bizarre contraption. It resembled a cluster of DVD players at strange angles, forming a rough-looking sphere. Blinking lights and flickering panels covered the sides. Atop the final segment sat a small satellite dish, in the center of which was a compact cube of circuit boards suspended midair by a titanium spider web of wires.

Take a moment and try to visualize that. Weird, right?

Taking great care to conceal my contraption beneath an empty cardboard box under the desk, I pulled its USB cord up behind my laptop and plugged it in. *Sorry Edge, but this is one program I always launch.*

```
[19:28:42 INFO]: Initiate Cyber Net Launcher Version 3.7.18
   [19:28:48 INFO]: Checking surrounding networks
   [19:28:49 INFO]: Launching Cyber Net Launcher
   [19:28:49 INFO]: Searching for routers
   [19:28:52 INFO]: Did not find routers
   [19:28:52 INFO]: Placing Cyber Net Launcher on hold
   [19:28:53 INFO]: Launching Central Network
   [19:28:56 INFO]: Central Network is functional
   [19:29:03 INFO]: Initiation complete
                              ~
>"Hello. I am Cyra, an AI created by Laelaps." Awaiting
                          input_
    <Cyra.Command = Site.Monitor: Teumessian.Database
           >Accessing "Teumessian.Database"…
           >Access complete. Awaiting input_
  <(Cyra.Find && Cyra.Stream {Function "ctrl.F"}) Keyword:
       "Project Plutonium" AndOr "مشروع اليريديوم"
                   >Commencing search …
```

In everyday words, Cyber Net Launcher is the program I use to launch my Wi-Fi networks. By using thirty-five signals, my online activity cannot be traced directly back to me. Since I haven't set them back up, though, Cyra didn't find them. Thus, Cyber Net Launcher was put on hold and Central Network was launched. Central Network is my own personal Wi-Fi, the one I use for everyday tasks. By commanding Cyra to "Site. Monitor: Teumessian.Database" and "Find && Stream Keyword: 'Project Plutonium,'" I was basically telling Cyra to go pace outside Teumessian's firewalls and eavesdrop on their conversations. If any mention of Project Plutonium was made, Cyra would tell me.

Sitting back in my chair, I gave a contented sigh. I would assign the routers new pathways tomorrow. Reusing the old pathways would just get me caught. Glancing back over the initiation process, I realized it was nineteen-hundred hours: 7 o'clock. I'd done enough work for one day. Edge would have the background check results by morning, Cyra would monitor information circulating around Teumessian through the night, and I'd get the full rundown from both in the morning.

Throwing a frozen macaroni and cheese packet in the microwave, I pulled out my journal and wrote down the highlights and lowlights of the day's events and the disastrous, daring escape in Colorado. I don't keep a journal so I can look back on my crazy emotional roller coasters. I keep a journal in case anything ever happens to me. At least the police will find it and understand why I do what I do. Or did. Or … tried to do. I didn't want to think about failing. Others could take my place, but still. No one else has a reason like mine.

No one.

Before I'd had my fill of leftover spaghetti, I was ready to hit the sack. I didn't even read a single paragraph in my book or bother to clean up the dishes. Usually I sit on the balcony when I read my Bible each night, but I opted to stay inside, under the covers, in bed, half asleep. I'm afraid it all didn't necessarily sink in, but one verse stuck with me.

> *Always be prepared to give an answer to everyone who asks you*
> *to give the reason for the hope that you have . . .*

While I waited for sleep to find me, I replayed the day in my head. It was like a movie: all the little, monotonous, inconsequential things were left out. I only saw what mattered, and I thanked God for the big and small blessings. *This day goes down in history as one of the best, odd, fun, and exhausting days ever. If I could do it again, I would.* I didn't move, my thoughts became incoherent, my mind shut down, and I drifted to sleep.

He's actually quite good. Will elaborate more later.

THE JOURNAL OF
AMBER MARIE GIBSON

July 14, Saturday

I had to flee Colorado early Thursday morning. Teumessian has never closed in so quickly and accurately; I actually spotted some on site. The only thing I managed to save was my laptop bag. Thankfully, Cyra and most of my important things were already packed and ready to go. I rented a car and gave them the slip. I hope. So, I am in Santa Barbara, California, in the Salt Breeze Apartment Complex on Driftwood Avenue.

The lady at the front desk is named Beatrice, or "Betty," and is a bit of a motor-mouth-Sherlock-Holmes. She deduced that this is my first time to CA. I don't feel that she is a threat; she just seems like ... ah, Sherlock. Still, I'll watch for any suspicious behavior.

"Jordan Tyler West," who lives in the room below mine, is proving to be quite the nosey one. Not only did he realize I must be new, but he also insisted I join him for lunch. Practically interrogated me the whole way there. I'm having Edge run a background check on him, he might be trouble. Teumessian has never actually seen me, but they might have in CO. Jordan could be one of them for all I know. They have spies everywhere. It is going to be entertaining to watch him surf, though, he's actually quite good.

I have successfully launched Cyra. Only Central Network is functional, and I will re-enter the routers and activate Cyber Net Launcher tomorrow. Current focus is *Project Plutonium,* but, nothing to report yet.

Project Plutonium is a series of experiments to test whether or not the full power of the rare element Plutonium can be harnessed. Problem is, handling it can be deadly, it's extremely radioactive, and it has a tendency to spontaneously burst into flames. But if the project succeeds, it could solve the energy crisis. The government is funding it and has invested millions. Failure would be economically devastating. I believe Teumessian might be targeting it.

How Teumessian found me so fast in CO is a mystery. Hopefully I will discover my mistake and correct it. I can't have them finding me like that again.

CHAPTER 6

The Salt Breeze Apartment Complex, Apt. 1407
Sunday, July 15, 7:23 A.M.

Amber

Waking to a buzzing sound in a strange place in a strange bed is, well, momentarily paralyzing. I had no idea where I was. About three seconds later, it all came slamming back to me. Colorado, California, Jordan, Cyra, and … *my phone?* I rolled over to find my phone throwing a temper tantrum, imitating the garbage disposal as it jittered across the bedside table. Grabbing it, I caught glimpse of the caller ID. *Edge?* Hesitating briefly, I answered.

"Hello?" I muttered. My voice was thick from sleep; I cleared my throat. Alas, the damage had been done.

"Are you honestly still asleep?" Edge scolded on the other side of the line. "The background check results have been sitting in your inbox since 6 and you haven't even opened them yet? Get out of bed, chug something with caffeine, and get on with things," he ordered.

I wished he could see me roll my eyes.

"Top of the morning to you too, Edge … " I murmured sarcastically.

"NOW!"

"I'm up, I'm up. Goodness, take it down a notch, will you?"

I punched the End Call button before Edge could lecture me anymore. I hadn't slept in a real bed since Wednesday, just in the back of a public bus or tiny car. Shouldn't that be taken into consideration? *As if Edge would remember.* As I started to get up—too late—I realized I had forgotten about all the tossing, turning, and rolling over, because I almost face-planted trying to step out of bed; the sheets were wrapped around my legs like chains.

I no longer needed coffee. The mini heart attack was motivating enough.

Cyra had nothing new to report and thankfully seemed to have run smoothly through the night. I would clean up the program later; it needed some love. Anyway, I still had to calibrate all thirty-five Internet routers to the machine again. I opened my email, and sure enough, there was a new message sitting in my inbox.

Edge

I checked your surroundings and there isn't too much to report. A few petty thieves and vandals, some gangs, and one scam artist. No fears there. Out of the seventy-eight people on that list (obviously that number doesn't include you, your background is far too colorful for this email) there is only one person of interest. We have a former, but fired, agent from our very own branch of the FBI. For some reason, his crime is "confidential"; all I know is that it was some form of treason. I need to appeal to a higher power to find out more. I don't know what level of trouble he got into; it could be minor or massive. You need to lay low and blend in until I find out more. Better yet, he lives three rooms down from yours. YOU MUST NOT DO ANYTHING UNTIL I CLEAR YOU, ARE WE CRYSTAL CLEAR???
On that happy note, here's what I dug up on Jordan West. You're on the wrong track here. He's done nothing; he hasn't even gotten a parking ticket. But I still included some information to appease you.

The more I read, the sicker I felt. Why had I shunned Jordan's kindness? He really hadn't ever done anything wrong. He was only being nice and I assumed the worst. As I scanned the document, I picked up little things here and there. Birthday, schooling, hometown, a PhD in marine biology. But there was one piece of information that stood out. *His family moved away to Las Vegas when he was nineteen ...* I looked back at his birthday and calculated it had been eight years. Edge had added notes and commentary the whole way through, and his comment for this section was: "No real contact since they left, though he corresponds letters with his little sister. Odd. Why not email or text? Anyway, the only other 'contact' he has with his family is sending birthday and Christmas gifts. Getting the sense they don't really care."

Hearing it all made me realize how wrong I had been. I had been so unfair to Jordan. Despite the actions of his family, he still loved them. From what I had seen, he was genuinely considerate and kind. And he cared about people, truly cared. In that moment, I made a resolution to be kinder to Jordan, to Betty, to all who I may have—and probably will—offend through the years. Yes, even to Edge—to some degree. I laid my head on my desk.

Already, I've made a mess of things, all because of my stupid paranoia. I'll make amends. Then go back to being invisible.

It was a wonderful day to be alive. I woke up to find I had two texts: one from the Ocean Front Rescue group chat and one from Dylan. Ocean Front Rescue was happy to announce that, "Whiskers, the Northern Steller Sea Lion, has survived the night, and will probably continue to do so. He has been cleared to be tagged and released after a couple weeks of rehabilitation."

"Whiskers," or "57NS4SL78," was found by a little girl, who got the honor of naming the sea lion, on Friday afternoon. Whiskers was beached, tangled in fishing line, malnourished, disoriented, sunburned from staying near the surface of the water, and had one flipper in the grave—metaphorically speaking. By the time I got to Ocean Front, everyone was saying Whiskers probably wouldn't make it. But after a few hours of care, various treatments, and buckets of dead fish, Whiskers began to improve. Now it sounded like he was in the clear.

Dylan had texted to inform me that the schedule for the next release had been moved up, and I needed to write the medical report on the whole affair within the next couple of hours; the transmitter/tagging process couldn't begin until I did, and time was running out. That was the only down side; I didn't think I could finish it and get to church on time. At least it was Whiskers and not some shark.

Also, I was teaching a group surfing lesson at noon: age range, 8-12. Those were always the best. Kids are typically eager to learn, and not many have the "my mother made me do this" attitude. It's wonderful to watch people discover something they love, a new and marvelous world to explore—especially when it's surfing.

It's going to be a fantastic day. The sun is shining, the seagulls are screaming, Whiskers is surviving, and I'm gonna teach surfing. I thought about this for a moment. *Wow, that sounded cool, like some sort of poem. Except, it didn't really rhyme.*

I would never admit it to anyone, but I missed my family. The deep, stabbing pain of losing them never subsides. Not many people really know what it's like to be suddenly torn from those you love most, leaving you feeling abandoned and alone. Even if Jordan's situation wasn't the same as mine, he'd doubtless had a splash of the sorrow I swam in. *I should go apologize for my rudeness yesterday. That might be a good place to start.*

It took a while for me to make myself knock on Jordan's door. I had no idea what I would say. When I did finally knock, the wait felt like hours. It was actually only five minutes; it took me that long to figure out he wasn't home.

I slid down the wall and sat there, thinking. *Now what? Should I wait and see if this whole thing will just sort itself out?* After a moment, I shook my head. *No, I'll try again, look somewhere else. I could ask Betty. She might know where he is. And if I can't find him after that, I'll just wait.* This sounded like a good plan of action.

Reaching the lobby, I hesitantly made my way over to Betty. Then I found the flaw in my idea. What was this going to look like? I sincerely hoped Betty didn't gossip, because I was about to give her some serious ammunition.

"Lookin' for something, Miss Amber?" Betty asked. Last chance to chicken out. I took a deep breath and crossed the point of no return.

"Actually, I'm looking for someone. Would you, ah, happen to know where Jordan West is?"

The look she shot my way was an expression I have never seen before. It looked like a cross between an *are-you-kidding-me?* face, an *oh-really?* face, and a hint of a devilish grin. And then there was the blasé mask attempting to cover it all.

"Afraid I don't. Did you check the beach? That would be my first guess."

I should have thought of that. "No, I didn't. Thanks." Betty looked like she wanted to say more, but kept her lips shut. I hurried off, wondering how I managed to get myself into this sort of thing.

I searched the beach, but Jordan was nowhere to be found. Instead of heading back, though, I stood rooted in the sand, looking out over the ocean. It occurred to me that I had never been to the sea before. I was spellbound. The stormy-green waves rhythmically drummed to some unsung aquatic melody. The sun scattered glittering diamonds from horizon to horizon.

Slowly walking toward the water, wondering what it was like, I put my foot beside the recently soaked sand. But I pulled back before the tide could reach me. What was I doing? I shouldn't get my shoes wet. I could come back another day when I was wearing something ocean-worthy. Halfheartedly, I turned away and went back inside. Betty glanced up when I came in.

"Did you find him?"

"No, but it's OK. Is there anywhere else you can think of that he might go?" I tried again. It wouldn't kill me to wait; it would only make things harder. I undoubtedly had Betty's undivided attention now. She tipped her head to one side, seemingly interested.

"And you're looking for Jordan because … ?" she pressed. Of course. Heaven forbid I should escape this unscathed.

"I … I think I need to apologize. I may have offended him yesterday, maybe even hurt his feelings a bit," I muttered. Betty looked surprised.

"Now what makes you think that?"

Why do you have to know? Can't you please just leave me be? "I was rather short-tempered and rude, and when we parted ways, he seemed … I don't know. I just know I owe him an apology," I concluded, feeling slightly flustered. Betty sat back a bit, calmly returning to tidying her desk.

"I doubt you have anything to worry about. Takes a lot to upset Jordan, and even if you did, he'll get over it. In fact, I'll betcha you won't even have to go looking for him. He'll turn up eventually, and when he does, he's probably gonna come looking for you," she said matter-of-factly.

"What? Why?" I asked, bewildered. Betty shrugged.

"It's just his way. Practically everyone within a three-mile radius is friends with Jordan, to a degree. Just wait, soon you will be too, I suppose."

"Oh. OK," was all I could come up with. What was I supposed to say to a thing like that? I decided I'd made enough of a fool of myself for one day. "Guess I'll just have to wait and see. Thanks anyway, Betty." I headed for my apartment.

Maybe I should keep my big mouth shut and just wait for something to happen. I have an alarming lack of patience, social skills, and backbone. Apologizing takes a kind of courage that is considerably foreign to me. Just one of the many reasons I don't fit in with regular society. People usually ignore me. But it's OK; I prefer to be alone.

I decided to work on Cyra. Even if I didn't use them yet, it would be nice to get the routers functional. It was tedious work, but would be well worth the effort. After steeling myself for the long task ahead of me, I dove in.

Even though this is at the very bottom of my what-I-want-to-do-list, let's just get it over with.

"Hey, Jordan!" Dylan called. "Wait up!" Walking backwards, I allowed Dylan to catch up. "Chloe and I are gonna hit the waves later today. Anything on your schedule?" I shrugged.

"Surfing group lesson in an hour, that's all. I can join after that." *An hour should be enough to get this to Amber, get ready for the lesson, and get out there—*

"What's up with the map? Are you going to explain that?" Dylan asked, forgetting the previous conversation. "OK, be straight with me," he teased. "Exactly when did you lose the last of your mental marbles?"

"Don't ask questions you already know the answer to."

"Humor me," he said.

"A very long time ago. Same goes for you," I pointed out. Dylan rolled his eyes.

"No, it's just you," he insisted. We both laughed. But Dylan wasn't about to let this one slide. "Seriously, though, what's up with the map?" I had picked up a local map and was scribbling all over it.

"It's a long story," I explained. "Yesterday, I ran into this girl, Amber. And I mean literally … ran into her. We seriously got off on the wrong foot. Turns out she's moving in right above me, and this is her first time to California, so the map's my attempt to get on her good side. She doesn't really like me right now."

At this, Dylan shrugged. "Already? And you think a map is gonna solve that? Oh well, it's only a matter of time before she hates your guts," he said, smirking. I punched him. Not hard, just hard enough to get my point across.

"Hey, just kidding!"

"I know," I said, "but you still deserved that. Someone's gotta teach you manners." Dylan and I have known each other since we were in diapers, so we are entitled to get on each other's nerves without actually taking offense.

Think, think, think. I glanced up and down the street for inspiration; I noticed a poster for a new exhibit at the museum. The art museum! Yes, that's an idea. I circled the spot and put a little 'M' by it. *And I assume she likes music. I heard it yesterday.* I made note of the beachside amphitheater and the bands that sometimes play there. Dylan looked over my shoulder and chuckled.

"Absolutely hopeless," he muttered.

"What, the map idea, or me?" Dylan snickered and said it was both. Pretty soon we were chatting about yesterday's epic waves. I hadn't been the only one to have a go at it.

We were almost to Dylan and Chloe's home. A while back, the siblings had reunited and moved back to their childhood home to be with their mom. That way, she didn't have to live alone, and they could help pay the rent.

"See you later, Jordan," Dylan said, turning toward home. "Good luck with your peace offering!"

I chuckled. "Whatever. See you later!" *Who knows?* I thought. *Maybe that luck will come in handy.*

I won't go into the technological, itsy-bitsy details. Simply put, I had to give all thirty-five routers a new cyber pathway. When the router's cyber signature changes, the "old" network disappears and the "new" network appears, thus becoming untraceable. It's like getting a makeover. You might as well be a brand-new person; no one recognizes or remembers you, but deep down, nothing has really changed. You're still your old self, just under a new look … or a new name. You're a blank slate. *I wish life were that easy to fix. Make a really stupid mistake? No biggie, just reroute yourself! That would be superb.*

Twenty-nine routers done, six to go. All the pathways had twists and turns, "area codes" that made it appear they were coming from all over the country. I loved watching Teumessian run my little rat race. They always found their way out—sooner or later—but until then, it was amusing to send them on wild goose chases. My fingers kept working, but my mind wandered off; I wondered if Betty was being serious. Why would Jordan come looking for me? True, he seemed nice enough, but I doubted he really cared whether we were friends or just neighbors. Especially after my abrasive demeanor yesterday. Glancing back at my screen, I grinned. Thirty down, five to go.

Halfway through the thirty-first router, I heard someone knock on my door. For a moment, I didn't move. *You've got to be kidding me.* Getting up, I went to go see who it was. *This must be some sort of coincidence.* I went up on tiptoe to look through the peephole. *He wouldn't …* but yes, there stood Jordan. *Betty was right! What do I say?* I didn't have to worry about saying anything, though, because the moment I opened the door, he started talking.

"Hey Amber! How's it going?" Jordan asked, grinning.

What is this? "Ah, pretty good, I suppose." I almost forgot to reply in kind. "How about you?"

"Fantastic! Thanks for asking. Anyway, I don't actually have much time, but, hold on … wrong pocket … ah, found it!" He pulled out a carefully folded piece of paper and handed it to me. Unfolding it, I discovered it was a map. He started to explain. "Being new here and all, I thought it might be useful. Sometimes all the buildings look the same; it's really disorienting. Anyway, I marked some of the more worthwhile places, like this cool little ice cream place around the corner. And if you go a couple blocks down and to the left, there's the movie theater. And then there's the art museum, and some great amphitheaters. Sometimes there are music concerts, free movies projected onto huge sheets, even fireworks!"

Honestly, it stunned me, looking at all the places he had marked. He had pinned so many of my interests.

"Wow. I don't know what to say. Thank you, really. This is … amazing," I stammered rather pathetically. Jordan just seemed thrilled.

"Great! I'm really glad to hear it. I wasn't sure if it was a lame idea or not," he added sheepishly.

"No, no, it's a great idea. Seriously, thanks," I insisted. He seemed to almost be blushing now.

"It was nothing. I, ah, gotta run. I have a group surfing lesson in—" He checked his watch. "Oh, less than half an hour. See you later!" With that he turned and started jogging off.

No! I'm gonna lose my nerve if I wait any longer!

"Jordan! Wait!" I called. Skidding to a halt, he turned to give me an inquisitive look. "I won't keep you long, but … I want to apologize about yesterday. I was terribly rude. It was unfair of me, especially with you being so kind. I barely thanked you when I honestly enjoyed it. So, thank you. For everything." I couldn't believe those words just came out of my mouth. It looked like Jordan couldn't believe it either. He seemed to be at a loss for words.

"Uh … you're welcome. You don't need to apologize, I know I can be a little … annoying. But, thank you. It means a lot that you would say something." Nodding, I permitted myself a small smile. He smiled back for a moment, then took off running again. *Group surfing lesson? I thought watching him surf was entertaining. This is going to be a blast.*

It didn't take long to finish the other routers. As soon as I started the activation sequence for the Cyber Net Launcher branch in Cyra, I prepared to wage war on the hammock again. This time, I studied my netted enemy and delivered a decisive defeat. Perhaps I was starting to get the hang of it.

Judging by the rate the kids' skill levels increased, I decided Jordan was a genuinely good teacher. Watching them go from terrible to terrific was inspiring, and their feisty determination was endearing. Before long, I found myself silently cheering them on.

Well, that was one of the best group lessons I'd taught in the past few months. Everyone had fun, caught some great waves, and avoided any serious wipeouts. The last of my class had cleared out, but I stuck around a bit longer, trying to catch a few more waves. But the tide was changing and the water grew choppy from the onshore wind. Perhaps it was for the better. The sun would be setting soon; stay out too late and you become shark bait. That's a lesson that shouldn't be learned the hard way, so I don't push my luck very often. Heading home, I went to see if Betty was still in her stronghold. She was, and I decided to go chat for a while. We both have a lot to say and not many people care to listen, so we listen to each other.

"Jordan! I was hoping you'd drop by! You shoulda been here this mornin'," Betty exclaimed as if she had the gossip of the century.

"What did I miss?"

"The question is who you missed," she chuckled.

Come on, Betty, you have my attention. "Alright then, who did I miss?"

"I thought you'd never ask," Betty declared, then hastily launched into an explanation. "Oh, you shoulda heard it. Miss Amber was down here, askin' if I might know where Jordan West was. And you know why? She felt she owed you an apology. Isn't that sweet? And then she went off looking … " I will admit, I zoned out a little. She lost me at "Jordan West." *I don't think I told Amber my last name.* "… just have to wait and see. Well, you should probably go find her, don't you think?" Betty finished. Quickly burying my curiosity, I nodded, smiling.

"You were right, I already talked with her today," I admitted. Thankfully, I had managed to keep track of what Betty had been saying. "She didn't seem as opposed to chatting as yesterday, even if it wasn't for very long."

Betty looked pleased, as if she had just been crowned chess champion of the year. I decided to let her play her little game for now; she'd won this round. But it was just that—a game. And I doubted she'd play forever. We talked a bit longer, then I returned to my apartment. It was a little weird Amber knew my last name. I shook my head. *There's probably a logical explanation. But, how could she have possibly known?* I couldn't figure it out, yet couldn't let it go. My tendency to curiosity could be such a curse. I wondered what tomorrow would bring. Time would tell. I just had to wait.

CHAPTER 7

Santa Barbara, Ocean Front Rescue
Monday, July 30, 11:47 A.M.

Jordan

I doubt many people can say they've had a staring contest with a loggerhead sea turtle big enough to block a sidewalk, fat enough to crush a watermelon, and close enough to bite your nose off—and with jaws built for cracking open giant clams and shellfish. It's pretty intense. And this particular loggerhead was still deciding whether it liked having a penlight shone in its eyes. Feeding time wasn't for another half hour, and Maximus the turtle was eyeing my fingers hungrily.

Sophie, my shadow for the summer and intern for the coming year, was rocking back and forth on her toes while peeking over my shoulder, her big brown doe eyes studying my every move through her thick-rimmed glasses. Her long, chocolate brown hair, despite being pulled back in a ponytail, refused to stay out of her way; she had to push it behind her ears every few seconds. Originally, she had been examining Maximus—until he got a mouthful of her shirt. Now it was my turn. Clicking off the light, I moved a safe distance from the testy turtle.

"So? What's the verdict?" Sophie asked. I grinned.

"Well, I think it's time to feed him. He wants to eat me. Other than that, I think he's ready for release, if that's what you want to know." That was exactly what she wanted to know, and she donned a smile big enough to split her face. Maximus was going home.

To Sophie, every creature that lives in the sea is as precious as a newborn baby, no matter how small, strange, or scary, and she was devoting her gap year between high school and college to taking care of them. Her quiet, gentle demeanor had earned the respect of sharks. A seal pup let her cradle it in her arms and pet it like a lost puppy. She'd caught a rogue pelican and coaxed it back to its cage with nothing but a tiny sardine. She's got loads of spunk and heart, that's for sure.

Glancing at my task list for the day, I scanned the lines in search of the next assignment. *OK: Maximus. Check. Now ... oh, this is going to be a blast.*

"Hey, Sophie," I said. "How about we get Maximus over to the tagging division, and then we go trick the porpoises into taking their medicine?" She feigned begrudging exhaustion.

"I suppose so. We do what we must. All in a day's work." The melodramatic act only lasted for a few seconds, after which she broke into another huge smile. "Can porpoises eat peanut butter?" she asked.

"Peanut butter? What?" I balked. *Did I miss something?*

"Peanut butter is what I use to get Sweet Pea to take her medicine," Sophie explained. "First I hide the pill in a spoonful of peanut butter. After she starts eating it, I run the spoon across the roof of her mouth and she spends the next half hour trying to lick it all off. It's really funny to watch. Do you think it would work with porpoises?" she finally finished. Now I was completely befuddled.

"What on earth are you talking about? Who is Sweet Pea?"

"My Boston Terrier."

I couldn't help it. I started chuckling, which made Sophie giggle, which made me laugh even harder, which, well ... It took a while to pull ourselves together. This is my job. Welcome to another part of my amazing life.

Maximus had the air of a regal king lounging on a lofty royal throne. In reality, he sat on his tiny table with wheels as we pushed it around like a shopping cart. Animals have attitudes. Personalities. It was almost as if Maximus knew he was returning to the majesty of the ocean and its splendor, to the colorful reefs, vast forests of kelp, sway of the great currents, and the lonely calls of whales in the deep. I could almost envy this reptile. Oh, the wonders he would see! Then again, he's a turtle. I'm happy being a human.

Before long, we were heading toward the porpoise tanks, debating the whole way whether peanut butter was bad for porpoises. How to describe Ocean Front Rescue? Well, take controlled chaos, puddles of seawater, and a wide range of creatures and stick them all in a pressurized bottle. Yes, that's what it's like. Open the wrong door or latch, and *BAM!*—suddenly there are puffins running down the hall. It's a good idea to keep all personal items at least two feet from the edge of the seal tank, because those flippered fiends will pop out of the water when no one is looking and steal a bagged lunch or baseball cap in a heartbeat. And the floor is almost always wet, so no running in the halls.

The bright, linen white walls are a few shades from perfection, and the speckled salt-and-pepper floor tiles have shiny flecks thrown into the mix. Tanks serve as the central point from which hallways and rooms branch, something like petals growing off the center of a flower. The roof is open above most of the tanks, filling the building with warm sea breeze. Flickering data constantly drags my attention from wall to wall as panels display the current information, as does the occasional muted *beep* or *ding*. Animals and humans alike call back and forth to each other, and electricity laces the air.

These days had been filled with challenges. The ocean was changing. Currents were bringing new animals to our shores, and the tables had turned for many species. Some were thriving, others teetered on the edge of extinction. It might be temporary; there had been some monstrous storms in the past few months: undersea earthquakes and volcanic eruptions. But no matter how long the change lasted, we would take action and respond to it as best as we could.

Seriously, though. Can porpoises eat peanut butter? I don't know.

What am I doing with my life? Actually, what life do I have? I need to get one. I mentally reprimanded myself for my laziness. Surely there is more to boring days than sitting around and playing video games. What would I do without my computer? Running through a few options, my brain stopped paying attention and my fingers took over; my little avatar darted around, slaying zombies and the forces of darkness in all the gory, 8-bit glory it could muster.

Until Edge said otherwise, attacking Teumessian was off limits. I didn't have any current programming projects. Drawing was off the table; I'd already filled two pages with intricate designs and miniature graphite-clad creatures. Perhaps it would be a good idea to get some colored pencils and paint. *Maybe paint pens. Paint pens are good. Especially the neon and metallic ones. I really like the silver—* My thoughts were interrupted by a descending *wong-wong-wooong.*

I glared at the "GAME OVER" banner for a moment, then hit the little red "X" button in the top right corner of the screen. *Now what?* Tilting my chair back, I stared at the ceiling as if someone had scrawled the answers to my questions up there. Glancing over at the empty bookshelf, I made an executive decision: I felt like reading. Finally, some purpose. A quick scan of Jordan's map showed there was a library nearby. I had been looking at the map, and there were a lot of interesting places marked; they seemed worth checking out. I wondered how many I would get to see. Who knows how long I would stay here? Already, things had fallen into an inconspicuous pattern. I only had to interact with a few people, and apart from Jordan, none of them asked many questions.

The moment my foot touched the pavement, I could feel it in the air: rain. Heavy, tangible humidity dangled down from the atmosphere, clinging to my skin. A storm was brewing. The sky had turned an orange-ish reddish gray, and fast-moving clouds rolled across the sky. I'd been under the impression California was mostly cloudless days and sunshine. Apparently, that wasn't entirely true. *I'm going to have to move fast. Books are not waterproof.*

I was halfway through choosing between a medieval historical fiction and a western romance when my phone started pulsating. Not vibrating. Pulsing. In that instant, adrenaline poured into my veins, starting at my thrumming pocket and spreading to every fiber of my body. Only one thing made my phone do this: an alert from Cyra. Whipping it from my pocket, I scanned the screen. The encrypted text message looked like gibberish, but I knew the cypher like the back of my hand.

Find && Stream "Project Plutonium" complete. Live communication feed intercepted. Detected threat level 10. Database is open. Interference maximizes at 67%, rate increasing. Stronger A.I. is fighting back.

For a moment, time seemed to slow and my heart began to race. Then the books hit the floor and I was running in an instant.

Teumessian was making its move. Cyra had slashed a hole in their firewall and was holding it open, but it wouldn't last long. Teumessian had a new toy: a superior A.I. It was interfering with Cyra's grip on the gateway. The fate of hundreds depended on how fast I could slip through that hole, grab the information, and get out before the doorway disintegrated and trapped me inside. I knew this was coming … I just didn't think it would be so soon …

The sounds of battle met me at the door: the hyper-speed whirring of my computer, overlapping measures of low humming and shrill beeping blending together—producing a chaotic, tangled music—and the clicks of Cyra channeling crackling electricity back and forth from wire to wire. Hurling myself into the chair by my desk, I evaluated the situation. Interference was fluctuating between 65% and 71%. Cyra was putting up a worthy fight. My original thirty-five networks were spitting out new ghost networks exponentially, shrouding my real location in a cape of swirling shadows. Their numbers would soar, then fall back as Teumessian's A.I. sliced through their shallow code.

The only way to make my location unclear was to have my computer switch back and forth from all the Wi-Fi networks as fast as possible. That way, Teumessian couldn't tell where they were being attacked from. But if a network was pinned in the 0.058 seconds I was on it, I could be discovered.

I froze, caught in the decision. Should I jump in? It had been a long time since I'd gone solo, without guidance or warning from Edge. If I failed … I shook my head. *No, that doesn't matter! My life isn't the only one at stake here.* When I put it to myself that way, there was no choice. With trembling hands, I dropped my phone into the charging dock, pulled on my headset, and started firing commands.

"Cyra: sync my phone. Contact Edge and feed the call through my headphones. On my command, activate my programs and start network hopping, top speed. See if the enemy A.I. is using any kind of methodic order, whether numerical, alphabetical, or cyber location to eliminate our networks. If it is, avoid its pathway. If interference reaches 85%, alert me; if it reaches 95%, pull out. At 100%, our firewalls will fall and they'll have access to my computer. If worst comes to worst … force a crash."

I took a deep breath. *Here we go. No turning back.* "Cyra: activate hacking program Laelaps."

```
>Launch in 3…
    >2…
    >1…
>Launch complete.
```

My fingers flew. I sped down the electronic hallways of Teumessian's digital database, making frantic grabs at all the files within my reach. When I wasn't fighting off the antivirus programs, I was racing through the maze of letters and numbers. *Come on … where is that live feed? Orders are coming in—why can't I find them?* Suddenly, from my headphones …

"Hello?"

"Edge!" I exclaimed, relieved. "Contact the chairman of Project Plutonium and whoever is in charge of the facility. We have a problem."

"Please tell me you're not hacking," Edge sighed, sounding like a displeased, weary mother of an unruly child.

"What *I'm* doing doesn't matter," I insisted, carefully steering away from the fact of the matter. "Cyra picked up a threat level 10. Teumessian's got their eyes set on Project Plutonium and there's a live feed out there. Whatever their plans are, they're carrying them out now." An ascending, shrill beep sounded through my headphones. Interference had reached 85%. *No, I need more time!* Unfortunately, Edge heard the alarm too—and the weary mother morphed into the iron-fisted father.

"You *are* hacking! Amber, get out of there! Pull the plug, shut it down, do whatever it takes—you're going to get caught! What the heck are you thinking? This is suicide!"

I defiantly ignored him. Edge sensed this and suddenly went deadly quiet; chills ran down my spine. "Amber, as your superior, I demand you back out now. Shut. It. Down." I faltered. His calm, poison-laced, icy words were like charm-speak, working deep into my mind and making me question my rebellion. Time froze for a moment.

"No. Not this time, Edge," I said suddenly, breaking free of the spell. "You forget: I hacked Teumessian long before I had your help. I did it then. I can do it again."

OK, maybe I went a little too far. Everyone who's ever met Edge knows he's dangerous when he's angry—me most of all—but even I didn't know he was capable of such profanity. I was tempted to hang up, but I knew I might need him.

Struggling to block him out, I turned frantic attention back to finding the live feed. Ghost network numbers were half of what they should be. Interference was at 92%. The protection programs Teumessian had put in place could pull the ground out from under my code any second.

This was the end of the line. Do or die.

I found the communication line. It was pure luck; I just stumbled on it.

The moment I saw the messages scrolling across the screen, I hit the "select all" function and the download button. An alarm went off: 95%.

"No, Cyra! Override, Override! Wait for my command!" I exclaimed desperately. The progress bar was moving too slowly. I glanced up at the stats: 97%. *Hurry up, Come on!*

Download complete.

"Cyra, escape. Get me out!" Code flew across the screen faster than my brain could fathom.

99%. Then, it was all over.

My screen flashed blue and the program went down. I did it. I dove through the metaphorical hole in time, just as it slammed shut behind me. But I made it out alive. Edge was still furiously trying to get my attention from the other side of the line, but I ignored him a bit longer. Opening the files, the magnificent loot from my escapade, I carefully scanned down the data. It confirmed what I had long suspected: Project Plutonium was going to be Teumessian's bombing target practice. Time was of the essence.

I took a huge breath and exhaled. "Edge, I did it. I'm out. They didn't catch me—and I was right. In less than twenty-four hours, the facility hosting Project Plutonium will be nothing more than a mushroom cloud, no silver lining. Get everyone out now. I'll even send you the files," I said, surprised at how calm my voice was. There was a terrifying silence on the other end.

"What you just did … don't ever do that again. You could have been caught. I will act on this information, but just because you played the hero, don't think you are escaping severe punishment. You will be hearing from me soon."

With that foreboding prediction of doom, Edge hung up.

Well, I still don't know if porpoises can eat peanut butter, but we found a jar in the break room and fed a bit to them anyway. I assume it's fine. They didn't sink to the bottom of the tank and die, choke, or turn purple. So, for now, yes: porpoises can eat peanut butter. They even seem to like it. Hey, you learn something new every day!

I heard the first raindrop. There were about twenty-three more, then the entire ocean started falling from the sky as a cacophony of rain pattered across the roof. It sounded like the angels were using power washers instead of watering cans to hose down the little garden we call earth. For most people, a drop in barometric pressure causes drowsiness, but it doesn't really affect me much. Maybe it's just the excitement and anticipation of the coming storm, but I feel more awake. It definitely was having its effect on the others, though; everyone and everything seemed to set aside their own conversations and noise, content to listen to the deluge.

It wasn't long before I found myself wondering if it was raining in Las Vegas, if Lexie was sitting at the window trying to draw the liquid crystals as they fell from the sky. She had always been good at drawing rain and water, especially when the sun shone through it, making it glow. It was like she had taped the rain to the paper and ordered it to stay there while she traced it. I was excited; it had been a week since Lexie's last letter had arrived and it was time to write back.

Lexie and I came up with a system when she had to move away: she would write a letter about her week. I would get her letter, wait a week to amass stories, questions, and comments about her last letter. She would get mine, wait a week, and reply. This was a ray of diamond sunshine in the midst of my gold and silver days. It was an old habit, but we kept on even after Lexie got her own email address and phone. It was fun.

Note to self: write more about Sophie and porpoises' newfound addiction to peanut butter. I wonder how her band competition went. She said she had to replace her cello strings and that they were taking some getting used to. I bet she did fine. I bet they won. I smiled. *I think they won.*

"A penny for your thoughts," Sophie called in a singsong voice. I decided to play along.

"OK, I'll take the bait. But why do you want to pay a penny for my thoughts? They might not be worth that much. For all you know, I could be thinking something really stupid right now, like, 'Oh my! The sky is blue!' or something," I said. Sophie giggled.

"I know you're smarter than that. You'd be more likely to be thinking about something cool, like whales' intuition of migration routes, or the fact that the sky is composed of nitrogen, oxygen, carbon dioxide, and—what is it?" she asked.

"Argon and water vapor."

"Oh, right," Sophie said, tucking this away in her mind, then lighting up and pointing at me triumphantly. "Exactly! See what I mean? But whatever you were thinking about, it made you smile, so it's got to be worth hearing." I couldn't help but smile again.

"First off, flattery will get you everywhere, Sophie. Thank you for that lovely compliment. Second, yeah, OK. I wasn't thinking about the sky being blue. I was thinking about my little sis, Lexie. She's the cellist in her local orchestra. They were going to a competition today, and my guess is that they probably won." I paused. "You serious about that penny?"

"I like you, Jordan," Sophie exclaimed, giggling again. "You're nice and fun to talk to. Lexie is lucky to have a brother like you."

"I sure am glad to hear that. After all, you are stuck with me for the rest of the summer," I reminded her. "You're not so bad yourself. I don't think anyone else is creative enough to try feeding peanut butter to porpoises or giving a rubber dog bone to a seal. That's just from today. Should I go on?" Sophie suddenly smirked.

"Flattery will get you everywhere, Jordan," she said.

I face-palmed. *Here we go again.* Tristan, the main ecosystem-oceanographer, geologist, and understood leader of Ocean Front, poked his head around the corner.

"Jordan, I've been looking for you. Come on, you should see this." He waved some papers in the air like a British kid trying to sell a newspaper. Grinning, I started trotting after him.

"Wait! What about me?" Sophie called out.

"I'll be right back. I think you've got things covered. They seem to really like you!" I insisted, then hurried on. An otter chose that perfect moment to steal a sea urchin from Sophie's hand and a small skirmish ensued.

I followed Tristan to the data central of Ocean Front: a break room that had been transformed into a four-walled map with pages of data, sticky notes, markings, and thumbtacks all over it. An old-style approach, true, but old-fashioned still worked. Anyway, there was a digital copy in the database. In the center of the room was a table rimmed with as many computers and chairs as possible. Every other inch of space was taken up either by more tables covered with various technological or scientific instruments, tall stacks of drawers brimming with files and tablets, or shelves of articles ranging from rocks to riptides. It was certainly hazardous, claustrophobic, and at times confusing, but it served its purpose well. We could track everything that was happening in the waters along the coast.

As of late, the map collected notes that spoke of some freak wave or surprise storm cell. But today, Tristan strode forward and pushed an orange pin on the tiny island of San Nicolas, then one in Avalon, then in Santa Rosa, all of which landed within one hundred miles of Santa Barbara. Snatching a long string of rubber bands from a nearby table, Tristan stretched it across the three points.

"Sensors picked up a level 5.5 tremor on the Richter scale in this triangle an hour ago," he said.

"What? Are you serious?" I asked in disbelief. Tristan handed me the papers. The data confirmed it. After scanning the details, I shook my head. "This is the third one in the past few months. What tectonic plate did it come down from?"

"That's just the thing: it didn't come from a plate. The tremor originated somewhere in this triangle," Tristan murmured, studying it.

"It doesn't make any sense. There aren't any fault lines in that zone. What could have caused it?"

"I don't know," Tristan said, running a hand through his coal-black hair. He turned to me. "What have you got? Have there been cases of heat trauma recently? What about chemicals? Are there any traces of sulfur anywhere at all? Deep sea microbes or plankton on the shores?"

"Heat trauma, sulfur, deep sea … you think an underwater volcano has erupted?"

"I didn't say that. Until I know more, I can't prove or disprove it. That's why I'm asking you."

I silently scolded myself. My binder—and all the information I had gathered in the past few months—was sitting safe and sound beneath Sophie's notebook in the otter unit, far out of my current reach. Tristan seemed to notice my hesitation and lack of a notebook.

"Just remember," he said simply.

"Pardon?"

"You don't need your binder. I trust your memory. You're always right."

"OK, thanks. I think."

What's it like to remember everything? I don't know how exactly to describe it. The closest thing I can compare it to is standing in the center of a hologram projector. I've never done such a thing, but I can imagine what it's like. When I close my eyes, there is … everything. Everything I have ever experienced. Images, sounds, places, strings of words, scents …

the list goes on. They sort of drift around until I decide what I want, like picking flowers in a field or popping bubbles floating through the air. *Wow, actually reflecting on this makes me realize how weird it is. I wonder, does anyone else have this, or am I just really different?* Brushing those thoughts aside, I pulled together the results in my head and started rolling them off.

"There have been nineteen animals treated for burns since May, but none of them were related to any sub-marine eruptions. No sulfur except the usual amount. But, yes: there have been some odd microbes floating around, but they aren't the type that come from volcanos. They don't really fit any categories we've seen before. Other than that, I think you can disprove your hypothesis now. Do you have any more?" I asked hopefully.

"Nope," Tristan admitted.

Looking again at the triangle, I counted twenty-eight tiny slips of paper, all half the size of a postage stamp, with the tag IDs of animals we had released neatly written across them. Every slip was a gravestone; each marked where a transmitter came to a grinding halt—where an animal had died. Tristan and I had noticed the signs months ago, but now there was no doubt. Somewhere in those waters, a new threat had emerged from the shadows and was challenging everything that swam past it. Bizarre disappearances, odd creatures, new currents, superstorm cells, and traces of chemicals all pointed to something big. *Whatever it is, it's really good at hiding—despite its size.*

So now the truth comes out. I am a master hacker. My enemy and I are named after creatures in an old Greek tale. My name: Laelaps. The hunter-dog from mythology that was destined to always catch its prey. I fight a group of terrorists named Teumessian: the mythological fox who was destined to never be caught.

We are the first paradox.

I work for the FBI. Well, sort of. I'm expendable and stuck under their thumb. It's complicated—and just got even more complex. *I am in so much trouble. I've defied Edge before, but never like this. He's gonna kill me ...* Yes, I might have just saved hundreds of lives. But if you're wondering: no, Edge does not care. You could throw a flaming crate of puppies from the top of a ten-story building and Edge would not care. I don't think he has a heart—or a soul. If he does, they're harder and blacker than a block of obsidian.

Even his appearance mirrors his personality. Though I hadn't seen him in years, the memory was still stunningly vivid. It was like someone had increased the "contrast" setting and decreased the "brightness" on a paint program. His hair was black as raven's feathers, and this contrasted against his marble-white skin. His eyes were like ice: bluish, white-like ice, harshly cold like ice, and sharp like ice. I often wondered what had shattered him, what made him so frozen. Perhaps nothing. Sometimes I'm all but convinced he was born that way. Now I could practically see his angry face glaring at me.

My heart felt like it was being rung out like a wet rag. The anxiety was overwhelming. My lunch was threatening to make a reappearance—and so was my breakfast. I paced the apartment, practically wearing holes in the carpet. Nothing could calm my nerves. I tried everything.

Gaming didn't last long. My computer was radiating fear, doom, and lag beyond reason; the motherboard was tired after waging war, and it made sure I was aware of its pain. It sent me plenty of error/"Please Wait"/crash messages. Music helped a little, but see point number one. I couldn't stay focused or sit still long enough to draw. Nothing was screaming "Draw me!" I couldn't hear anything whispering it, either. Nothing was worth watching on TV. I wasn't into the cartoon channel or sketchy chick flicks. The only reading material I had was my journal, Jordan's map, and some random magazines. My journal was a terrible option, I'd already looked at the map, and I need more than a grain of salt when it comes to magazines.

I darted around for at least two hours. It felt like a millennium. But life likes to laugh at me, because guess who eventually showed up? Yep. I was wound tighter than a spring on a loaded gun, so when Jordan knocked, I almost leapt through the ceiling.

"Amber? Are you OK?" Jordan called out after a long, awkward silence. I didn't go to the door, but he knew I was home; I accidently yelped when he knocked. *Oh great. Now he probably knows that the crazy girl upstairs is going to have a mental meltdown.*

"What is it, Jordan? I'm busy," I called back.

"Nothing. Just thought I'd say hi. OK, I'll … see you later?" I didn't answer, so I assume he eventually left, and I returned to my worrying.

What kind of punishment is Edge thinking of? I've never been in this kind of trouble. What could he do? I'm here, and he's far away. Oh, but I don't fully know what he is capable of! What is he going to do?! More lame activities were exhausted. I found myself growing drowsy; the rain was washing away my energy and sanity. The pacing and fretting started all over again. I lost track of how many times I went through the agonizing cycle, but it was shattered once again.

"Hey, Amber. Are you still busy?" Jordan called through the door. *Why is he here again? What does he want?*

"Yes."

"Oh. Alright."

Back to my misery routine. I even plucked up the courage to call Edge. My call went straight to his voice mail. At the first prerecorded word, I promptly hung up, but after approximately 124 more laps around the apartment, I tried again. Voice mail. Again.

"Edge, look, call me. I didn't ... it's not like they caught me. What was I supposed to do? What kind of trouble am I in? Don't be mad. Would you ... never mind." An awkward pause. "Come on, Edge. I know you're there!" I angrily punched the "End Call" button, then realized that probably only made things worse. So I worried more. Evening shadows were creeping up the walls and the storm persisted. And it wasn't the only annoying thing that wouldn't go away.

"Are you OK, Amber?" Jordan called through the door. "Have you been pacing? I can hear you, you know. Is something wrong?"

"I'm fine! Go away!" I snapped.

"OK! I'm sorry!"

I should have been grateful that someone seemed concerned about me, but I was stretched too thin to care. Eventually, my restless legs betrayed me, and I flung myself on the couch. Before I could fight off its attacks, sleep captured me.

Should I be worried? What's going on? Why is Amber upset? I don't think I did anything wrong, so why did she get mad at me? I pondered all this. *No, something else must be bothering her. I'll see if she's OK tomorrow. Maybe by then I can think of something useful to say to cheer her up. It's worth a shot.*

I was absolutely determined to make friends with Amber. She seemed lonely, whether or not she realized it. I loved making new friends. I love people. And I hoped she wouldn't misunderstand my intentions. *Good grief, Betty better stay out of this. I don't even know which side of eternity*

Amber is standing on. Yet. I'll find out; she is my neighbor, after all. I just have to wait for the right opportunity.

I looked down at the paper in front of me, covered with sentences stretching from margin to margin: my letter to Lexie. Everything I could think of had been jam-packed into the space of a single page. It was hard to narrow my ideas down, but if I didn't, Lexie would be reading for a very long time. I sealed and stamped this small treasure. By the way, envelope edges taste really, really nasty, don't they? Why? What kinds of chemicals do they put on those things? I don't know, and maybe I don't want to.

Dear Lexie,

First things first. Today of all days, it's a good thing you like reading and writing, because I have a lot to say and ask. Here it comes!

How did regionals go? I looked up the song you were going to be performing and it floored me. It's so beautiful! And did the new girl Karen get in? I bet the prospect of another cellist is exciting. Is it still just you, Maria, Trever, Benjamin, and the violinists in the strings section? The world needs more musicians.

Are you still driving Hunter around to finish your hours for the DMV? Is it really worth it? I remember when I was learning how to drive, he was a real pain to have in the car because he would point out my every mistake and alert me when the light turned green. Oh goodness, please don't let him read that. This is what I get for writing in pen — I can't erase dangerous comments. How are Mom and Dad doing? Did Dad get those vacation days? Have they decided where you all are going this year?

Remember Sophie, my assistant/shadow at Ocean Front for the summer? Well, random fact: usually, I get the water mammals to take their medicine by stuffing it down the throats of dead fish during feeding time, but today I fed it to them in peanut butter! Yes, you read that right. Peanut butter. They really like it, too. Sophie has some crazy ideas, but they usually work. Oh, also, she has a Boston terrier named Sweet Pea. Isn't that a creative name for a dog? There are a lot of strange things happening off the coast. Tremors and earthquakes where there are no fault lines, creatures that belong miles away, and unusual currents.

And, I have a new neighbor! Her name is Amber, she's moved in above me. Granted, she is a little strange. It's probably just a coincidence, but she somehow knew my last name despite the fact I'm sure we've never met before. Weird, right? Who knows, maybe she's some sort of spy. Just kidding. She listens a lot more than she talks, but what she has said is certainly intriguing. She's a graphics designer, and she has twelve siblings! And I thought you and Hunter were enough! She says most of them are adopted, but still.

Okay, I'm pushing the limits of this page. I hope you have a wonderful week! I'll be praying about prepping for the finals. I'm simply assuming that you made it past regionals. I love you!

~ Jordan

CHAPTER 8

The Salt Breeze Apartment Complex, Apt. 1407
Wednesday, August 8, 10 A.M.

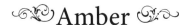Amber

I can't do this. I'm going to come apart at the seams. It's been over a week.
Edge had yet to reply to any of my calls, texts, emails, spam voice mails or
anything else I sent his way. So, either he had forgotten, which was terribly
unlikely, or he was cooking up something truly awful, which was extremely
likely. I would probably be relocated again, banished somewhere very, very
cold, and far, far away, like Alaska. Some crazy side of me was tempted to
jump on a fishing boat and sail across the ocean. Onward! To freedom! But
I was paranoid about leaving the apartment, and they would find me—
whether it be Teumessian or Edge and the FBI. I stayed put.

Jordan wouldn't leave me be. I had to tell him to go away at least once
a day, often more. There's almost a childlikeness about him, yet it doesn't
lower my opinion of him. It's like he's somewhat exempt from the laws of
life. No, I suppose they don't bother him. But he just can't take a clue.

Leave. Me. Alone.

There was something different about Jordan, in more ways than one,
but I couldn't put my finger on it. So many evenings, I'd see him sitting on
his balcony, swinging his feet over the edge without a care in the world,
pouring over the same old leather-bound book. I have yet to decide what
he's reading, but it must be good. I searched his computer with my old
F1R3ST0RM hacking program; I was too scared to use Cyra. I didn't steal
or delete anything. I simply observed. Honestly, I was impressed; he wasn't
like other guys. No porn, violent games, cursing, weird love letters, hate
mail, or anything like that at all. A human being who actually sticks to his

self-set standards! Now I've seen everything.

I also hacked the computer of the former FBI agent down the hall. He was a false alarm. There was absolutely no connection between him and Teumessian. His "treason" was selling information to the media anonymously, but the government decided to dismiss him secretly since he was once well respected. If I wasn't worried about Edge slicing my head off, I might have even gone and introduced myself. We'd just be two rogue FBI agents, chatting about the good old days when the government knew a good thing when it saw it.

I was feeling more tired than ever. When sleep did come, it was shallow and broken with strange, nonsensical nightmares, composed of scrambled horrors from my past—like always, like every night of my life—but the dreams were worse than ever before. I woke up with less energy than I had when I lost consciousness. The only things really keeping me awake and alive were fear, coffee, and Jordan's little visits.

"Morning, Amber!" *Speak of the devil.*

"Hey, Jordan. What is it?" I asked wearily from the safe side of the closed door.

"I gotta get to work, but are you doing anything later? How's your project coming along? Are you almost done?" he asked hopefully. I don't like to lie, but I'd told him my boss had given me a big assignment.

"It's going fine, I suppose," I lied while fingering a sharp, unwritten circuit board in complete boredom. "That's why I'm already up. This will, ah, probably take all day." I flipped the green slip of metal in the air and caught it.

"OK, then," Jordan said. "Well, I have to go. Good luck!"

"Bye, Jordan," I muttered.

For a minute, I listened, making sure he was long gone, then let out a heavy sigh. *I wish getting a huge assignment was the worst of my worries. I love hacking Teumessian.* My goal: to repay at least half of the suffering and torment they have imposed on me, to make sure they reap exactly what they have sown, to avenge those they've taken, and to make sure they never take anyone else.

Thomas Edison once said, "I have not failed one thousand times. I have successfully discovered one thousand ways to *not* make a light bulb." OK, let me rephrase that: I have not been rejected eleven times. I've only discovered eleven different conversations that don't get me anywhere closer to making friends with Amber. *That ... sounds a little better. Not by much, but a bit.*

I was pretty sure there was more than an art assignment on Amber's mind. I heard the faint moaning bend of the floor boards all the time: Amber pacing. She was staying up crazy late, and whenever she answered the door, it was like there was a dismal cloud of darkness, dread, and despair shadowing her.

It had rained on and off for days, and the ground seemed to be tiled with scattered mirrors as the puddles reflected the morning sun. The sky was a hazy blend of pale yellow and bluish grey, and the wind was cool, as if to hail in yet another storm. I don't know what to compare it to. I don't think there's anything else like it. It was a lovely morning.

When I got to Ocean Front, I knew something was up. There was none of the usual hustle and bustle, and the faint chatter was missing. For a moment, I simply stood just inside the door, looking around, confused. Did I overlook something? Did we have the day off? *No, there are lights on. Someone is here, somewhere.* I started walking. If there were others here, I was bound to run into them eventually.

I was considering phoning Dylan when I heard a distant commotion. It didn't last long, but it was enough to point me in the right direction. Soon the sound was constant and distinct. *The map room. I should have thought of that. But why is everyone ...*

When I slipped in, I froze in my tracks, gaping at the scene before me. I hadn't seen the map room this busy since the oil spill four years ago. It was crazy. Every single computer and chair had an occupant. There were a few people clustered around each set of lab equipment. There was some serious-looking science going on. File drawers were squealing open and shut. Tags dating from months back had made a reappearance and the walls had doubled their thumbtack count. The rubber band triangle from last Monday's tremor was gone—a new one had appeared. *That doesn't look good.*

I spotted Sophie rummaging through the bottom of a filing cabinet. She must have seen me, but before I could warn her, she sprang to her feet—and her head found the bottom of an open drawer. *Thud.* I closed the distance between us.

"Oh, my goodness! Sophie, are you OK?"

"Yeah. 'Look before you leap' just took on a whole new meaning," she muttered, shoving the drawer closed with a *bang* as if in retaliation.

"What on earth is going on?" I asked. Sophie gave me a stunned look.

"You haven't heard? Didn't you get the message?"

"Message?" I pulled my phone out to see if I had overlooked a text. It was dead. Apparently I remembered to plug the charging cord to my phone, just not to plug the cord into the wall. "Ah, no. I didn't. What did it say?" I asked, casually slipping my phone back into my pocket. Sophie launched into an explanation.

"There's been another tremor, but this time it's a level 6.5! A whole bunch of that weird spongy rock stuff is floating around, and there's been an explosion in that strange bacteria population. If the tremor causes a tsunami, Santa Rosa would be right in its path. Tristan says we need to pull together enough information to decide whether the islands are in danger and if the microbes and chemicals pose a threat."

We were right. Tristan and I were right. Something huge was going down. There was the threat of a tsunami. Earthquakes. Equilibrium and balance had been thrown into chaos. Everything was changing. We were right—but I wished we were wrong.

"I have to get these files over to the lab techies," Sophie added.

"Oh, of course. Don't let me keep you. Hey, you sure you're OK? I know that really hurts."

"I'm OK. That's not the first time that's happened today. Thanks." With that, she vanished into the sea of people.

I looked back at the map; so, the new triangle was a shock radius. I knew I should probably go ask Tristan where I fit into all of this, and what I should do. But the map was having a magnetic effect on me. Weaving through the madness, I made my way over to it. I'm not sure how long I stood and stared at it, pointlessly reobserving absolutely everything. The different shades of blue, the creases and wrinkles in the paper, the tack marks, paper slips, coordinates. No lightbulbs were going off. There was a lot going through my head. Sadness, frustration, curiosity, disbelief, astonishment. It just didn't make sense. There had been so many tremors, only weeks apart. What could cause something like that? It didn't fit together. What were we missing?

So many complex problems and mysteries can be unraveled by one little thing. The smallest revelation can bring it all together and make everything fit. The map held the key, and it was right in front of me. *No, the question isn't what we are missing—it's what we're overlooking. The answer is here somewhere, it has to be! There must be something that fits it together ... yes, a pattern! There has to be a pattern! Think back, start at the start ...* I closed my eyes, blocked everything out, and stepped into my mind.

I'd pulled together the maps of the first, second, third, and fourth tremors when I realized there was no way I could hold them all. OK, new idea. Connect the dots. Literally. Every pin ever stuck on the map had left a mark: a tiny pinhole! My observations weren't so pointless after all. I opened my eyes and grabbed a nearby pencil. *This better work.*

The pencil met paper, and I knew it had found its mark: the top of the first triangle. As I followed the outline in my head, I could feel the pencil slip in and out of hole after hole, matching each of the points of the triangles. Memory-guided motion. It was working.

When I opened my eyes to inspect my handiwork, I knew I had found something. There was a pattern. All along, the tremors had been looked at chronologically and seemed to be randomly scattered around. But, side by side, I could see the pathway. Despite the gaps, there was no question. The path began and ended on fault lines, taking a detour that looped in and out of the Channel Islands, forming a jagged border around them. These tremors weren't coming down from any tectonic plates. They were silhouetting a *new one*.

"No way! You're arresting *him*?! No-no-no-no-no, you got the wrong guy! The actress is the killer, not him! Do your homework, idiots! He has a solid alibi. Nothing links him to the crime scene, and he barely even knew the man. She's the one with the motive and opportunity: the dead guy cheated on her, and no one can confirm her whereabouts at the time of the murder! *Come on!*"

Here I am, sitting on the couch, yelling at some crime shows I had stashed away in my computer's archives, which I had connected to the TV. Occasionally I would glance down at Jordan's map, which was spread out across my lap, but mostly I criticized the dim-witted detectives. *I have been reduced to actual trash,* I told myself. *All because of Edge and Teumessian's pyromania problem. I hate them both.*

It only took forty more minutes before the investigation turned and headed in the right direction. Pretty soon they had a confession, the little psycho was dragged off to jail, and back in reality I debated watching another episode. I finally decided I'd been around enough crime. I could probably crack all of these cases before they even knew the victim's full name. The screen went dark as I clicked the off button on the remote and retrieved my computer from the chair beside the TV. Returning to my desk, I plugged Cyra back in. The moment the cord was in the computer, a warning popped up. Cyra had detected a virus. When I saw the source, my heart almost stopped. I'd seen this pathway before. Its origin: FBI headquarters.

Suddenly, Cyra made an alarming, strange sound. I tried to get into its base code to throw the firewalls up, but neither my mouse nor keyboard were responding. Diving under my desk, I wrenched off the cardboard box covering Cyra. None of the little lights were on. There was no hum or buzz. Nothing happened when I pushed the on button.

"No! What have you done? What have you done!? No! Why have you taken Cyra from me?" A distinctive *ding* rang out. The sound that plays when I have a new message. As I pulled myself up off the floor, I found my email page up and a letter waiting for me. I realized the truth: *I ... really have been hacked.*

I always thought I was tough, hard to shake, even harder to break, a force to be reckoned with. But within the space of a minute and a few lines of binary code displayed as words, my entire world came crashing down.

```
Amber Marie Gibson, in light of your defiance and direct
disobedience of orders, you are banned from hacking. The
extent of your punishment has not been finalized, but expect
a year at the least. Your Laelaps programs and Cyra have
been remotely shut down. They will be reactivated at the end
of your punishment. Do not try to initiate them. Though you
are not currently in the service of the FBI, you are still
bound to the laws you have agreed to: you may not leave the
United States of America. You are forbidden to disclose
any information regarding your involvement with the war on
Teumessian. You may not hack for any organization other than
the FBI. If you do, your contract will be terminated and you
will be immediately arrested for your crimes. All communica-
tion will be cut off in 19 days, and you will not be able to
contact any FBI agent until the end of your punishment.
                              X
```

The foundation I had built my life on crumbled. My only power in this world, my only defense, offense, fallback, purpose, and the force that pushed me on … all gone. I couldn't fight Teumessian for a year, probably longer. I would much rather be banished to Alaska. Yanking my phone from my pocket, I hastily speed-dialed Edge. *Why does it take him so long to answer his phone?*

"I was wondering when you were going to call," Edge muttered when he finally picked up.

"Edge, you have to do something! This isn't fair! I saved lives. I didn't get caught. I averted a disaster. And now I'm grounded! This is ridiculous!" I exclaimed in a furious rush.

"Calm down. You're going to blow a circuit," Edge ordered. I attempted to squelch the frustration in my voice and tried pleading instead.

"Please, do something. You're influential. The very least you can do is shorten my sentence. Please. Don't do this to me," I begged. Edge sighed, almost disappointedly, from across the line.

"You did this to yourself. If you're ever caught, it puts the FBI in a dangerous position. You can't take risks like that. Anyway, it's out of my hands. I simply reported your actions and the board settled on a verdict. There's nothing I can do."

A surreal numbness washed over me. There was nothing left. I lost sight of who I was, what I wanted to become, what was going to happen to me, and where I was going. I simply ended the call, let my phone fall to the desk, stood, and walked out.

Even though I was seeing, I was having a hard time believing. A new fault line, a new tectonic plate. Here, off the coast, just a few hundred miles away. Wow. *Impossible …* No, it was possible. The path did converge on volcanos and deep trenches; a violent tremor could have started a crack that passed beneath them, triggering the recent catastrophic marine events. *Is this really happening? I can't think of any other expectation.*

If my hypothesis was right, surely someone else would eventually come to the same conclusion. I found myself asking if I was willing to be the first to speak up and run the risk of making a royal fool of myself.

I needed more than some triangles on a map before I considered telling someone. My mind took a snapshot of the updated map and I mentally watched the sequence of events play out, from first to last, from strongest to weakest, the widest shock radius to smallest. It took me a while, but I finally found something. There was an undersea cavern and a volcano that the line passed by, but there had been a strong tremor on either side of the spot, and the newest tremor was one of the two. The crack was working its way down to this point. It had to be. If it was, then the next quake would come from there.

It was no longer about my own reputation; this dealt with the lives of others. Judging by the strengths of the surrounding tremors, there was enough tension building up to cause a massive earthquake, perhaps a level 7.5 or even an 8. A quake that big could produce a tsunami. The Channel Islands were in danger. I had to say something.

I scanned the room for Tristan. He was caught in a debate group clustered around one of the nearby computers. *Time to be brave.* I made my way over to the outskirts of the circle and waited quietly, searching for the right moment to say something. Everyone was arguing in an intense free-for-all.

"Nope. It's wrong. Test it again," someone was saying.

"How do you know it's wrong?" a woman challenged. "Alright then. How about you tell us what it is, since you're so confident and smart."

"Your tests say those samples match a species of algae that's only found *beneath* the deepest sea caverns. Explain that. No, there's no way that's right. Test it again," the first one insisted.

"The tremor could have disrupted more than just the sea floor. Maybe it pushed a current through a shallow cavern or something," a timid voice piped up.

"But what's the likelihood of that happening? And even if that did happen, it wouldn't bring very much algae to the surface. Why, then, is it all over the place?!"

Tristan stood, silently listening to this dispute as if he was to judge who the winner was—if it ever ended. There didn't seem to be a solution in sight. He didn't appear totally involved, so I decided it would be OK to interrupt. Thankfully, no one else paid me any mind; they just kept squabbling.

"Tristan? Do you have a minute?" I asked.

"What is it, Jordan?" He sounded low on patience and didn't even take his eyes off the scene before him. I pressed on.

"Can I talk to you? I think I may have found something."

"You're already talking to me, Jordan. Just spit it out," he said, irked. *OK then. Here it comes.* Taking a silent, deep breath, I stepped into total abandon.

"I know where the next quake is going to be."

Target acquired, bomb dropped, bull's-eye. Yes, I had every ounce of his attention now. He spun to face me, looking like I had just informed him that I was the president in disguise. It seemed he was about to say something when another voice cut him off.

"And how do you know this? This is not the time for jokes! You can't possibly predict something like that!"

Tristan wasn't the only one who had heard me. Every eye within two feet was aimed my way. I had an audience. My brain broke under the stress and abandoned ship, and so did my voice. It became one of those rare occasions when I couldn't think of a single sensible word. Finally, I managed to force out an answer.

"There's a pattern." I found a shred of courage and pushed on. "The next tremor will be about … roughly fifty miles southeast from the most recent one, possibly a 7.5 or stronger."

Finally, Tristan spoke. "You found a pattern. Show me." He wasn't smiling, but there was an eager light in his eyes.

Nervously, I led the little troupe toward the map. I had been careful not to make the pencil marks dark in case I utterly failed. Throwing caution to the wind, I drew a bold line through the centers of all the triangles.

"OK, I know this is going to sound crazy, and you probably won't believe this, but just hear me out. I think I know what's causing all these tremors. Something started a chain reaction months ago, a crack that's connecting weak points in the ocean floor. One of the quakes joined the crack with a fault line. It forms an almost complete loop—except for this spot." I pointed to the gap. "This is where the next quake will probably be, and it'll be big. Once the line's complete … I think it's a new tectonic plate."

The stunned silence hurt my ears. I wanted to disappear. Almost everyone was wearing their opinions on their faces: disbelief, scorn, uncertainty. I couldn't tell what was running through Tristan's mind, though. All I knew was that his thoughts were running deeper than the deep blue sea. He studied the map with great interest and seemed to be honestly considering my proposition.

Everyone began to bicker among themselves again. I heard phrases like "absolutely ridiculous," "impossible," "out of his mind," and "the freak." I know I'm different … weird, even. My memory makes sure I stand out, even though I try to hide it. Some people don't mind, others can't stand me. *Everyone's unique, and unique is just a synonym for different, so I suppose it isn't that bad.*

"Well, I believe you, Jordan." I turned to find Sophie standing beside me, wide-eyed and sincere.

"Thanks, Soph. You'd be the first," I said quietly.

"I won't be the last. They'll see you're right when that tremor happens. I think it makes perfect sense! It explains everything," she insisted. "Can I tell 'em off? Between the two of us, we'll have them convinced in no time!" I found myself smiling. I hadn't realized what a loyal little fighter I had by my side.

"No, Sophie, though that's quite noble of you. If you're looking to stay here, you can't be that feisty just yet. Wait until you are officially on staff, then maybe."

I was glad Dylan wasn't here; he too might try to defend me, and then it would be us three against everyone else. I didn't want him to go down with the ship. Suddenly, Tristan turned and faced the group.

"Call the Coast Guard and issue an earthquake and tsunami advisory for the islands. Jordan's on to something." Chaos erupted; Tristan was none too pleased with this. "Enough! Everyone quiet!" Silence returned. Tristan huffed an exasperated sigh, then seemed to mend a few of his frayed nerves. "Thank you. Now, it may seem unlikely, but none of the data we have collected contradicts this. Every aspect of Jordan's hypothesis will be tested, but unless it is disproven, we move forward as if this is solid fact. Understood?"

I didn't care if everyone thought I was crazy for a couple of weeks. Sophie was on my side. Tristan believed me. The islands would be warned. Even though today had its metaphorical and literal dark clouds, I could still feel the sunshine.

I walked for hours. I just kept going, with no idea where I was headed and forgetting where I had been. I wandered toward anywhere and nowhere, anywhere but here. It seemed nothing would be the same again.

Teumessian was weakening the USA in preparation for war. They grew stronger every day, creeping closer and closer to their goal. So often, I had been the only one standing between them and victory. I was being hunted because I was the only survivor of one of their attacks. Once I began to fight back, there was no escape. I had to run, run—always run. It was only a matter of time before they found me. I braved day after day just so I would live to see their destruction. Now I wasn't part of the equation. I knew their secrets better than any FBI agent. Teumessian would gain so much ground without me there to stop them …

More teens would lose their families in a blazing inferno, have their best friend executed in front of their very eyes, be betrayed, hunted, live in fear … die. A year's worth of death and destruction, death and destruction that I could help prevent.

There seemed to be a gray haze over everything, the motion around me was blurred, and all noise sounded distant. Memories were escaping the prison cells I had locked them in. I thought I had thrown away the keys, but apparently not.

Ashley, how did we escape the flames? Why? What was the point? … No, I'm glad I'm a Gibson. It's made me who I am. But even that life didn't last! Katlyn, Akoni, Aida, Johnathan. Khari, Liesel, Zachary, Cameron. Baisil, Elizaveta, and Tongo—your name means "always stay the same," doesn't it, dear Tongo? I miss you all more than you'll ever know. Why … why did you leave me? No, you didn't leave. You were taken from me.

And what about Eric? I owe him so much—I owe him everything. I wish we could trade places, that things didn't end the way they did. Eric, forgive me … I'll never forget you, I promise. Oh, it's all my fault! Then, Jessica. Oh, I should have been more careful. It wasn't her fault. She couldn't see any other way. I can't hold it against her; she was only doing what she had to. She thought she was doing the right thing, right? I'm sorry. I'm so, so sorry. Please, could you ever forgive me? I only ever wanted to—

An uneven piece of sidewalk made me trip and I landed hard on my hands and knees. I almost cried. Sitting back, I realized there was no one around. It was starting to get dark. Nothing looked familiar. I was lost and alone. I sat on the curb, fighting away tears, trying to bite back the pain, when I realized there was something in my pocket. Something paper. I reached in and pulled out … Jordan's map. As I looked at it, I began to get an idea of where I was and how to get back. *Thank you, Jordan. Thank you so, so much …* I cried. I haven't cried since forever. And there was no stopping: years of sorrow had finally found their way out.

I was still crying by the time I got to Driftwood Avenue. It felt rather good to let it out, but I was a mess. Instead of going inside, I headed to the beach. It was dusk. No one was out. Pulling my knees up to my chin, I watched the waves come and go as the burning, red-orange sun drifted just below the horizon.

Surprisingly, my hypothesis was holding up. Despite all the tests, research, and criticism that had been hurled its way, it was still standing. But I wouldn't be able to stand for much longer. Sinking into a computer chair, I looked around at all the night owls starting their shifts. *How do they do it? When do these people sleep?*

I practically never work past 9:30 P.M. I'm just useless after nightfall. But it's good to push your limits now and then, so here I am, two and a half hours away from turning into the hypothetical pumpkin. *Come on, don't be lazy. Get up … keep going! I don't have to stay here all night, just most of it. Come on, I haven't finished …*

"Uh, Jordan?" My head snapped up. *Great. How long have I been out?*

"Oh! Hey, Tristan. Sorry. Oh, I got the results on the secondary chemical tests. There's a match in the northern region of—"

"Go home, Jordan," Tristan interrupted, shaking his head and smiling faintly.

"Why?" I asked, bewildered.

"You could have left hours ago, I doubt you could make it through the night, you can't sleep here, and the main reason is you've done far more than your fair share of work today. You're only human." I found myself searching for an excuse.

"But I'm pretty sure I could squeeze in another hour! There's no telling how long the islands have before the next tremor," I said hopefully. Tristan shook his head again.

"I don't want to come in tomorrow and have to mop you off the floor. No. Just go home. You're too motivated for your own good tonight." After a moment, I sighed in relief and nodded.

"Alright. Thanks, Tristan."

As I neared the apartments, I was seriously debating what to do when I got home. Yes, I would eventually get some rest. My body was tired but my mind was still racing. I could log on to the archives and keep researching. If I concentrated, I was pretty sure I could recreate most of the graphs and charts. *If all the new findings are posted before morning, that will give me a head start for tomorrow. But I can't last forever. I wonder how long …*

My hand was almost to the front door handle when I heard it. It seemed to come from behind me.

"Wait."

I whirled to find what I already knew was there. Nothing. *What am I meant to see? What's out there?* For a moment, unmoving, I gazed intently through the misty darkness, searching for anything special, unusual, or out of place. The smallest movement caught my eye. There, sitting on the beach, directly across the street, was a solitary person looking out over the sea.

Perhaps it was my curiosity, or maybe I sensed something was wrong, but I decided to go see who it was. As I got closer, I decided it was a girl … about my age. Her hair was past her shoulders, and it was a sandy brown color. *Wait. She looks like …*

"Amber?"

In the milliseconds between Jordan saying my name and when I turned to face him, I felt frustrated, self-conscious, and embarrassed. Why did Jordan, of all people, have to show up? But it all dissolved when I saw the way he was looking at me. He was so concerned, so worried. And when he saw my face, he immediately noticed the tear stains.

"Why are you crying? Are you OK? You're not hurt, are you?" he exclaimed, eyes going wide.

"I'm fine," I whispered, blushing. I heard what sounded like a tiny, squeaky sniff, and was horrified to realize it came from me.

"What's wrong?" Jordan asked gently.

"It's just … work problems. In a way … I'm temporarily fired." This apparently was a bit of a shock for Jordan, who seemed to radiate empathy.

"I am so, so sorry. Was it something to do with your project?" Jordan seemed to catch himself and suppressed a cringe, as if expecting a reprimand. "Sorry, you don't have to talk to me if you don't want to. I shouldn't have asked—"

"No, I don't mind," I interrupted, shaking my head. "I guess it is sort of related to the project. I don't know. It's complicated." I surprised myself by silently admitting: *I actually … want … to talk to him.*

I wanted to tell him everything; I wanted to trust him, someone, *anyone*! But I'd heard it from Edge and experienced it firsthand: it's smarter to stay away from others in general. I just put them in danger and drop them like they're hot when I leave without a trace. It's not fair to them. *I should just be quiet. He'll go away after a while. It's better this way.*

There was an awkward silence, then Jordan plopped down on the sand beside me. I couldn't believe it. I shot a glance his way, trying to decide what had just happened. He seemed somewhat sad. It was like he was trying to share in my troubles. Staring at the sand at my feet, I grasped for an explanation. *Why does he really seem to care? I highly doubt he's attracted to me. I'm not pretty. He might be curious, but I'm not a very interesting person. And he's not oblivious or bored, so why does he keep pursuing me?* I mulled it over in my mind for a while, but just couldn't make sense of it.

"Why are you still here? What do you want from me?" I finally asked.

"I don't want anything," Jordan answered simply. I sighed a little louder than I meant to. *Denial. He's human. Of course he's after something.*

"Everyone wants something, Jordan, and they persist until they get it. Be honest with me, what do you want?" He thought for a moment before answering.

"It's not what I want for myself," he said carefully. "It's what I want for you."

In that moment, the shattered remnants of my old life, the life of a confident hacker girl who didn't need anyone, were turned to ash. That's twice now that Jordan has blown my mind with a single sentence. I found myself fighting off a sob; no one had ever said anything like that to me. There was another long stretch of silence—but I had to know.

"Jordan, may I ask you something?"

"Sure. Ask away," he said.

I hesitated briefly. "What makes you different? You're not like other people. Why?"

This is it! That verse—"Always be prepared to give an answer to everyone who asks you to give the reason for the hope that you have," the one from a

few weeks ago—that's now! I was trying not to react too quickly or seem overeager. This was exciting.

"What do you mean?" I asked. "How am I different?" Amber seemed to be searching for the right words.

"You're … kind. You keep coming to talk with me, even though I don't really reciprocate. Nothing seems to bother you; you have this air of joy at all times. Yet you seemed somewhat distressed just now—simply because I am."

Why thank you. That's the nicest definition of "different" I've heard all day. "Well, if that's different, what would you call normal?" I asked. Emotionless, Amber gazed at the indistinguishable horizon.

"People usually follow the crowd. They don't actually care about others; they only have motives for their own good. As long as there is something to gain, people will feign courtesy and kindness. But they drop the act when they cross paths with someone disagreeable. Like me," she added dejectedly.

"Don't be so hard on yourself," I insisted gently. "I wouldn't say you are disagreeable. Perhaps a little shy, but that's not a bad thing. And surely I am not the only 'different' human being you've ever met." That warranted the smallest of smiles from her.

"Well, no," she admitted quietly. "I guess my close family wa—" A slightly choked expression flashed across Amber's face. " … Is. Is like you, and I suppose there have been a few others." That jolted me a bit. *Did she almost say "was"? Wow, she must really miss her family if she's talking about them in past tense … I could empathize.*

"What do you think makes me different from others?" I asked. Amber shook her head.

"I don't know," she admitted, then looked at me expectantly.

Here I go. "This world … it's not my final home. That's why things don't bother me. I care about you because I don't live my way. I'm a Christian, so I live my life God's way."

"Christian," Amber muttered, seemingly saddened again as she turned her attention back to the ocean.

"What is it? Did I say something wrong?" I asked, confused.

"No, it's OK. I did ask, after all. It's just …" Amber sighed. "When I was still living at home, that's all I ever heard about. Every day, all the time, it was always something. They were always trying to talk me into it. Please don't do that too." An understanding smile crossed my face.

"I'm not going to preach at you or shove my beliefs down your throat. But I do hope you will hear me out one day," I said. That seemed to be what she needed to hear.

"Someday. Not today, Jordan."

"OK."

We sat in silence once again. My mind was swimming with everything that had just transpired. I now knew what had been bothering Amber. Perhaps the project was a make-or-break kind of assignment, and that's why she had been so stressed about it. I dearly hoped I hadn't interrupted her too often. Without moving my head, I watched her for a minute.

Success at long last; I had made a difference. Amber appeared almost tranquil—to a degree. She still seemed discouraged, but she wasn't crying anymore, and maybe, just maybe, there was a tiny hint of a sad smile on her face. Grinning inwardly, I turned my attention back to the ocean— thinking, wishing I could do more.

I could come up with something to keep Amber's mind off the whole ordeal. But what? She seemed so lonely. It was my guess that it was gonna take a while before she came out of her shell. She didn't strike me as the kind to go looking for friends … more of a lone wolf. But everyone needs friends. *Hmm … I wonder if Amber would like Chloe.* I thought on this for a moment. *Yeah, I think so. Chloe is charismatic; she's easy to get along with. If Amber wouldn't come out of her shell for Chloe, then she must be stuck in there.*

That caused an unwelcome smile to flicker across my face for a moment. Thankfully, it seemed as though Amber didn't notice; it would be hard to explain that the smile came from a mental image of Amber as a turtle. Meanwhile, an idea was starting to form in my head. A crazy idea, but it just might work.

"Amber?" I asked, and she turned to me. "Are you … does this mean … ah, do you have any plans for tomorrow?" Amber gave me a mildly confused look.

"None whatsoever. Why?"

Realizing I didn't have a response ready, and pausing awkwardly, I sighed, gazing back at the ocean, then replied in total honesty. "I'm not sure I have a good answer for that one yet," I admitted. "Give me about half an hour or something." At this, Amber smiled a little. *I think I'm starting to get the hang of this!* Just as I was about to return to my planning, Amber stood.

"Thank you, Jordan," she said simply.

"You're welcome," I replied. "But what are you thanking me for?"

"For caring about me," Amber said quietly. Then she smiled—really smiled. "And for being the good kind of different." With that, she walked off.

I waited a bit longer before heading home myself. Time to put the plan to the test. Plugging my charging cord to the wall and my phone to the chord, I powered it on and pulled up the group chat.

Group Chat: Jordan, Dylan, Chloe, Matt

Jordan

Hey guys. OK, I have an idea. It's a bit spur of the moment, but I think it's worth a shot. Tell me if I'm crazy or not.

Dylan

I already know the answer to that one.

Jordan

Hey, I'm not finished yet! Just giving an explanation before I send a mile-long text.

Chloe

Oh boy, here it comes.

Dylan

If it's a mile long, I think we're gonna be here a while. I predict an hour. Maybe two.

Matt

Patience Dylan, patience.

Jordan

I've already told you about that girl Amber moving in above me. Well, her boss assigned her some big project a week ago, and apparently it wasn't what they wanted. She got fired today. I think. It sounds like it may be temporary...? Anyway, I talked with her, and for the first time she wasn't against chatting with me a little. (Even got to witness to her a bit!) Amber needs some serious cheering up. She's really down about the whole ordeal; she doesn't really have any friends here yet… tomorrow is Thursday. I think you can see where I'm going with this. Are you all okay with her tagging along?

Matt
I'm game.

Chloe
Yes!

Dylan
Sure.

Jordan

Great! I'll see if I can convince Amber. She's rather shy. I think she will naturally gravitate toward you, Chloe. Don't interpret her quietness for disinterest, it's just her way. Dylan, do try to keep a lid on the inside jokes. I don't want her to feel like we are a clique. And Matt … I think you're good.

Chloe
I am more than fine with that.
I'm excited, this is going to be fun!

Matt
You said something about witnessing to her?

Jordan

It sounds like she's from a Christian home, but she's not a believer. She doesn't want to hear any more about it. She's not convinced, but deep down, I get the feeling she is willing to be convinced. Actions will speak louder than words for now, though. All in?

Dylan
All in.

Chloe
All in!

Matt
All in.

Jordan
All in.

After a few more messages, the plan was complete and a strategy was in place. Now all that was left was convincing Amber. *I sure hope this works.*

I sat on the side of my bed, staring down at my journal. The pen quivered in the air above the paper, but I just couldn't find the words. *Where do I start? I don't know what to say.* It was all a mess in my head. I couldn't focus. If I was thinking about my phone call to Edge, thoughts of Jordan's map would find their way in. When I thought about Jordan, I found myself missing my family. As I thought about all my brothers and sisters, I remembered I was grounded. If I thought about Teumessian, images of the ocean pulled at the corners of my mind.

I closed the notebook and let it tumble from my hands onto the sheets. *Forget it. This isn't going anywhere. I'll try again in a bit.* Flopping back, I stared at the ceiling, letting my chaotic thoughts run rampant. A few minutes later, there was a soft knock at my door. Take a guess. This time, I didn't hesitate to open it.

"Hey, Amber. Good thing you're still up. I was worried I might wake you. I came up with an answer!" Jordan exclaimed.

"An answer? For what?" I asked, confused. Jordan grinned.

"Remember on the beach when I asked you if you had any plans for tomorrow, and I wasn't sure I had a good answer yet? I found one. You're still free tomorrow, right?"

"Right."

It was only when I agreed that I noticed Jordan had been hiding something behind his back. He handed over his little surprise. It was an admission ticket of some sort, the kind you print off the computer; beyond that, there was no telling what it was.

"What's this for?" I asked, inspecting it. Jordan's grin graduated into a smile.

"Well, you're going to have to find out yourself. All I'm going to tell you is that it's amazing fun. I'm going with some friends, but I think you would really enjoy it too. You should come." He seemed eager. At this, I shook my head.

"I'm intrigued, really. And, yes … I'm not doing anything tomorrow. But … I couldn't. You're going with your friends. I don't want to intrude." Surprisingly, Jordan's light smile turned into an impish grin.

"Actually, ah, they're good with this. I was just messaging them. You're kinda already in. I promise they won't bite," he added jokingly. For a moment, I could only stare at him in disbelief. *Absolutely unpredictable. I can't believe it. He already … but, they don't know me! Yet he said they are fine with me coming along.*

"I suppose that means … " I began, then thought better of it. "But I don't think—"

"Please?" Jordan interjected. Before I could finish forming a good excuse in my head, I realized something: I could go. Why not? Honestly, I couldn't think of a reason not to. After a long pause, I tried to smile and nod, an awkward combination for me.

"OK."

The Journal of
Amber Marie Gibson

August 8, Friday

I hope this makes sense. I don't exactly know what to write. Last week, I hacked Teumessian on my own. They were going to bomb Project Plutonium. Truly, I had no choice. But "Mr. Ice-E" had ordered me not to hack. He reported my actions, and, I have been grounded—for a year at least. The FBI de-activated Cyra and my Laelaps programs. In 19 days, which I assume is how long it will take things to be finalized, all contact with E. will be cut off. I don't know what I'm going to do with myself.

The only bright side in the cyber world right now is that I still have my old high school F1R3ST0RM hacking program. There is no way under the sun it could get past Teumessian's programs after all these years, but it can break through most secure sites, and originally made me infamous, so I suppose it's good enough for now.

I know there is a local hacking group here, and, since I'm out of a job, I might join …? I don't know. I need to see what kind of hackers are in this community. It's been years since I last joined a group. I'm not sold on this.

I misjudged Jordan. He is not a threat to me in the least. In contrast—I haven't had any one act this kindly to me in years. Honestly, I'm ashamed of being so suspicious of him. He's a Christian but has promised not to preach at me, so I'm okay with this as long as he keeps his word.

A couple minutes ago, he gave me some sort of ticket. I can't figure out what it's for. All I know is that something is going on down on the pier by the boardwalk tomorrow at 5 P.M. Apparently, he was going to go with a couple of his friends, but he says they are OK if I tag along. I'm a tiny bit … excited. I think. And extremely nervous. Oh, what am I getting myself into?

I suppose I have a year of freedom. I don't have to really hide. I can actually walk free. Yes, this is sort of a vacation. As long as Teumessian waits one more year before they start waging war, maybe I can still stop them.

Here, I made a countdown.

<u>Days of Punishment Remaining</u>: 365

CHAPTER 9

The Salt Breeze Apartment Complex, Apt. 1307
Thursday, August 9, 5:30 A.M.

Jordan

I was up at dawn, ready to tackle the day. In fact, it was so early that Betty wasn't even at the front desk yet. The acute silence was bizarre. It was a good thing I slept well, because I was going to need it.

I raced to Ocean Front, clocked in, and plunged ahead. I didn't actually need to be there for about another four hours, but I was determined to figure it all out. The data I found could just as easily disprove my hypothesis as prove it, but I didn't care. If it was wrong, my hypothesis should be abandoned as a possibility. But if it was right ...

By the time I finished my usual responsibilities with the animals, it was nearly 9:30. Though it was still packed, there wasn't as much concentrated chaos in the map room. I slid into one of the computer chairs and got to work. The end was in sight when I felt someone fold their arms on top of my head.

"Wow, Jordan, you actually beat me here today. Early bird gets the worm?"

I grinned. "Yes, Dylan, do try and keep up," I answered. "And find your own armrest," I added, swatting him off me. Dylan chose to sit on the side of the table instead.

"Just heard about yesterday. Alright, I'll admit, I've always known you're crazy, but this—this is slightly insane. A new fault line? How'd you come up with that?"

"Have you seen the new marks on the map?" I responded. Dylan shrugged a little.

"Yeah. What of it?"

"Those are my handiwork," I admitted. "It might seem random, but if you look at them all at once, it's evident the tremors are actually following a pattern." Dylan thought about this for a moment.

"How do you know the volcanos and such reach far enough down? Do they actually come close to tectonic depth?"

I smiled. He couldn't have asked a better question. Ignoring him a moment longer, I typed a few more lines into the computer and hit enter. A scatterplot materialized out of pixels before my very eyes, graphing the known depths and positions of the fissures. They were much deeper than necessary.

"Yes," I replied, grinning. Dylan leaned forward, eyes wide.

"Now, *that* is cool. How'd you do that?"

"I'll teach you some time. It's not that hard. You just need a lot of data in number form."

Turning back to the screen, I sent a copy of the graph to the main database. Documents, sonar images, chemical reports, charts, tables, hypotheses, and new developments flooded the recent files. Everyone was pouring themselves into getting to the bottom of this; tiny bits and pieces were falling into place. With all of us working together, it was beginning to fit like a picture puzzle. I couldn't wait to see it all come together.

"You're going to be famous. Maybe they'll name the new plate after you!" Dylan exclaimed, punching the air for emphasis. At the mention of such a thing, I felt a bit of color leave my face.

"Oh, please no. I've had enough attention to last me a lifetime," I murmured. "I'm really glad you weren't around when everything went down, Dylan. It was pretty bad. And don't count your eggs before they hatch. None of this is solid yet. We still need loads of proof."

"Alright then, genius. Just don't forget to mention me when you're on TV explaining why there is a tectonic plate named after you. Once you're done playing with the computer art, let me know. I want to take a crack at it," Dylan said, a tease in his voice. I shook my head, chuckling.

"In the rare event I end up on the news, I'll make sure the world knows your name. And have at it. I'm done. If you're working with locations, take the X and Y coordinates and plug them in. Depth works best with fathoms, and distance uses either meters or miles."

I decided to hang around for a little longer to show Dylan the ins and outs of the program. Once he had it down, I was off. Sophie would be here soon. Her thing was microbiology, so she would probably want to hang with the chemists, and though I had already helped her with most of her daily chores, she still had things to do. Everything goes faster with two people, so onward to the manatee tanks!

Most of the solutions to my problems have always been just a keystroke away. But for the life of me, I could not trace where this mysterious ticket came from. What new dark magic was this? *Anything* can be tracked if you know where to look. But after a while, I allowed myself to realize the ugly truth: I had no idea where to look. It was absolutely maddening.

OK, yes; now I was intrigued. Somehow, it seemed the ticket didn't originate from the Internet. Sighing, I realized the only way I could find out what it was for would be to … actually show up. I was terrified, though. I really didn't fit in. But Jordan said he had already told his friends, and they were expecting me. No pressure.

I couldn't believe how quickly life had managed to boot me out of my comfort zone, landing me in the deep snow drift called the normal world. It's disorienting and cold in here. I'm not quite sure which way is up. *I better get my bearings soon. I won't be able to go to Edge for help much longer. Speaking of, maybe I should phone him. I do have to clear a few things up.* There was no point in putting off the inevitable, so I called him.

It was a pain from the very start.

"What is it now, Amber?" Edge snapped on the other side of the line.

He's mad. "What on earth, Edge?! Why are you frustrated with me?" I exclaimed, indignant. "Considering the circumstances, I'd say I have executive rights to being upset. I'm not, so why are you?" Edge sighed as if I was treading on his last, frayed nerve.

"Dang it, Amber, you haven't annoyed me yet. Someone else is ticking me off today. Just, what is it?" At this, I took a moment to tip my chair back, smirk at the ceiling, soak in the moment, and ponder the possibilities. *Someone else is irritating Edge? To the point of making him emotional? Wow, I wonder what they did. Maybe they swapped his coffee creamer with lard or something.*

"Look, I won't take up much of your time. I just want answers," I said, swallowing my smug smile. "Exactly how long am I grounded for? The email said it hadn't been finalized yet."

"You are suspended for 365 days," Edge replied, as if stating the weather. "Well, 364 as of today. You can thank me later. They wanted to add four months."

"Thank you, Edge," I breathed. This seemed to surprise him.

"Learning your place, I see. Good."

You could just say: You're welcome. "Whatever," I muttered. "What if Teumessian somehow finds me? Where do I go? They're developing new tracking technology all the time. We still don't know how they caught up with me in Colorado. What if they've found a way to trace my programs?"

"If they find you, flee to Seattle. If you drop off the map, then I'll know that's where you'll be." There was a commotion on the other end of the line. Edge must have covered the phone for a moment, because I heard a muffled shout and a few swear words. *Meanwhile, at FBI headquarters …* I smiled. Life didn't seem so messy when I realized I wasn't the only one falling apart. A moment later, the ruckus faded. "I'm back. You're not my only subordinate who's being a pain. Are you almost done?"

"Yes, just give me a little longer," I said, trying to massage away an inevitable headache. "Why won't I be able to contact you throughout the year? It seems rather ridiculous."

"I don't know why. Likely a safety precaution. I think it's excessive, but I'm not telling that to the board. They do what they want. Just go with it," he muttered. I could practically see him burning a hole in the wall with an icy, displeased gaze. Shaking away the mental image, I pressed on.

"OK, last question: how am I supposed to support myself? My source of income is hacking for you. Now what?" Edge yelled at someone again. Whoever crossed him today was probably regretting it.

"Look," he snapped. "Get off your lazy butt, go be a useful part of society, and get a freaking job. That's how you are going to support yourself, Amber. I have to go." The line went dead.

For a moment, I just frowned at my phone. *Excuse you, Edge. I work hard, thank you very much. You can keep your rules and regulations. Hacking is my job; it always has been and always will be. You may have me on a leash, but I know how to slip the collar.*

Pushing aside my frustration, I turned my attention to the world of local hackers. Rumors of the "V0RT3X" society flooded the web, but no one seemed to agree on anything. Some people claimed they were all corrupt, destructive black hat hackers, and should be eradicated. Others said they were all white hats, helping the community like heroes. Then, some people were content to call them gray hats. There was hardly anything known for sure about V0RT3X. The police had begrudgingly worked alongside them on occasion, yet the cops were keeping their hopeful ears open for tips on the hackers' meeting place. But no such luck for them so far.

After about half an hour of searching, I stood. If they really did exist, they were good at keeping a low profile. My guess was that most of them were street hackers. If so, then I'd have to take to the streets to find them. Before I went exploring, I decided to see if Betty somehow knew about the mystery ticket. Sauntering into the lobby, I made my way into her field of vision. She noticed me and beamed.

"Mornin', Miss Amber!" she chirped.

"Hi, Betty," I said. Pulling out the ticket, I handed it to her. "I was wondering if you know what this is for." She studied it a while, then shook her head.

"Well, I've never seen the likes of it before. Sorry, darlin'." She handed it back.

"That's OK. Thanks anyway. I'll figure it out." *Eventually*. Bidding Betty good-bye, I slipped out the front doors.

Pretty soon, I was navigating the streets in search of clues about the hackers. Usually, there are encoded messages in graffiti or stray Wi-Fi signals near the stronghold of a hacking group. If you can crack the code or password, it will lead you to the central meeting place. I disturbed a lot of stray cats and ignored plenty of "No Trespassing" signs, but I finally found something. There, on an old cinder block wall, sprayed in electric blue, was a code of some sort. Binary code. A long string of numbers stretched for about six yards. Behind the numbers appeared to be some sort of symbol. Upon closer inspection, I decided its shape resembled a hurricane. The arms of the spiral were dark, purplish-crimson, neon blue, and cyan. The center was black, except for a single silver spot. It looked like a nebula from outer space, or the death of a star. It must be V0RT3X's signature.

Stepping back, I pulled my gaze across the stretch of ones and zeros, and the message began to form in my head. *"Join our cause. Fight back."* I pondered this for a moment; sounded good to me. But what exactly were they fighting? I glanced around. If V0RT3X was leaving messages around here, then they must be nearby. Wherever they were, there would be a lot of concentrated signals—modified signals. They were hackers, after all.

I slipped my phone from my pocket and opened the Network Scanner app. Network Scanner is a program I designed to help me locate incoming and outgoing cyber signals. I can locate phones, count how many televisions are turned on in the surrounding area, or find out if someone's computer is connected to the Internet. Setting the search function to "laptops," I watched as the screen lit up with glowing star-like dots of varying size, shape, and color, based on the strength of the connection or the type. *They can't hide forever. I will find them. It's just a matter of time.*

Sophie is so smart—either that or she has a fantastic imagination. Perhaps both. I have to work so hard to wrap my brain around what she's saying sometimes—especially when it's coming out of her mouth at sonic speed.

"So, it makes sense! The microorganisms have a symbiotic relationship with the algae, and when the tremor disturbed the layers of organic debris in the sea caverns, it dislodged the seaweeds, and the vacuum created by the sudden rupture of the air pockets in the hardened magma pulled it to the surface. And! That's why those fish were displaced. They were caught up in the current, got disoriented from the sun, and stayed near the surface. Then, when the algae pods were exposed to sunlight, they withered and died, and the exoskeletons of the diatoms in the peat cracked and fused with the bacilli in the algae, causing it to have a spongy-like texture. That's what the floating rock stuff is!" I stared blankly at her, trying to fathom what she was telling me. *Too fast. Just too fast.* She sighed. "Am I doing it again?"

When Sophie gets excited, she flits from idea to idea like a Mexican jumping bean, her words-per-minute count hits three thousand, and the scientific terms floating around in her head come pouring out all at once.

I nodded. "Yeah. I might have gotten some of it, but I'm not entirely sure. Try again," I encouraged. Sophie thought for a moment.

"The floating things are clumps of dead algae that have a rare bacteria growing out of them," she said carefully.

"Oh! OK, that makes sense now. I get it." I considered the idea. "Wow, that's amazing! It explains a lot!"

"You think so?" Sophie asked, uncertain. "I don't know. What if I'm way off the mark or I say something really dumb?"

"Go ahead, tell them! Though this isn't the area of my expertise, I think you're on the right track."

"OK. I suppose it's worth a shot," she said hesitantly, then smiled. "Thanks, Jordan!" With that, she scampered off toward the chemists.

Grinning, I watched her go. *There she goes again. I'm like Peter Pan. My shadow occasionally runs off without me.* I looked around the room. I wasn't sure what to do with myself. Since I'd arrived at Ocean Front so early, I'd already done most everything. It was only—I glanced at my watch—eleven, not even noon. *Good grief.* Perhaps I was too motivated for my own good.

Sighing, I went over to the task board to see if there were any miscellaneous jobs that needed done. As I was scrolling down the list, out of the corner of my eye, I saw Laura scowling at her phone. She smacked a button on the screen, shoved it in her pocket, and glared into space. I decided to go talk with her.

Laura handles all our dealings with the rest of the world. She does everything from contacting the Coast Guard to calling an electrician. She's collected and organized, never loses her cool, knows where to find a missing binder or coworker, and has her fingers in just about every metaphorical pie. I have no idea what Ocean Front would do without her.

"Hi, Laura. Is everything OK? If you don't mind my asking, is something wrong? You seem frustrated." Laura sighed, her glare softening a little, yet she kept her frown trained on the ground.

"Hello, Jordan. No, I don't mind you asking." She turned toward me. "We have a potential problem. You heard that Governor Brenton stepped down a couple days ago, right?"

"Yes. Do you know why?"

"I'm afraid not. It seems nobody does. As you know, Ocean Front Rescue is government-funded. Well, the governor was our main patron. Now that he is no longer in power, I need to get in contact with the new governor to confirm the arrangement is still valid."

"But I thought the runner-up from the election was in support of us as well. Is there reason to believe she's changed her mind?" I asked. Laura shook her head.

"There's been a shift in power. For some reason, the position has been given to a Gregory Damon. I've never heard of him before. I can't get ahold of his secretary or anyone else in his little brigade. It's like he's avoiding my messages," Laura muttered.

"Oh. That … that changes things," I said lamely. Laura simply nodded. A slight sense of dread settled over me, but I brushed it off like sand in the wind. *Everything will be just fine. Stop your fretting,* I scolded myself. Then I had an idea. "Laura, do you by any chance have anything that needs to be done?" I asked. "I'm not quite sure what to do with myself right now."

"Nope, sorry," she answered.

Bother. Well, it was worth a shot. "That's alright, thanks anyway. I hope Mr. Damon's people answer their phones. I'll see you around!" Now to find something to do …

There must be a mistake. I shook my phone, then tried smacking the refresh button. The readings didn't change. *Are there really over fifty hackers in there? Could this be V0RT3X's stronghold?* Peeking around the corner of a Dumpster, I studied the building across the street. At first glance, it appeared to be an abandoned warehouse that hadn't seen a human for decades. But my phone had led me here, and after scrutinizing every inch of the place, I found no reason to believe that bugs and birds were its only occupants. There were people in there.

Network Scanner had found a few weak, obscure signals, yet only when I got within a hundred yards of them were the real signals revealed—once I hacked them. The original few were fakes. Now my screen was blazing with the bright, neon blue dots of strong, altered Wi-Fi signals. Small pale-yellow particles were scattering from a few of the blue ones: ghost networks. They must have some pretty decent equipment in there.

I was impressed. Not all hackers used the fake Wi-Fi trick. The "normal" signals were like reinforced blankets that covered all the soldier networks hiding beneath them. V0RT3X had been careful to conceal their presence in the warehouse, and the location was perfect: just a short distance away was a treacherous, rocky shore with a broken pier jabbing out into the rough dark-jade sea. Other old structures dotted the area, and a couple were marked for demolition. It was the side of town that everyone had forgotten.

I needed to know exactly what kind of security programs these hackers were using. It was slightly risky, but I launched my hacking app and started prowling the cyber world. My phone wasn't nearly as sophisticated as my laptop, but it was better than nothing. As long as I went undetected, I could remain in the hack, but if I was discovered, there was no way to fight off counterattacks. Within a few minutes, I had pinpointed the type of protection they were using and found a weak spot; my phone began deciphering the log-on code. If I ended up joining V0RT3X, I would have to help them with all the holes in their firewalls.

"Hey, let's be friends so I can fix those flimsy firewalls of yours, eh?" The memory hit me in the back of the head like a firmly packed snowball. *Eric … how long ago did you tell me that? Ten years? No, eleven … I'm so sorry things happened the way they did. Please, forgive me …*

I must be turning soft, because the threat of tears pounded my eyes. But before they could escape, I pulled the back of my hand across my face, balled my fists, and gritted my teeth, allowing my sorrow to morph into wrath: my survival technique. *I swear on my life, I won't rest until I make them pay for what they did to you.* Taking a shaky breath and letting it out slowly, frowning, I looked back down—and grinned mischievously. On my screen was the layout of a computer desktop, files and icons littered here and there. I had entered a single computer and was now in control.

First, I observed. It would seem the owner was away; there hadn't been any activity for eight minutes and twenty-four seconds. Next, I used commands to make the mouse pointer invisible—you know you are being hacked when there is a rogue mouse flying across your screen. Last, I set my systems so that if the mouse was moved manually, it would reappear and I would lose control. It was better to lose connection than lose my anonymity.

Soon I was browsing the files and cyber history of the little PC. The laptop had a powerful core which devoured electricity like a ravenous lion, yet it ran smoothly. It could process multiple tasks at once, and its records stretched years back. I had found a treasure trove.

V0RT3X is a vigilante group of "Robin Hood hackers" trying to make the community a better and safer place. They were like the undercover police, except some of what they did was definitely illegal—but it did have good results. Exposing political fraud, convicting criminals, attacking black hat hackers, diverting funds from ritzy, upper-class clubs and giving to nonprofit organizations and hospitals were just a few of their daily exploits. *Join our cause. Fight back … I think I will.*

Suddenly, my connection dropped and my phone returned to its home screen. The computer's owner had returned. I quickly powered off my phone in case they saw they had been hacked and tried to search for nearby signals. After a few minutes, I decided the coast was clear. When I turned my phone back on, I slipped a tiny tracking bug into V0RT3X's overall system; even if they decided to relocate, I wouldn't have to hunt them down again. Then I noticed the time. I knew a good hacker-spy must be patient, but perhaps I had been a little too patient. It was 3:47. *I should probably head back. I still have to convince myself to go out tonight.* Reluctantly, I took one last look at this warehouse that was pretending to be lonely.

I would return to match my skills with the hackers—to win my way in. It was only a matter of time before I was one of them.

Why do we even keep these? Yes, this species is endangered, but maybe that's a good thing. Despite being the same size as a housecat, they make sharks look safe. Sea spiders are scary enough in pictures, let alone face-to-face. Or, face-to-fangs. These are the kinds of things nightmares are made of.

I had managed to get myself one of the most obscure jobs possible: feeding the invertebrates. The few times I've done this, I end up saving the sea spiders for last. I don't know why. It's chilling yet slightly interesting to watch them sink their fangs into the tiny minnows and eat them whole—and I can safely watch all of it with my face less than a foot from the action. Glass tanks are wonderful.

Even with the glass between us, you spiders are still terrifying, I thought, aiming a slightly disconcerted frown at one particular arachnid; it had stopped maiming a minnow to watch me with its glinting, pitch-black eyes. I didn't doubt it would attack me if it had the chance. *Thank heavens you only live underwater*—my heart almost stopped. Icy electric shivers shot up and down my spine and I let out a very undignified shriek.

"*DYLAN!*" I yelped. Beaming, my supposed friend released my shoulders from his pounce claw-attack and started to laugh as, fuming, I regained my balance, sprang to my feet, and exclaimed: "I will string you beneath the pier and use you as shark bait!" This did not help my cause, for Dylan was now laughing even harder.

"That was new!" he said, delighted. "I'm a little scared, considering the pier is where we're headed." A moment later, his teasing smile turned devilish. "Oh, and that was a lovely scream. I've found your weakness, Jordan. This is gonna come back to haunt you." I tried to gather the remaining scraps of my dignity.

"Not fair," I huffed. "And is it really already 5 o'clock?"

"Yep," Dylan affirmed, nodding happily. I knew I'd look back on this and laugh, but I was still flustered.

"Next time the demon arachnids need to be fed, you're going to have to do it. I resign," I said, shoving the empty fish pail into Dylan's hands.

Before long, we were trotting down the boardwalk to the pier, chatting excitedly about the night ahead of us. The street was a bustling mass of people, and faces blurred past me like autumn leaves in a playful wind. Most of the community had shown up for the festival, like always, despite the main attraction being still three and a half hours away.

"Dylan! Jordan! Over here!"

Toward the middle of the pier stood Matt and Chloe. Matt was grinning, a light of anticipation in his eyes. Chloe was waving to us and bouncing on her toes, her pink streak of hair bobbing among the pale gold sea that skimmed the tops of her shoulders. Grinning, we went over to join them.

"How are you already here, sis?" Dylan asked Chloe. "I thought you were going to meet up with us half an hour from now." Chloe smiled.

"I begged off work early. I didn't want to miss anything. Anyway, there were hardly any customers; everyone's down here tonight." Chloe is a waitress at—get this—a restaurant named The Chubby Pelican. (And people think The Flying Turtle is an odd name.)

"Hey, where were you yesterday evening, Jordan?" Matt asked. "We got a message from an unknown number saying Samuel would have to step in for you and take the lead because you weren't going to be able to make it. What happened?" Matt and I were involved in the youth group at church. He was one of the leaders; I was on the music team.

"Well, first, let me ask: how did it go? I barely gave you a heads-up."

"It went fine. He did great," Matt affirmed.

"I knew he could do it," I said, smiling. "My phone was dead, so I borrowed one to send the text. And, well … it's chaos at Ocean Front. I don't know where to start."

"Yeah, 'chaos' is an understatement," Dylan jumped in. "Here, I'll explain. Let me start with this: Jordan's breaking new and dangerous ground, and the ground is breaking in dangerously new ways." That earned some confused looks; I found myself wondering how long it took him to come up with that. I gave him a warning nudge. Unfortunately, he wasn't finished, and ignored the hint. "And I have discovered that someone is terrified of sea spi—" I clapped my hand over his mouth before he could do any more damage.

"What he's trying to say is that there may be a new fault line forming. All those tremors near the islands—well, I found some new data, and now they are being reinspected." I gave Dylan a look of warning before letting him breathe again. *Don't you dare finish that other statement. I know where you live, and I know your fear.*

There was a long pause. Chloe opened her mouth to say something, but had evidently lost the words. Matt was taking his time thinking this through, and appeared rather stunned. I sighed.

"Could someone else please volunteer a crazy story? The silence is unbearable." Chloe finally spoke.

"Does it have to be real, or can it be fiction? Give me a couple minutes and I can come up with a pretty good tale." She had a playful look in her eyes.

"Never mind." I sighed and chuckled. "I miss normal life." At this pathetic statement, Dylan grinned impishly.

"Jordan, 'normal life' died years ago, about the time we all met. It's never coming back. Sorry to break it to you." I rolled my eyes.

"Alright, smart mouth, you win. Can we move on now?"

"Sure." Dylan turned to the others and grinned again. "OK, my turn. You wouldn't believe what happened this morning. The janitor was cleaning the shark tank today and slipped and fell in. The ladder was broken, and he almost got eaten—but someone pulled him out just in time. One of the tiger sharks found his baseball cap on the bottom of the pool and ate it instead. You shoulda seen the look on his face … " Apart from the chuckles of the others, I couldn't believe my ears.

"Dylan, why haven't I heard about this, and why didn't you speak up earlier? That definitely qualifies as a crazy story." Dylan just shrugged.

"I was gonna bail you out eventually, but it was fun to watch. You survived. No rescue needed."

I stared at him in disbelief. The rascal. Chloe started giggling. Matt's grin grew. Soon we were all laughing. Looking at my friends, I knew deep down that there was nothing else I could ever want. We were a team—forever. I wouldn't trade this for the world.

I had been watching Jordan and his friends for a while. They were so happy. It was like an inviting pool of light and laughter surrounded them. It was like a dream, like I had stepped outside of time and space to observe this gathering.

The courage I had gathered was gone, though, and I couldn't convince myself to go over. Yet neither could I convince myself to leave. It was tearing me up inside. I was trapped in the shadows, at the edge of the river of people, gazing at the far shore, longing for and fearing the same thing: to be accepted again.

If Jordan's friends were anything like he was, they might not mind me. But I didn't want to ruin this night for them. They were all having fun together and I was an outsider. I looked down at the ticket in my hands. *What is this for? What are they planning? Would it be rude to not show up? Are they counting on me?* No matter how much I tried, I couldn't move, call out, or make up my mind. *I should have never come. I want to go over, but would doing so be selfish of me? Or would it be worse if I left? I don't know what to do.*

Maybe it would have been better if I hadn't discovered the truth about myself that night. Until that moment, I had never realized it, but there was no denying the truth now: I was lonely.

I glanced at my watch. *Amber should be here by now. I don't think she's planning on coming.* Sighing, I shoved my hands back in my pockets and looked at my friends.

"Looks like Amber's a no-show. Sorry to keep you all waiting. Shall we move on?" My statement was met with halfhearted agreements and shrugs. Matt offered a small smile.

"Hey, we gave it our best, and can always try again," he pointed out. I nodded and we were off. Matt was right, and I knew there would be other opportunities. But I felt a vague sadness. Tonight was special …

Then, two things happened in the space of a heartbeat. I sensed someone approaching behind me, and a quiet voice called my name. Even before I could get my feet turned around, I knew who it was. Amber had come after all.

I don't know what possessed me, but when the little group started to leave, a feeling of desperation hit me. If I didn't go, I would always wonder what I had missed. In a moment of bravery, I dashed after them. Four pairs of eyes were suddenly on me, though, and I went back to being scared.

"Hi. Uh … sorry I'm late. I got a little turned around," I muttered, trying not to fidget and thus give away my lie. Jordan simply smiled.

"That's OK. I'm just glad you found us," he said, and seemed to be about to add something else when a voice cut him off.

"Oh! The map girl!" *The map … girl?* I was already blushing, but now my temperature reached melting point. *I wanna go home.*

Jordan looked irked with the younger guy, who was shrugging and muttering something. The other one simply looked confused; evidently, he hadn't heard of the map. But the girl didn't seem phased. She strode forward, grabbed my hand, and shook it enthusiastically.

"Don't mind him. He can be an idiot. I would know; he's my brother. I'm Chloe. You must be Amber. It's great to meet you!"

"Nice … to meet you too." I was still mortified from a moment ago, but Chloe's eagerness made me feel a little better. *I can do this. It will be fun.* And with that, the night began. It wasn't long before I could put names to the rest of the happy, glowing faces I had watched just a short while ago.

Matt was the oldest. He was quiet and thoughtful—and very thoughtfull. He would mull something over in his mind, then make a stunning observation or an amazing comment. It was interesting to listen to what he had to say. He was quite engaging. His hair was nearly black as charred oak, and his eyes looked like dark chocolate, but they sparkled brightly whenever he laughed.

The blue-eyed, dirty blond-haired boy's name was Dylan. He and Chloe were siblings. It seemed to me he was the youngest—or perhaps I was misinterpreting his silliness. Before long, I came to see him as a sort of class clown of the group, but despite the occasional lame joke or pathetic play on words, he was good at it; he made us all laugh. He knew when to make a pun, when to duck Chloe's warning smacks, and when to be quiet. Well … most of the time.

I could see the resemblance between Chloe and Dylan; it was rather obvious. Though her hair and eyes were lighter in color, she looked just like him. She had dyed a section of her hair neon pink, though, as if to make sure they weren't too similar. But if I was judging by personality, I would have thought Chloe was Jordan's sister. She was like a hyper female clone of him, except she was a little more distractible, slightly sassy, and loved pink things and kitties.

And Jordan … was being Jordan. He was the same person around his friends as he was around others, a rare and wonderful trait. They all listened to him, and though there didn't seem to be a definite leader of the group, I would say he was suggesting—if not calling—most of the shots. He made sure to include me in everything they did. I wasn't stuck in the cold, silent background or part of the scenery; they didn't forget me.

Still, the first half of the night, I was wishing to go home. But as time went on, I enjoyed every minute of it.

She came. She actually came. I can't believe it worked! Thank the Lord. Tonight of all nights … I can hardly wait! This is the same feeling I got as a kid on Christmas morning. Everything had aligned perfectly. This festival only came around once a year. Since the date changed slightly each time, and since Amber had only been in Santa Barbara for a few weeks, there was no way she could have already known about it. But she came anyway— and I got the feeling she would love it.

Occasionally, I noticed the others looking at their watches or checking the time on their phones. Soon, excitement was lacing the air all around us. People were finding little spots to stake out for the show. I snuck a peek at my watch. 8:56. *Yes, finally—just four minutes!* I caught Matt's eye and gave the slightest nod. He grinned and nodded back. The two of us subtly guided the others off the pathway and onto one of the piers. Dylan and Chloe caught on and followed our lead, chatting with Amber the whole way. She didn't notice our strange route until we came to its end.

"Why are we stopping here?" she asked. *Come on. Start! Any second now …*

"Keep your eyes on the horizon. You'll see." I had a hard time pulling my eyes off the sky to meet Amber's inquisitive gaze. From over the water came a brief hiss, then a *boom!* as a single white firework lit up the night.

The pause felt like eternity.

Then, it finally began.

What was that all about? What are we waiting for? There was a long stillness. No matter how much I searched, the only thing I could see was darkness. I was about to turn to Chloe when something caught my eye. Up out of the sea drifted a speck of pale yellow light. Then another. And another. Slow-moving, glowing orbs dusted the sky for miles, some drifting overhead. My mind balked. *They look like ...*

"Welcome to the Firefly Festival, Amber." Jordan's eyes had been fixed on the sky, but now he turned to grin at me. The mysterious lights threw glitter down from above, setting his dark brown hair ablaze with dancing lights, and his eyes sparkled with excitement. "It's only just beginning."

Suddenly, a multitude of fiery stars exploded into the sky, taking my breath with them. I'd never seen anything like it. Fast-moving streaks of scarlet, orange, and golden-yellow surged up from the sea, as if the water had ignited, and the flames leapt higher and higher, reaching for the stars.

Gradually, the hue of the spots changed and the fire morphed into shifting clouds of blue and green, like the waves had chosen to leave the sand bed and go crash in the sky. White mingled with the turquoise, like bubbles, and spun a curtain of water and light. The ocean reflected the glow, the whole world surreal.

The white temporarily washed over the rest of the colors, leaving spots of pale lilac and violet in its wake, which wove in and out of the teal. It looked ... exactly like the Aurora Borealis. My brain was trying to convince me that my eyes had a glitch. This was impossible. But it was real, it was right there, just over the water. If I reached far enough, maybe I could even touch it. To my disappointment, the lights got fewer and dimmer and seemed to dwindle away.

Then, right when it seemed to be over, the sea burst one last time. All the colors of the rainbow took to the sky in the brightest array yet. Neon pinks, poppy red, crimson, orange, yellow, lime, forest green, light blue, navy, indigo, and violet. Behind the curtain of dots, white fireworks emphasized their beauty and everything was covered with radiant light. It stopped as suddenly as it had begun, and the pale-yellow, lazy, glowing "fireflies" returned to brush the darkness again.

Though I had been to the Firefly Festival every year since I was born, it still left me breathless. Even though the actual show lasted for a good ten minutes or so, it felt like mere seconds. Chloe was saying something about the finale, Matt was agreeing, and Dylan was adding commentary. But I didn't pay it any mind. Not really.

I had never seen Amber this way before. I had expected her to enjoy the festival, but I had no idea it would mean this much to her. She was wearing her first genuine look of happiness. She had grinned, smiled, and giggled before—but now she was beaming. Her eyes were slightly glassy, as if she was fighting tears, and her face was just as radiant as the display had been.

"So, what did you think of it, Amber?" Dylan asked, leaning over the railing a bit, trying to catch a glimpse of her expression. Slowly, she pulled away from the edge and turned to him and the others.

"That … was the most amazing thing … I have ever seen in my life. It's … " she gazed back over the sea, searching for the right words: "astoundingly beautiful," she concluded. That made me grin. *Astoundingly beautiful. Wow, I'm using that phrase from here on out.* Amber tipped her head slightly to one side. "What were those? They weren't real fireflies, I know that. How did … what happened?"

Matt grinned and launched into an explanation. "There are boats out on the water carrying tarps full of balloons. Each balloon has a small light inside it. The color of the glow depends on the color of the balloon skin. Like a synchronized fireworks show, there is a pre-established order by which the boatmen release the tarps or cut the strings. The first and last parts are called the 'fireflies,' and over time, more segments have been added, but the original show consisted only of fireflies."

"How many years has the festival been around?" Amber asked, intrigued. Matt looked to me for help. I shrugged.

"I don't know. It's been here longer than me," I answered. *That was less than helpful. Oh well, I'll look it up some time.*

"It's been here your whole life … " Amber whispered as she gazed with wonder at the last of the lights fading into the black night sky. Something about her statement didn't sit right with me, though. I couldn't put my finger on it, but something was off. *Never mind. You're just tired.*

"Oh! Wait, what about this?" Amber asked, pulling the ticket out of her pocket. There was a pause, during which we all tried to decide how to answer. Eventually, Dylan's sneaky grin turned into muffled snickers. Amber noticed. "What is it? I was supposed to bring this. What is it for?" she pressed.

"I can't believe that worked. She brought it! Matt, you're a genius," Dylan exclaimed through hiccupping laughter.

Amber's look of utter confusion was rather amusing, but I fought the urge to smile, let alone join Dylan in his laughter. I didn't want to hurt her feelings. After glancing at the rest of us, Matt sighed thoughtfully.

"It's fake," he explained. "We weren't sure how to best convince you to come. It was spur of the moment and you had never met us, so the tactic we voted on was the intrigue of the unknown. Keeping the festival a surprise seemed like the only thing to do, but Chloe came up with the idea; a ticket would divert your attention from the actual event. That way, even if you heard about the Firefly Festival during the day, you would still think we had something else planned. I plead guilty. I'm the one who designed it. In my defense, Chloe thought it up, Dylan was the deciding vote, and I sent it to Jordan to print. We're all guilty. Sorry."

"It wasn't my favorite plan. I'm so very sorry to trick you, Amber," I muttered, feeling even worse now that I heard it all explained. She turned to me, her face an unreadable, blank look of shock. *I think this was a bad idea. I should have never gone along with it—*

"Thank you," Amber said hesitantly, smiling sheepishly.

"What?" I asked, surprised.

"It worked. I was curious and I came. Thank you." Silently, I released the breath I had been holding on to so tightly. *It didn't upset her. It did work. She came. Thank you, Lord.*

If I closed my eyes tightly, I could still see a dim picture of the tiny lights shining in the night sky. But I couldn't look at it for long; if I didn't pay attention to where I was going, I might walk into a lamp pole or accidently bump Jordan off the sidewalk. Even with my eyes open, it was hard to focus. Though I tried and tried, I couldn't wrap my head around the fact that I had been *accepted*. It was too good to be true.

"I am so glad you came tonight, Amber. Please, I think I speak for all of us when I say we would love to do this again!" Chloe hadn't hesitated in saying

this. No matter how many gaps in the conversations there had been or how many social skills had been forgotten on my part, she barely seemed to notice. She treated me like … a friend. Chloe would not let me leave until she had some assurance that I would be back. I have not exchanged phone numbers with anyone in years. I felt like a silly college girl. But I didn't want this feeling of naïve happiness to disappear, so I didn't push it away. Instead, I cherished it while it lasted.

My thoughts were interrupted as Jordan lightly cleared his throat.

"Well, I don't see any teeth marks, so I assume they didn't bite." I grinned. *That is a conversation starter if ever there was one.*

"You're clever with words. You know that, Jordan?" I said. This brought a pleased smile to his face.

"Thank you. But only sometimes."

"Sometimes? I would say most times, and I still have all of my fingers, so I guess that means you're right. I can see why Chloe, Matt, and Dylan are your friends. They're amazing." That practically made him glow.

"I think so too. They are amazing. And I'm so glad you enjoyed the festival. You did like it, right?"

"Yes, very much. It brought back an old memory," I said.

Jordan turned a curious gaze on me. "How so?"

I hesitated for a moment. "When I was little," I started slowly, "there was a huge open field behind our house. My siblings and I called it the Firefly Field. I don't know why, but every single firefly seemed to stay there during the summer. We would take willow branches, run through the grass with our 'magic wands,' and light up the night as hundreds of fireflies flew away. To the mind of a child, it was the best thing in the world."

"Wow. That sounds … " Jordan suddenly grinned triumphantly. " … astoundingly beautiful." It took me a moment to realize those were the same words I had used just a short while ago to describe the festival. I felt a smile spread across my face.

"Again with the cleverness! How do you do that?" I asked.

Jordan shrugged. "I don't know. It comes and goes. I actually tend to be open-mouth-insert-foot more often than not." Looking up, I realized we were almost to the apartments, and felt rather sad. All good things must come to an end, but I didn't want it to end this soon. "Matt, Dylan, Chloe, and I hang out on Thursdays. You're welcome to join us anytime," Jordan said.

Is he actually inviting me to the group again? "Jordan, I appreciate the offer, but I don't think you can speak for the others like that. How do you know they don't mind me being there? I better not. It would be intruding." Whenever anyone says that kind of thing, they are sincerely hoping that someone will deny it; I sure was. And Jordan sure did deny it.

"No, it's not like that at all! It's actually the opposite. They loved you! I liked having you there, the others did, you evidently like it, all of us did, ah … I'm not doing so well with the words anymore. Please say yes so I can stop rambling."

This was just too good to be true. Did they all really want me to come? "Well, I suppose we will have to wait and see," I answered coolly. "I'll think about it." That was all it took to get Jordan smiling again.

Once I got back to my room, I messaged the number Chloe gave me. Within a minute I had a reply and added Chloe as a contact. But before I put my phone down, another text lit up my screen: Chloe welcoming me to the group chat. *What have I gotten myself into? Who is on the chat?* I soon had my answer. Messages from three unknown numbers popped up.

"Matt"
"Dylan, present and accounted for!"
"Jordan here"

Numbly, I saved their numbers. I wasn't sure how to feel about all of this. Insecurity washed over me, as if the ground wasn't trustworthy. *Too good to be true …* I was treading dangerous ground. They were growing on me, and I didn't have the willpower to push them away. I knew it was best to avoid normal people; death followed me around like a lost puppy, yowling for my attention and nipping anyone who got too close. But I also didn't want to spend a year in utter solitude. Without hacking, I didn't have anything to do—not really. Perhaps there was room for a few friends in my life now.

Only a year. Then, I'm sorry, but you all won't be seeing much of me anymore. I don't want you to get hurt.

The innocent, free happiness settled back in my heart. I found myself wondering what kinds of things Matt would say next time I saw him, how many jokes Dylan would make, where Chloe would run off to so she could inspect cute things, and what Jordan would say to make us all smile. At these thoughts, I decided I'd try and go next Thursday. And if not next week, then the one after that.

My computer exclaimed its feelings about being temporarily ignored by quickly *ding*-ing four times. A message from Edge. *Great. What does he want?* Freedom was forgotten as I read his email.

Edge

I found you a project. This encrypted letter was intercepted earlier today from a major illegal firearms bust. It is possible that there are others linked to the group. I do not feel like doing this right now, so I will let the night owl take a crack at it. Have it done by morning and I will see if I can get you a side hacking job.

view.attachment.docx

The air was pulled from beneath my wings, but I didn't feel myself hit the ground. A chance at hacking! I had to decipher the document in time, even if it took me all night; I just had to! Algorithms, codes, and symbol patterns were my specialties in math. They were like puzzles, except earning the "high score" meant learning an important secret.

Despite this wonderful offer, I was still irked with Edge. He too spoke in riddles; the only difference was that he didn't want me to crack his code. He couldn't swallow his pride enough to admit he needed help, just like every other FBI agent. "I do not feel like doing this right now" actually means "I have scrambled my brain trying to figure this out, but I'm stumped." Oh, and "have it done by morning" means: "This was assigned to me and there is a deadline. Get it done so I don't get in trouble."

Queuing up some fast-paced electronic music through my headset and grabbing a caffeinated soda, I stimulated my brain to its sharpest, most energized state, and dove into the arduous task of deciphering the message.

CHAPTER 10

Somewhere near The Salt Breeze Apartment Complex
Friday, August 17, 7:15 A.M.

Amber

Well, that good-for-nothing "partner" of mine—more like slave master—used me! I should have known. I deciphered the message on time, but Edge was bluffing; there was no reward waiting for me. But I'll bet my right arm there were more than a few words of praise waiting for him. After all, "he" cracked a code that led the FBI straight to the meeting places of a huge weapons and drug ring. The code had been a tough one. Really tough. Since it tripped up my system, I even had to work part of it out on paper. Even after I'd cracked the code, it had taken me all night due to its sheer size. By the time I had finished the whole ordeal, dawn was breaking. I didn't sleep. At all. Needless to say, it was brutal. If I ever saw Edge again, face to face … well, I had till then to think of my revenge.

After that disappointment, my week ended up chock full of what the new normal would look like. Friday was stuffed with … nothing. Drawing, exploring the city, programming a simple AI for fun, talking with Jordan, and messaging the group. Nothing profoundly important.

Saturday was mostly empty, except I went ocean swimming for the first time. It was actually quite enjoyable. I dove under waves, found shells, and watched a seagull eat a dead jellyfish. That was amusing. Also, between my clothes and hair, I think I gained about two pounds in sand.

Sunday, Jordan was gone in the morning. Since I had no one to chat with, I grabbed some coffee at The Flying Turtle then spent the whole day on the docks, sketchbook and pencil in hand, attempting to draw the waves. Later, I went to the library and got both the historical fiction and the Western romance I had been debating over when Cyra messaged me. Win-win.

Monday was the beginning of a stretch of Jordan's surf lessons. I wasn't sure if he'd noticed I was watching him. To be honest, I wanted to try surfing. It looked like skateboarding, but on water. I skateboarded all the time when I was in high school. Later on Jordan and I chatted, and, of course, more messages with the others—mainly Chloe.

Tuesday was just like Monday, except it felt longer because I had to go shopping. I may be female, but I have an inborn hate for shopping. In the evening, I heard music coming from Jordan's balcony. He plays the guitar. Sometimes, I seriously question what I'm doing with my life; I'm not sure I can even play a kazoo.

Wednesday, I was a lazy couch potato and did nothing but game, binge on TV shows, and read. The only productive things I did were a bit more research on V0RT3X and watching another surf lesson.

Thursday, I decided to go hang out with the others. The more I talked with them, the more I felt I could be myself. I had to be careful; I couldn't get too comfortable. We voted on a movie and went to see it. It was edge-of-the-seat kind of exciting, yet there were also parts that made me laugh. I'm glad I went.

Now … today.

Most of my morning was spent setting up the remainder of my F1R3ST0RM software and charging up my computer's extra power supply. After some test runs, I decided the old program was still strong enough. Today I would wage war, play a game of chess. Or, checkers. (I never learned to play chess.) *I will be a V0RT3X member by this time tomorrow. All I have to do is win my way in.*

So, I found myself crouching behind the rusty dumpster, just like on the day of the Firefly Festival. Except this time, there were guards by the warehouse. They weren't obvious, but I could see them leaning against the side of a nearby building, watching the door. V0RT3X must have realized I hacked them. That was unfortunate, but not unworkable. I could still pull this off; I just had to be smart. Until I got inside, I was at a serious disadvantage. If I simply walked out into the sentries' field of vision, they would be on me in moments. There was no way I could sneak past, and I wasn't strong enough to overpower them. I would have to get the hackers' attention from out here—without, that is, getting myself clobbered and thrown into the sea.

Flipping open my laptop, I stared at the screen, pondering what to do. I could use some of my tricks to get part of the way, but the real show wouldn't start until all eyes were on me. If my little games didn't get me in, I would be stuck halfway, exposed and vulnerable. Turning to the main F1R3ST0RM branch, I started pounding out code. It would be a gamble, but I targeted every computer in a 150-yard radius. Hopefully, there were no PC-using civilians nearby; if so, this would probably freak them out. I finished my creation, my little monster, and prepared to release chaos.

The virus would only disintegrate on my command. It would cause all the information stored in the circuit boards to flash across the screens of the computers it affected, over and over again, rendering the system inaccessible. Sliding the little package of pain into the hole in VORT3X3's cyber firewall, I took a deep breath to calm my nerves, then launched the program. *I hope this works.*

I am so glad tomorrow is Saturday. It's time to move my clock back within smacking distance. The only time my alarm works is when it is across the room. That way, I have to get out of bed to turn it off. Though I hadn't watched the sun rise, I was still up early. Strangely, Amber was awake before I was—I think. I'm pretty sure I heard her moving around; the floorboards creaked faintly in protest of her hurried footsteps. I wondered what she was doing up so early.

Even more surprising was the scene that met me when I arrived at Ocean Front. Curled up at the edge of the pinniped habitat was Sophie. She was holding a gray seal pup in her arms and stroking it gently; whenever she stopped, it would nuzzle its head under her hand as if to remind her to keep petting it. But Sophie wasn't really paying attention. She was staring into nothingness, a faraway yet slightly disturbed look on her face. The usual twinkle in her eyes was missing.

"Good morning," I called. Sophie jumped slightly and seemed to snap out of her daze.

"Oh, good morning, Jordan." She frowned a bit, as if she had forgotten something she wanted to say. The seal, slightly startled by my arrival, tried to wiggle away, thus regaining Sophie's attention. "Sorry, little one. I should probably put you back now."

"How long have you been here?" I asked, noting her shirt was damp but not truly wet, as if it had been drying for a while.

"About an hour, I suppose."

"An hour! Why?" *And I thought I was early.*

Sophie shrugged, absentmindedly tracing her finger through a puddle on the tiles. "My neighbors were noisy this morning. I couldn't get back to sleep, so I came here." She began to brighten a bit. Turning, she carefully placed the seal on a rock in its lagoon. It dove into the water and swam off happily. Sophie stood and her strange, spacy look finished disappearing; she looked fine again. "So, what are we doing today?"

"Mostly medical assessments to see if any animals can be released," I said. Sophie smiled broadly.

"I like these kinds of days. I want to help all the sea creatures get home again. Will I ever get to see a reintegration team at work? Oh, could I ever tag along? That would be amazing—wait, have *you* ever seen a release? Have you ever helped in one? Is it exciting? What is it like?" *And Sophie is back to being Sophie. In full force.*

There was a good chance I was being a pain in the neck. Fantastic. I needed the hackers' undivided attention. Even though I had already released the virus, I could still tweak it, and I made sure it was as annoying as possible.

Let's see … Uh, make it repeat random sound files, maximum volume level. After launching the new branch, I soon heard a commotion in the building. The guards heard it too and, confused, two went inside to see what all the ruckus was about. *I can target a few systems to crash …* Twenty-four computers went down for the count. *Pause virus for a few seconds, just long enough to give the illusion of control … OK, that should be enough.*

I closed my laptop and returned it to my messenger bag. Now I had to wait until the hackers discovered they couldn't shut it off. Then they would need me. Once I deleted the virus, I would show them what I was made of and plead my case until they allowed me to join. The question was: when would they give up? If I timed it wrong, it could ruin everything.

My timing was decided for me.

"Who are you and what do you think you're doing here?" Turning toward the alley entrance, I found myself looking down the barrel of a handgun. The hands that held it were shaking. My eyes traveled past the quivering barrel and up to its wielder.

It was a boy. He seemed about eighteen, rather skinny and homely looking. He stood alone; his pals hadn't noticed me yet. There was a hardened resolve etched in his face, but beyond that mask I could see fear. I felt a pang of pity for him. I knew this species of human well. I was once one. Slowly, I began to stand.

"Don't move or I'll shoot!" he stammered. I knew deep down he wouldn't. Judging by how he was shaking, I could tell this was the first time he had ever pulled a gun. It appeared he was about to call for help, but I stopped him.

"Wait! No, I'll … " *Turn yourself in. He will take you to the hackers.* "I'll come with you. Don't shoot me. I won't run. I surrender." Keeping my hands in the air to prove my sincerity, I carefully continued to get up. This presented quite a dilemma for him. What to do with a spy? He motioned to the street with the gun.

"Start walking. And don't try anything stupid, or I will shoot you. I swear."

"OK, OK," I consented, then grinned inwardly. *This will earn you popularity points with your friends, and I'll get to be in a hacking group again. This is our lucky day, kid.*

The moment I stepped onto the road with my escort in tow, the other sentries came running. Soon I lost the right to use my own two legs as they grabbed my arms and dragged me off. It was then that my confidence faltered and I had the first notion that this might end badly. When the door opened, I found myself in a huge room decked out with high-tech equipment. *So, this is V0RT3X's stronghold.*

A huge server stood as the axis on which the rest of the room spread out, wires snaking away from it, reaching to the far corners of the building. The sound of a generator humming quietly from somewhere above made me realize there was a second floor. Pockets of tables and chairs took up about half the floor space, and the ground was covered with cords and duct tape. On the far wall was a large screen, data flying across its face. It would seem my virus had infected everything, because everyone was busy at their computers; I went mostly unnoticed. The boy approached a man in the far corner. After an intense conversation, he strode over, leaving the small-fry scrambling to keep up. One of my captors stepped forward.

"Ender, Jason found this girl across the street. She may have something to do with the glitch." He threw me down before him, as if I was a sacrifice. As my knees hit, I gritted my teeth, biting back a harsh retort. *You'll regret that later today.* I began to get up, but was pushed back to my knees.

I looked up at Ender's cross face and wondered once more how many pieces they would cut me into if I failed. We locked eyes for a moment, both glaring, neither backing down. Suddenly, in one quick move, he shoved me to the side, slipped my bag over my head, and tossed it to one of his friends.

"Crack the password and shut the virus down," Ender ordered, then turned back to me. "Who are you?" he asked. I hesitated. *No way am I giving them my real name. If they look me up, I'm done for.*

"That's not important yet," I said cryptically. He gazed steadily into my defiant face, doubtless debating whether he should just shoot me now.

"I assume you are the one responsible for this fiasco. Are you working for a gang or an enemy hacking creed? Are you with the police?" he pressed.

"No. I answer to no one," I replied, smiling slightly to keep calm. "My reasons are my own. For now." *I just have to be brave and stall a little longer. Please don't kill me.* Ender's frown deepened and he tried a different route.

"How did you find this place?"

"I searched." I could tell my vague answers were seriously testing his patience.

"This is your last chance to comply. After that ... well, I will decide what will happen to you," he declared after a painfully long silence. *Time is running out. Please give up on my computer. Please, please, please ...*

"Jason?" I asked. Jason froze under the spotlight of my attention. "How are they doing with my laptop? Have they unlocked it yet?" Jason glanced nervously at Ender for instructions. After a nod of approval, he hurried off. I turned back to Ender. "I will talk when you appreciate what I can do. Until then, to pass the time, we can play this game again if you want. Maybe I'll throw in some new adjectives." *Where am I getting this sass? It's fantastic.*

"You are in no position to be negotiating. I could have you killed for infiltrating us. Is that what you want?" Ender threatened. I shrugged, trying to maintain my rebellious, disinterested air.

"Not exactly," I admitted, pretending to inspect my nails. "Life is relatively enjoyable. It could be better, but it's good enough for me. I don't exactly want to lose it. How about you put me in a position where I am allowed to negotiate—"

"Shut up." Ender cut me off, rubbing his head and grimacing. "No, you'll be lucky if you have a miserable life after this. That's best-case scenario. Worst case: you die." I shut up. *Time to put a lid on it, Amber. Don't get carried away.*

Jason returned, looking almost pale. "Ender, the computer—they're part way. But the systems, they … "

"What is it? Spit it out!" Ender exclaimed, exasperated. Jason threw a terrified glance my way. Once again, I felt empathy for this poor kid.

"What he is trying to say," I explained calmly, "is that they can't seem to crack the password and that your systems are beginning to overload. You see, my computer is designed in such a way that if it is connected to a decoder, it will sidestep the program and jam the system. It will go critical if I don't shut it off." The lights flickered and the power surged. I smiled at the perfect timing. "It would be a shame if your entire mainframe disintegrated."

"Ender … " Jason looked like he wanted to disappear, but pushed on. "Please, let her fix this. She's right. It's pretty bad." Ender looked between Jason and me with shell-shocked, furious disbelief.

"Yes, Ender, do listen to Jason. You can't save your systems without me. Now, I will put an end to all of this, and you will give me a status at which we can negotiate. Deal?" After a pause, Ender huffed a reluctant sigh.

"Fine. But make one wrong move and it's over. I'll have you shot."

"Hey! No! That's rude!" I paused my scolding to wipe the salty seawater out of my eyes. I had gotten blasted in the face by a dolphin. It was laughing at me now—and so was Sophie. "What was that for?"

"You skipped over it just now. It thinks you forgot about it," Sophie said through giggles. I looked down at the slimy, nasty mackerel in my hand.

"Well, if that's my only crime—" I threw the fish into the air and the dolphin shot up to grab it. "I plead guilty. I think I paid the price, though."

Sophie chuckled and gingerly pulled a cod by the tip of its tail from the fish pail, tossing it to another dolphin. She was having a blast. I was glad to see her smiling again; I was starting to get concerned. Heaven knows what had gotten into her earlier.

She had been acting strange on and off for hours. We were headed down one of the hallways past the shark tanks. Then, for no apparent reason, Sophie stopped in her tracks. When I realized she was no longer by my side, I turned to find she had gone absolutely pale and was staring into space, as if in a trance. I actually had to shake her a bit to get her to snap out of it. When she came to, she seemed confused. When I asked her if something was wrong, all she said was, "No, I'm fine. But, I think something is amiss with the animals." Well, what on earth was that supposed to mean? I decided not to push it, and instead distracted her with the dolphins.

I mulled the event over in my mind, speculating what could have caused it. *She did wake up unusually early. Maybe she's just overtired. Maybe it's like falling asleep while standing up and then dreaming. That sort of thing used to happen to Lexie now and then when she was younger. I don't know. That was weird. I hope it doesn't happen again.*

"I love dolphins! They're so amazing, and so talented!" Sophie chattered excitedly. "Even without training, they literally do back flips for our attention and their food. Amazing! And that one could see that there was a pattern to your distribution of the fish, so when you missed a beat, it got offended and splashed you. Oh, that was so funny. It's almost like—" Sophie suddenly faltered and stopped, midsentence.

"It's almost like, what?" I urged.

"I don't know. I forgot." She seemed slightly puzzled and distressed. *Please, not again …*

"Don't worry, you'll remember in a minute," I reassured her. I reached for another fish, and for a moment I thought I had a live one, because it was quivering. Then I noticed something concerning: the fish wasn't moving, the pail was. And Sophie was holding it. She was shaking. "Sophie, what is bothering you today?" I asked. "You're starting to worry me."

She stopped to think. "It's almost like I feel … fear. But it's not mine. Someone *else* is afraid."

"Who?"

"I'm not sure." Her eyes widened and she froze. *That can't be good.*

"Sophie?"

Suddenly, my cheeky dolphin friend came shooting to the surface and started splashing around, spooked by some unseen force. It flicked its head from side to side, clicking and whistling shrilly. The rest of the pod darted about, then swam toward the bottom of the tank and cowered. I gazed confusedly over the edge of the tank. It was like they sensed Sophie's fear. Turning back to her, I found she had returned to reality.

"I'm OK. I'm fine." She looked up. "But something bad is going to happen."

"Like what? What makes you think that? Sophie, you're safe, I'm OK, and the animals are fine. What is frightening you?"

"I don't know," she said simply.

I sighed. This was getting out of hand. There was nothing in Sophie's personality to make me think she was pretending or fretting, so it made me wonder if I should take what she said seriously. Maybe she had some kind of premonition. But what should I do? What disaster was I supposed to avert?

"Alright," I conceded. "But I don't know what to look out for, so until I do … just stick close, OK?" She nodded and attempted a smile. *I hope she's wrong … God, please help me protect her, whatever might come.*

This was certainly not how I imagined my debut to the hacking creed. I should have sent Jason to check on my computer sooner. It may already be too late; it was going to fry the electrical grid. Even though I had already told my antivirus systems to stop terrorizing V0RT3X, the damage was spreading. It had started a chain reaction. Code was going corrupt. The whole system was crumbling. Somehow, I had to stitch it back together and heal it. I destroy things much better than I fix them, so my future was looking more elusive and more bleak—maybe nonexistent. As if the stress of possibly destroying the group I needed to join wasn't enough, I could sense Ender glaring over my shoulder. People were noticing me now and a sizeable group was clustered just out of the range of danger.

My fingers stopped flying and I let my brain catch up. *Calm down and think. I can't keep fixing the code line by line; it's being corrupted just as fast. I'll be here for eternity. There's got to be a way out of this mess.* Taking a deep breath, I slowed my thoughts and tried a more logical approach. *OK: identify and isolate the problem. The power keeps surging and sputtering. So, how do I stop that?* I tilted my chair back on two legs, a dangerous but effective habit to force ideas to come faster.

Turn it off.

"What are you doing? Don't just sit there. Fix it!"

"Please stop fussing, Ender," I murmured. "I'm trying to think. Do be quiet." *Don't get angry again. I didn't ask for this either.*

The lights went off for the third time in the last four minutes, pausing to give me a heart attack before coming back on. If a strong enough volt hit the circuitry, all the wires would be fried and the lights would go out permanently. When they died, so would I.

I had to restart the grid, then prime it so it worked properly. But the generator wasn't reliable. Once the system was shut off, I only had thirty-eight seconds to get a steady stream. If I couldn't hold that for twenty-one seconds, the power would blow and fry the server. All the data would be destroyed. If there was ever a good time to panic and make a break for it, now would be that time. But I couldn't just give up. I had done this; I had to undo it. Theoretically, I just had to rinse out the generator with a little spare electricity, and all would be well. Except, I didn't have enough.

A reliable, steady supply ... come on ... think! ... my extra battery! Bingo! I closed my screen and flipped my computer over. Pulling off the fake bottom, I slid out the reserve of pure energy. It was thin and long, like the cover of a hardback book painted silver.

I insisted they tell me where the generator was. Second floor, southeast corner. Scrambling to it, I knelt and started searching. Finding the wire that ran to its core, I remotely switched off the power. Grabbing alligator clips from my bag, I hooked them to the main cord and the battery's output, then started counting in my head. After twenty-one nerve-wracking seconds, I turned the generator back on. There was a long pause, and then ... it began to run normally again. Scrambling back to the first floor, Ender close on my tail, all eyes turned from me to the big screen as data popped up, indicating computers were reconnecting to the system. I let out a heavy, silent sigh. *Good heavens, that was close. I'm never doing that again.*

Bringing my nerves under control, I turned to face Ender. He was evaluating me skeptically, irked with this enigma of a girl who had stumbled into his territory.

"You fixed it," he said simply.

"Yes, I did. I kept my word. Now, am I allowed to negotiate? At least let me state my case." After a pause, he sighed, completely exasperated.

"What else am I supposed to do with you?" Ender gestured to my computer. "Fine. Go ahead. Impress me."

That I can do. As I looked out over the crowd of hackers, I realized my original, planned "inauguration speech" no longer applied. Everything had changed. I not only had to impress them, I had to blow their minds. And they did not look very … interested. They watched me with annoyed, blank, even bored expressions. Fear returned to lodge in my throat, and my words stuck. *I can't do this.* Unwanted panic started taking over. But then, I noticed Jason.

Beyond his messy milk chocolate hair, I could see his big brown eyes. They were wide with anticipation, curiosity, and excitement … almost admiration. I blinked, my gaze resting on him. *Why does he seem so eager? Did I inspire him or something? How?* He noticed my staring and froze. A long moment passed, in which I could feel Ender growing impatient, the hackers growing bored, and Jason holding his breath. Then I grinned at him. *No, I can do this. Time to be brave, one more time.*

"I got my first computer when I was fourteen and started hacking that same year. Since then, I've lived my life through keystrokes on a keyboard. It's my income, my hobby, the air I breathe. But that's not why I'm here." I moved back to my computer, plugged it into the now steady stream of power, and started hacking. "Go put up your firewalls. Make this fun for me." After some hesitation, everyone scattered, typing away on their respective computers. *OK, here we go. Just like always.* "Does anyone feel like volunteering? Do you think you're … un-hackable?" Snickers spread across the room and a few hands went up. That invited a smug smile from Ender. *Now to wipe that smile away.* "Alright, that's not enough. I'll just have to hack all of you."

Pulling up the cyber map of the electrical currents in the building, I targeted all the paths leading to PC processors and entered the commands "<System.Lock>" and "<System.Beep>". Dings rang out around the room.

"If your computer just beeped, you're out. Game over for you. I'll reset it later, though."

People were noticing that their touchpads and mice weren't responding. The annoyed looks I got were amusing. *Sore losers.* I turned to the remaining systems. Only seven were down, leaving thirty-six. I upped my strength and the *dings* popped out around me. Now, this was where it all began.

From that moment on, my fingers didn't stop flying. Command after command, divide and conquer. Small clusters went down and others fought back. I was one with the cyber world. I was an enchantress, fighting a legion of mythical beasts, bending the magical forces and crackling energy to my will, soaring with my dragon named F1R3ST0RM. Oh, I've missed this.

Twenty-eight remaining. Releasing a stream of irrational, repeating loops of contradicting commands, I watched the number drop as computers scrambled to obey my orders but tripped as they collapsed in confusion. *Eighteen. Fifteen. Eleven.* Sections of my firewalls crumbled, but with a swipe of code they were not only patched but reinforced, and the attackers were swatted off with a fist of steel. The more I hacked, the stronger my systems grew. Oh, I think I forgot to mention: my AI *learn*.

Both Laelaps and F1R3ST0RM have transcended all but seven AI entities in the entire world—unknown to most, naturally. I must remain hidden. But I still have a metaphorical trophy with my signature on it. My name would be known someday. For now, I remained anonymous and undiscovered. But I still got to play with my toys.

"Cheers to all still standing. But it's not over," I called out. I glanced down at the stats on my screen. "It hasn't even been a minute."

Nine remain. Now to target them specifically, yet still keep the others occupied. If I was actually waging war with these hackers, I could have annihilated them more than twenty seconds ago. I could just overload the electricity and fry their computers.

I pulled another system under and began to besiege yet another when it suddenly dropped off my grid. Scanning the room, my gaze settled on Jason's glowing face. He grinned at me and waved his unplugged power cord in my direction. *Smart. I'll come back to you later.* A few more systems dropped off my map, and I knew it was time to switch entirely to the cyber world. Slipping out of the currents of electricity, I entered the world of 1s and 0s—pure code.

Within seventeen seconds, all but four computers had cried surrender in their native language of *ding* or *beep*. I released the command "<System. Locate>" to see who my opponents were. The map showed me their relative positions in the room. Ender, Jason, a hooded mystery boy, and a red-haired girl. *OK. Let's end this.*

I found the boy's weak spot and his walls crumbled. *Beep.* I lowered a cage of whirling code down over Jason's data center. *Ding. Sorry about that.* The girl was harder. She had an AI. F1R3ST0RM and it danced, but soon it was pinned under my dragon's claws. *Ding.* Everyone was watching.

Now for Ender, who was being quite a pain. I had to congratulate him on that. He too had a strong AI. A scout report popped up on my screen. It was self-modifying, just like my programs. *Impressive. But we'll see who goes home with the gold.*

Our attacks went toe to toe, nose to nose, each blow was blocked, and each attack met with a perfect counterattack. Mirrors. I felt myself grinning. *This is entertaining. We should do this more often. But—it's time to win. I see your weakness.* His weakness was also his strength: his offense. I wove a wall of electricity, commands, and spastic bursts of code that served as land mines. If he so much as sneezed on them, they would collapse on him and freeze his systems. After some convincing counterattacks on my part, I ordered the guard near my trap to temporarily abandon defenses. In less than a second, it was all over. Ender drilled through the wall and stumbled right into my web.

The next keystroke brought our war to an end. *Ding!*

I can't figure her out today. One minute she's catatonic, the next there's no end to the carefree chatter. I was sitting across from Sophie at one of the tables in the map room. She was jabbering away, running outlandish but creative ideas by me, looking for approval and advice. Thankfully, she didn't seem to mind me keeping my head on the table. Between lack of sleep and Sophie occasionally giving me heart attacks, I was exhausted. With a great deal of willpower, I refocused on what she was saying.

" … and she was super skittish, like a cat on a hot tin roof. Two feet of water was too deep. When I asked her why she was being so ridiculous, she said she had seen some movie called *Jaws* and had no intention of ever swimming in the ocean again!"

"Yeah, *Jaws* is scary," I agreed. "Don't ever watch it. Hunter showed it to me when I was little and I didn't sleep for days."

"OK, I won't. She summarized the story for me, though, and I got curious. How did they do it? Did they train a shark? I already know the answer, but do you think it was a real shark?"

"No."

"Right! I found out it's actually an animatronic! There were three built, and they used weird stuff like chopped-up walnuts or something to give it texture. But when they put it in the water for the first time it had issues with electrolysis. Anyway, it got me thinking: it must have been really nerve-wracking to be an actor in that movie. Despite it being fake and all, what if it malfunctioned and went rogue? Like I said, it did act up when it got wet at first. I don't know. Even without seeing shark movies, I don't like sharks. Except for shark rays. I mean, their real name is bowmouth guitarfish. That's just beautiful. And they aren't really aggressive, so they … are on my good side."

Sophie slowed and finally came to a crawling stop. Then, the semi-sad and scared look returned. It was her turn to put her head down.

"No, Sophie. Don't zone out again on me, please."

"I think I'll be OK this time. Just a little … nervous," she said, gazing tiredly at the table's surface.

"About what?" I asked.

"Don't know," she answered.

This is exasperating. "Maybe you should just go home and get some rest," I offered.

"I'm fine. But thanks." She frowned, closed her eyes, and was silent.

I waited. And waited. And waited. Nothing. Then, I finally realized: she had fallen asleep. I smiled. This was probably a good thing. I'd wake her up later. As long as she didn't snore, I doubted anyone would notice. With nothing better to do, I got to work on medical reports I had been procrastinating on.

For a moment, time stopped. No one moved. A shocked, awed stillness had washed over everyone. Ender stared at his screen. Surely he now saw his error, but was too startled to admit it. I had beaten them. I had won. *Now for the bonus round.* I stood, and all eyes turned to me.

"Game over," I announced, my proud smile spilling into my voice. "That only took two minutes and twelve seconds. Good match." There was a long silence.

"How did you do that?" the hooded boy asked.

"Like I said, hacking is my life. But it's more than that. And now!" I exclaimed, clapping my hands together. " … to dole out rewards." *This is going to be great.* "What is the name of your rival hacking group here in Santa Barbara? I know you are at war with another creed. What is their name?"

"Why do you want to know? Let our computers go. You still have them on lockdown!" someone in the back called out.

"Not yet," I smiled. "I won't betray you. Let me do this. Now. A name. Tell me."

Chaos erupted. People tried to free their computers, others were arguing with each other. Ender was still gazing at his screen in disbelief. *How does he feel about all of this, I wonder? I need someone who will trust me ...* My gaze landed on Jason, and I raised an eyebrow, anticipating an answer. Turning to my screen, I singled out his computer and sent this message: *"I'm going to give everyone a little gift, courtesy of your enemies. Will you help me surprise your V0RT3X friends and annoy your enemies? Type the answer."*

He thought long and hard about this, then, very slowly, his hands rose to his keyboard and pecked eight keys. *C3RB3RU$*. My mind blurted a definition. *Cerberus, the three-headed hellhound of the underworld.* Apparently I wasn't the only one with a Greek-originating alias. I smiled at Jason and gave a little nod of approval.

"Cerberus. Thank you," I said cheerfully. That freaked everyone out. Now Ender's head snapped up, a look of alarm in his eyes. "Don't worry, Ender, I'm not here to steal your crown and empire. I may be champion today ... " I started hacking C3RB3RU$. " ... But, you are still the king."

With one voice, all the computers around the warehouse chimed, and I unlocked their systems.

"Cerberus just ran into some financial difficulties," I announced. "I have added seven hundred and fifty dollars to each of your personal accounts, but if you were among the last fifteen I defeated, I added a high-score bonus. One hundred dollars more with each increasing rank. Also, there is now ten thousand dollars in V0RT3X's overall systems. Cerberus was loaded, but they have much lighter electronic wallets now," I explained, smiling slyly. Ender slowly stood and searched my eyes for a long time, at a loss for words.

"Why are you doing this? You had our systems frozen. You could have sold us out, but you didn't. Why? Who are you?"

"My name ... is Firestorm." I sent the characters "*F1R3ST0RM*" to the big screen on the far wall. "I will not give you my real name. I'm doing this because I've heard of what you have done for this city. You have my utmost respect. I searched you out, not because I want to conquer you, but because I want to join you."

That all but floored Ender. "You want to join Vortex? *That's* what all of this is about?"

"Yes," I answered. Ender looked unsure. "Look, I'm sorry about all the trouble I've made. My intent was only to get your attention so I could show you what I can do. It got a little out of hand and I almost lost control. I'm sorry. Please, let me join you. I want to fight political and social corruption and help this city. Will you accept me?"

Sophie was out for so long that I finished all my work. I couldn't believe it. There was actually time to organize my messy binder. Somehow, no one seemed to realize that my intern was sound asleep. I just nodded and smiled at anyone who passed by; I had laid an open book in front of Sophie so it looked like she was just deep in thought. *Hmm … If I don't wake her up, will she sleep till tomorrow morning?*

She seemed to be dreaming about something. Thankfully, she didn't start talking or twitching, but she kept grinning. It was kind of cute. Curious, I watched her for a while. *Where are you right now, I wonder?* For some reason, she muttered something that sounded like "wheat bee." What is *that?*

Wheat bee. Wheat be. We be. Wet bee. Eat bee. What? Before long, Sophie lifted her head and found the open book in front of her. There was a blank expression on her face for the longest time.

"Why am I … was I reading about the lifespan of a jellyfish?" she asked slowly.

"No, you weren't. I put that there." Now she seemed to be legitimately reading the book, and I decided to test the waters. "How are you feeling?"

"Good, I guess," she said distractedly. Suddenly, she whipped her head up to look at me, her eyes wide with horror. "Why are you asking? Wait, did … how long … did I fall asleep?!"

"Yes. Don't worry, it's fine. You really needed it, and I got free time. My binder is neat now, so this is a win-win," I assured her.

"You sure it's OK?" she asked anxiously.

I nodded.

"Thank you, Jordan," she said, giving a huge sigh of relief. I decided to ask.

"What does 'wheat bee' mean?"

Sophie looked perplexed. "Wheat bee? I have no idea. Is there such a thing? Does wheat have flowers? And why is the bee exclusive to wheat?" She rambled on for a minute with several odd questions. I stared blankly at her for a moment, then abandoned that line of inquiry and tried another.

"Actually, if I may ask: what were you dreaming about just now?" Sophie thought for a moment.

"My dog. Why do you ask?" Then I realized what "wheat bee" was. It was supposed to be Sweet Pea—her Boston Terrier. I started chuckling, I couldn't help it. *This is like that game Mad Gab. Wheat bee, that's hilarious.* Sophie looked confused. "What's so funny?"

"Well—you know what? Never mind. It's nothing." She just shrugged, then smiled.

"I just found out a group of jellyfish is called a smack. Smack! How did they get a name like that?! And they don't have brains. That's just weird. This is interesting. Thanks!" *Sophie's back to normal …*

Once again, I found myself in a staring contest with Ender. Except, this time, the longer I watched him, the less I felt endangered. An agreement was traveling back and forth between us, growing and changing ever so slightly at each turn; I could sense it. What its terms and conditions were, though, I didn't know.

"You've caused chaos today," Ender said. There were no clues in his voice as to what he was thinking.

"I'm sorry."

"You almost killed our systems."

Where are you going with this? "I'm sorry for that too."

"All our computers went on lockdown—because of you."

"I unlocked them … "

"I'm more interested in the first part."

"OK," I said, looking down at the floor. This was not going well. *Maybe I annoyed him a bit too much. Grudges tend to stick around when it comes to hackers. Trust is a risky characteristic.*

"But, you did all these things … to join us." That regained my attention. Ender wasn't done. "You caused chaos because you realized we would need you. Your computer is so finely built that our decoder almost died when it got too close. You not only brought our entire mainframe to the brink of destruction, you brought it back. You defeated all of us. Including me. No one has done that in years. And then you gave us all gifts from Cerberus. So many times, you could have finished us with the click of a button. Vortex would be history. But the very fact you did all of this just to get my attention shows me where your loyalty lies."

"Does that mean … " I couldn't bring myself to say it.

"I'm going to keep a very close eye on you. But, for now … welcome to Vortex, Firestorm."

He held out his hand to shake mine; I accepted. I was in! Half the crowd dispersed, shrugging off this turn of events as if they were as insignificant as an increase in gas prices. Ender turned to the red-haired girl.

"Sonja, enter Firestorm's computer into the database and give her the rundown." Sonja seemed to huff and shrug in a "whatever" kind of way. I picked up my laptop and went over to her. She snatched my computer—an action that usually brings a rapid decline in health—and plugged it in to the main server. She started typing.

She reminded me of a dangerous, assassin-oriented agent I saw in an old comic book when I was a kid. Both she and Sonja had names of Russian origin. Sonja's eyes were a dark penny brown. Her short, scarlet hair was a near perfect match for that heroine. There was an aura of danger surrounding her; she held herself with a ninja-like stance. On top of all this, her leggings and jacket were black. I secretly nicknamed her Ninja.

"Hi. I'm Firestorm—"

"Yes, I am well aware of your name and you know mine. There. No need for introductions. Now, come on. I don't like babysitting and I'm not good with children, so let's make this quick," she said coldly, keeping her attention on my screen.

"Look, I'm sorry about earlier. One of us had to lose. But you put up an amazing fight; your software is impressive."

"Oh really?" she asked with dripping sarcasm.

"Actually, yes." She threw me an incredulous look. *Here, let me clarify.* "It took me approximately 3.7 seconds to pin your AI. My record is 3 milliseconds after connection, and my average for disabling AI programs is 1.2 seconds. It's been a while since someone broke my average." Sonja was silent for a moment, then regained some of her swagger.

"You sure are ambitious. You seem young. Heck, how old are you anyway?"

"Twenty-five," I answered, unsure whether to feel complimented or offended.

"You *are* young." She snickered. "I haven't seen anyone rattle Ender's cage like that in years. Actually, that was great." She kept her voice lower as she said it.

"Surely he isn't still angry at me. Is he?" *Can I please get a little bit of goodwill from you people?*

"Doubt it," Sonja muttered, smacking a wad of neon pink bubble gum. "Anyway, it's good for him. He's gotta get a taste of his own attitude once in a while. I'd say he's indifferent to you now. As long as you're serious about your intentions and not hiding anything, it'll stay that way. He'd never have harmed you anyway. He's all talk. Gotta be to run this team and all." She unplugged my computer and handed it back. "There. You're connected. Now I gotta get your brain on the same page as the rest of us."

Sonja marched off. After a moment, I realized I should probably follow. She vaulted herself into a swirly chair; it skated nimbly across the floor, coming to a stop in front of a two-screen computer set up. *Fancy. I need to get some more monitors.* She clicked on a file, spreading documents, pictures, news clippings, and audio files across the screens.

"We are always at war with Cerberus, but right now our main focus is on the whole ordeal with James Brenton," she said flatly.

"James Brenton? Who is he?" I asked. Sonja spun her chair around and looked at me like I had happily admitted of my own free will to being a geeky freak.

"What rock did you crawl out from under this morning? Are you seriously saying you haven't heard about all this?" she challenged. I nodded, now feeling nervous once again. *They can't know I'm new here. Not yet.* Sonja sighed in exasperation. "He's the governor. Well, was. He stepped down about a week ago—for no apparent reason. He's the best political nut California has seen in ages."

Time to wing it. "Oh. Right. I think I've heard something about him. I don't … go out that much." Sonja rolled her eyes and turned back to her computer.

"Alright, whatever, geek. Maybe look up from your screen and observe the real world once in a while, OK?" I frowned at the back of her head. *You are so rude. Hey, Edge isn't the last of his kind!* I hid a snicker. *If these two got together, maybe their species wouldn't go extinct.* Sonja went on. "Everyone thinks that being governor was just stressful for him and that he simply wants to retire. But they're wrong. We have reason to believe he was blackmailed."

"Blackmailed? By who?" I took a wild stab. "Like, whoever got the position?"

"Very good! You are learning!" Sonja praised, lacking even a hint of sincerity. "Yes, the new governor, Gregory Scott Damon, is a very shady character. There is no available file on him, but from what we've hacked, we smell a rat. He doesn't even have roots in California. What he is doing here is a mystery. He arrived only two weeks before Brenton quit. And within a few days ... surprise! He's governor. His team is trying to feed this crap to the media about him being an old friend of Brenton's and that it was Brenton's request that Damon take his place."

"Have you hacked him personally yet?" I asked, leaning a bit closer to the screen.

"Not him yet. Vortex is trying to get in touch with Brenton first. We want to offer our help. If we can nail Damon, we slide a little closer into Brenton's favor. When he returns to power, maybe we can actually get a good rep among the puppeteers of the political world."

"Smart move. I take it he has optimum security, though."

"Exactly. We can't just barge into his computer; this is a delicate matter. It must be done when he alone is present at the monitor. We have to ensure that he won't copy the video feed and sell us out and, somehow, we have to get past his programs without triggering the security system. It will notify the police directly. If we're caught, we're done for."

"So, program recon is probably the best option right now, I suppose."

"Yep. You any good at that kind of thing?" Sonja asked, spinning her chair once again to regard me with slight disapproval.

Are you kidding me? I spy on Teumessian at least four times a week. "Yeah."

"Good. Check the main database for the info and get to work." Sonja pushed her chair back, got up, and looked across the room distractedly, muttering. "Babysitting duty is done. Yay."

She wandered off, leaving me to wonder where she was going. *Never mind. I finally have a purpose.* After scrounging around for an unclaimed stretch of tabletop and finding a spot, I slid into the chair and set up base.

Brenton is a good guy? Good. Damon is a bad guy? Also good. I'll help VORT3X take him down. With people like him, it's only a matter of time … he will fall.

Glancing at my watch, I sighed and looked up at Sophie. *Oh, I hate to rain on her party, but we still have six assessments to go.* Turns out, the book Sophie was reading was not only about jellyfish, but the phylum Cnidaria, including—but not limited to—corals, jellyfish, hydras, and various parasites. Sophie was so intrigued with these strange creatures that she was taking notes on one piece of paper and doodling invertebrates on another. I could probably balance a cup of water on her head and she wouldn't notice.

"Hey, Soph?"

"Hmm?" She hardly looked up.

"Sorry to be a bit of a wet blanket, but the day's not over yet. We still have a little bit more work to do." Reluctantly, she closed the book.

"OK. Hey, if we work fast, maybe I can come back and finish this!" Turning to the back of her binder, she slid her masterpieces behind a tab labeled "Cool Stuff." That made me grin. Every other girl Sophie's age was into famous movie stars or the latest fashion trends, but she was curious about things like microbes and whales. Grabbing the book off the table, she started toward the shelves. "I'll go put this back."

I slid my notebook into my bag and stood. Suddenly, there was a loud *thud.* Whirling toward the sound, my heart faltered; the Cnidaria book was on the floor. Sophie stood over it, her empty hands quivering and her knees knocking. It seemed to be the same thing as earlier—but this time, she wasn't zoning out. Absolute terror registered in her eyes, and she seemed to be having a hard time catching her breath. I dropped my bag and raced to her.

"Sophie!"

She looked up, right at me, and whispered: "It's here." She jerked her head toward the door. "They're in danger—they need me! Nessie's tank!"

Before I could ask her to elaborate on the meanings of "it," "they," and "Nessie's tank," the floor … jumped. An earthquake! A shriek rang out from somewhere across the room. The lights swung and blinked off. When they surged back to life, Sophie was gone. The door caught my eye. It was swinging closed. *Sophie, no!* What was she thinking? This was the safest place in the building! I darted after her, calling out the whole way. *Did she know the quake was coming? Is that what "it" was supposed to mean? But who needs her help? And, "Nessie's tank" is …* Nessie's tank was what Sophie called the group tank! That had to be where she was heading!

The group tank is where all the rehabilitated animals are put until a release can be scheduled. It's also their final lesson, a reminder of how to interact with other sea animals when they return to the ocean. How big is this tank? 310,500 gallons—spread between two sections. Sophie and I joke that it could hold the fabled Loch Ness Monster, or "Nessie" for short. The tank has been around about a year. Only the left side is complete. The right side has yet to be filled with sand, fake rocks, plants, current simulators, and lighting. But they're both filled with water. *I don't like the words danger and Nessie's tank in the same sentence.*

I flew down the flight of stairs to the experimental sublevel of Ocean Front. Skidding around a corner, the door came into my sights. It was open. Sophie was at the control panel, her hand hovering over a button. The wall between the tank's two sectors was down. There was a mass exodus of marine animals from the main left side to the lesser right side. *Why are they all leaving the nicer side?* Then, light glinted through the tank and I saw it. A crack. It was spreading, crawling across the face of the glass. The left tank was going to burst.

"*Sophie!!!* Get out of here, now! It's gonna blow!"

She paused. The last two turtles and a sand shark were escaping the tank. The moment the tips of their flippers had cleared the boundary, Sophie smacked the "up" button. The divider wall began to climb. She turned and fled toward me, her footsteps sending a desperate echo through the empty grate beneath her feet. It was like time became heavy and sluggish. Either that, or my mind had an energy spike. I looked up to see the space between cracks closing, a tiny trickle of water spilling out. Sophie was more than 70 feet away from me. She wasn't going to make it.

In half a millisecond, I made my decision.

Abandoning all hope of escape, I sprinted toward her. The cracks grew closer. Fifty feet. *Danger.* Thirty feet. More water. Twenty feet. Inches between the center cracks. Seconds remained. *God, help me!* It was like pure energy poured over me. Never before have I run so fast. I doubt I ever will again.

I lunged for Sophie, grabbed her, and spun, shielding her with my body. The ground sent shock waves up from the depths.

The cracks met, and the tank shattered.

CHAPTER 11

Santa Barbara, V0RT3X stronghold
Friday, August 17, 4:47 P.M.

ᙅᙍ Amber ᙍᙂ

At the rate things were going, if we were lucky, we would be contacting our political friend by Christmas. Maybe. My brain is more productive and creative when I'm drawing, so I was secretly doodling with my art program. To my annoyance, the table on which my computer sat shuddered and my steady hand jerked, messing up my perfectly straight lines. I glared up and down the rows, thinking someone had bumped the table. But everyone looked as irked or confused as I was. Something caught my eye and I glanced up. *Wait, why are the lights swinging?*

BOOM! Suddenly, loud, roaring thunder resounded up from the ground and the entire room jolted.

"Everyone out! This building isn't stable enough to withstand earthquakes! Get out! *Now!*" Ender shouted, directing people toward the doors. I balked. *Earthquake!?* Leaping up, I shoved my laptop into my bag and made a break for the door. In front of me, I saw someone stop, turn, and start running back. Jason.

"Jason, *no!*" Ender cried out and started to push against the flow of people to get to him.

"No, Ender, go! I'll get him," I yelled and raced toward Jason. He was at the main server, holding on to a USB stick, waiting for data to transfer before pulling it out. Just as I reached him, he snatched it from the port, yet remained frozen. "Come on!" I exclaimed, grabbing his arm and dragging him after me. His legs seemed to wake up and he started running.

With lightning speed, I perceived motion over our heads. I yanked

Jason backward. A beam pounded the ground where he had been just moments ago. He stared at it in shock, but I kept going. Ender was at the door, motioning frantically and calling for us to hurry. *Hang left!* I pulled Jason; another board fell from the second floor, almost taking him down again. *Faster!* The ground shuddered and cracked behind us. *Right!* I whipped away from a ceiling light that fell, shattering with a burst of crackling electricity. *Almost there …*

My foot caught in a crack in the floor and I went down. I sucked in a breath. My forearm had found a jagged piece of glass; it was bleeding. Gravel and splinters rained down. The crack was widening. I was slipping. Time was up. Jason lunged for me, grabbed my arm, and pulled me out of the yawning hole. Our feet hardly touched the ground between that spot and the door. A huge chunk came crashing down from the second floor, nearly catching us as we dove out. We stood with the others, hands on our knees, gasping for breath as the building quivered.

"Jason!" Ender came over, a scolding in his eyes. "What were you—" Jason cut him off by holding up the USB stick and smiling a little.

"The server. It's all here," he panted. After a moment of surprised silence, Ender took it from him.

"Well done." Jason beamed at this bit of praise.

Suddenly, Jason's feet left the asphalt as Sonja grabbed a handful of his shirt and lifted him up, her face inches from his.

"What were you *thinking*?! Just how stupid are you? You could have been killed!" She swatted him upside the head with her free hand. "I swear, if you ever do anything like that again you'll be sleeping outside for a week! You're lucky you still have all your limbs!" After glaring at him for a moment, Sonja released Jason and turned to me. There was a new look in her eyes. *Is that … gratitude?* "Thank you, Firestorm, for saving my brother."

"Brother?! You two are siblings?" I exclaimed in shock. She gave me a "well, duh, yeah" face, and Jason nodded, looking rather sheepish. Now I could see it; they did resemble each other. And, of course, there was no way Sonja's hair was naturally that deep a shade of red.

The earth decided to interrupt this turn of events by crippling a nearby building. We all retreated further into the street and watched as the rubble rained down.

I hope our building doesn't fall …

A tidal wave of water, chunks of glass, and doom came crashing down. It was like being trapped in a wave, except this was much worse, and waves don't carry boulders made of glass. I was shoved to my knees under the driving force of the water. It slipped through the grates in the floor, but within moments, it had risen above our heads. The sound of the door being swept closed sounded like the pounding of a judge's gavel, sentencing us to death. The good news was the rest of the floor wouldn't flood—but we might drown. I clung to the metal grid, trying to stay firm in the strong sway of the water. If we were pulled away we'd be dashed to pieces ...

Neither of us could hold our breath forever. I could already tell Sophie was losing the fight; she was starting to tense up. A piece of glass glanced off my shoulder. *Please, God. Please protect us.* Sophie started struggling, but I held on. *Just a little longer!* Finally, the wave hit the opposite wall and doubled back, beginning to cancel out the flow. *Now!* Tightening my clutch on Sophie, I pushed off the bottom and started for the surface. My lungs were bursting. Sophie let go of her breath. *Almost—*

We broke the surface, coughing and gasping for air.

"Kick off your shoes! Come on! Just keep your head above water. You can do it!" I encouraged.

I could tread water for at least an hour, but I wasn't sure how good a swimmer Sophie was. As long as we stayed up, the room would drain and we could get out. Miraculously, the secondary tank remained intact. If it burst, we would drown for sure. The ceiling was close enough as it was.

The water was lowering too slowly. The current was wearing my energy down rapidly and Sophie was dipping lower and lower with each surge. Suddenly, we dropped. The pressure on the grates must have finally registered on the system! The floor had sensors in it; if the lower level ever did flood, the grates would expand, draining the water much faster. It was working. My feet touched the ground as the last of the water disappeared. I grabbed Sophie's hand and bolted for the door, but not without noticing something very special: all about us, glass covered the floor ... except where we landed. *Thank you, Lord. Thank you!*

Out the door, through the corridor, up the stairs. The ground shuddered. Down the hall, the goal within reach—we burst into the map room. Calls of "Jordan!" and "Sophie!" rang out and a few people came scurrying. Sophie slid down the wall, pulled her knees up, hugged them, and sat quietly shivering.

"Jordan! Are you OK? And Sophie! What happened?!" Dylan asked anxiously as he came to a skidding stop in front of us. Sophie simply nodded. I turned to him.

"Sophie channeled all the animals out of the main segment of the group tank, then it burst." Dylan's eyes got big and I hurried on before he flipped out. "We're both fine. Just, well … soaked." I looked down at Sophie. She hadn't lifted her head and was still quivering. "It's a miracle. I'll explain more later." Dylan seemed to notice my worried glance at Sophie; a silent understanding passed between us and he gave a little nod.

"I'll see if I can find some towels so you two can get somewhat dry."

As he jogged off, another tremor hit, but the floor absorbed the shockwaves. I watched him go, then joined Sophie on the ground. *Thank you, Lord. Thank you for helping me keep her safe …*

It seemed I wasn't the only one who had grabbed my laptop before making a break for it. But I was certainly the only one using it. I suppose Ender was testing my usefulness, which was probably good, but I felt conspicuous. I glanced down at my screen.

"There still aren't any broadcasts on the air. Everything's down," I said, turning to Ender, who was scuffing at the ground impatiently with the toe of his shoe.

"We can't stay in the dark like this. We need to know what's going on!" he exclaimed.

"There's no way to tell when the news stations will get back on their feet," I pointed out. "I suggest we dash in and grab what we can if there isn't another aftershock for … five minutes. Or send runners in," I hesitantly offered.

"Fine," Ender said, then turned to the other hackers. "Start fighting over who's the fastest. I want ten volunteers. The timer starts now. If there isn't anything alarming for five minutes, I'll send you in. But be careful; use your heads. I don't want any more accidents today, alright?" He frowned at me and Jason, who was sitting close by. I frowned back and Jason looked embarrassed. I nudged him.

"Hey, don't let Ender's negativity get to you. I think we're gonna need that data. I doubt the servers are still standing."

"You think so? What if it was all for nothing?" Jason asked.

"Come on, you saw that chunk of upstairs fall."

"Yeah, I guess you're right." He sighed and looked at the old warehouse. "I wish it hadn't. I hate moving." He paused. "Thanks … for saving me back there." I wasn't quite sure how to respond to this, so I just nodded.

After five minutes was up, Ender sent the runners in. Before long, they were back, and they didn't look particularly happy. One of them—I believe named Lenny—stepped up to give a report.

"Not much left. The servers were destroyed, the stairs are precarious, and the front entry is almost blocked. The whole place is structurally unsound. If another aftershock hits, it could fall." Ender paced in a tight loop for a moment, then huffed in annoyance.

"Alright. Try and get as much out as you can. Send a lightweight up to throw things down from the top level." Ender paused to glance at Jason, then seemed to think better of it—probably due to Sonja's warning glare. "Keri. Send Keri up. She's small. See if you can set up some sort of safety system first. Catch her if you have to, but no matter what, that child does not hit the floor. Got it?"

Lenny nodded and beckoned to a little raven-haired girl who looked no older than eleven. She got up and followed, a determined look in her eyes, pride in her step, head held high. I watched her go, amazed by her courage. Surely she was terrified, yet she was being so brave. Ender turned to Sonja.

"Go check the secondary location. See if it's stable. We can't stay here."

"Ugh. Must I be the one to go?" she whined. "Send someone else. I've already done my fair share of work. Yesterday I ran an errand, earlier you made me babysit the newbie, and now you want me to inspect a dang building that's over a freaking mile away!" At this, Ender raised his eyebrows.

"I'll keep an eye on Jason if that's what's holding you back. But I think you're just being lazy, so you better start running, because if I can still see you in fifteen seconds, my boot will find your backside, and trust me, it's gonna hurt—"

"OK, OK!"

With that, she jogged off. Ender muttered something that sounded like "lazy, stubborn, mouthy mule." I swallowed a laugh. *Those two have the most amusing relationship.* Jason seemed to be thinking the same thing, because he was trying to hide a grin behind a forced look of innocence. I let out a grin of my own, then returned to my computer. *There has got to be a report somewhere. What are we dealing with?*

The earthquake was a seven. Well, at its epicenter. From what I heard, the island of Santa Rosa suffered the most. Buildings went down, the surf was wild, and huge chasms covered the ground. Thankfully, the earthquake only registered a six by the time it reached Santa Barbara, but some damage had still been done. When I came back from my scavenging for information, Sophie still hadn't moved, except to pull her towel closer around her shoulders. I sat beside her again. She didn't say anything.

"You OK, Soph?" I asked. She nodded. "You did almost drown a while ago. Are you sure?" She nodded again. After a long pause, I realized what I should have said a long time ago. "That was very brave of you." Sophie slowly lifted her head, a dejected look in her eyes.

"They were so scared. So, so scared. It was awful … and, I scared you. I'm so sorry. Are you upset with me?"

"No, not at all! Just don't do that again, OK?" I said.

She sat bolt upright. "You think the other tank might burst?! Is there going to be another earthquake? I would have to do that again! The animals would need me!" she exclaimed firmly. I sighed, feeling slightly exasperated, yet amused.

"No, I mean—never mind. Just be a bit more careful."

"OK." She put her head down again. *No, don't clam up. Come back.* "Animals can sense earthquakes before they occur. You felt their fear, didn't you?"

"I guess so." She lifted her head and frowned. "All I could hear was this … no it wasn't hearing, more like *feeling*, I suppose, but … it was like I was one of them. I felt their emotions. There was a silent hum, a buzzing, as if they were all whispering like nervous ghosts. I could feel it in the air. It was loud … yet *silent*. I don't know how to describe it. I couldn't tell exactly what they were trying to tell me, though. If I had listened better, maybe things wouldn't be as bad as they are now."

"Oh, Sophie, you couldn't have prevented this," I insisted gently. "You did make a huge difference, though, even if it was risky." She thought about this for a while.

"Why could I hear the animals? Was I really the only one? But that's crazy. I'm … imagining things. No one can hear animals," she said in a nervous rush. I smiled. A memory came to mind: a precious story that had been magical to me when I was a kid.

"When I was little, my mom told Hunter and me a legend. A legend about a supernatural gift." This piqued Sophie's curiosity and she turned to me. "The ocean chooses one living person at a time to have the ability to empathize and communicate, to be on the same level as the creatures of the sea. All the animals love their protector. The person has to be very special and tenderhearted. Without this chosen guardian, the ocean would lose its voice and mankind would forget about it, abandoning its shores, never to return. The gifted one has one foot in the sea and one foot in the sand, thus keeping the harmony between humans and the great ocean." Sophie's eyes were full of wonder, soaking in this fantastic tale. Her smile returned, as did the happy glow that seemed to follow her wherever she went. "Don't get me wrong, it's just a story, and I don't believe in the mythical side of it. But I am convinced you have the gift. You're not crazy, but you are one of a kind. Don't ever stop being you, OK?" I said gently. Behind the huge brown saucers staring at me, I saw the familiar fire ignite once more.

"OK!" Sophie agreed. Her smile grew as big as the sky.

"I got something!" I exclaimed. Ender seemed to teleport; he was at my side so quickly. I scanned the data filling my screen. I had sent F1R3ST0RM out to search for any references to the quake, so if anyone posted anything, I would know about it via automatic hacking. Ender started reading it out.

"It was a seven! But no—that was in the Channel Islands. We suffered a six. There's a cautionary advisory; there might be a few more repercussions." He stepped back and sighed, then smiled. "A level six. Yet everyone's OK."

Ender was a good leader. I originally interpreted his strictness for irritability. But now I could see he was only worried about his team. He wasn't so bad after all; I rather liked him. I turned back to my computer. *Who am I getting this information from? They're being quite helpful.* Temporarily slipping out of the information feed, I checked the source. Ocean Front Rescue. I frowned. Why did that sound familiar? After a while, I shook it off. No point in racking my brain over something trivial.

Lenny and eight others returned. *Eight plus Lenny, that's only nine! Where's the other runner? Where's Keri!?* Then I saw the ninth, with Keri high on her shoulders. Keri, despite having scrapes on her knees and arms, was smiling proudly, carrying a stuffed dolphin in her arms. Lenny trotted over to Ender.

"We got most of the important things. The pile's a couple yards away from the side door." Ender nodded and turned to the other hackers.

"Go find your laptops, but don't go a step closer to that building than absolutely necessary." Everyone scrambled off. "Now," Ender said, turning to Keri, who was still perched on the runner's shoulders, "what happened to you?"

"I got everybody else's stuff, but then my dolphin was stuck, and I fell a bit. But I got it out," she said, holding up her little friend.

"Agh, what is it with you kids and danger?" Ender asked, a reprimand in his voice. She watched him nervously. But then he allowed a small grin to break through his stern mask. He lifted Keri and put her feet on the ground. She giggled and scampered off.

I gave a silent, contented sigh. *This is how things should be. Just like in Maryland. Oh, how I miss—* I jumped as a *ding* rang out. I pulled out my phone. Chloe was texting me. But why? *Oh, it's a group message.* Just then, an exceedingly breathless Sonja returned, and I put my phone on stealth mode so there wouldn't be any more interruptions.

"The secondary location's fine. It's good. No damage. Still safe. I swear, Ender, if you do something like that to me again today—"

"Thank you, Sonja. Good! OK, great, we still have a base." Her half threat didn't even seem to register with him. "I'll rally the others. We move tonight."

"Tonight!? Ugh! But I'm tired now!" Sonja called out after him. I chuckled and she turned on me. "What's so funny, eh? What are you laughing about?"

"Do you really want me to answer that?" I asked.

She stomped off, muttering and swearing a blue streak, which made me laugh even more. Jason gave her a wide path, avoiding her line of sight as he returned with his laptop and a backpack.

"I'm glad my computer's OK. I'd be useless without it," Jason said, plopping down beside me and opening it.

"I doubt you'd be useless. What's in the bag?" I asked. Pulling the backpack around, he unzipped it and showed off his loot.

"Well, my headset, two comic books, a jar of shark teeth that I collect, this hat—" He paused to pull on a UCSB Gauchos baseball cap; I believed this to be the popular local university team. " . . . a few games for the younger ones, my lock pick, a little GPS thing I use to explore the city, and … my marbles."

He lifted a large sack of marbles out, untied the top, and carefully laid it on the ground. I didn't mean to, but I gasped. They were stunningly gorgeous! Hundreds upon hundreds of multi-colored balls caught a stray sunbeam and set the bag aglow with dancing spots of light. They all seemed unique; some weren't even made of glass. Jason pointed out a few of the odd-looking ones.

"This one is a stone, that one is clay, this one is made of metal, and there are even a few wooden ones." He picked out two and handed them to me. "Guess what these are made of?" I inspected them for a moment.

"One looks like glass, the other looks like rock, but there's something different about them." I handed them back. "I give up. What are they?"

He grinned slightly. "A sea stone and a piece of sea glass. Sonja and I used to scavenge from the streets to the beach, looking for marbles. Then we'd come home and play with them." His smile suddenly turned to a sigh. "She isn't fun like she used to be. I don't think she likes me very much anymore."

"Why do you say that?" I asked, confused. Jason shrugged, turning his attention to the sea glass marble he was fingering.

"I don't know. All she ever does is harp on me about stuff and tell me not to screw things up, like I always do. I think I'm like a burden to her."

I shook my head. "I highly doubt she feels that way. Didn't you see how upset she was earlier? She was upset because you almost got hurt, not because you did something crazy." I sat back a bit, remembering the night Ashley lectured me after I snuck out to meet up with Eric. "Sonja's only trying to look out for you. Trust me, a sister is the best gift life has to give. She cares. You'll see." *You don't realize what you have till it's gone.*

"You really think so?" Jason asked, unconvinced.

I nodded. "I know so."

I don't know why, after all these years of owning a cell phone, the thing is still capable of stopping my heart. Being extremely tired and having a near brush with death earlier only made things worse. When my phone went off, I jumped about four inches and gave a quick gasp, sounding like a dying fish. Sophie looked at me inquisitively.

"How on earth does your phone still work? The water didn't ruin it?"

"No, my phone's waterproof. It has to be. More than 80 percent of my activities in life involve water, and I have a tendency to drop things," I explained, feeling slightly foolish.

The message on the group chat was from Chloe.

Group Chat: Chloe, Amber, Dylan, Matt, Jordan

Chloe
That was a big earthquake, is everyone alright!?!?

Matt
I'm okay.

Jordan
I'm still breathing. Dylan's here too, just on another floor, but I've seen him since the quake.

Dylan
Yeah, I'm okay.

Matt
Damage report?

Chloe
A palm tree fell across the street and down the block a fire hydrant exploded. It's a mess. Things fell over. All is good other than that.

Matt
Lots of things fell over. Windows shattered and we had to temporarily evacuate the building. A few people went to the ER with minor injuries. Building across the street crumbled.

Dylan
Half of the group tank shattered on Jordan and Sophie.

Chloe
WHAT!?

Jordan
…

Jordan
Don't worry. Seriously, everyone's OK here. Dylan, stop volunteering my stories.

Dylan
Sorry, I was just filling out the damage report.

Chloe
Amber, are you okay?

Chloe
Amber?

Chloe
Where is she?

Matt
I just tried to message Amber outside of the group chat. It didn't go through. My phone got really laggy, then said her number doesn't exist.

Chloe
But she's messaged us from that number. It does exist.

Jordan
Matt, you're tech-smart. What could cause a phone to do that?

Matt
I can't think of many things.

Dylan
So there are a few, what are they?

Matt

…

Jordan

Matt, what are they?

Matt

I don't mean to alarm you all, but this doesn't look good. Either her phone has been disconnected, it lost satellite connection for over six months, or … was destroyed.

Destroyed?! I leapt up.

"Is something wrong?" Sophie asked, looking concerned.

"I hope not. I have to go find out. I'll be back."

This was one of those times I wished I drove to Ocean Front. I tried to keep calm, to walk normally, but I found myself running, racing toward home. Despite Amber being relatively distant, withdrawn, and, well, new—I already considered her a friend.

Perhaps she just put her phone down somewhere and forgot. Or maybe it was dead and she was charging it. But, no—the message would have still gone through! Yet, her phone wasn't disconnected, and it was working the other day … I really didn't like the last option. Maybe I could find her. Her apartment was the only place I could think of. *Oh, please be there!*

The ride to the fourteenth floor was way up there in my mental list of longest elevator rides. I came to a skidding halt in front of Amber's door and knocked. Nothing. I tried again. Nothing. I called out her name. Nothing. I hurried to my room, went onto the balcony, and looked up. There weren't any lights on in her apartment. Through the cracks between the boards, I could see that her shoes were gone. I had seen them up there yesterday.

The elevator ride back down to the lobby was also memorably long.

"Betty, are you OK?" I asked, finding her at the front desk.

"Yes, Jordan. Thank heavens this place is sturdy. I think everyone's fine. What about you? I've not seen a quake like that in a coon's age!"

"Agreed. That was big. I'm alright. Have you seen Amber today?" Betty looked like she was about to comment, but then stopped and thought.

"Actually, yes. Real early this mornin' I saw her leavin."

"Have you seen her since?"

"No."

I thanked Betty and wandered off, drowning in the unknown. *Why is her phone not working? Does she know it's nonfunctional? Will she come back? Where did she go? Is she OK?* I sighed. *Where are you, Amber?*

I was so occupied with Jason and his marble collection that I didn't notice the hackers slowly gathering their belongings and heading down the street.

"Jason, where's everyone going?" I asked. Jason looked up, watched a few of them go, then groaned.

"I guess we really are moving tonight. I hate moving." He put his marbles back in his backpack, slung it over his shoulder, and motioned for me to follow.

"Wait, really? This is happening now?"

"Yeah. Don't worry. I know the way," Jason assured me. We walked on and on, past old structures and broken water towers, standing as haggard, dirty gray skeletons from the past. Eventually, I could see our destination ahead.

The old warehouse was made of rusty, corrugated metal sheets, reminding me of an apocalypse game I once played. It was smaller than the last base, with what appeared to be only one and a half floors; also, the sea was just a few steps from the back door. The only improvement was that this building was still standing. Inside, the dirt floor had been trampled flat years ago. The walls were cracking and flaking. The roof was low; if I stood on a chair, I could easily touch it. A few boarded windows let cracks of dusty evening sunlight in. Even so, it was still quite dim.

The others were already hard at work, gathering tables, setting up equipment, and reassembling the generator and servers. Or, what was left of them. There were plenty of circuit boards, wires, solder guns, and sparks. I was surprised at how quickly the repairs were going. I turned to Jason.

"How long has Vortex been around? You all work together like clockwork. It's amazing."

He shrugged. "I'm not quite sure. A long time. Ender's the best leader Vortex has ever had. He came up with most of the current systems. Everyone has their assigned places. We only keep as much as we can all collectively carry; that way, we can leave at a moment's notice and never come back."

"Smart." I looked over at the broken servers. "I can fix that. Should I just … jump in and start helping?" Jason shrugged again.

"The sooner the generator and servers are back up, the better. I doubt Ender could find something better for you to do." He grinned and jerked his thumb over his shoulder. "I'm gonna go upstairs and barter for a rafter or corner." With that, he trotted off.

Pulling tools from my bag, I got started on the first server. It was just like the good old college days. I hadn't done any serious mechanical stuff like this in ages. It was coming back to me already. After all, this was my third language. First: English. Second: hacking. Third: electrical engineering. Fourth: Arabic. *It's been awhile since I got a paper cut from a circuit board or got molten solder in my hair. Let's do this.*

When I got back to Ocean Front, I told Dylan and messaged the others about my findings. None of us could think of where Amber might have gone. There were a million options. And though it might just be a coincidence, I didn't like the fact that Amber had dropped off the grid right after a massive earthquake. I couldn't help but be worried.

Lexie risked a super short phone call to see if I was OK. I wish we could have talked longer … I miss her so much. I could hear it in her voice; she's growing up so fast. Our parents don't like us communicating, but they tolerate the letters. They know I'm a Christian, and they also know that, because of me, so is Lexie. They say believing in God is worthless religious gibberish, but Lexie and I disagree. I'm thankful for that. At least my sister loves the truth. I wish Mom and Dad and Hunter would, too.

The rest of the evening passed in a blur: clean up, report, round up the puffins, check on other tanks, try not to slip in the puddles, reboot the systems and, generally, restore order. When everything was said and done, I was almost reluctant to go home. What if Amber was still missing? It was getting rather late. Surely she would be back by now … right? I hadn't learned the full extent of the damage in the surrounding area, but I knew a few buildings went down and cracks had opened up. What if she … ? No, I didn't want to think about those possibilities. This time, the journey home seemed short, even though I dragged my feet the whole way. I wanted to give her more time to get back. If I got there and she was still missing, I would worry.

Upon returning home, I sat out on the balcony, looking up, waiting, hoping, and praying I would see the lights come on so I would know Amber was OK. But the stars came out—and I went inside. *Wherever you are tonight, Amber, I hope you're safe.*

After melting a hole in my shoe, dripping molten solder on my hair—as predicted—getting shocked by a wire, and, also as predicted, getting some paper cuts from circuit boards, I eventually finished with the last of the servers. It was surprisingly enjoyable working side by side with other electrical and cyber geeks like me. It was like being part of a team. Pretty soon, the power was back and the systems were up. V0RT3X was alive and well. I decided I was earning my keep.

Apparently, Jason's efforts really did save the day. Most of the circuit boards had to be replaced; there was hardly any data remaining. If it weren't for him, V0RT3X would be back to square one.

Deciding my work was done, I wandered upstairs in search of my young friend. The ceiling was higher on the second floor than it was downstairs. Along each wall were giant, empty shelving units, and ladders had been secured to the sides of them. I spotted Jason swinging his feet over the edge of one of the cubbies, working on his GPS gadget. After some ninja-like skills on the ladder, I landed on his platform.

"Hey, Jason," I said. He glanced up and grinned slightly.

"Hey."

"The systems are back up. You can connect your computer again," I announced. His smile grew a bit and he turned to his laptop.

"Done. Thanks, Firestorm." He paused, looking for the right words. "And thank you for saving my life, back at the other stronghold. You really did save me. Thank you." Nodding, I sat down beside him.

"No problem. Anyone would have done as much." I noticed another drop of solder in my hair and picked it out. "It was great. Working on the servers, I mean. I like that kind of stuff." I glanced down at the ground far below. "It's really cool up here. This thing is like a giant bunkbed."

"Yeah," Jason agreed. "You're not scared of heights?"

"I live fourteen floors up from the ground. No, I kind of like high places." Suddenly, Jason looked up from his gadget and regarded me inquisitively.

"You came to talk to me. Why? I'm just a kid." That made me smile a little.

"Well, for starters, I'm new here. You've been a great help. You're the person I know best out of everyone here. Ender's busy, and Sonja's complaining about how small and scrappy the place is."

Jason chuckled a bit at that. "Yeah, she's not in a good mood right now."

Then, grinning smugly, I added, "And, as a side issue, you did point a gun at me today." Jason sighed.

"I'm sorry about that. I thought you might be from Cerberus, or with the police or something. I'm sorry." I laughed.

"I'm just teasing you. It's fine! You were doing your job, and I think everything turned out perfectly. No worries."

"Thanks," he said, then cocked his head slightly. "Can I call you Storm? It's not as big a mouthful as Firestorm is."

"Sure."

"OK." Grinning, he picked up his GPS and showed me his handiwork. "Check this out. So, here's the layout of the city—" He pressed a button and the city spread across the screen. "Here's our general location—" The picture zoomed in. "And here's the 3D model of the warehouse." Using his fingers to make the screen zoom in and out and pivot, he did a speed walk-through of the entire place.

"How did you do that? It's amazing!" I exclaimed, wide-eyed. It looked so real!

"It's like sonar, I guess; I scan sections of the building one at a time, then put them together." I was going to ask more, but Sonja chose that moment to come scaling up the ladder.

"Jason, we're going home tonight. There could still be a few more after-shocks. Get your hide down here. I'll be waiting at the front." Jason seemed to slump a bit.

"Fine. I'll grab my stuff," he muttered. This seemed to satisfy Sonja; she slid down the railing and strode off. *What was that all about?*

"What did she mean, 'tonight'? Don't you always go home at night?"

"No. Usually we crash at the stronghold for weeks on end," Jason said quietly.

"What? Why?"

"It's better than going home. Our parents don't give two flying monkeys about what we do. As long as we check in now and then to prove we haven't gone completely AWOL, they don't question where we've been. They don't care." He shrugged, stuffed his computer and GPS into his backpack, then slung it over his shoulder. "See you later, Storm." With that, he clambered down the ladder and ran after Sonja.

That hit me hard. While I was back in Maryland, I was lucky to have a loving family. Some of my friends didn't have a good home to return to, though, and would live at the stronghold, just like Jason and Sonja. I remembered what I was here fighting for. *Try to make everyone's life brighter, and make the world a better place.* I sighed. It was late. Time to go home.

Thankfully, the new base was a lot closer to the apartments than the last one. I trudged to my building, went straight to my room, flopped onto the bed, and was out before the sheets settled.

CHAPTER 12

The Salt Breeze Apartment Complex, Apt. 1307
Saturday, August 18, 11:35 A.M.

 Jordan

Amber was still nowhere to be found. None of the lights were on in her apartment, and there was no answer when I knocked. Betty said she didn't see her come or go in the morning. Neither Dylan nor Chloe nor Matt had heard from her. I was seriously starting to get worried. I couldn't help it. She was just … gone.

My morning surf lessons were cancelled due to rough, choppy waves, so I decided to go help at Ocean Front. A few windows had shattered and some shelves had fallen over, but there was nothing major. Ocean Front was built to withstand level eight quakes. The damage to the group tank was by far the worst area to begin cleanup and repairs. It was discovered that the glass had a tiny fault in it. If it weren't for the divider, the entire thing would have burst. As I went about doing this and that, I picked up on stress among Tristan, Laura, and some of the directors. Add that to the bucket of nervousness balanced precariously on my heart.

Also, just about everyone was debating the idea of a new fault line. The events matched the predictions. There was talk of trying to get an official thesis together. Using sonar, recon submarines, and robotic probes to prove it were all possibilities to be discussed. It seemed unreal. I tried to keep to the shadows. I had done my part; I had started this. Now, others would finish it. I was truly hoping things would go back to normal—at least for me. At least a little. Anyway, I didn't know about complicated tectonic and seismic stuff. I just took care of animals; that was what I did.

My head was still spinning at the thought of Sophie's unusual ability.

Though, honestly, I probably shouldn't have been surprised. She was special; I'd seen it from the start. She was like some kind of aquatic angel with a loving, motherly instinct for ocean animals and a passion to match. I'm not quite sure how I got volunteered, but at the start of the summer, I had come in to work and found Sophie waiting for me. I had no idea I would be mentoring an intern, so I ended up winging it. But everything was going well. She was a quick learner and already getting the hang of things. I was glad she was my shadow.

Anyway—back to the present—I had wandered home after a while. And now I was bored.

"The waves are too choppy to go surfing; the rest of my lessons still might get canceled. Chloe's picked up extra hours today and won't be off till later. Dylan's still at Ocean Front working with the radar tech. Matt's busy. And Amber is missing. So, I'm a tad bored." While I was saying all this, four pairs of oblivious, wide eyes stared at me, watching my every move. I sighed. "I wish you guys could talk."

If my goldfish could speak, they would probably only say things like "Human, feed us more!" Or, "Food is good! It makes us fatter." Maybe, "You look strange. Where are your fins? How do you breathe?" Or perhaps, even, "Human, is your entire species as crazy as you are?"

Sitting back, I shook my head as if to clear my thoughts. *Why am I thinking about this?* The whole stranded-alone-on-an-island scenario would kill me. Apparently, I couldn't even keep my sanity for one afternoon. *I wish Amber would come back. I hope she's OK. … Maybe I should go look for her again. I still have a mental picture of the map I gave her; I could check those locations. Yeah, that's what I'll do. If I stay here much longer, I will truly go a little crazy.*

The first sensation that met me when I stepped into reality was panic. I couldn't hear, see, or breathe very well. Disoriented, I lashed out desperately. The fight only lasted a second. My pillow went flying and the bright light pounded my eyes. *My pillow? What?* … I remembered; a sound had begun to wake me this morning, so I had covered my face with my pillow.

Glancing at my phone, which was devoid of notifications, I was surprised to see it was already past noon. I hadn't slept this late in forever. It wasn't as if I had any obligations or work, so it didn't really matter. *If Ashley was here, she'd scold me so much ...* I smiled at the thought. Ashley always woke me up at some ridiculously early hour, school or no school, weekday or weekend—she'd pinch my nose so I couldn't breathe. Such an efficient but slightly annoying wake-up call. *Where did she learn that?*

Shaking away the tiredness, smiling at this memory, I swung my legs over the side of the bed and stood, glancing around, searching for a purpose. Usually I'd be doing a job for Edge or stealing data from Teumessian— if this was a normal day. There wouldn't be any of those for a year. I wasn't used to my mind being so unoccupied; it was awful. Without something to focus on, I felt miserable. Eventually, after a few pointless tasks, I decided to go to V0RT3X.

As I neared the old warehouse, I saw some of the younger kids playing a game of tag down by the water. How they got past the treacherous drop, I had no idea. I could pick out Keri, nimbly darting between rocks and dodging the tide, giggling all the way; Jason was down there too, running alongside the younger ones, catching them if they tripped, calling encouragement, making them laugh. He noticed me and waved, pausing long enough for the chaser to catch up with him. I think she yelled something like, "Tag! You're it!" because Jason groaned and took off after the kid. I couldn't help but chuckle. *Ah, that made my morning.*

I assumed this was what a casual day looked like at V0RT3X; people were setting things up, chatting, hacking, programming, and running around. No one paid me any mind as I sat at a table and got to work. An idea was forming in my mind. It needed lots of work, but it was a start: a self-assembling virus.

The more I inspected Brenton's security systems, the more I realized they were impenetrable. Unless, that is, damaging them wasn't a problem. We needed to freeze up most of his computer if our plan was going to work, yet nothing hostile could get past his walls. But what if the malware came in harmless bits and pieces? It would seem insignificant to the protection programs, and when all the parts were past the walls, they would assemble and become a full-fledged virus. Theoretically. Now to actually make one. I dove into the code.

Within a couple of hours, I had programmed the virus, split it into smaller pieces, and taught them how to move through security walls. But once they got past, they simply sat there, doing nothing! They were oblivious to their counterparts sitting nanobits away from them—either that, or they didn't get that they were supposed to merge. They reminded me of dead paramecium I saw under a microscope in fifth grade.

This is terribly annoying. What am I missing? After tweaking the code a bit, I sent it through another simulation. One through, two, three … seven, eight—nothing. *Alright, that does it.* I shoved my chair back and stalked off. The program would have to wait a while; otherwise, I would blow a mental circuit and delete the whole thing.

Pretty soon, I found myself staring at the raging sea and the brave children taunting it. Now some of them were playing a mixture of hide-and-go-seek and freeze tag. A few of the older kids had clustered near one of the sea boulders and seemed to be inspecting a tide pool.

"Hey, Storm!" I glanced down to see Jason waving at me. Keri and another boy were with him. She looked up and waved enthusiastically. *I think these kids actually like me.* I don't consider myself good with people, but children—I love children. I'm free when I'm around them; I don't have to be suspicious or worry about what they might think of me.

"Firestorm, come see this!" Keri called.

"OK. How do you get down there?" I asked. Keri stood, dusted the sand off her knees, and scrambled to my left. I watched her go, then lost sight of her under the overhang. *Where did she go?*

"Here!" I almost jumped out of my shoes. There, standing behind me, was a very sandy Keri. She giggled. "Come on, follow me!" Turns out, there were small ledges sticking out of the rocks. The top ones were covered in sand, and the lower layered in sea slime, so I had to hold on tight—but I got down in one piece. Coming to a sand-spraying stop, Keri pointed proudly at the boy beside Jason. "Firestorm, this is Aiden, my big bro! He's a master hacker. I'm gonna be just like him when I grow up!" She looked to him for affirmation. He shrugged a bit, as if unsure how to handle this praise.

So, that's why Keri was with V0RT3X. Though I had seen some exceptions, Keri, being only eleven, was too young to be a true hacker, so I had assumed she had a sibling.

"Hello, Aiden. Nice to meet you."

"Hi," he said simply. Aiden appeared bored and was probably only sticking around for Keri's sake. She, however, was enthralled with some sort of contraption Jason had set up.

It was a marble track. It was made of shells and bits of cardboard, held in place on a wooden base by twisted coils of wire and string. At one end was a long, adjustable track with a rubber band launch pad. In the middle stood a shell with a little hole in the center of it, after which were multiple curvy trails, all leading to a bowl with a magnet in the center. I could see a few tiny metal BBs stuck to it.

"Here, Keri, try this. I think it's fixed now," Jason said, moving out of the way. Keri slid forward and got down on eye level with the contraption, thus getting even sandier.

"Watch!" she exclaimed excitedly. "I'm getting better." Keri took her time, tweaking the position of the starter track little by little. I turned to Jason.

"Is it a game?"

"Yeah. The goal is to try and shoot the little ball through the hole. If you overshoot or undershoot, it misses the track. If it reaches the magnet in the center of the basin, you win."

Keri held her breath, slowly pulled the rubber band back, and let go. It slammed into the BB, sending it flying down the track. Curving left, right, dipping, then launching into the air, it sailed through the tiny hole and onto one of the tracks. After an impressive display of twists and turns, it slid down the sides of the bowl and came to a stop with the other balls on the magnet.

"I did it!" Keri giggled in delight. "Here, you try!"

"Me? I don't think I'll make it."

"I'll help you," she said proudly. "I can do it."

She is so cute, I thought. "OK." I swung the launch track to what I thought looked like a good starting position.

"Left a bit," Keri said. A moment later: "Right a teensy weensy bit ... no, too much ... no—there! Shoot it!"

Left, right, the drop, then it went airborne—and it made it! Soon the tiny ball was cruising down a complicated trail, then, right at the end, it seemed to hit a bump, because it skipped a little and landed on top of four other BBs, forming a tiny pyramid. The magnetic force held it in place. Even when Keri picked it up, the structure retained its shape; it had become magnetized.

"You did it! And you built something!" I didn't totally comprehend her words.

There's something to be learned here ... this is important. But, how? I stared at the tiny stack, and it hit me. Something to bring the pieces together! A catalyst, a common tie, a destination! *The balls all end up in the same bowl, but the magnet is what unites them!*

"That's it!!!" I leapt up and started for the slippery staircase. "Keri, Jason. You're geniuses!"

"What did I do?" Jason asked, looking puzzled.

"Tell you later!" I called over my shoulder.

I knew how to fix the virus. I felt foolish for not thinking of it before. All I had to do was find something unique about Brenton's computer—or more precisely, something stored in it. Once the virus had a specific object to target, it would serve as a rendezvous place for all the pieces!

I climbed the rocks and ran as quickly to the building as I could, then leapt into my chair so fast it almost slid away from the table. *Come on, this is it!* I sent a timed search bot into Brenton's real systems, one that disintegrated within five seconds—thus leaving it untraceable—and waited impatiently. Five seconds later, a copied file popped up on my screen.

Adding an entirely new branch to the code, I programmed a string of commands, targeting the file I had found inside Brenton's computer. After adjusting the simulator, I sent the virus through one more test run. The new line of code didn't prevent the pieces from getting through the walls, and ... it was working! The virus began to come together, merging like drops of oil floating on water, becoming one. It grew and grew. The simulator began to glitch. Suddenly, the screen went dead and a blank video chat popped up. The virus had frozen the simulation and, now, awaited input.

I stood, drinking in this moment of victory. *A magnet. An ending point. It worked.* I reclaimed control of the system and ordered the virus to reset. Sticking the little monster into a file, I jumped onto the main database and sent the file to Ender with the title "ONLY OPEN INSIDE THE BRENTON FIREWALL SIMULATOR." I released the attachment and waited.

The thing about living in Santa Barbara is this: you better like people, because there are thousands. Usually, I don't mind; I rather like it. But today, I couldn't help but wonder if I had passed Amber by, perhaps a few feet away, and not seen her due to the crowds. I had gone farther inland, toward the center of the city, and the streets were a bustle. I checked the beach, the ice cream shop near the apartments, the art museum, The

Flying Turtle, the library, and by the park. I looked everywhere. Amber was nowhere. I despaired of running into her on the streets. Well, hopefully I wouldn't ever actually run *into* her again. But if I was going to find her, it probably wouldn't be this way.

The remainder of my surf lessons had been cancelled, just as I suspected. Everyone was still occupied. Then I noticed my watch. 2:36. *Wait—Chloe gets off soon!* Today felt like a good day to surprise her; I hadn't done that in a while. I decided, if she wasn't too busy, I would go say hi. Perhaps she had heard from Amber; if not, maybe we could team up and start our own search party. If we didn't find her, we could come up with something else.

By the time I was peering through the front windows of The Chubby Pelican, it was almost three. It didn't appear to be busy. *Let's see how long it takes Chloe to notice me. This is going to be fun.* I waited for Chloe to go to the back before walking in. No doubt she heard the bell, but at least she didn't see me arrive. Choosing a table in the blind spot of the kitchen door, I slid into the booth and pretended to be looking at the menu. Within the minute, I could hear footsteps aimed in my direction. *Right pitch of heel clicking, right pace … yes, it's Chloe. Wait for it …*

"Welcome to The—" Instant, delighted recognition flashed across her face. "Jordan!"

"Sorry to disappoint, but I'm not here for food. Are you busy?" She grinned and sat down across from me.

"Not anymore, thank heavens."

"I take it it's been crazy?"

"Yeah. I've heard that bell over the door more than my own voice today. But I'm doing fine. What have you been up to today? And what exactly happened yesterday, the whole 'group-tank-shattered-on-Jordan-and-Sophie' thing?"

"Ah, the group tank is a long explanation. I'll tell you a bit later," I murmured, chuckling. "And not much is happening today. I went by Ocean Front this morning, went home, and then did nothing for about an hour. Ever since, I've been wandering around looking for Amber."

"Have you heard anything from her yet?" Chloe asked anxiously.

"Nothing. Have you?"

"No," she admitted, then seemed to wilt a little. "It's … I'm starting to get worried. Please tell me I'm just worrying too much."

"No, Chloe," I said, shaking my head. "You're not. I'm worried too."

Chloe sighed and sat back, looking out the window with a distant, disappointed look in her eyes

"You know, I've only known her for a few weeks, and yeah, she's super withdrawn, quiet, reserved, and all, but I already feel like we're friends in a way. I don't know."

"Yeah, I feel like that too," I agreed. It appeared Chloe was about to say something more, but she was interrupted by the *ding* of the bell above the door.

"I better get that. Hey, don't go anywhere, I won't be balancing trays up and down my arms for much longer; I get off soon."

"I know. No worries. I don't have to be anywhere today." Chloe started to walk off, then backpedaled and dropped a basket of chips in front of me. "What are those for?" I asked. She winked.

"Technically, you have to order something to stay, so those are there so the other waiters don't boot you out."

"Oh, thanks. You sure this is OK?"

"Yeah. And, thanks for stopping by. You're the best. I'll be back before long."

Chloe walked off, and I heard her enthusiastic sing-song voice call out greetings to the new customers. I couldn't help but smile. *She's like walking sunshine. I must be the happiest person alive. My friends are the best. I'm set for life.*

I decided Ender was beginning to trust me a little. Once he tested the virus, he wasted no time and jumped into action. All of V0RT3X was thrown into full throttle. Hundreds of search bots were being sent into Brenton's computer. The simulator was upgraded bit by bit and the virus was sent through test runs at every turn. If it had a glitch or hole, we had to find out now. I had to tweak the code a couple of times, but for the most part, it was perfect. No matter how the simulator grew, the virus got through without a hitch.

The plan was to secretly turn Brenton's face cam on and wait till he alone was at the monitor. Once he was, the virus would be released in the form of an email. Never mind the fact that it was a private address; we found it easily. He didn't even need to open the email: the virus would simply slip out and hijack his system, freeze up the controls, and open a live video feed. On our side of things, Ender would do the talking. We would use a voice distorter and an instant face recognition program, one that would keep Ender unidentifiable. Also, he would be wearing a low hood in case something went wrong. The rest of us would be monitoring the system and Brenton's phone in case he tried to record the video or contact authorities.

Problem was, there was no telling exactly when we could put the plan into action. At the moment, Brenton wasn't even home. He was visiting a retired ambassador in Los Angeles. Furthermore, when he did return, not only did Brenton have to be alone at the monitor, he also had to be alone in the room. Possibly the whole house. Why? Because there was a speaker com system. All he had to do was push a button and the entire household could hear what was happening. Thus, I ended up syncing my phone to the V0RT3X system. That way, if an alert was sent out, I would be notified instantly.

It had been a long time since I felt like I was making a difference. Yes, fighting Teumessian saved thousands of lives daily, but I didn't get to see immediate, obvious results. Now I was fighting for the community in which I lived. When all the hard work paid off, I would get to see it with my own eyes.

This feels like the good old days when I was a member of R0GU3C0D3. I'd say that's the only thing I miss about Maryland. At this thought, I sighed. *That was a sad statement.* I grinned slightly at the mental image of my past self: the child who had won her way into a secretive hacking group. I remembered the sweatshirt two sizes too big that went halfway to my knees, the hair that wouldn't stay out of my eyes, the nervous fear of being rejected, the small voice, the clumsy behavior. I had been so disappointed that the hackers had been indifferent toward me. Well, everyone except Eric.

This time, the memory didn't hit me as painful, just bittersweet. *You were my only friend, and a good one. The best. I don't think anyone else in the world is cut out as perfectly as you. Eloquent, a carefree and irresponsible air, yet mature when the situation demanded it. Maddeningly annoying, yet … irresistibly endearing. Us two outcasts, roaming the cyber streets, not taking the real world seriously.* I sighed, the manifestation of longing loneliness and a recollection of peace. *You're the only one who ever understood me, Eric. Oh, how I miss you.*

"Hey, fire girl!" I jumped. Sonja was headed toward me, looking, as usual, bored. She flopped sideways into the chair beside me, her legs swinging over the armrests. "What'd you do?"

"What? What did I do? What do you mean?" I asked, wondering if I was in trouble.

She snorted. "The virus, dummy. How did you come up with it? I wanna see your base code." She paused, looking at me expectantly. "Today, please. Come on! Pull it up!" Feeling rather stunned, I numbly opened the program. Sonja slid forward and regarded my work with an unimpressed, skeptic gaze.

"I was—"

"Hush it," she interrupted, her eyes fixed on the screen.

"OK." *Wow, the Ninja is testy today. What did I do to make her dislike me so—*

"Impressive," Sonja stated simply, sitting back. My mind balked. Did she just compliment my work?

"Pardon?" I asked.

"You heard me. Or are you deaf as well as slow? I said 'impressive.' In simpler, smaller words, that would be 'not bad for a newbie.'"

"Thanks ... I think," I stuttered. She noticed the slightly offended and confused look on my face and huffed an irritated sigh.

"Yes, I know my social skills suck. Get over it."

"Mine aren't so great, either," I murmured. I have no idea why I felt the need to respond. For a millisecond, Sonja appeared pleased with this. Then she returned to her usual rude, bored self.

"Yeah, nerd. Whatever." She seemed to run out of snarky comments for a moment. "Oh, Ender says good work. When it's the real thing, he wants you to be backup; if the virus fails, you'll start hacking manually." Another pause. "Alright, science-fair-show-and-tell is over. I'm done." Sonja stood and walked off, her stride silently screaming attitude. I shook my head. If this place was a bee hive, she would be queen.

I was still lost in thought. My mind was far, far away, on a time long, long ago. I couldn't focus anymore. *I think my work here is done.*

Done. Another book, done. I set it down, closed my eyes, and started sorting through this new information. Chloe and I had wandered around and chatted for a while. We even looked for Amber a bit. But eventually we parted ways and went home. I'd been here a couple of hours. At my back was the balcony railing, and by my side waited a stack of books, three of which I had already finished. I brought up my mental binder; to the left of it, the image of a trash bin. *Trivial information to the left, useful stuff to the right.*

Yes, I have to sort my memory. It's a bit of a pain sometimes, but if I don't, it gets hard to find the information I need. Despite remembering everything, I can still forget. I go through a process of sorting everything. It's something like turning pen marks into pencil. It isn't instantaneous, but eventually, things will fade.

It took a while to figure out how to control my mind. It's amazing I passed elementary school. But I had a handle on my brain by middle school and total control by high school, thank heavens. From there, it was simple trial and error to figure out how to delete, keep, sort, categorize, and recall all the info I stuffed into my head.

Hmm … do I need that fact? I don't know, it's kind of interesting. To keep or not to keep? That is the question … My eyes snapped open. There was a faint sound above me. I hardly dared to hope. Could it be? I glanced up. I couldn't see anything from my position. Slowly, I stood, leaned over the railing, and looked up. There, arms folded on the rails, hair blowing gently in the breeze, eyes searching over the ocean, was Amber. Relief washed over me like a tidal wave, and my breath caught in my throat. She seemed to hear my little gasp, and looked down.

"Oh. Hi, Jordan."

"Amber! I'm so glad you're alright! What happened? Where have you been?" A look of confusion flitted across her face.

"I've been … uh, around. What do you mean, 'what happened?' Why wouldn't I be alright?"

"The earthquake. You weren't on the group chat, Matt tried to text you, and his phone crashed. We were worried you might have … we couldn't find you. You just dropped off the grid." I paused, then asked: "Did you know your phone isn't working?" Now Amber appeared absolutely mystified.

"My phone?"

I pulled out my phone. No missed texts or any indication of a problem.

Opening the messages, I noticed a symbol at the top of the screen. The hidden icon. *Oh no. Friday, after the earthquake—I enabled stealth mode. I never turned it off!*

"Oh, here. I'll restart it." Pretending to hold down the power button and pausing in a convincing way, I flicked to the settings and ended the incognito option.

Ding-ding-ding-ding-ding-ding … My text count soared as messages from Chloe, Dylan, Matt, and Jordan came in. Titles of, "Amber? You there?"; "Are you okay?"; "Where are you?"; "You're not hurt, are you?"; and "Please answer, I'm getting worried"—all flooded my inbox. *They … were really worried about me.* My gaze dropped from my phone down to Jordan's smiling face. I didn't know what to say. I *had* disappeared for more than a day. I *had* ignored Chloe's text. I *hadn't* even wondered if they were OK. Yet they had been concerned about me.

"I'm sorry I scared you. I … well, I don't know what to say."

Jordan gave a contented sigh. "Don't worry about it. You're here now." He grinned. "Maybe you should message the others. We don't want them planning a search party."

Numbly, I nodded, and sent a message on the group chat. Replies poured in, and I could dimly pick out the echoing dings of Jordan's phone from somewhere below.

"Welcome back, Amber," Jordan said quietly, and I could hear the smile in his voice. "I'm so happy you're safe."

CHAPTER 13

Ocean Front Rescue
Monday, August 27, 11:45 A.M.

Jordan

For a couple weeks, I got my wish. Life went back to normal. Apart from little things, it was as if nothing weird had ever happened. New fault line? There was talk of that, but it had died down. My neighbor was acting strange? Well, she seemed normal soon after. Earthquake? It felt like a distant memory. Amber went missing? She'd been around ever since. What could possibly go wrong?

I don't like that question. Disaster follows whenever I ask it.

I'm so glad things have stopped changing. Good heavens, I was starting to worry "crazy" would be the new "normal." It still felt a little odd having Amber in the group, but it wasn't a bad odd. Just different. Ever since Dad and Mom left, taking Lexie with them, it'd just been Matt, Dylan, Chloe, and me. Now there was Amber, too. Chloe was seriously enjoying having another girl to hang with. My prediction was right: despite their differences, the two of them had become good friends.

Amber had started to become less of a hermit crab. She was still super shy, and now and then would do something strange, or something unexplainable would happen, but other than that, nothing out of the ordinary. Except for the fact that she still watched every surfing lesson I taught. What's up with that?

With no group tank, releases were being scheduled all the time, but they were difficult; the waves were still dangerous. Though none of them could compare to the earthquake, there had been aftershocks. The ocean wouldn't be calming down anytime soon, and neither would the waves.

Any chance I got, I was out surfing. I think I have some sort of daredevil death wish.

"Hey, Jordan! Meeting with the bigwigs in the map room in five," Dylan called to me as he passed.

"Got it. Thanks."

This was nothing new. There had been loads of meetings of late. Progress reports on the group tank, scheduled release dates, and stats on the repercussions of the quakes—all were being discussed at length. As long as we kept up the pace, everything would be fixed within a month or two. I turned to Sophie.

"Hear that?"

"Yep! High gear activated." She held the list on her clipboard next to the electronic depth maps and continued to make corrections.

Sophie was totally back to normal. There was no doubt the earthquake had been the source of her anxiety. It baffled my mind still. She had been able to sense all the major aftershocks before they happened, and thus we had been a little more prepared for each of them. Of course, not many people readily believed her at first, but once her predictions started coming true, precautions were taken at her suggestion. I grinned. *Ah, they grow up so fast. Already influential. Well, to a degree.*

"With all this data coming together, I bet there will be an official thesis with supporting facts within a couple weeks! The tectonic plate will become solid reality!" Sophie exclaimed excitedly.

"I haven't really thought it out yet. You really think we can pull it all together that soon?" I asked.

Sophie nodded. "I'd say it's pretty convincing already. We don't need much more."

"You've been keeping tabs on this whole thing, haven't you? Has any other organization released info of their own yet?"

"Nope! I think we're in first place!" Sophie declared happily.

This was too much for me. Surely there were others who were beginning to explore the possibility, but it would seem we were ahead of the game. *Could Ocean Front really be the first to take credit for the discovery? Goodness, what have I started? But I suppose it's held together this far. I guess I was right.* Brain bomb! I looked up at the ceiling and shook my head.

"Please tell me I'm not 100 percent crazy."

"No, you're only 99 percent crazy. In a good way," Sophie said, smirking.

"I shouldn't have asked. Even if my sanity is just an illusion, it's a rather comforting one," I teased. Sophie laughed, and we went back to adjusting the electronic database.

Well, this is it. End of the line, at least for a year. *It's been nineteen days. Edge is supposed to call me soon …* I was glad I had a little foothold in the cliff called the real world through Chloe, Jordan, Matt, and Dylan, but I still wasn't ready to sever my lifeline: connection with Edge and the FBI.

All morning, more memories had resurfaced, reminding me why I became Laelaps in the first place. When you lose people you love, you find you want them back—if only to say good-bye. And to tell them you're sorry for failing.

I will avenge them, each and every one that Teumessian took from me. Just not for the next … 346 days. By then, I'll be ready to take them down. I won't rest until— I jumped as my phone started ringing. Edge. Like I said—the end. I answered the call.

"Hi, Edge," I muttered, quieter than I had intended.

"Amber," he said curtly, only acknowledging my existence. "We both know why I'm calling."

"Are you sure there's nothing you can do to shorten my grounding?"

"Positive. I tried. But I'll survive without my hacker kid for a year."

Excuse you, Edge. Stop treating me like a child.

"I don't know what else I was supposed to do," I said. "I'm sorry."

"Me too. Contact will be restored at the end of your punishment, as will your programs." I felt a bit of my spunk return.

"Stay up late, then, because you'll be getting a call from me in 346 days, at one minute after twelve midnight, August the ninth, which I believe will be a Friday. I'll be expecting a full rundown. You better have me up to speed within ten minutes, and I better be hacking within fifteen."

"You don't get to order me around, but fine," Edge said. "Have it your way. Keep out of trouble, lay low, don't do anything stupid, and try not to get yourself killed. Over and out."

Before I could answer, the line went dead. Just like that, Edge was gone. I sighed, staring sadly at my screen for a long time, my mind swimming. The memories began to assault me once again, but I wasn't ready to deal with them.

I've got to get my mind off of all this …

We all filed into the map room, notebooks out, chattering about new findings, exchanging hypotheses. Plenty of scientific gossip was floating about. Dylan and I were in the middle of debating whether migration patterns were purely instinct or instinct mixed with intuition, and thus changeable, when I noticed Tristan slip in. Something in me froze. There was a well-hidden look of distress in his face. He was keeping to himself. I scanned the room. Laura was exchanging glances with one of the board members. Tristan headed toward the front and sat on the edge of a table, looking out over the room. A hush fell over everyone, but I seemed to be the only one who was picking up on the fact that something was very wrong.

"Report," he said. "Group tank progress, current projects, release scheduling, average expenses, and where we are with the research." One by one, people volunteered their findings and statistics. Tristan nodded, quietly taking all of this in. His eyes flicked from side to side as he calculated and estimated in his head.

"Dylan?" I whispered.

"Yeah?"

"Something's wrong."

"What do you mean?"

"Look at Tristan. He's acting … skittish." The change in Dylan's face showed me that he saw it too. "Something's up."

We glanced at each other. He shrugged nervously and we turned our attention back to the reports. Kyle was elaborating on the current focus of the tech division, and Sarah was filling in the details he missed. They finished and no one spoke for a while.

Tristan sighed, glancing at Laura. She nodded grimly. He turned back to face us.

"I'm afraid I have some bad news."

I found myself sitting on the beach, watching people splash around in the ocean. My mind was mirroring the motion of the water, memories rising to the shore of my consciousness, then pulling back, occasionally clashing with each other. Names, faces, phrases, conversations, and events flooded my head.

"Once upon a time … once upon a time, there were two sisters. One was named Mae, and the other was named Marie …" One of Ashley's stories. *I hated the feeling I got when I heard we would be going to stay with another family, after we had been stable for so long … I didn't want to go to the Gibsons. But … they loved us.* Finding my place in the world.

"Hey, let's be friends, so I can fix those flimsy firewalls of yours, eh? You teach me your tricks, and I'll teach you mine." Eric. *When we graduated, Ashley—oh, we were so happy … life was finally ours. We were free, truly free! We dreamt of that for years …* One of the best days of my life.

The fire … the heat of an explosion strong enough to shatter the very foundations of my world, to reprogram my very existence … Who knew it could leave such scars? … One of the worst days of my life. *"Amber, if what you say is true, and I don't doubt that it is, you are in unimaginable danger. I know it seems soon, but I need to take drastic steps to keep you safe."*

If it wasn't for Eric, I would be dead now.

"I'm up to my neck in debt, and you're my only way out! You sure fetch a good price … At school, they always called you weird, different, maybe even dangerous. I should have seen it sooner—Laelaps!" Jessica taught me not to trust. *"Amber, Amber, calm down! I won't deny this is your fault, but flipping out isn't going to help anything. I warned you; stay away from normal people. You just put them in danger and drop them like they're hot when you leave without a trace. Sometimes they even end up dead."*

And Edge: he reenforced the whole "no one can be trusted" concept.

Everything that brought me here … Well, I never could have imagined it would take me so far away. I don't know where I would be if only I had turned in the … No. Don't think about that.

I frowned. I'd come out here to get my mind off the past, not to wallow in it. Sitting and doing nothing only made it more difficult to keep my memories in check. I had to occupy myself with something. Standing, I began to pace the beach. Then, after a while, I sat again to watch a cluster of surfers. Before long, I found myself wondering … *How hard can it be?* And that's when I started scheming.

Everyone went stock-still. No one spoke, even whispered. All eyes were on Tristan. There was a heartbeat in time. Then, he sighed and pressed on.

"We finally managed to get in contact with Gregory Damon's secretary to finalize where Ocean Front Rescue stands. We are on his 'terminating relations' list. Funding has been cut."

The world slowed to a grinding stop, only long enough for the meaning of doom to sink in, then everything was hurled into hyperspeed. Everyone started talking at once. But I was frozen, absolute shock working its way to my gut. *This can't be happening.*

"Stop! Stop!" Tristan called above the din. The noise simmered. He sighed, discouraged and frustrated at the entire situation.

"Why was Ocean Front terminated from the financial aid program?" someone called out. Tristan's shoulders seemed to slump even more, if that was possible. Laura spoke first.

"Damon said, and I quote, that he 'will not pay for an oversized, private aquarium with no relevant output to the public or scientific community. As far as it concerns him.'" *But we're among the leading groups of oceanographers on the west coast …*

"How much time is there before our savings run out?" one of the microbiologists asked from somewhere near the back.

"Three and a half weeks at best, two and a half weeks at worst," Tristan answered. "The damage to the group tank and overall system repairs are mostly to blame for the shortage in funds, but there's nothing we can do about that now." *Three and a half weeks. That's hardly any time at all.* I heard a voice from somewhere behind me.

"Does this mean … we're all fired?"

There was a resigned sorrow in Tristan's eyes. I know Tristan. I've known him for years. And I knew this was tearing him up. Ocean Front Rescue was his life. It was falling apart at the seams, and there was nothing he could do about it.

"No, but you should all start looking for new jobs. You're welcome to stay as long as you'd like. We're not sunk yet, but the ship's going down, and even as captain, I advise abandoning it." He gave a sad laugh. "It would take more than a miracle to turn this around." I hadn't realized Sophie had come to stand by Dylan and me until she spoke up.

"What about the research on the new tectonic plate?"

"I suppose someone else will have to pick up where we left off," Tristan answered.

"Then what about the animals?" Sophie pressed. "What will happen to them? We can't release them until they're ready."

"We will work toward releasing as many as we can with the time we have left, and after that … " Tristan paused. "I don't know." There was a long silence. Tristan appeared to be about to say something to Laura when Sophie spoke in a voice I had never heard before. Quiet, yet strong—and determined beyond measure.

"No." That gained everyone's attention; heads swiveled around. "No, we don't give up." She was so calm, so sure of herself. She didn't break away from the gaze of the leaders. "We give it our best to get the animals released, but we shouldn't abandon the research."

"We don't have a choice, Sophie. I'm sorry. It can't do us any good now. The research is not finished," Tristan pointed out.

"You're right, it's useless incomplete. But we can pull this off. We're close. We only need a couple more weeks of concentrated research. If we come up with something truly substantial, something impressive, and present it to Damon, we could convince him we're worth funding. And if he's not interested, we take our case somewhere else." She waved her hands as if trying to encompass the whole state. "Surely! Surely there is someone in this region who will help us once they see what we can do."

It was so small. Just a tiny scrap of hope. But it was the best idea yet, and I could feel people thinking it over. A long time passed. There were plenty of exchanged looks and whispered opinions.

"Sophie … it's a very long shot," Tristan said slowly. "I appreciate the idea, but the chances are slim."

"But it is a shot, even if it's a crazy one. And there is a chance." A tiny flicker of hope flew across Tristan's face. She was getting to him. "As you say, we've got nothing to lose. Why not?"

The room filled with chatter once again, but Tristan just let it go. He was considering the options, inspecting the different endings this story might have. The noise level rose. Dylan and I glanced at each other. I read confusion, shock, and disbelief in his face—and hope, excitement, and a willingness to give it a try. I felt the same way. A determined smile pushed at the corners of my mouth.

As I glanced around the room, I could see there were others considering the idea. I looked up to see Tristan staring directly at me, thinking hard. He raised one eyebrow and waited, as if to ask what I thought about all of this. In less than ten seconds, my mind churned through the possibility.

OK, we're almost out of funds and no more will be coming in anytime soon. So, either we give up or try to get funds another way. Sophie was talking about the research just this morning. She really is serious; it can be wrapped up in a handful of weeks if we all work together. But is that enough time? And if it falls through, then we'll be sunk in the deep end for sure. We've only got one shot. Is it worth a try?

The thoughts spun faster and faster, roaring like a whirlwind. Finally, I commanded silence in my mind. It all disintegrated in an instant, leaving a single, quiet thought drifting down like a feather in the breeze: *why not?* Meeting Tristan's eyes, I gave a single nod. Tristan said something. I couldn't hear it over the din. He waited until he had regained everyone's attention, then spoke again.

"Report," he said slowly, not taking his gaze off Sophie. "Status on the research of the new tectonic plate. Where do we stand?"

Hesitantly, people began to speak up, telling everything they knew and noting the things we needed to know. As this went on, I could feel a shift in the mood of the group. *This just might work.* The popcorn-style commentary eventually settled down. If brainpower could be harnessed, there was enough energy in that room to light the city of Paris. Sophie was grinning, a look of victory on her face even though she had not yet won, and Tristan was thinking. Still thinking. He glanced over to Laura for guidance. She tipped her head slightly to one side, unsure. Suddenly, Tristan made an executive decision.

"Continue as you always do and also get ready for the storm, but ... anyone who is willing, give all you've got to figuring out this puzzle. If Sophie's plan fails, it fails. But if it works, it could fix everything. We don't have much to lose, so ... " he smiled. "Why not?" With that, the crowd began to disperse. Everyone was talking. It was so noisy. Sophie turned to me and beamed.

"It's going to work! I know it!" she called through the din.

"It sure is the only bit of hope we've got, but don't let that hope get too high. Tristan's right: this is a long shot," I reminded her.

"I know," she admitted. "I'm going back to entering the depth maps. Time is of the essence!"

I could sense Dylan had something to say.

"OK, Sophie," I told her. "I'll meet up with you in a minute." She nodded and ran off. Dylan turned to me.

"I don't think … maybe we shouldn't tell the others yet," he said hesitantly. I gave him a confused look.

"Why not?"

"Well," he began carefully. "For starters, I'm not looking forward to telling Chloe. She has a tendency to worry too much and she's gonna tell Mom, who will also worry like crazy. I get the feeling that if Matt knew, he would walk dangerous ground to try and pull some strings for us. And Amber … well, I have no idea how she would react." He stopped, then hurried on. "I'm not saying we should hide it from them, but for once—well, I know I won't be volunteering this story."

I nodded slowly. "Good point. I see what you mean." I thought for a moment. "Agreed. For now, we don't say anything, though it's just a matter of time before they figure out something's wrong." *A matter of time. How long?*

"I know," Dylan said.

"Hey," I joked, poking him. "This might be the longest stretch of time you keep a secret! And you're the one who decided it should be this way." I smirked. "Who are you, and what have you done with my best friend?"

Dylan grinned.

Dear Lexie,

Only five more days till finals!!! I knew you'd make it that far. I can't wait to hear all about it. It's hard to keep from bragging on you in advance! Oh, I ran into Mrs. Sparrow the other day. She says hi and was quite pleased to hear that you're still rocking the cello. Is she still your favorite music teacher?

I heard Las Vegas got hit with a huge windstorm Friday. Did it knock the power out? If so, is it back? Writing challenge! In 20 words or less, describe what it was like as vividly as possible. Here, I'll try:

Today, the raging ocean glistens of emeralds and sapphires, the sun encasing it in a brilliant blanket of golden light.

That was harder than expected.

I didn't really elaborate on the phone after the quake, so I guess I should give a more accurate account of what's going on. Sophie had some kind of intuition about the quake; I think she could sense the animals stressing out. Anyway, when the quake started, she ran to the group tank and channeled all the animals to the safer side, and—don't freak out, we're both fine—the other side shattered on the two of us. So, there have been a whole bunch of repairs, and ... I don't know exactly where to go from here. It still just feels like a bad dream.

Funding's been cut from Ocean Front. For some reason, the governor stepped down a few weeks ago and the new one isn't in favor of supporting us. I haven't even told Matt, Chloe, or Amber yet. Tristan predicts three and a half weeks until we're sunk. But, there is a chance we can survive.

I know it sounds absolutely crazy, but there might be a new tectonic plate off the coast. All the tremors are following a line, a pattern, and they're connecting fractures in the sea floor. Ocean Front seems to be the first to explore this. If we're right, if we can pull together undisputable evidence, maybe we can convince someone we're worth funding. Time is what we need most, so pray we can make it.

Running out of page space here. Have fun at finals! Don't forget the 20-word-description challenge. I don't know how all of this will turn out, but it'll be an adventure either way. I love you!

~ Jordan

CHAPTER 14

Santa Barbara, V0RT3X's stronghold
Thursday, August 30, 1:28 P.M.

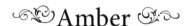 Amber

That was a cool drop-in. He's cutting it really close … Wait, no. He's trapped inside! That can't be good … he made it! That was risky. I hadn't realized surfing could be so dangerous. I was secretly watching how-to videos and beginning to wonder what I was getting myself into.

Oh my goodness, I am excited. I am also a terrible friend …

I had schemed up the best plan ever. I told Chloe, Matt, Dylan, and Jordan that I had other things to do today—which wasn't a total lie—and wouldn't be hanging with them that afternoon. They hadn't taken issue, and I got the sense they had a backup plan. Good. They would go do whatever they had in mind, and meanwhile … I would try to surf.

I rented a board, and it was taking up my living room floor. If I had put it out on the balcony and Jordan somehow saw it … Anyway, I needed to occupy myself with something non-hacking-related, it looked fun, and as long as those four musketeers were off somewhere else, I wouldn't have to worry about making a fool of myself. *Just try to focus for now, OK?* I scolded myself. *You're not here for the Wi-Fi; you're here to hack.* I closed the video and returned to my search.

It was a mystery how Damon got the position of governor so easily. V0RT3X suspected corruption elsewhere in the system. He didn't seem to have any connections in California. He was just here to take advantage of the situation. Already, we had seen that he had sent sections of Santa Barbara into chaos by changing little rules, cheating on negotiations, pulling the ground out from under companies, cutting financial support from hundreds of small or private organizations, and stuffing his pockets full of cash. These are the types of things the public would never see, but in the hacking world, we could. It was my job to hunt down the people in the most dire situations. That way, V0RT3X could help.

The list was growing rapidly, but names were checked off just as fast. It felt good to even out some electronic wallets, like a modern Robin Hood. Restore order and peace, fight back. It was our job to keep the government accountable; the government serves the people, not the other way around. Even if we didn't play by the rules, it felt great to know I was one of the good guys.

Also, C3RB3RU$ was raging, posting furious threats on the local cyber bulletin board. They knew they had been hacked, but they didn't know where their money had gone. I hadn't been part of V0RT3X's systems when I hacked them, so they only knew me as F1R3ST0RM. They got wrecked and didn't even know who to beat up over it. As long as I stayed out of their clutches, all would be well. Even if someone from C3RB3RU$ saw me, they wouldn't know I was F1R3ST0RM. *I'm going to be just fine.*

Keep it up, and everything will be fine. Focus, come on ...

"Bother! I lost it."

"Come on, Jordan. You can do it."

I'm trying. The database glitched and some of the files were missing. So, Dylan had recruited me to help reconstruct them. But my head was swamped in a swirling data storm from all the research I'd read over the past few weeks; I was having trouble finding things up there.

"Isn't there a way to recover that sort of thing?" I asked.

"If I was Matt, yes. But, no. I'm only a little techy." Dylan paused, as if counting to ten to calm his nerves. "Found anything yet?"

"I'm trying ... " *Good grief, where is that info?*

It was getting harder and harder for everyone to keep their cool and not worry. It was so discouraging when the help line was disconnected. There was no point in keeping it open if we couldn't take in any animals. All work on the group tank had been suspended. No more system repairs. Extra expenses had been cut off. Time and resources were still slipping through our fingers like sand.

"Dylan, I don't think—wait, no, I've got something." *Don't let go, no—get over here.* I mentally pulled the memory back, something like dragging a fish by its tail. "OK, here, move," I said, stealing the computer chair, typing furiously. A couple minutes later, I finished and sat back, a job well done.

"You do realize you could have just read it to me, right? I think I'm a faster typer than you are," Dylan pointed out.

"It wasn't an image, it was motion memory. Guess I was the one who wrote it up in the first place." I sighed. "I'm sorry, I don't think I have the rest. It's gone."

"Well, you've got an entire document to show for all the brain wracking. Better than what I could do." Suddenly his faint grin turned to a huge smile, and he switched to a happier subject. "You excited for this afternoon?"

"Are you kidding me? It's been forever!" I exclaimed. "Don't get me wrong. Having Amber with us on Thursdays is a blast, but I am so ready for this."

"Same. And the weather's great today. I can hardly wait," Dylan agreed, grinning. Kyle came hurrying down the hall.

"Dylan! Come on, I heard we got another critter ready for tagging."

"Got it. Coming." Dylan playfully nudged me. "Three and a half hours. Try not to get eaten by anything before then, OK? Like sea spiders." I frowned.

"You're not going to let me forget that, are you?"

"Nope."

"I'll get my own wild card on you some day. And, yes—only three and a half hours." I glanced down at my watch. "Wrong, actually three hours and twenty-one minutes." Dylan grinned and trotted after Kyle.

"Lights! Camera! Action!" Jason exclaimed, flinging his arms wide. I chuckled at his mocking impression. Sonja poked him in the ribs.

"Quiet!"

"Ow! Sorry," he muttered. We had been using recognition programs to edit video feeds for what felt like forever; it was high time for some enter-tainment.

Some of the companies we were helping were going to notice an extreme spike in their bank accounts, so we were sending a video message with it: *This is a gift; this is not a scam. See, we're human; just take it and go, no ques-tions asked, please.* A handful of the messages were live feed. We were here to make sure the speaker couldn't be recognized and that the connection didn't drop. Jason suddenly looked up from his monitor, smiling.

"I pity the brainwashed kids out in the world, fitting the mold. They're getting A's on tests, following curfew, always doing what they're told, and shuffling around like dumb sheep in a flock. They're just alive. This—" Jason moved his hands to encompass all of the V0RT3X world . . . "This is true living. The thrills of hacking are new each time you turn on your computer, the power and sway you hold, the freedom! I wouldn't trade this for the world."

"You hit the nail on the head," I said.

"Someone had coffee this morning, so his brain's actually turned on for once," Sonja murmured, pushing Jason right off his high cloud.

"Jason, how did you learn how to hack?" I asked.

Sonja snorted. I turned to her inquisitively. "Well, I taught the pip-squeak," she said. "A fact he often forgets." Jason frowned at her, but she kept on. "Got my folks' old laptop when they got a new one. I upgraded it and taught myself. Found I was wicked good at it, so here I am. Master hacker."

"Yeah, but I've taught myself lots too," Jason muttered.

For a moment, Sonja seemed to turn some honest attention my way. "How about you? What got you started?"

My mind flew through the story. *Is there anything that might give me away? I don't think they should know about Eric—at least not by name. There was a big fuss and investigation over his death ... I don't know if I was ever placed at the scene. I left before the full story got out. And I probably shouldn't mention R0GU3C0D3; they might want to know where it is.*

"I got my computer for my fourteenth birthday. In ninth grade, there was a programming class offered at my school. It was like my second language from day one. Pretty soon, I started messing around with it and discovered I could program in reverse, break down code and rewrite it. I didn't get really good until two months later, when I found another hacker. We built off each other's technology, teaching, and tips. So, yeah ... " I hurried on, eager to keep their attention away from Eric. "It's a hacker's life for me." The words had barely left my mouth when Sonja's fingers started flying.

"Live feed. Connection's unstable. Come on you two, get with the game!" Grinning, I joined the overall system and started to defend the cyber base.

I can hardly wait. Only an hour, forty-eight minutes—and thirty seconds! Twenty-nine, twenty-eight …

"You're doing something later today," Sophie observed in a dry tone.

"How did you know?" I asked. She grinned.

"Well, you only look at your watch every ten seconds. I don't know. It's just a hunch at this point." That made me laugh a bit.

"I'm hanging out with my friends later. It's gonna be just like the good old days. Sorry, I'll try and focus."

I turned my attention back to the task before me. Sophie and I were checking all the animals' conditions to see if any more could be released. And I mean it—*all* the animals. The ones that weren't ready to return home required a report filled out as to why they couldn't, and information on how long until they could. Eventually, we finished the rounds and started filling out the remaining papers. About a third of all the animals could be released within the week thanks to some concentrated care. But, that still left too many. If Ocean Front shut down … I tried not to think about it.

So many data gaps had been filled. If everyone hadn't been convinced about the new fault line already, they certainly were now. The question was if it was convincing enough to present to someone like Gregory Damon. He might not understand or appreciate what we had found. There was still time, no matter how short it might be. There was still time.

I peeked at my watch. *Speaking of time, those rounds knocked out a chunk of waiting! Only fifty-two minutes, seventeen seconds left! Sixteen, fifteen …*

It was almost time. I had to get back to the apartment so I could be in my room before Jordan got back; that way, I'd know exactly when he left. I couldn't afford to run into him. Glancing around the room, I decided it was time to break away. I started to pack my computer into my bag.

"Leaving already?" Sonja asked without looking up from her screen.

"Yeah, I gotta be somewhere," I answered. She shrugged.

"Whatever. Just keep your phone nearby. If Brenton gets back, we need you here."

"OK," I muttered distractedly, my mind reviewing the surf videos and lessons I had watched. I tucked away that half-compliment of "we need you here" for later; kind words from Sonja were few and far between.

"Bye, Storm," Jason said. After acknowledging my two hacker team-mates, I slid out the side door and started jogging toward the apartments.

Back in my apartment, I sat cross-legged on top of the newly waxed surfboard, patiently waiting for Jordan to leave; I had heard him get in just after I did. There was nothing new in wearing a swimsuit, or a T-shirt, but I felt a little strange in the short-shorts. They were so … short. *It's better than going in just the suit.* Imagining the horror my parents would have felt at seeing me in a swimsuit caused a naughty smile to flicker across my face. *Well, times have changed,* I told myself. *Maybe they would have changed, too … if they were still here …* I felt the smile melt. But before the sadness could sink in, I heard Jordan's door closing beneath me—and my grin returned.

I had to remind myself not to rush out. It would be better to give five minutes to be sure he was gone. The moment the clock hit the mark, I was off. I tried to carry the board under my arm, but I was too small—or I had gotten a board that was too big—and I found myself holding it on top of my head. It was bright yellow and long; I decided to call it "the banana board."

Now—about Betty. I gathered that she and Jordan chatted a lot; I couldn't let her see me heading out to surf. I paused to assess that thought. *I'm so paranoid. Whatever, this is a good skill-building technique. Sneaking.* I rode the elevator to the first floor, then used the stairs to get to the lobby. They opened to the ground floor at an angle that was slightly out of Betty's line of sight—if she had her head turned the right way.

I watched her carefully. *Wait … wait … now!* I walked as casually yet quickly as I could. She didn't look up. I picked up my pace. Bursting out the doors, I headed for the beach: over the little wooden path, over the yellow sand dunes, and then I was greeted by the huge waves, shining sun, and the endless, glistening crystal sea.

I met up with the others at the end of the pier west of the apartments. High-fives all around, Chloe's giggle of excitement, the look of adventure in Matt's eyes, Dylan's constant movement, my own anticipation—it was finally here. It was about time White Water got in some practice. And it was going to be a blast.

I'm not usually one to pat myself on the back, but I'm not too bad at this! It wasn't quite like skateboarding, but it was somewhat similar. My skateboard skills certainly helped with balance. And all my observing paid off. Over the past few hours, not only had I been staying up on the board, I had begun to try a few basic tricks.

The waves were huge. It was unbelievably intimidating at first. It didn't really look scary until there was a wall of water over my head. The first wave I took pounded me; I ended up with a mouthful of salty seawater and a shirt full of sand. That was extremely unpleasant.

Now I was getting better. I hadn't wiped out badly in a while. Thankfully, all my running—both in preparation for Teumessian, and actually fleeing them—meant I was in pretty good shape. Even so, I often found myself lying face up on my board, desperately trying to catch my breath.

This is a blast. Why have I never done this before? I wondered, gazing up at the sky. *Also, no one has really noticed me. Thank goodness.* At this realization, I grinned. I had a new secret life. An underwater breeze swept the bottoms of my feet. Sitting up, I returned my focus to the water. A wave was coming; it was farther out than normal. *I think that's called an "outside" wave.* I decided to take it. The excitement sped my heart and I started paddling. The drop, pop up, and I was off. I was standing, weaving up and down the wave.

Suddenly, seemingly out of nowhere, a surfer appeared directly in front of me. He had come from under the wave that preceded mine and had a deer-in-the-headlights aura. *Bail!* As I turned sharply and jumped off my board, my brain tripped on something—a feeling of recognition—and adrenaline shot into my veins. I hit the water at a painful speed and the wave crashed over me. *Well, there goes my stretch of perfect rides.*

I pulled on the tether tied to my ankle, bringing my board toward me, broke the surface, and held onto the board to keep from going under. After coughing some seawater, I looked up, and came face to face with . . .

Jordan.

Wha … what? It can't—but … what? Amber surfing?
Amber was staring wide-eyed at me, her mouth slightly agape, but no

words were coming out. She had the look a child gets when you catch them with their hand in the cookie jar before dinnertime.

Neither of us knew what to say.

"Amber?" Chloe asked from somewhere behind me. Amber looked frozen.

"Hi, Chloe … " she said weakly.

"I didn't know you surfed!" Chloe seemed more intrigued than surprised.

"I don't. Not really … " Amber's eyes locked on something behind me, and the blush in her cheeks turned blood red. "Hi, Dylan. Hi, Matt," she squeaked. She was met by stunned silence.

I still didn't know what to say. Finally, my brain turned back on and I quickly took in the details. I recognized the markings on her board as a rental, and it was a slightly larger size, recommended for beginners. She chose to come out here today of all days because … she must have assumed we wouldn't be around. Her current level of embarrassment and general self-consciousness made me realize she was far from her comfort zone … Finally, I got it. *She knew we're all surfers, and she wanted to try, but was too shy to say anything!* Suddenly, I found myself chuckling. *That's why she's been watching all my lessons. I get it now!* Amber looked mortified.

"This is the 'other thing' you had to do today, isn't it?" I asked. She glanced at me, thought for a moment, and gave a single, sheepish nod. "You didn't tell us because you felt like we might judge your skill level?"

"Well, not when you put it that way," she murmured, looking like she wanted to drown. "I'm just … " She stopped.

"Oh, Amber, you don't have to be so shy!" Chloe exclaimed, grinning. "Yeah, it can be rather clumsy when you're just beginning. I would know. But you don't have to worry about what we'll think of you! I think it's exciting." Chloe's mind then jumped to another track. "It's exhilarating, isn't it? Surfing, I mean." That seemed to make Amber perk up the tiniest bit.

"It is. I like it."

"You've gotten up enough to decide you like it. Alright!" Chloe said, eyes shining. "Then let's see what you've got so far." Amber looked absolutely trapped. Finally, she nodded slowly. As we all headed farther out toward the lineup, I came alongside her.

"You could have just asked me. I teach surfing, you know." Amber, blushing profusely, whispered:

"I know, that's exactly why I *didn't* ask." I shook my head and smiled. Her extreme timidity and embarrassment was slightly endearing and almost amusing. She was just so shy.

The irony of it all, of course! Just my luck. I knew they all surfed, and sometimes together, but a team? And out of all the ocean, they chose *here, today*?

Chloe didn't seem to realize this was a potentially uncomfortable situation and was forging ahead. Dylan appeared bemused, but was keeping it to himself. Matt was just surprised. And Jordan was still baffled that one girl—me—could possibly be so very shy. He kept chuckling and shaking his head, gently assuring me that it was fine and that I could stop blushing now. Even if they didn't see it, the whole ordeal was just so embarrassing. I could be such a klutz. Then, escape was provided in the form of a huge wave, and I swung my board around and got ready.

"Um, Amber, I wouldn't take that one," Dylan warned.

Watch me. The embarrassment fueled my inner kamikaze, and before any of them could keep me from my suicide mission, I shot forward, paddling furiously, and got in front of the wave. *Here I go.*

I couldn't believe her spunk. Yes, that was brave, but she was going to get flattened. That wave didn't look it yet, but it was going to be absolutely colossal. Amber plunged over the edge and took the drop. To my complete surprise, she was up within moments and seemed to be having no trouble keeping her balance. The wave was folding in on itself behind her, and for a second, it looked like she was going to get caught inside. But at the last second, Amber pulled ahead and aimed her board at the top of the wave. *No way. Is she actually going to try a trick?* She broke the top of the wave with just enough velocity to clear the water for a second—by about an inch or two—then came crashing back down. She seemed to falter, but still, she didn't fall. *Unbelievable.*

She wasn't done, though.

As she began to run out of wave, Amber finished off with a slash, a rapid turn off the top of the wave. A good slash throws loads of spray off the top; it was a relatively decent one. But she didn't quite recover after this final move. She lost her footing, flew through the air, and landed in the water with a less than graceful *splash! Unbelievable. Amazing. What just happened?* Amber paddled back, looking sheepish. No one could find any words. After an awkward moment of acute silence, she frowned.

"I know I'm bad, but close your mouths. You're gonna catch flies." I hadn't even noticed my jaw was hanging open until she said something, and apparently, neither had the others.

"It wasn't that bad," Dylan said, a tease in his tone. "But! The wipeout! Now, that was—" His joke was cut short as Chloe hooked her foot under his board and flipped him.

"Amber, that was amazing," Matt said, as though he couldn't believe what he had seen. "Are you sure you haven't surfed before?" She seemed surprised at this comment, and nodded slowly.

"Never." She hesitated. "I used to skateboard to school. The balance thing is similar. It's like skating halfpipes, I guess."

"Still," I said. "That was absolutely unbelievable. When I started, it took me a day or two before I could keep from falling, let alone do any fancy moves!"

"I wouldn't call those fancy, really. I just saw some people doing it … "

"Amber, stop being so modest and take a little credit," Chloe scolded. "That was amazing. End of discussion." Dylan came spluttering to the surface, turning his board over the right way.

"Yeesh, Chloe. I was just kidding," he muttered, once again perched on his board. He turned to me. "Really, Amber, that wasn't bad at all. It was great. You're a natural." Amber seemed stunned.

"Thank … thank you."

The rest of the day crawled by in a blur. It felt agonizingly slow, but looking back, it flew by. It felt so uncomfortable at first, but things got a little better. I just blocked out the situation and focused on the surfing.

Something seemed a bit off with Jordan and Dylan, however. I couldn't figure it out. They were quieter and would sometimes exchange silent, grim glances. Two of the chattiest chatterboxes were silent and uneasy. It made me nervous.

Chloe was evidently quite a tomboy at heart, especially out on the waves, and thus didn't mind the company of guys. Having a brother can do that. I would know; I had seven. But Chloe was absolutely ecstatic to have another surfer girl in her social circle, and once again, her enthusiasm made things seem not so bad.

Hours later, on my balcony, I reviewed the afternoon's events while thoughtfully rubbing wax off the surfboard. *I'd say that was 60 percent disaster, 40 percent success. That's what I deserve.* I sighed. *I better get used to it. I'm stuck here for a year. I can't just up and leave when I feel like it. Invisibility is definitely no longer an option. Just fit in, OK?*

Matt Created New Group Chat: Matt, Jordan, Dylan, Chloe

Matt
Conference time.

Jordan
Here.

Chloe
Here.

Dylan
Breathing.

Jordan
What's up?

Matt
Alright, here's something we might want to consider: at the end of last year's competitions, it was announced that this year, teams are now allowed five members. Like we decided awhile ago, we are at a serious disadvantage with only four to team White Water, but we don't really know anyone who fits the bill of a fifth member. Judging by the fact this was Amber's FIRST day surfing and she's already pretty decent at it, well, maybe we should keep an eye on her skill level. She might be a good candidate for the fifth.

Dylan
Good point. She's already hanging with us most Thursdays as it is.

Chloe

I like Amber. She's sweet even if she's a little socially awkward at times. She seems relatively comfortable hanging with us and she really likes surfing already. I say it's an option.

Jordan

Agreed. Only time will tell for sure, but I think you're on to something Matt. This might just work.

CHAPTER 15

Ocean Front Rescue
Friday, September 14, 3:35 P.M.

Jordan

It didn't seem real. We were almost out of time. We now all believed that only two or three days stood between Ocean Front and disaster. About three-fourths of the staff had abandoned ship, and more were leaving every day. Even I was beginning to lose hope, as was Dylan. Yet, somehow, Sophie remained sure that everything would turn out alright. I wished I shared her confidence. The few of us who were left were throwing ourselves into finishing the research. It was decided that by this time tomorrow, Tristan and Laura would take our case before Damon and hope he took it, whether it was finished or not. It was all or nothing.

Along with a handful of others, Sophie and I were amassing all relevant information and organizing it into presentable form. Despite the overwhelming amount of data we had, I found myself focusing on the data we *didn't* have. *I wish there was more time, even just a few more days. It's amazing how little time is needed to uproot and unravel. I don't know if it can ever be fixed.*

"Chin up, Jordan. Don't look so down," Sophie said cheerfully. "It's going to work." I turned to her.

"How are you so sure?"

"I just know."

"Sophie … I mean, I hope it does. But I don't think … oh, I don't know. I mean, if there was going to be a miracle, don't you think it would have happened by now? Ocean Front needs direct, immediate, solid cash in the bank within a day or two. Even if Damon answers our plea for help, it might take him a week or so before he can get everything arranged."

"There is still time, Jordan. Don't give up hope. Our God is strong enough," she insisted calmly, a distant smile on her face.

Sophie's nineteen, so she's no child, but she certainly has faith like one. I envy that. I'm so glad that, out of all the people in the world, Sophie is my shadow. I'm probably one of the most blessed men on earth. On top of the rest of the wonderful things in my life, many of my close friends are Christians. *It's good to be constantly reminded I'm not alone.*

"And even if Damon doesn't help, there are others we could go to," Sophie continued. "We just gotta keep our heads above water until then." I nodded, half convinced, and returned to the computer screen.

One of the thickest walls we'd run into was the fact that there hadn't been an accurate sonar imaging of the area around the fault line for three years, so there wasn't remote, visible evidence to be shared. To convince people to have a scan done two years in advance would take solid evidence, which is why we needed the image: to get solid facts. Which is needed to get the facts: an image. Which is needed for facts …

This is frustrating. It would be the quickest, most efficient way to get proof, but it's not an option yet. I sat back, frowning a little, my brain grasping at straws. *Perhaps if enough of the animals we've tagged went deep enough, it would show that chasms have opened up due to the shifting earth. But the tracking devices run off the electrical charges emitted by the beating of a heart. Living marine mammals don't go down that far.* Well, there went that idea. Deep down, I was pretty sure the information wasn't going to be enough. We needed a plan, an idea. We needed a breakthrough—or a miracle. Preferably both. *Please. We're running out of time …*

"Oh, Brenton's on his way back," Sonja said matter-of-factly, as if stating the weather. My brain balked.

"What?! Really?" I exclaimed. She looked at me calmly.

"Yes, really. I just said so."

"How'd you find out?"

"The database."

I pulled up the V0RT3X database and started skimming. Past the recent hate mail from C3RB3RU$ and the help list was an incoming feed from the built-in GPS in James Brenton's car. Destination: Sacramento. Coordinate tag name: home. *Finally! This is it!* Sonja started typing.

"Ready for chaos?" she asked.

"What?"

"I'm sending this to Ender. I assume he hasn't noticed yet. Moment he does, he's gonna start ordering people around, so keep your head down, OK?" With that, she hit enter. Sure enough, within ten seconds, Ender sprang to his feet and—of course—started ordering people around. Sonja nudged me with her boot and tipped her head toward the second floor. *Escape is that way.* Evidently, she wasn't in the mood for any hard work.

Sonja wasn't so bad after all. Yes, she needed a serious attitude adjustment, and I pitied Jason being at the end of most of her verbal jabs, but she was just a normal—well, as normal as a hacker can be—girl who simply had a bad disposition. She was starting to consider me a fellow teammate and wasn't treating me so poorly. As I said, she still had attitude problems, but other than that, she wasn't taking personal issue with me.

We found Jason on his high perch in the shelving unit, working away on his exploration gadget, which he had plugged to the computer. Sonja slid her laptop into her bag and scaled the ladder; I followed.

"Hey, runt," she said, pinching Jason when he didn't respond right away. I frowned at her.

"Ow. What was that for?" he asked, rubbing his arm.

"Your head's in the clouds again." She sat against one of the backboards, pulled out her computer, and lifted her headset from around her neck. "Look, don't bother me. I'm just here because Ender's running around playing boss." I heard faint music come from her headphones and knew she wouldn't be paying attention for a while. *Correction, Sonja. Ender isn't playing boss, he actually is boss.* I turned to Jason.

"What are you doing?" He seemed to forget the rude behavior of his sister and had totally reimmersed himself in his work.

"I think I might have found another safe house option."

"That's great! What's it like? Is it better than this one?"

He shook his head. "I don't know. I haven't been there yet." I gave him a puzzled look.

"I thought you had to be physically present at a location to scan it into your device."

"Yeah, I do," Jason affirmed, returning to his gadget. "But, I've been messing around with the satellite connection. I bounced a signal off an old forgotten satellite." He held up the screen. "And this image came in an hour ago."

It displayed a sketchy map of the surrounding area. It was glitching around; there were strange splotches of blurred color. As Jason moved it, pixels fell out of place and rearranged themselves. It was barely staying together.

"Here," he said, pointing to a zone without any color. "The orange and green spots mean that there has been movement or activity of some sort in that area, past or recent. This building doesn't have any movement readings within a good half-mile radius, it's structurally sound, a tiny bit more inland, and it might even have an underground level, like a hidden bunker. But—" He smacked the side of the device and it glitched out. Suddenly, it was ablaze with color, both green and orange. "It could also have satellite cloaking technology and be a gang base. Based on the size, possibly Cerberus's."

"Oh. That does present quite a problem," I murmured, inspecting the screen.

He shook his head. "Either way, it could be really good for Vortex. We could find the best stronghold ever; this could just be an old imaging system or an imprint from the past. Or … it could be Cerberus's base. We could rat them out to the police. Problem is, I don't know which it is."

I nodded. I saw the dilemma. If it really did have that bunker, and there wasn't any activity for a half-mile radius, it would be the perfect base. But if someone went to check it out and it happened to be the base of the dreaded C3RB3RU$ gang …

"What's your plan?" I finally asked. He sighed.

"Well, originally I was going to ask Sonja if she could sneak me nearby so I could get a better reading, but I know she would never help me." He paused, glancing at Sonja, ensuring she still wasn't paying us any attention. "Don't tell her about this, but … I'm thinking of checking it out on my own." I didn't mean to, but I gasped. That would be suicide!

"Jason, no. If that is Cerberus's stronghold and you got caught, they'd pulverize you without hesitation. And, if they get their hands on your GPS, they could find our base. No, you can't go alone."

"But the possibility! Think about it: I didn't even know this part of town existed until I found the satellite image. It's an old restricted area. No one would ever find us there. We'd never have to move again. Come on, Storm,

I trusted you enough to tell you my plans, now please trust me. You don't understand how important the base is for group hackers. You're a solo hacker—for the most part. And I would get into Ender's good graces if I could find out for sure. Maybe he wouldn't put me on patrol as much. I wouldn't have to point empty guns at people like you."

He trusts me a bit. Good to know. I sat back, mulling this over. Maybe I could ... *No, Amber, don't do it. No, don't—* Just do it. I glanced at Sonja. She was still listening to music, not us. *Good.*

"I was a group hacker once, so I do understand," I started, hurrying just in case. "Confidentiality and location is everything. I left because things got complicated. But I'd like to keep the details of my past between the two of us, OK?" He nodded. "Thank you," I continued. "Now, I see what you mean. On one hand, we have a base that most hackers wouldn't even dream of. On the other hand, we could eradicate our enemies." I could see him lighting up, hope blossoming. "But no, Jason, you can't go alone." He seemed to melt. *Amber, don't do this ...* "Which is why I'm coming with you."

Jason's eyes went big. "What? You? But, you don't know surveillance skills, do you?" I had to chuckle to myself. *I've got every FBI-related skill set imaginable, kid. Edge made sure of that.*

"I have a lot of abilities you don't know about. Another thing to keep between the two of us." I looked back at the screen. "How far away is it?" Jason looked like he was going to fall off the platform from surprise, but he pulled his attention back and started to calculate.

"We would have to go around the main hub of town activity, so about ... seven and a half miles."

"OK, to get there and back would take about six hours." I started planning in my head.

Jason was the type of kid who would carry out his plan no matter what I said; he would go with or without my blessing. So, I had to go with him. I couldn't let him go alone—and warning Sonja would just make his life miserable.

"Alright. A week sound good?" I asked. He nodded. "Good. That'll give me enough time to get some things in order. Jason, I'm dead serious. Do not do this without me. Wait just a week and I swear on my life we'll go. Understood?" A grin spread across his face.

"Don't worry, I'll stay put—as long as you promise not to tell anyone.

Especially Sonja."

"Deal," I said.

"Deal," Jason agreed.

Now I have to get ready for a rogue mission. Great, I better write up my will.

I stared at the far wall of the meeting room, mulling over a scrap of hope. Sarah had found out that a small research team was going to be launching a drone submarine to collect samples from the sea floor about fifty miles from where we suspected the trench to be. If we could convince them to upgrade it with a small sonar scanner, they might be able to get the information we needed. Problem was, this wouldn't be for another month. *Well, it's better than waiting three years ...* If Ocean Front could make it that far, it might be the answer. I sensed someone enter the room. Tristan. Within a minute, the chitchat died down and all eyes turned to him.

"Anyone who knows what to do, I need you on the reintegration team. We leave in twenty minutes. It's the last one," he announced. I turned to Sophie.

"You still want to see a release?" I asked. She lit up, nodding enthusiastically. I found myself grinning. "Alright, I'm gonna go pull on my wetsuit. And from there ... well, you heard Tristan."

"Really? Oh, this is going to be amazing! I can't wait. Do hurry back! Hurry!" she exclaimed, bouncing out of her seat and scrambling to get her things together.

"Sophie, Sophie ... " She looked up at me. I chuckled. "You still have nineteen minutes. There's no need to hurry." She sighed.

"OK."

Though time must have dragged for Sophie, it raced for me. *The last release. This is it, the last one.* When the wheels hit the sandy shore, we all filed out. Sophie watched excitedly from the shore. Soon, I was holding a tarp full of dolphin. It kept clicking and squealing, as if it knew it was finally returning home. The waves, though smaller in this particular cove, were still bothersome, and slammed into me and the others. But we kept on. Coming to a stop in chest-deep water, we lowered the tarp. The dolphin swam free, heading toward the deep ocean. As I watched it go, I couldn't help but wonder if it knew how lucky it was. *Be free. Go home. Don't forget us.*

Two more dolphins, two seals, four turtles, and a nerve-wracking sand shark later … it was over. The sun sank lower, toward the sea, as if to meet the animals that had returned to frolic beneath its glow. It was then that I realized: another day was ending. Already, so soon. Just like that. Gone.

Time was almost out.

Sonja eventually returned to reality. Ender calmed down, I hacked some more, and life went on. Typical day. After making Jason renew his promise and once more swearing on my life that we would explore in a week, I went home. My work for today was done. I was on my phone like glue, though. Once Brenton was alone at his home desktop computer, we would know. And we would be there. *I dearly hope Jason and I survive that long,* I mused while walking home. *I can't believe I'm actually doing this. He better not run off without me. By himself, it's suicide. But if it works …* I grinned. *Good things are ahead.*

Within two hours, I had finished reading my Western romance book. I knew I'd wake up tomorrow with the depressed feeling I got when I finished an amazing book because I no longer knew what to do with my spare time, but it was worth it. I walked out onto the balcony, tripping on the high clouds of fantasy literature. Suddenly, my mind was yanked to earth by the sense that something was wrong. I looked over the edge. There was Jordan, unmoving and unblinking, watching the waves come and go. He was zoned out, something I'd never seen before.

"Hey, Jordan," I called. He snapped out of the trance and looked up.

"Hi, Amber."

"Great waves today, I see." He seemed slightly confused for a moment, then apparently recalled what he had been watching.

"Oh, yeah. Right." He was clearly distracted.

"You gonna hit them tomorrow? Last week and yesterday were amazing." I waved my phone in the air. "Got a group message a minute ago. Chloe's going to be out there all day, and Matt for most of the day too." A thought hit me, and I frowned a little. "I haven't heard from Dylan." All the while, I watched Jordan's reactions. Something was wrong. Something subtle changed when I mentioned Dylan.

"Actually, I've got to go to Ocean Front, and Dylan too. I don't know if we'll be coming." He was trying to sound casual, but I could hear something in his voice. This was scripted, rehearsed. *Wait, Ocean Front … Dylan works at Ocean Front Rescue, too. They have weekends off. Then why …*

"Is something wrong, Jordan?" I could almost hear his heart speed up.

"Ah, I don't think so. Why do you ask?"

"So nothing's wrong?" I pressed. He didn't answer. I watched him calmly for a minute. *Just maintain eye contact; first one to break has to take off the mask.* It didn't take long. Jordan seemed to deflate as he dropped his gaze. "Jordan?"

"Funding's been cut from Ocean Front. By this time tomorrow … we're out of time."

My heart tripped and plummeted. I had never seen this side of Jordan. There was such hurt in his voice. And he hadn't said anything was wrong until I had pushed him. Neither had Dylan. Why? *Because they didn't want us to worry.*

"Jordan, I'm … I'm so sorry."

He shook his head. "Almost all good things must come to an end," he said, trying a sad smile. "We had a heads-up. We knew this was coming. Dylan and I didn't say anything because, well … you don't need to carry this burden too. Please, Amber, don't tell Matt or Chloe." He sighed. "I'll survive. I've got enough in savings, and I'll find another job. I just really don't like change. Especially this kind." *No. Nothing will change if I can help it.* I had a solution. I could save Ocean Front. I had to get back to V0RT3X. After an uncomfortable silence, I finally came up with an escape.

"I'm sorry, Jordan. I'll, uhh—I'm going to go back inside now." That was super lame. *Whatever, I'm running out of time.* Jordan nodded sadly and I hurried back. *Nothing will change for the worse. Not if I have a say in the matter. Hang in there, Jordan. It's my turn to repay some of your kindness to me.*

I wished Amber had stayed. I didn't blame her, though. What does one say after a bombshell like that? I felt so frustrated with myself that I had broken down and told her. *Well, it won't matter soon …*

My thoughts were interrupted by motion beneath me. I strained my eyes, watching the ground. There, running from the building … wait, *Amber?* She had a computer bag over her shoulder and was all-out sprinting. Confused, I watched her melt into the distant, growing darkness. *Where is she going?*

There was no time to waste. If there wasn't a cyber package of cold hard cash sitting in Ocean Front Rescue's inbox by morning, they would close shop and give up! I remembered how considerate Jordan had been to me when I "lost my job," the kindness he showed when I needed it most. Now the roles had been reversed. It was my turn.

I used my phone to get the stats on Ocean Front while I ran. They needed an estimated $83,650 each day. And I thought my water and electrical bills were high! They had about $12,914 left. Based on their discovery output, size, and tech, there was no doubt: without government help, it would be impossible to keep up. *It takes time to scrape together money like that, and it's ticking down. Oh come on, Amber. Hurry!*

Reaching the stronghold and slipping through the side door, I scanned the room for Ender. He was typing away at a console near the main server. *This better work …* Hurrying over to him, I waited impatiently for him to notice me. For about a minute, he didn't seem to.

"I'm listening, you know," Ender muttered without missing a keystroke or taking his eyes from the screen.

"Oh, right. Thanks. I've found another victim of Damon's spending spree, and they really need our help."

"Why are you coming to me? Just put them on the list like all the others," Ender said. I gathered my persuasive powers and courage, then pressed on.

"It can't wait. It needs to be done tonight." Ender looked up at me, a disapproving frown on his face. But I wasn't about to give up. "They're running on fumes. The hack won't be an issue; it's the money. I need your help, or at least some other hackers. I can't fix this one on my own." Ender stopped typing and straightened, inspecting me.

"You care about this one. Why?"

There were two options. If I told him it was for a friend, he would decide I wasn't neutral in this affair—I was biased. Or, I could try to convince him of the overwhelming good Ocean Front had done for the community. Thank goodness I had done my research; I chose the latter.

"Because it is by far worth saving. Ocean Front Rescue. It ranks among the top ten teams of oceanographers on this coast. They help injured sea creatures recover, study changes in the marine ecosystem, predict things like earthquakes and dangerous currents, and discover revolutionary data.

Four years ago—remember the oil spill? They were the first to act, coming up with methods and machinery for the cleanup, containing the spill so it didn't spread, and they prevented two species from being officially labeled endangered. When the earthquake hit a month ago, they were the ones that we hacked. They put out the information. They've been government funded since day one, and they can't survive on their own. Tomorrow they run dry and it's end of the line. Please, help me save them." Ender was listening carefully. He nodded slowly.

"How much are we talking?" Drat. I was hoping he would ask that after he agreed to help.

"They're going to need a rather steady supply for a while, and to get them through one more day." I paused. "At least seventy-one thousand for tomorrow alone." To my surprise, Ender didn't even flinch. He just watched me for a while.

"You wouldn't happen to have any ideas, would you, Firestorm? Because numbers like that are hard to achieve." I nodded nervously. I had a small idea, but it was just that. An idea.

"There is no one place we could take that kind of money from without doing some real damage. But—if I can track where the money has been rerouted to, I can slowly draw it back. It's probably been spread over multiple locations, and if I move carefully, I could even replace the missing money with ghost sums. Unless those organizations suddenly withdraw a large amount, they won't notice anything missing. Also, I can track down money that's been lost in transactions. It's undefined, floating around. Between those two methods, it should be enough."

Ender thought a moment longer. "Sonja!" he suddenly called. I almost jumped from my skin. Sonja came over.

"What?" She sounded none too pleased.

"I need you to gather a group of twenty hackers. Follow Firestorm's orders and move fast. There isn't much time." Sonja looked a bit incredulous at this, but did as she was told. *Thank you, thank you! Yes! It's going to work!* Ender gave a nod of approval, then began to walk away.

"Ender, wait!" I exclaimed. He stopped and turned. "If I could, I would like to be the one to arrange and send the video message."

"Why?" he asked. I grinned.

"Just consider this one my pet project." After a moment of thought, he shrugged.

"Sure. Just make sure you've got someone running the scrambling software. And wear the hoodie."

"Thank you, Ender," I said. He smiled, nodded, and walked off.

Soon I was seated in front of the wall, hoodie over my head, scrambling software on, and a camera aimed my way. *This is it, Jordan. This is for you. And you'll never even know.* I had recruited Jason. He sat at the computer, monitoring the software and camera. He motioned to me and counted down. *Three, two, one.* I looked up at the camera and smiled.

"Hello, Ocean Front Rescue."

CHAPTER 16

Ocean Front Rescue
Saturday, September 15, 9:58 A.M.

Jordan

When I woke up, my first thought was: *Well, this is it. Doomsday.*

Except for Sophie, who sat by my side, calmly reading a book, it seemed everyone at Ocean Front shared my sentiments. The overall mood was despair. It was so quiet; there was little noise above a whisper. Most of the tanks were empty. The halls felt lonely without the calls of the seals and the squeals and clicks of dolphins.

Tristan and Laura were pulling together the last threads of the presentation, tying them up in a neat little bow, hoping Damon would take the package. Along with most of the others, I was in the map room, chatting nervously or gathering last-minute files. I sat by one of the computers, remembering the events that had led me to Ocean Front, thinking about all the amazing things I had learned and been part of … and the fact that it was now coming to an end. *I don't know how this fits into the big picture. There's got to be a good reason. But what good could come from this? It just doesn't seem right …* Dylan was brain diving, too; his chair teetered dangerously on two legs beside mine.

"Feels like we're gonna wake up soon, doesn't it? This has all got to be a dream," he whispered.

"Correction: nightmare," I answered miserably.

"Agreed. But … I don't know. There is still a little chance we can pull this off," Dylan said. I didn't answer. "Hey, what happened to my hopelessly optimistic Jordan?" He paused to think about this. "Hopeless. Optimist. Alright, no pun intended. But, I'll take it and run, because the optimist is feeling rather hopeless, I see. But even if this whole endeavor is hopeless, do try to be optimistic about it anyway, okeydokey?" I felt myself grinning. Leave it to Dylan to brighten up a dark situation.

"You know, half of that went over my head. But, point taken. Thanks. You're right." I started chuckling. "Hopeless. Optimist. Really?" Dylan started laughing too.

"I didn't even catch that until after I said it. That was one of my best unintentional puns ever."

Suddenly, Tristan raced into the room. He was holding his laptop, a look of disbelief on his face. Flipping the screen open, he clicked a few buttons and the projector whirred to life, displaying Ocean Front's account information on the wall. Sophie gave a little gasp, and Dylan sat up so fast his chair nearly tipped.

The overall financial numbers in our account were sporadically climbing. The amounts were small, but they were adding up quickly; the numbers were rising and continuing to rise. I couldn't believe my eyes, and a glance around the room told me I wasn't the only one seeing this. *Is this really happening? But how? Where's the money coming from? What's going on?*

All of a sudden, the power went out. For a moment, there was almost total darkness, save for the glow from the windows and Tristan's computer. Then, the lights blazed back to life. Just as everyone was beginning to get over their shock, the projector started up on its own … and then things got even weirder. There, cast on the wall, was the image of … someone. Something was off, though. Everything was sharp and defined except the person's face. It was slightly out of focus and pixels morphed into a more static-like state, especially around the person's eyes. He or she wore a deep hood and the background was nondescript. *It looks like … I think … it's a girl.* The image began to move. It was a video.

The person smiled a kind, warm smile.

"Hello, Ocean Front Rescue." The voice was undefinable. Male yet female, young yet old, high yet deep; clearly, this was a voice scrambler. "This is a prerecorded message. All satellite connection has been temporarily blocked from the building and your phones have been locked down, so do not try to record this or contact any outside organization until the message is complete." The … girl—at least, I think it was a girl—paused, as if to give us a chance to see for ourselves.

I snuck a peak down at my phone. It was glitching. The connection bars weren't empty; they were nonexistent. I tried to unlock the home screen, but my phone flickered and powered off. *What on earth is going on?!* She continued.

"My name is Firestorm." The word "F1R3ST0RM" flashed across the wall for a moment. "I am a member of Vortex, a group of vigilante hackers here in Santa Barbara. Our focus and concern is the welfare of this city and its citizens. We heard of your plight. Your research and goals are commendable, and you ought to be proud knowing that you are making this earth a better place. You have our respect."

The video feed's sound glitched momentarily, and everyone seemed to be holding their breath. Then the message played on as if nothing had happened.

"Change is coming. Things will soon be restored to the way they were. I do not advise you pursue your negotiations with Governor Gregory Damon. It will come to nothing in the end. Therefore, until you have a steady patron once more, this is our gift to you. You can rely on us and our funds to carry you through this time of unrest. You are in no legal danger for having this money. You can accept it."

The pixel filter seemed to falter just the slightest bit, and I got a better glimpse of her smile. It was rather … angelic.

"I wish you the best of luck. Thank you for all you have done. It won't be long before this is a distant memory and everything will be as it should." The pixels glitched one final time, into the rainbow array of a static complex, and the girl's eyes seemed to shine with it. "Thank you again." It was like she looked right at me, and her smile widened a little. "Good-bye."

The power crashed again, and when it came back on, the video feed had been replaced by the climbing account numbers. They had hit $94,275. Everyone was too stunned to speak for a minute or two. I could barely process what had just happened. Before it started to sink in, I felt someone pin my arms to my sides in a hug. I looked over to find Sophie, beaming with a smile, eyes shining like stars, as she whispered:

"I knew it'd all be OK."

Everything snapped into focus and it finally sank in. *We're safe. We're gonna make it. It's over, the nightmare is over. Ocean Front's going to be OK!* A cloud chose that moment to pass away from the sun, and the room lit up even brighter, a warm, summery glow filling it. Suddenly there was excited chatter, laughing, cheering! Sophie was giggling, Dylan and I were exchanging looks of disbelief—but mainly joy—and I wondered: What was I ever worried about? I should have known that God would orchestrate a last-minute miracle in His mysterious ways, as if He just wanted to remind us that there was nothing to fear. *Thank you, Lord. Thank you so very much. I promise to trust you better from here on out. Thank you …*

I closed my laptop, my heart swelling as high as the sky. The look on Dylan's and Jordan's faces had made it all worth it, as if the very act wasn't reward enough. I had hacked into a central camera a couple minutes before 10 A.M. so I could watch the action. I wouldn't have missed it for the world. Sitting back, I reviewed the events in my mind.

I assume the girl was Sophie. Her reaction was just as wonderful! She seems really sweet. Also, Tristan's face when he saw the account info. Then Dylan! I chuckled. *I thought he was going to fall out of that chair. And . . . Jordan. Now you get a taste of your own kindness.*

I smiled. All was as it should be. Soon, Brenton would return to power and things would go back to normal. Until then, Ocean Front would remain safe. Well, as long as they didn't make a big fuss over the whole thing. That realization made me frown a little bit. *They've come this far. Hopefully they won't make any dumb decisions.*

The wait is going to kill me. What exactly is going on? Tristan, Laura, and some of the other leaders had gathered and then left the room, intensely debating this turn of events in hushed tones. It had not yet occurred to me that this could actually be a problem instead of a solution; I had been too excited and relieved to look at it logically. Can a hacker be trusted?

I had heard of Vortex, or "V0RT3X." Good things and bad things. They really were vigilantes; not everything they did was legal. But it wasn't like we chose to have their help, right? Could we get in trouble for this? How could we know if that girl was telling the truth? Others were realizing the insecurity of the situation, and once more, the room was filled with nervous, whispered conversations.

Over and over, I replayed the message in my head. It was so haunting. The way the money was climbing, little by little, spastically. When the room was thrown into darkness and the projector turned on. The connection and glitching phone. The girl, "F1R3ST0RM." There was something distantly familiar about that girl, as if I had passed her by in a dream once, long ago. It was the smile; I knew that smile. But I couldn't place her. *Well, seeing that she used a scrambler, it's no wonder she's unrecognizable. You can't see the big picture with just a few pixels.*

"That hacker person. Wow, that was crazy, huh?" Dylan muttered.

"Yeah. I certainly didn't see that coming," I agreed.

"I couldn't get a good look, but he—or she—seemed ... I felt like I know them. No, *knew*—like I knew them long ago. It was weird," he said, thinking hard.

I turned to look at Dylan. "It was a girl. And me too, Dylan. I feel like I'd met her in another lifetime or something."

"Who do you think it could be? Could we really know her?" Dylan asked. I started to shake my head, but stopped.

I quickly flew through the images of people we'd known through the years. I hadn't been expecting to find anyone. Granted, it wasn't an exact match, but as I ran down my own personal hall of pictures, I tripped over one.

Amber?

She and this F1R3ST0RM have the same smile. Could Amber . . . ? No, impossible. Really, it couldn't be. She only just arrived here a couple months ago. And she's not a hacker, she's a graphics designer. I shook the thought away.

"No," I said, as much to myself as to Dylan. "No, I don't think this Firestorm matches anyone I know." Sophie, who had been listening all along, leaned forward and put her elbows on the table.

"Well, I didn't recognize her, but I get the feeling she's a very good-natured person, whoever she is." Sophie tipped her head to one side. "You're right, this is a very strange miracle. What do you think Tristan and the others are going to do about it?"

I shook my head. "I really don't know."

"That was amazing, Chloe! What was that called? It looked like dancing!" I called. Chloe grinned and paddled back toward the lineup. I had dragged the crazy banana board out and was surfing with her.

"Cross-stepping. Just run from one end to the other, foot over foot. And yeah, it does kind of look like dancing." *I've got to try that.* Chloe glanced up at the sun, which was already past its peak. "I estimate it's around one-ish. Matt should be here before long. I haven't seen or heard from Dylan today, though, or Jordan. Do you know where either of them are?"

I was caught in a decision. If I told her, then I might end up giving away some of what was actually going on. If I didn't tell her, she would be none the wiser, but I was trying to stop lying. *Just move the conversation a little.*

"You haven't seen Dylan today? How's that? Don't you both stay with your mom?" I asked.

She nodded. "We do. Usually he wakes up right as I finish making breakfast, but when I came downstairs this morning, Mom said he was already gone."

"Oh," I said, preparing for the plunge. "I'm pretty sure they're both at Ocean Front." Chloe seemed thoughtful.

"Strange. They don't do that very often—a Saturday. Do you know why?" she asked. I shrugged. "You think they're gonna show up?"

One can only hope. "Yeah, I think so," I said, taking a risk. *Come on, what's taking you two so long? Get down here ... please?*

After an unbearably long wait, eventually the door opened, and Tristan and Laura quietly slid back in. Everyone was watching them. Tristan seemed puzzled, as if he was stuck on a problem, but not frustrated about it—simply amused that he couldn't figure it out. Even Laura seemed surprised. By what, I didn't know.

"We've reached a verdict ... for now," Laura said, finally acknowledging us. "After much discussion, it was decided the best course of action would be to go straight to the authorities and see if anything should be done about Vortex." My nerves spiked, and I wondered if this was the end after all. *No, this isn't the end,* I decided. *Do try and be a bit more trusting, Jordan. Come on.* Tristan picked up where Laura left off.

"I'm sorry for the long suspense. After we had explained the situation, the police put us on hold for a long time." Suddenly, I saw a sparkle in his eyes. "When they came back to the line, they admitted nothing could be done. There have been thousands of similar stories about Vortex helping organizations from all over Santa Barbara for about a month. It's too much for the local authorities to handle. The money is absolutely untrace-able." He let the smile out. "Ocean Front Rescue won't be sinking today, tomorrow, or any time soon. The money can't be traced, so it's ours, and it's enough—for now."

Matt had joined Chloe and me, and we were having a blast. I kept my eyes on the shoreline, though, hoping to see Jordan and Dylan coming over the sand dunes. I was beginning to worry they wouldn't show up after all. The problem had been fixed hours ago. There shouldn't be any complications. *Shouldn't be.* That didn't mean there weren't. I went ashore to check my phone from time to time, for either a message from V0RT3X, Dylan, or Jordan. Nothing. Staring at the distant shore, deep in thought, I frowned. *Come on, you two. I took a risk and said you'd be here soon.*

Oh look, a wave.

Shoving my thoughts into a mental junk drawer, I got in position and launched into the ride. After trying cross-stepping and almost falling, I focused on staying up. Instead of leaving the wave, I angled my board toward shore to finish out the ride and check my messages. But as my foot touched sand, I forgot about my phone. There, trotting over the old wooden pathway to the beach, were Jordan and Dylan, with smiles as big as the sun. Chloe called and waved, and Matt teasingly asked them how they managed to be late to something fun. Jordan's eyes met mine. I tipped my head to one side, asking the silent question. *What happened?* His smile grew and he gave a quick wink. As he passed me, he whispered …

"I'll explain later."

I nodded and followed them to the water. I would act innocent when Jordan told me about it all, but I would be inwardly grinning. *Oh, the things you will never know, the things I'll never tell you, wonderful things.* I grinned. *If only you knew …*

CHAPTER 17

V0RT3X's stronghold
Friday, September 21, 2:15 A.M.

᪥Amber ᪥

As long as I get a good rest the night before, I love early mornings. It's breathtaking to watch the sun rise into the golden rose sky. The world is still; most people are sleeping, as are the birds. Love it. Poor Jason didn't like mornings, though. He looked like he could fall asleep standing up. But he was still there, waiting for me behind the stronghold, packed and ready to go. There was a fifty percent chance this was a suicide mission. Fantastic.

I tried to remember all the fighting skills Edge had forced me to learn. Hopefully, I wouldn't have to use them. If worst came to worst—if this was C3RB3RU$'s base and things went awry … I had my phone ready with a distress signal. If that worst-case scenario did come, though, it probably wouldn't matter if the cops found us. We'd likely be dead. Either way, if we came out of this alive, Sonja would still kill me. Even though she didn't know how to show it, she loved her little brother like crazy. She was so protective of him. And she would hate my guts if she ever found out about this.

"You ready?" I asked.

"Yep," Jason said, nodding tiredly.

"Are you *sure*?" I pressed.

Jason frowned. "Yes, seriously. Let's get going." We started, but then I turned and smirked at him.

"Did you say all your good-byes, dictate what you want in your eulogy, and write your will just in case?"

He chuckled. "Just how scared are you, Storm?"

"Only a little on edge. Actually, I'm really scared, but not about Cerberus. I'm scared of what your sister will do to me if you get so much as a single scratch." Jason nodded slowly, looking as if he was imagining how that would go down.

"Yeah. She can't ever know about this."

Thus began our long trek. I had calculated it out: three hours there and three hours back, including ten minutes for wiggle room plus time for exploring. That way, we would be getting back sometime around nine, and hopefully, most everyone would just be arriving. Jason said that Sonja had a tendency to sleep to at least 8:45, and usually later; she probably wouldn't even miss us.

I brought a small backpack with energy bars and water bottles. My pockets were full of fun stuff, too. Phone, pocket knife, lock pick, and an active cloaking device that made me cyber-invisible. Jason would be, too, as long as he stayed within three yards of me.

We passed by the outskirts of the busier side of town and kept to the shadows, because … Jason was holding what looked like either a bomb, a mini computer with enough upgrades to kill, or a freak gaming device. I was in a deep hood. Needless to say, we stayed away from normal people. Jason mapped the route by GPS. With any luck, this new place would be empty; if I came at it directly, it wasn't far from the apartments.

I hope I can keep Jason safe. Oh, this is crazy! I worried as we walked. *I shouldn't have let him do this. What was I thinking?* It was like another side of me answered. *You were thinking you would keep him safe.* I had to keep him safe, I just had to … My warring thoughts were interrupted as Jason held up his device.

"Almost there. It's just down the street a bit and around the corner," he said. I nodded.

"Alright. Stay close, and whatever you do, don't do anything reckless. From here on out, no more talking unless absolutely necessary, OK? We can't be heard."

As we walked the last stretch, I couldn't help but feel nervous. We crept forward and cautiously peeked around the edge of a nearby building. The warehouse wasn't very run-down. The siding appeared to be reinforced with some sort of metal, like it had been remodeled. *Strange.* Why would a building this side of town be so well built? A tall, thick, strange-looking tower, one that appeared to be tiled with mirrors, rose from somewhere inside the building, right through the roof. We were in a blind spot; I couldn't get a good enough look at the place. I nudged Jason and motioned to the side.

Despite a new vantage point, I still couldn't get a good fix on the size of the place. As we rounded another corner, I noticed a sliver of light coming from beneath one of the side doors—and froze. *There are people in there!* That discovery alone was enough for me. This was not a potential base. Time to get out of here. I pointed out the light to Jason and started to retreat. When he didn't follow, I turned and grabbed his arm. To my horror, he yanked out of my grip, looking right at me.

"No," he whispered defiantly.

"Jason!" I hissed. "Keep it down! We have to get out of here. There are people in there, and there is no reasonable explanation, apart from the truth, as to why we're snooping around!"

"I'm not sure. It doesn't add up."

"What do you mean?" He showed me his device. The image wasn't glitching now, but apart from that—nothing. "It's the building. What about it? I don't see anything, Jason."

He nodded. "Exactly. There is nothing to see." This time, I understood. *There aren't any green or orange dots. But, we're within range; surely they would show up.*

"It doesn't add up," Jason repeated. After hesitating slightly, he snuck forward. *We're gonna get caught …* Sighing miserably, I followed.

As we got closer, I realized there didn't appear to be any signs of life. No footprints in the dirt, no movement, no sound. I soon confirmed this by listening intently beneath a window. Between the faces of glass, metal strands had been woven; doubtless, that window wouldn't shatter easily. *Why is this place so well built? And Jason is right—I don't think there is anyone here.*

I used network scanner to check for active signals. There were no cell phone or computer signals, but there was a large amount of electricity flowing in this building. Yet it was unlikely there were people nearby. Ignoring the voice in the back of my head screaming that this was a bad idea, I crawled closer to the door, slid my lock pick from my pocket, and got to work. After five minutes, I sat back and quietly huffed in frustration. Suddenly, Jason began chuckling. He reached forward, turned the knob, and … the door opened.

"Come on, Storm. You can't pick an open lock," he whispered. I stared in disbelief at the door, feeling like an idiot. I had simply assumed a place built like Fort Knox would be locked. Carefully, I stood and stepped in.

A corridor, lit with a dim, ghostly glow, stretched out in front of me, like a wing in an abandoned hospital ward. The lights sent a bluish-white filter over everything, and the acute silence was, frankly … deafening. The tiles on the floor were dusty, but I couldn't see any footprints. So far, so good.

The main room had a span that was as wide and long as half a football field. Just like the upstairs of our current hideout, rows of tall, empty shelving units covered most of the floor space. Something caught my eye. In one of the corners was an unfinished machine and a strange-looking pillar. I walked over to it. Suddenly, it all made sense. Jason came over beside me.

"Everything's been cleared out except for the shelves. I love the shelving setup; they're great. What are these weird-looking things?"

"Look up," I said, smiling. He tipped his head and realization dawned on his face. Mirrors. *Correction: solar panels.* "That's what that tower is, Jason: solar panels! And this machine—" I touched a button and a generator whirred to life beneath our feet, sending a quiet, low-pitched hum that reverberated through the walls as it booted up, then went silent. "This controls the rest of the power. That's why there are lights on. They're solar-powered." Jason looked around in awe, then turned to me and grinned.

"Wanna go find that generator?" he asked.

"Absolutely."

After exploring the rest of the room and a few side doors, we discovered a long staircase leading down deep into the earth. As I cleared the doorway, I came to a halt and suppressed a gasp. It was pointless, though, because Jason gasped anyway. The place was huge! The roof was probably at least a story above our heads and as big as the floor above. The generator was one with the server, in the center of the room, reaching up to the ceiling like a great, blinking metallic tree, a modern wonder to behold. Metal tables and chairs had been bolted down in neat rows across the remaining space. If there were computers and geeky tech stuff in there, it would look a bit like NASA headquarters.

After inspecting the generator, I found the right controls and turned on the full power. The ghostly haze was eaten up in a strong glow as the generator cranked out energy reserve. Jason pulled out his GPS scanner. A moment later, confusion flitted across his face.

"What is it?" I asked.

"Look." He held up the screen. "It doesn't see us. There aren't any green or orange dots." Sure enough, there were no signs of activity.

"What does that mean? Why isn't your device-thingy picking up our presence?"

Jason thought for a minute. "This bunker must have been … a high-profile location. Perhaps government-related. There's a satellite cloaking device in that generator, I think." Something clicked into place in his mind and he lit up. "That's why there was residual activity at first, why there were so many dots! The last memory satellites have of this building is when it was being built, so there were people running all over the place!"

"Jason, this is amazing. We've got to tell Ender. This is a fantastic base!" To my surprise, he shook his head.

"Not yet."

Not yet? You risk your life finding this place, and now telling Ender about this treasure trove is a "not yet" option? "Why on earth?" I blurted. "Why not?"

"I have reasons." Jason held up three fingers. "One: to get everyone and everything to this base would take a slightly-longer-than-normal trek. Two: Vortex doesn't move unless absolutely necessary. Three: I think there should be a bit more time and space between this little adventure and telling Sonja about it." I nodded slowly.

"OK. Good points. But how long do we wait? How often does Vortex move?"

Jason shrugged. "Based on the structural soundness of the current base, I doubt it will be super long till we need a new hideout. I don't know for sure," he admitted.

I sighed. "Alright. Let's just not wait too long. I really want to earn some brownie points with Ender as well, and I'm ready to get out of that silly little hovel we call base and move into this palace." That made Jason grin.

"Me too."

After a bit more exploring, we went back to the surface. Sitting on the edge of one of the shelving units, we refueled with our snacks and then headed back. I couldn't wait for V0RT3X to move, one last time. I was glad the place hadn't been C3RB3RU$'s base. After a bit more searching, we discovered an eviction note; the entire area was restricted. The surrounding area was the nesting ground of an endangered species of albatross. The building crew would never return. Everything had turned out much better than expected. *Eventually, someday … soon, this will be our new base.*

Though I didn't know it yet, we would have to move sooner than I had imagined. And not under the best of circumstances. It was coming … soon.

CHAPTER 18

Ocean Front Rescue
Thursday, October 4, 3:35 P.M.

Jordan

Finally, at long last, progress was being made. Now that Ocean Front was safe, Tristan wasted no time in making arrangements to further our search for answers. Already, we were consulting a team of geologists and ecologists and learning what we lacked. But today was special; it might provide proof instead of just facts. This was the day Ocean Front would be negotiating with the phycology research team (phycology is the study of algae) that would be sending a drone submarine to the ocean floor.

Everyone was running around, gathering and giving information, listening to and spreading hopeful rumors, and basking in the metaphorical light at the end of the tunnel. Even though the actual sonar images weren't going to be taken for a while, the excitement was real. This might provide the proof we needed.

Working at Ocean Front had always been just that. Work. Yes, it was fun, and I wouldn't trade it for the world, but save for a select few, no one paid anyone else much attention. But now, we were a team. Even though it was chaos more often than not, it was orchestrated chaos; no one got in each other's way. It was like we could anticipate what was needed, or when to step aside, or which files might be useful to the person beside you. Some of those who had left to look for other jobs had come back. Even so, we were still few in number. Yet, this wasn't much of a problem. Everything seemed to magically get done by the end of each day. Each morning I was met by a long list of tasks and responsibilities, but if I took things twenty-four hours at a time, it wasn't overwhelming.

Since the tech division was on the negotiation team, Dylan was going. After much begging and Bambi eyes, Sophie had managed to get permission to tag along. Since she was going, so was I. It would be interesting, yes—but I felt kind of bad, with both Dylan and I bailing on the others again. It was Thursday after all. *Not much I can do about this one. Sorry. Don't have too much fun without us.*

I was on top of the world; I had landed a graphics design job! Every single image—from the grass to the glint of a sword, from a squirrel to a demon monster to an angel to a human, every health and hunger bar—all mine to design. Granted, the game was small, as was the pay, but I wasn't in it for the money. This master hacker is set for life. I was in it for the art. After such a long stretch of no offers, I was pouring my best effort into this.

Not to pat myself on the back, but I decided these were going to be some of the best, most well-designed entities these programmers had seen in eons. Oh, how I missed this! I wished I could get my name out there, "artist for hire," because I could do this for months on end. But, no. According to the archives, I don't actually exist. I'm dead. Thankfully, these programmers didn't do their homework in depth; I sent them some links and they didn't look any further. All they knew was that I had a major in art, a couple animations and games with my name in the credits, and free time on my hands. If they had looked up my name, bad things would have happened, but ... they didn't. Perfect.

I was finishing up the animation loop for the iridescent shine of the delicate wings of a moon fairy, a design I was particularly proud of, when my phone chirped.

New Message: Chloe

Chloe
Hey Amber! What's up?

Amber
Not much. You?

Chloe

Not much either. Do you have any plans today?

Amber

No. Why do you ask?

Chloe

I don't think there's going to be any action with the others. Matt's tied up at work, so are Dylan and Jordan. They won't be getting back until, like, 7-ish I think. The tide won't be going out for another few hours, so surfing isn't an option right now. When the tide does go out, though, we could go surfing. Until then, if you want, you should come over! Let me say in advance, 'cause I know you'll ask: it's no trouble at all. I think I'm going to talk Mom's ear off, so she definitely won't mind me having someone else to chat with. I finished baking some cookies earlier, and since Dylan isn't home, there are actually still some left. That little cookie monster… Also, we have coffee.

Chloe

Hehe. I'm bribing you with cookies.

Amber

If you're sure I won't be a bother … you are sure, right?

Chloe

I'm positive. Sometime around 4 sound good?

Amber

Yep. See you then! ☺

Chloe sent me the address; I felt myself grinning. Keeping up the act of "normal" was getting easier, and I was actually starting to feel like … I belonged here. I had found a little nook of friendship in the world. *Cookies, that's great.* My smile grew as I remembered a phrase I had heard when I was a kid.

"Come to the dark side … we have cookies!"

Which was answered with:

"I've been to the dark side. I came back, because they lied about the cookies."

"Jordan, isn't this cool?" Sophie whispered. After flitting around the room for a minute, she returned to hover by my side, another half-page of notes scribbled across her notepad. "I could live in a place like this."

"No, you couldn't," I teased. "Because you'd never sleep a wink."

Despite the place being rather small, it was impressive. What had started as a pet project for a group of college kids had turned into a stable research facility. They had named it The Torres Center of Phycology after their beloved professor, who had inspired them to search out and discover new things in the depths of the ocean. *That teacher must be so proud.*

Before long, a lady with short, brown hair approached Tristan, a spring in her step and an air of surety about her. She was followed by two men and a younger woman. She stepped forward and held out her hand to Tristan.

"I presume you are Tristan Wells?"

"Correct."

"Well, Doctor Wells, welcome to the Torres Center. My name is Kirsty Evens." She turned to the people behind her. "This is Jacob, Colton, and my assistant in training, Lizzy." Tristan nodded and introduced his crew. Lizzy noticed Sophie, and the two made eye contact. I grinned. *Uh-oh. Instant friend alert!*

"Call me Tristan. Thank you for having us, Dr. Evens. As I said on the phone, we have a proposition to make regarding your deep sea search drone." Kirsty motioned for us to follow her down the hall.

"First off, call me Kirsty. And yes, you said something about adding sonar technology. Why? What is your purpose, and how could we help you? Excuse the bluntness, but what's in it for us?"

Tristan launched into an explanation, laying out our research thus far and the missing proof we needed. We could help fund the new tech if they added some modifications to the submarine's path. However far the information took Ocean Front was also as far as we would take their name with us. Evens was willing to see where this would go, and even allowed us to take measurements on the drone. It was a good one. The different pieces had been so expertly welded together that it appeared to be made from a single sheet of metal. It was optimal size. It could go deep. Its navigation system relied on satellite positioning, yet it had coordinates programmed in as a fail-safe.

As we assessed the different systems and protocols for the sub, I knew this could work. It was accurate, sturdy, and a good size. If Tristan could convince Ms. Evens to help us, we could have everything we needed.

This was it. Chloe's house. Even though there were similar homes up and down the street, this one strived to be unique. With the light blue siding, yellow door, and a lovely little flower garden out front, it stood out as a bright, welcoming haven among commonplace things. I knocked, and it didn't take long for Chloe to answer.

"Hi Amber! Come on in."

"Hey Chloe. Thanks for having me over." I stepped in, slid out of my flip-flops, and followed her as she practically skipped off. She threw a grin over her shoulder.

"I'm glad you could come!"

The interior of the house was just as beautiful as the outside. Behind the many hanging pictures of happy memories, the walls boasted a lovely pastel green with a white border running near the floorboards. Windows steered sunlight to every corner, chasing away shadows. There was a gentle coolness in the air, like an autumn night under a full moon. Rounding the corner, we came to the living room. There on the couch, knitting away, was who I assumed to be Mrs. Lynn.

"Amber, this is my Mom. Mom, this is Amber," Chloe said. Mrs. Lynn looked up from her work and smiled.

"So this is the girl I've heard so much about! Finally, Chloe has someone else to talk to other than me." I laughed a bit.

"Yeah, she sure does like to talk, but I like it." I could feel Chloe smile at that. "It's wonderful to meet you, Mrs. Lynn," I said, holding out my hand.

There was a strange pause, in which I wondered if I had somehow slipped and said something in Arabic or some kind of geek dialect. Then, Chloe quietly reached forward, lovingly took her mother's hand, and placed it in mine. That's when it hit me. *She's … blind.* Mrs. Lynn shook my hand enthusiastically.

"Thank you, Chloe," she said, chipper and bright. "You're surprised, no?"

I found my voice. "A little. I mean … I didn't know … But, you're knitting, you don't look like … " *I should shut up now.*

She chuckled. "I'm not totally blind. You don't need to see things to know that they're there. I know this house, and I know my knitting needles and yarn. Plus, I've got Dylan and Chloe. Anyway, I'll see again someday. I shall see His face ... " She seemed to get a slightly faraway look for a moment, a peaceful smile, then returned to reality. But I understood. She was a Christian as well. Time to wrap this part up.

"You have a wonderful daughter, Mrs. Lynn. And Dylan. He's amazing. They're a credit to you."

"OK, stop it," Chloe said, giggling a little and blushing a lot. "We're not that great. Mom, please don't elaborate on that fact." Mrs. Lynn laughed.

"Go on, you two. Go have fun."

Soon, Chloe and I were laughing and chatting at the kitchen table. Chloe makes amazing cookies. And coffee. Absolutely magnificent.

"Chloe, it's no wonder Dylan can't keep his paws off these cookies, they're delicious. You have a gift. And extraordinary self-restraint." She grinned.

"Well, they're not that hard to make. I bet you could do it." I didn't mean to, but at this, there was a sudden lapse in my manners. I practically snorted and simultaneously choked on my coffee. Chloe looked confused.

"No, no I couldn't," I insisted. "I don't make food of any kind. I can't bake or cook, not even when the ingredients come out of a frozen box with only three steps of instructions on the side."

"Come on, Amber. You can't be that bad," Chloe tried.

I shook my head. "I set things on fire, Chloe. Often. I am that bad."

We both laughed at this and exchanged cooking horror stories, like setting the stove ablaze and the fire alarms blaring, forgetting to take the plastic wrap off a frozen pizza before sticking it in the oven, putting an egg or something metal in the microwave, and trying to use a mixer on flour and powdered sugar. And the monstrous messes that resulted from said mistakes. Eventually, the stories died down. For no apparent reason, Chloe's mind jumped to a totally random train of thought—and she chose the worst possible conversation topic. I think she must be psychic.

"Amber, when's your birthday? I don't think I ever asked you." *You've got to be kidding me.* I hesitated too long and she jumped on it. "It's ... it's not today, is it?!"

"No, it's not today."

"Then when is it?" she asked, eagerly awaiting my answer. Evidently, she could tell this was going to be good. After another long hesitation and much fidgeting, I gave a nervous and flustered sigh and shook my head, feeling super embarrassed.

"Your timing is unbelievable," I muttered. Chloe's grin was a mile wide now, amused and excited.

"It's this month, isn't it?" she pressed. I nodded, cringing and smiling at the same time. "When?"

"It's … " I couldn't tell if I wanted to laugh or hide. "Monday." Chloe looked so amazed, pleased, shocked, and downright ecstatic—all at the same time.

"This Monday? Like, in four days, the eighth of October? *This* Monday?" *Why does this sort of thing happen to me? I just want to simply exist, to live a simple, quiet life …*

"Yes, this Monday," I confirmed. Chloe looked as though she might squeal from delight.

"Oh my goodness! Why didn't you say something? You should … No, I should—"

I cut her off. "Don't you dare tell the guys." Well, that poked a hole in her umbrella.

"What!? Oh come on, Amber! Please? It's not like we're gonna sing or anything!"

Thank goodness. "No, Chloe. Don't you dare. Please, for my sake. You can make as big a fuss as you want next year, but do me a favor and don't say anything for now." She looked rather displeased for a while, thinking long and hard about this.

"You sure I can't change your mind? You sure I can't throw you at least a *little* party?"

"I'm very sure," I insisted. Chloe sighed, then grinned playfully at me.

"If you don't like birthdays and cake and parties, you need mental help."

"I'm happy the way I am, thank you very much," I said, laughing. She pretended to pout a little, then her ever-present smile returned. I decided it was time to change the subject. "You and Dylan are good to your mom, you know?"

"Well, we could be better, but thanks."

"How long have you been staying with her?"

"Oh, almost five years now. When Dad died, Dylan and I had already moved out, so Mom was left alone. Her eyesight was beginning to deteriorate, and she knew she couldn't live on her own. She almost sold the house. But Dylan and I decided to come back. She needed us, and … " Chloe stopped to think on this for a moment. "I guess we needed her."

"What do you mean?" I asked, nibbling another cookie.

"I mean, Dylan's my brother, so I still saw him after we went our separate ways, but we were seriously starting to grow apart. I don't really know why," Chloe explained, reaching for another cookie. "I guess I got so occupied with my own life that I forgot about the real world. But coming back home with a common goal was a bit of a wakeup call. It was like, 'Oh! That's right, I have a bro.' Even though he can still be a pest at times, it's good to actually act like siblings again." *That was very insightful.* A faint smile tugged at my lips.

"I guess I kinda know what you mean," I mused. Chloe seemed intrigued at this comment.

"How so?"

"Well, even though I was close to home while, and after, I went to college, I was so distant from my family. I like how you put it: I forgot the real world. I didn't really wake up for years, and I miss the time I lost. I love my brothers and sisters. I wish I could do it over again and be there for them."

"You don't really … talk about your family much. May I ask why?" This was a dangerous question, and I took my time thinking out a safe answer.

"I guess … "

Suddenly, something brushed against my leg. My heart almost stopped. Whatever it was, it made some sort of sound. I made a very girlish gasp and jumped about three inches. Pulling my legs up onto the chair, I ducked, pulled up the table cloth, and peeked underneath it. I felt like an idiot. The sound? Purring. The critter? A fluffy white cat, who was now rubbing against the chair, meowing for my attention. Chloe quickly glanced under, too, and started laughing. She scooped up the culprit and straightened.

"Amber—" She chuckled. "I'm so … I'm so sorry. I forgot—" Another giggle. "I'm so sorry to startle you. Are you OK with cats?"

"Yeah, cats are great. I just, uh, didn't know you had one." I put my feet back on the ground and my heart slowed. The cat watched me curiously with its bright, lime-green eyes, then pushed its head under Chloe's hand.

"Yes, this is Winter." Chloe glanced down at the mewing poof of fluff in her arms, which was now playfully swatting at the pink streak in her hair.

"Winter? That's an unusual name for a cat, especially when you live by the sea," I remarked. Chloe smiled.

"Winter's a Christmas cat. There's a story behind the name." She raised her eyebrows, as if to ask permission to launch into the tale. I nodded, and she continued. "When Dylan, Jordan, and I were kids, there was a colder than normal winter. On Christmas day, Jordan found a stray kitten. For some reason, whether from fear, hunger, or actual cold, it wouldn't stop shivering and mewing. Jordan's parents wouldn't let him in the house with it, though, because his big brother Hunter hates cats and his mom's allergic. But you know Jordan; he can be so stubborn. He just wouldn't leave it be. He came to our house, looking for advice. I managed to convince Mom and Dad to let me keep it until they could find the owner. No one ever claimed it, though, and after much debate, the three of us kids decided to name it Winter the Chilly Christmas Kitten—Winter for short."

I grinned. "Winter sure is special. How long ago was this?"

"I suppose about fifteen or sixteen years ago."

"I knew you and Dylan and Jordan had been friends for a while, but that's a long time," I said.

"We've known each other longer than that. We practically grew up together. Jordan lived two houses down the street when he was little. He and Lexie came down to play all the time."

"Ah, yes. The famous Lexie," I said, smiling and leaning back a bit. "I feel like I know her even though we've never met. Jordan talks about her so much." Chloe nodded.

"Yeah. I miss her. She was so sweet." Chloe seemed to falter, and the sparkle in her eyes flickered. "It was hard to see Jordan so down and lonely after she left. You two would have been good friends. I wish you could have met her."

"Who knows? Perhaps someday I will." Chloe looked as though she was about to say something when her phone chimed. She glanced at it and smiled.

"That was a weather notification. The tide is out and the waves are good. Do you want to?"

"Surf? Definitely."

Chloe grinned. "Alright. I'll get my stuff together and meet you at the normal spot." I nodded, feeling excited.

"See you there. I'll show up eventually. I've got to drag that ridiculous banana board out. It might take a while. I've got to exchange that thing."

According to the calculations, there was no doubt: the drone was compatible with sonar scanning technology. Soon, the tech division had narrowed down the different options and models. Now, apart from small things, the only thing left to do was wait. Tristan and Evens stood off to the side, carefully discussing each new finding. An agreement seemed close.

I sensed there was excitement on both ends of the deal. The Torres staff had been waiting for an opportunity like this for a while. They wanted to establish connections with other organizations in the community, so not only did they now have a friend in us, if our research got attention, they might also be known by others.

Sophie and Lizzy had edged their way toward each other. Occasionally they would scribble something on their respective notepad or clipboard, but finally they dropped the act and chatted in hushed tones, efficiently covering every scientific conversational topic imaginable. It was fun to watch them; they kept finishing each other's sentences. Two young ocean-ographer girls, smart as they come. I'm pretty sure they exchanged email addresses and phone numbers.

Eventually, Tristan and Evens shook hands. A minute later, Tristan gathered us and we were off without another word. Just as we were leav-ing, I heard Evens call for attention from the others. The moment we were out of earshot of the drone hangar room, Tristan, energy bubbling near the surface, turned and faced us.

"Within a couple of weeks, the submarine will launch, and it will be carrying with it the sonar tech. We'll have the proof we need in a few months."

I sat on the balcony, watching the waves go in and out. My hair was still drippy and the back of my shirt soaked, but I didn't care. I was exceed-ingly tired, yet peaceful and happy. It had been a good day. In fact, it had been a good week and a good month. The more time I spent with Chloe, Dylan, Matt, and Jordan, the more I felt there was still some humanness left inside me. Because, hey—if those four liked me, how bad could I be?

What if … I defeated Teumessian and stayed here? Wouldn't that be amazing? For the first time in a long time, it's as if I could belong somewhere. I have a nice little home by the sea with plenty of sand and sunshine to go around. There's both a hacking and a programming community, one in need of a hacker and one in need of a graphics designer. I have friends. This struck me as a profound revelation. *I didn't think I'd ever have any again. They accept me, don't ask too many questions, and are only a text message—or a floor—away. It feels like … home.* Yes, that's what this was. At long last, I had a taste of it again.

I had a home.

Chloe Created New Group Chat: Chloe, Dylan, Jordan, Matt

Chloe
Hey guys, anyone there?

Matt
Here.

Jordan
Yeah, I've got a minute.

Dylan
Me too. What's up? You do realize you missed Amber in the recipients list, right?

Chloe
Yeah, I did that for a reason.

Chloe
Okay, I have an announcement and an idea…

CHAPTER 19

V0RT3X's stronghold
Monday, October 8, 11:09 A.M.

⸙Amber⸙

Hey, look at that! In twelve hours, two minutes and forty seconds, I'll be 26 years old! I imagined the sound of a paper party noisemaker and grinned. Yes, I was born at 11:11 P.M. Cool, right? I have an affinity for eleven. It even looks nice, in both word and number form. *But why am I counting down the time? I haven't really cared about my birthday since I was a teenager. But I miss those days. It was way more fun when I had Ashley to share it with ... even if she was older by four minutes.* I found myself smiling again.

"Judging by the fact that you keep grinning, I take it you're making progress?" Sonja asked.

"I was just thinking about something," I muttered.

"Focus, fire girl. Good gracious."

I swallowed my smile and turned my attention to the dilemma at hand. V0RT3X had been trying all morning to disable the com system in Brenton's house. But in doing so, we had momentarily set off the silent alarm and his home had been crawling with cops for the past two hours. Hopefully, this didn't mean there would be added security. Also, tension was building between V0RT3X and C3RB3RU$. Trouble was brewing. They had tried to hack us, so we hacked back—and they were not happy. We won.

We had obtained around twenty of their handles—a hacker term for fake name—and busted about half of them. C3RB3RU$ was, to a degree, threatening war. I wasn't entirely sure what all that would entail, but from what I'd heard, these people were dangerous. So much so that, on a few occasions, the police had actually cooperated with V0RT3X in order to track some of the members down.

I hoped all this would somehow motivate Ender to order a move. That way, Jason and I could show off the new base, which we had come to call "the palace." It was a surprisingly good code word; Sonja still didn't have a clue about the whole ordeal. I had a feeling she'd forgive me once she saw how amazing the place was. It bordered on extravagant.

I was mid-keystroke when I saw a notification from the F1R3ST0RM AI in the bottom corner of my screen. *What is this?* I clicked on it and my heart froze—cold. Ice took up residence in my veins. Shakily, I rose and began to pack my laptop. I felt like the world was spinning. *I need to get home, now!*

"Sonja … Sonja, I have to go." I was gone before she could answer. *I have to get back …*

Who knew I'd ever say this, but … I've missed wrestling my clipboard away from a hungry turtle. I don't think I'll mind the ruckus the seals make at feeding time ever again. It sounds like music now. Also, getting splashed in the face by a dolphin isn't so bad. I've decided to take it as a sign of friendship. The animals were back, and happiness had returned to the halls of Ocean Front. The very walls seemed to pulse with life, the air dancing with the songs of the sea creatures.

One of the creatures was especially unique.

"Squeaker" was the newest, youngest male bottlenose dolphin, and the chattiest of them all, though usually not to anyone in particular. When he was first picked up a few days ago, it was discovered that he couldn't echolocate. He couldn't even click or whistle. All he could do was make a squeaking sound, which earned him his nickname. Since he couldn't navigate or communicate, he had been separated from his pod, and thus found his way to us.

Squeaker found his voice a few hours ago and was quite pleased with this long-lost ability. But he still couldn't echolocate. If he got too excited, he would swim around in circles, sometimes colliding with walls, fake coral pillars, or other dolphins who didn't move out of his way fast enough. Something was wrong, but we couldn't figure out what exactly. It seemed

Squeaker had some sort of ear/nose infection. Anyway, he seemed to like me, truly like me. Squeaker could tell me apart from the others. The only people he would accept fish from was me or Marissa, his main rehabilitator.

I sat on the edge of the dolphin tank, trying to learn dolphinese with my fish-loving friends.

"No, don't grab. I have plenty … " I watched as a little dolphin promptly shot off into the deep side with its stolen prize. Turning my attention back to the more patient members of my audience, I continued to dole out the fish, quietly mimicking the whistles and clicks they made.

Whistle, click-click, click, click, whistle-click. I wonder what that one means. It could mean "thank you." I do hear it a lot. Or it could mean "give me more." Hmm. The little thief returned, squealing for more. I tossed a fish its way and it swam off.

Pretty soon the food was gone and the dolphins dispersed. I gathered the fish I had set aside and walked over to one of the corners of the tank, where Squeaker hovered, rubbing his nose in a patch of algae.

"Hey, Squeaker. I've got fish," I said in English, then tried to greet him in dolphinese.

Every dolphin has a unique whistle. If the sound is recorded and played back to them, they respond. It's their name. They whistle it to the rest of their pod, as if answering a silent roll call or telling their friends they are still there.

Squeaker turned toward my voice, clicked a few times, and swam over. Slowing at the wall's edge, he cautiously lifted his head out of the water and made a sound that started as a whistle but ended in a squeak. I chuckled and threw him a chunk of cod. After a few more, I held one underwater and waited. Squeaker seemed to sense that the next bite was no longer above his head and began to look around. I could feel the sound waves. The water was full of the fine vibrations of echolocation. But I could tell—he still couldn't see. After missing a few times and bumping into my hand, he finally found it.

"Don't worry, Squeaker. You'll get your bearings again soon." It was as if he could understand I was sympathizing, because he squeaked and clicked, chattering away to me. *Poor little guy. Well, at least he doesn't have to chase his food for now.*

"He likes you." I almost fell into the pool. Turning, I found Marissa standing behind me, watching Squeaker's antics. "Sorry, Jordan. Didn't mean to startle you." She knelt down at the edge and held out her hand. Squeaker nuzzled it in search of food, then snorted a plume of water droplets out his blowhole when he didn't find any, backing a bit further into the tank. "Squeaker has a healthy fear of humans, but he's a little too afraid around me. He's not scared around you, though, Jordan." *How long has she been watching me?*

"I'll take that as a compliment," I said, smiling.

Most times, Marissa is better with animals than she is people, as if the price of speaking the language of sea creatures is that she can't speak the social language of her own race. She's rather withdrawn. But I don't mind. She's an amazing person. You just have to take the time to get to know her.

"I see Sophie isn't here today?" she asked.

"Yeah, she took the day off." Marissa nodded, watching Squeaker; it would seem she had run out of conversation topics, so I continued. "How long do you think it will take Squeaker to be able to use echolocation again?" She shook her head, her voice quiet, almost sad.

"I don't know. Even after his ears and vocal chords are back to normal, I think he will have to relearn how to hunt."

"Relearn?"

"Yes. His behavior tells me it's been a long time since he has used echolocation. For some reason, he chose to stop. Perhaps this sickness made it painful. I don't know. But, he will have to be taught again. It won't be as difficult as it would be if he was an adult, but it could still take a while. I've been working with him, but he isn't responding as much as I hoped."

Squeaker snorted, as if clearing his throat to recall our attention and remind us he was hungry. Absentmindedly, Marissa picked up a fish and held it out to Squeaker. He approached warily, snatched the morsel, then retreated a safe distance. He sang out the common sequence—*whistle, click-click, click, click, whistle-click*—and scarfed down his snack.

"Marissa, do you by any chance know what that means in dolphinese?" I asked hopefully. She nodded.

"It means 'Thank you.'" *Score! I know how to say "thank you" now!* I looked up and realized Marissa was watching me, her head tipped ever so slightly to the side, thinking hard. After a strange moment of acute silence, she held out a fish.

"What is this for?" I asked, taking it.

"A test," she answered. With that, she held a fish of her own out over the water. Slowly, I followed her example.

Squeaker took in the situation. Marissa's chunk of fish was larger than mine. She had a salmon, I had a cod. I was further away. Logically, Marissa's offering was more appealing. Slowly, he edged closer, inspecting the options. He whistled, a unique whistle, one that I had only heard him make—*low, shrill-trill, down, shrill*—but it wasn't his name. I didn't know what it meant. For a second, Squeaker went absolutely still. Then he shot forward, slicing through the water like an arrow flying through the air, and lunged for … my fish.

Wondering what this all meant, I slowly straightened. Marissa put the salmon down. She looked almost pleased with this surprising turn of events. *Now what? Was the test for me or Squeaker?* Giving a little nod of satisfaction, Marissa turned my way.

"I want to officially recruit you to help rehabilitate Squeaker." My heart, which had been trotting along at a normal pace, suddenly took to the clouds.

"Really? Can I? Is that OK? I'm not a certified rehabilitator."

"You've befriended Squeaker in a way I cannot. I know you know how to work with disabled animals. You may not have the title, but you have the skills and you have the knowledge. Yes, it is fine," she assured me. A smile spread across my face.

"Alright."

I raced home. I hardly felt the ground beneath my feet. The sky threatened to crush me. A political speech was being held in Massachusetts. More than three hundred people were attending. And they were all being held hostage by Teumessian.

The facility had been sent into lockdown, trapping everyone inside. Teumessian had employed signal scramblers over the surrounding area; no one within a mile radius would be able to hack in. The FBI was having trouble getting access to the building. Reports said the gunmen were only willing to barter for time; as long as the FBI kept their distance, they wouldn't start shooting people. There was no way out. There was no way in. The three hundred were captive in a building full of killers.

I'd intervened in crises like this before. Without my help, the FBI would have failed on multiple occasions to save hundreds of lives. F1R3ST0RM couldn't hack accurately from such a huge distance. But my Laelaps programs were strong enough not only to hack a computer or camera in the facility, but to hack into the very code that kept the electric doors barred shut.

The moment I was closed in my apartment, I whipped out my phone and called Edge. Straight to voice mail, as expected. But there was still a chance I could get his attention.

"Edge! Listen! There isn't much time. I'm sure you've heard about the panic in Massachusetts. I can help. Get me my programs and I can get access to the building. I can disable the lockdown! If not that, I could get into the security camera feed so you can see what's going on in there. We both know I can do it. My programs are strong. Please! Convince someone to let me help! You don't even have to respond to this; I'm setting up my computer at this moment. Simply turn Cyra back on and I'll know I have the Laelaps programs. You can take them back after everyone's safe; just let me help now." I ended the call. Turning to my computer, I sent the news to my secondary monitor and the secure footage I'd hacked to my main screen.

There are families in there. Fathers, who might never return home. Mothers, whose little ones depend on them like the air they breathe. Children, their parents' pride and joy. Siblings, friends, lovers, neighbors. Please … let me help save them …

I hoped with all my heart to hear Cyra whir to life and see the little lights blink on. My hands hovered over the keyboard, waiting impatiently. My fingers started twitching, then began to type in the air, reaching for invisible keys that weren't there—a nervous habit of mine, spelling out every thought that flew through my head. *Fathers. Mothers. Children. Siblings. Friends. Lovers. Neighbors. Please …*

Images of my father and mother, of my siblings, my friends—all dead—flashed before my eyes. These were the images that always weighed on me. Their horrible deaths were all on my account, lives I couldn't save. Every soul that fell into Teumessian's grasp was another Ashley to me, another Eric, another Jessica, another set of brothers and sisters, another pair of parents. Rescuing them redeemed me. I couldn't let them slip through my fingers.

Until now, I'd always been the other half of Teumessian's paradox, going nose to nose, raising my shield to block all their attacks, foiling their plans. I'd dived into the fray, claws out, teeth gleaming, the growl of the hunter wolf-dog—the growl of Laelaps—heard by all. But now my paws were tied, my jaws muzzled. I couldn't fight. My enemy was advancing. *Please, let me help* …

Suddenly, the video feed grabbed my attention. Whoever had the camera was moving forward with a group of SWAT agents. One went for the door. It was unlocked. Inside, a dark, eerie corridor stretched out on the other side of my screen. They rushed in, rounding corner after corner. Soon, they reached their destination. Gathered by a set of doors, they crouched out of sight, and—*3, 2, 1*—rushed in.

My heart, which had been swelling with hope, was stabbed with a dark dagger. Sorrow flooded my soul, sinking me beneath the inky waters. They were dead. All dead. The flickering light illuminated the gruesome scene, searing the gory image into my mind like the imprint left by the blinding flash from a camera. Teumessian had escaped.

Slowly, I stood, stumbling away from the computer. My back found the wall and I slid down, horrified. *If only I could have done something … it's all my fault. I could have saved those people. It's all my fault* … It was like a cruel joke. In the thinning air, it was as if Teumessian had found its voice, and I heard a whisper: *Happy birthday, Amber.*

Silently, I wept, tears sliding down my face like driving rain on a window. I had failed again.

I can't believe I'm doing this. This is amazing! I had changed into my wetsuit and was hurrying back to the dolphin pool. It was hard to keep from running down the slippery halls. It had been so long since I had helped with coaching animals. I'd missed it.

When I got back, I found Marissa already in the tank; long, wavy, raven hair tied back, navy and black trainer's suit on, and a silent slider-whistle around her neck. Marissa tried bribing Squeaker with a fish. Swinging my legs over the side, I slowly eased into the water so as not to spook any of the dolphins. Within moments, a few of them came over to inspect this newcomer who had entered their home; they soon dispersed and went back to frolicking, deeming me unimportant. Squeaker noticed me, whistled the mysterious whistle—*low, shrill-trill, down, shrill*—and darted over, circling me playfully.

"Hey buddy, good to see you too." I mimicked his name. He repeated it, as if to agree, then repeated the other thing—low, shrill-trill, down, shrill. I turned to Marissa. "Do you know what that one means?" She shook her head.

"I've only ever heard Squeaker make it. Perhaps it's the name of another dolphin from his pod. Possibly his mate, or a sibling, or even close friend. My guess is he calls it when he's excited or looking for comfort." That made sense. *Hmm ... low, shrill-trill, down, shrill ... You'll be seeing your mysterious friend again soon, Squeaker. I'll make sure you get better.*

After a few hours, Marissa left to take care of some of the other animals. But I stayed, oblivious to the rest of the world, until ...

"Jordan, you lucky goose! Since when do you get to swim with dolphins?" I looked up from Squeaker and found Dylan.

"I only just started today. I'm helping rehabilitate Squeaker. It's a blast. What's up?"

"This," Dylan said, waving his phone in the air. "Chloe has a question for Mr. Memory." I climbed out of the tank, shaking water out of my hair, and made my way over to Dylan. He smirked. "You smell like fish."

"Small price to pay for hanging out with dolphins. Anyway, that can be fixed. What's Chloe's question?" Dylan held up his phone and flicked between two pictures for me to see.

"She wants to know which one is the right size for Amber."

"But ... I'm not sure I've ever seen her wear one."

"Which is probably why she's asking you; you can figure it out. It's better than what I could do."

I nodded. "OK, give me a minute. I think I can calculate an estimate."

I closed my eyes, thinking hard. *Get a size too small, and it won't fit; get a size too big, and it will come off in the ocean ... Alright, use the collar of the T-shirt, the orange one. Yes, that's the closest.* After some brain math, I got it.

"The second one. That's the right length," I said.

"Great. I'll let her know."

"Wait, let me see that again." Tipping the top of his screen back so I could see, I noticed the upside-down time, mentally flipped it over, and grinned. "Prep for show time starts in less than an hour!"

Eventually the tears stopped, leaving me a red-faced wreck, emotionally spiraling downward, feeling like an utter failure. *You are a disappointment. You are a terrible person,* a silent voice scolded. *Who are you kidding? People don't change. You are still an unlovable failure. Unlovable ...* I couldn't let those thoughts float around for long before I started crying again. So I distracted myself with art. Even so, I couldn't shake the heavy chains on my heart. I couldn't get the image out of my head.

Stop thinking about it. Focus on the art. Shaking my head as though to sweep my mind clean, I looked back at my screen. *OK, I need to use a more unique effect here. Oh, I remember when the moonlight hit that tree back in Colorado, the one with the thin layer of pure ice—that magical look, I'll use that.* I was working on the graphics for a guardian angel. Ever since I was little, I've loved things with wings, dragons and angels in particular. I always wanted to see one. Heaven knows I'd never meet either.

The wings look right. No, bigger. Two more rows of feathers, one more column. And ... there should be more— My thoughts were interrupted as my phone chirped.

Phase one was beginning. I got ready to play my part.

Group Chat: Chloe, Amber, Dylan, Matt, Jordan

Matt
Surf anyone?

Dylan
Sure.

Jordan
Yeah!

Chloe
Yep.

* * *

I was practically holding my breath. This was the deciding factor. If this failed …

* * *

Amber
Yes.

* * *

Yes! Perfect! Thank you, Lord! It's going to work! I could imagine Matt, Dylan, and Chloe sighing with relief on the other sides of their phones.

* * *

Dylan
Usual spot? Are the waves good over there, Jordan?

Jordan
They're great. See you all there in … 15?

Chloe
Yep!

Matt
Sounds good.

Dylan
Affirmative.

Amber
I'll be there.

* * *

Phase one, complete. Now for phase two. The others were probably already waiting. Now I just had to intercept Amber and make a slight tweak to the destination. I got into position. Standing in the doorway, I listened closely for her room door. Before long, I could pick out the faint noise of it opening and I raced to beat her to the elevator. Once I heard it pass me and reach the floor above, I hit the "down" button and waited. The elevator came back down for me … with Amber in it. All was going according to plan.

"Hey, Jordan," she said, a small, tired smile on her face.

"Hey, Amber. Oh, um, how to? … one sec." She giggled a little as I tried to figure out how to get into the elevator with my board without smacking her or falling over. "OK, there," I said, grinning triumphantly as I managed to squeeze in beside her. "Excited?" I asked.

"Yes. This is the best part of my day so far," she answered. *Just you wait. You haven't seen anything yet.* We reached the lobby and made our way to the doors. Once outside, I turned toward the back of the apartments where the big open-air gazebo was.

"Hey, Amber, I almost forgot—I wanna show you something. Come on!"

"But the others will be waiting … "

"This won't take long. Really, you should see this," I insisted.

After a moment of thought, she trotted along beside me, curiosity goading her on. I had to work hard to hide my grin; she might suspect something was up. *Just a little more … almost there …* Just as we were about to round the corner, I slowed a tiny bit to allow her to round the corner before me. And the moment she did …

"Happy birthday, Amber!!!"

My first thought was a blank one. Then I felt an overwhelming mix of shyness, embarrassment, anxiety, surprised happiness—and did I mention embarrassment? There, standing in the gazebo, were Chloe, Dylan, and Matt, all smiling wide with laughter in their eyes. Dylan promptly stuck a paper party noisemaker in his mouth and gave a hearty exclamation, the wonky *AOO!* sound those silly things make. I clapped my hands over my mouth and felt the fire rising in my cheeks; it threatened to melt me into a puddle.

"Chloe!" I shrieked in horror. "You promised you wouldn't say anything!" She grinned.

"Think back. If you will remember, I never agreed to anything." I wracked my brain and discovered it was true—she only asked if there was any way she could change my mind. After that, she was silent. "You're not mad, are you?" she asked, suddenly a bit concerned. I felt both a frown and a smile tug at my face, so I stuck with neutral.

"I'm still deciding," I muttered, and a small grin broke through. *Goodness, I hate attention.*

"Come on, Amber. Humor us for four little things," Matt said. "Please?"

"What little things?" I asked, after which I immediately felt like I had just agreed to sell ten years of my life.

"Happy birthday to you! . . . happy birthday to . . . "

Oh no. No! I threw a desperate glance at Chloe, pleading for rescue, trying to telepathically remind her this was the one thing she said they wouldn't do. She thought for a moment, after which she shrugged and joined in the song. Eventually—an eternity later—the song ended. Distantly, numbly, I felt Jordan chuckling beside me.

"Don't worry, Amber. The worst is past," he assured me, gently urging me forward; I hadn't moved since I rounded the corner. I had been too frozen with shock. After sticking his surfboard along the outside wall of the gazebo, Jordan came back and joined the group. Dylan grinned.

"Alright, now that that's over, how old are you today?" he asked.

"Twenty-six," I muttered, feeling bashful as ever.

"Well then, that makes you monkey in the middle, age-wise." *Makes me what now?*

I sensed that Chloe had moved behind me, but before I could turn, she looped something over my head and around my neck. Reaching up, I brushed my fingers over it and felt ... cowrie shells? Chloe came back around to face me, digging for something in her pocket. She held up a small compact mirror so I could see. It was a necklace. A tightly woven row of cowrie shells hung around my neck. They were held by what appeared to be some type of hemp string, a very sturdy cord spun from strong fibers. It had been stained a pale pink, and between each of the shells was a light, rosy tiger's eye bead.

The last time I had a necklace was ... I don't know. Apparently, my face conveyed my emotions well, because Chloe smiled wide.

"It's a surfer's necklace. Designed in such a way that it won't unclasp or come off in the ocean."

"It's beautiful, Chloe. Thank you," I whispered.

"I'm glad it's the right length," she mused.

"That's two," Matt said. "You ready for three?" I didn't have to answer, because Chloe grabbed my hand and pulled me off with enough excitement to fuel a rocket.

I had noticed the others' surfboards leaning against the side of the gazebo, but I hadn't bothered to count them. But as everyone moved around the edge and came to a stop in front of them, I felt … ashamed. Because … I didn't deserve this kind of love and attention.

There were five boards.

Beside Matt's dark red and orange board was Dylan's green board, beside which was Chloe's pink and white swirled number, and beside that was Jordan's dark navy and light blue board. Beside that was a fifth board. Teal, with slightly more blue than green; teal is my favorite color. It was about the same size as the others, small and light. It had a little bow affixed to it.

I was absolutely floored. My heart felt as though it would burst, brimming with a feeling of undeserved joy. Walking as though in a dream, I slowly approached it. The rest of the universe was temporarily forgotten as I took in this unbelievable sight. Hesitantly, I reached forward and touched it, afraid this dream might dissolve if I got too close. But it was real. And as it sunk in, the words, *You are loved,* drifted through my mind. I thought I might cry. *They did all this … for me?* In a daze, I turned back to face them. Chloe, Dylan, Matt, Jordan—all smiling.

"You didn't," I breathed, too shocked to form a complete sentence.

"Too late," Dylan admitted. "We did."

"Do you like it?" Chloe asked, a light in her eyes. I don't know what possessed me.

"No." For a moment, well—there really aren't words to describe their surprised, confused, and rather hurt faces. A smile lit up my soul. "I don't like it. I love it." I was treated to their beaming smiles again.

Jordan had been strangely silent during most of this whole thing, and now I realized he had been gathering his nerve. He took a little step forward, and though he was looking at me, he spoke to the others.

"Last chance. Any objections? Speak now, or forever hold your peace." Grins were exchanged, but no one said a word.

"What's this?" I asked, wondering what else could possibly be left.

"Part four," Matt said.

"Amber," Jordan started, and his voice told me he was pleased with what he was about to say. "You are a good surfer. You are a quick learner. But, most of all, you are a fantastic friend. The vote is anonymous: you are welcome to join team White Water."

I think my heart did burst after all. "But, I … I'm not … " I stuttered lamely. "My skill level. Won't it bring you all down?"

Jordan shook his head. "First off, your skill level is rapidly approaching ours. Second, no; lower scoring does not affect the overall points of a team. No matter what you do, you can't bring the numbers down. You'd be contributing points no matter what you did. In the competitions, the performance of the group isn't averaged, the points are simply added up. So even if your tricks and stunts were significantly lower in value than ours—which I highly doubt—it wouldn't have a negative effect." He paused. "Don't worry about that sort of thing. It's all fine."

Jordan seemed to have run out of things to say and chose to instead plead with me with his big emerald eyes. My gaze went beyond him to the others, who were smiling and nodding.

"Will you?" Jordan asked.

"Yes," I breathed, locked in a fight to hold back tears. "Yes, I would love … yes, I would love that!" The looks on everyone's faces! *You are loved …* This kept going through my mind. I felt the strength—the strength that comes when you belong—fill me up, and I didn't feel so shy anymore. Smiling, I asked, "Does this mean I get to try out the second, third, and fourth surprises now?"

It's been such a great day. It all went so well. Thank you, Lord. I wouldn't change a thing if I could. I frowned lightly. *Well. I might change this. This is a little annoying.* I couldn't sleep. It was, like, 11 o'clock, and I couldn't get my mind to shut off. It was still racing from all the excitement. Bother.

So, I'm sitting on the balcony, stuffing my head full of fantasy with an amazing book. I realized too late that this would not help my insomnia; I was hooked and would likely be up all night. But I could survive on coffee for a day. I'd done that plenty of times before. Suddenly, I stopped midsentence and listened. There was a quiet padding noise above me, then a slight *Scrkkk*, as if … I wracked my brain to understand the sound. It was as if … Amber had come out on the balcony, barefoot, and the scratching sound meant she must have rubbed her fingers across the sand-encrusted wax on her surfboard. *Nailed it.*

I was about to call out a greeting but stopped short. I felt I shouldn't say anything, as if someone had shushed me, telling me there was something I was supposed to hear first. I got the sense she hadn't discovered my presence yet. Tipping my head back, I caught a glimpse of her. She was leaning over the edge, looking out at the sea. The fringes of her T-shirt fluttered in the breeze, as did wisps of her hair, which were dancing and kissing her face. But she didn't bother to brush them away. Concern hit me when I saw the look in her eyes. Emptiness. Longing. Sorrow. Within a few moments, her phone lit up, illuminating her sad face. She looked down at it and smiled a little bit. And quietly, so very quietly, she began to whisper.

"Happy birthday, Ashley." My mind balked. *Ashley? Happy birthday? But, it's Amber's birthday. Then who is … ? Wait, does Amber have a twin?!* "What's it feel like to turn twenty-six?" Amber went on. "Same as last year, or does it get better? Well, I guess you were twenty-six four minutes ago. I was only just 'born' now," she said with a small chuckle.

I glanced at my watch. 11:11. *That's a cool time. And I guess Amber does have a twin. Amber and Ashley. That has a nice ring to it. I wonder if they're identical.* I frowned. *I hope I've been talking to the same one all along …* I felt bad for eavesdropping, if that's what it was, but I couldn't help but feel I was somehow meant to hear this. My attention returned to the present. Amber sighed.

"Oh, Ashley, I miss you so much. You'd love it here. It's not cold," she said with a little laugh. "It's sunny and warm. None of that miserable slush we used to trudge through. I can't help but hope … that I can stay here. Not just for six months, or seven, or even eight. I want to stay. Forever. If life has any pity left, it won't tear me away from this place." She was look-ing up at the sky now, as if … *as if that's where Ashley is.* "The people here, they care about me. Yes, your hopelessly antisocial sister has made some friends. Chloe. Dylan. Matt. Jordan. I told Chloe not to tell them about my birthday, but that scoundrel told them anyway. And they … "

It was only when Amber sniffed that I realized she was crying.

"They gave me a surprise party. This necklace—" I noticed Amber was fingering each of the cowrie shells. "I haven't had a necklace in years. It's so beautiful. A surfboard of my very own. It's perfect in every possible way. And! Oh Ashley, Jordan's invited me to their team! I didn't dare dream of that!" I felt a smile spread across my face. *I'm glad to hear that. I'm so happy she liked it.* "Oh, and they all sang." Amber chuckled. "I'm still embarrassed—but it meant the world to me. This has been the best birth-day I've had since I was parted from you."

A tone of bitter remorse suddenly filled Amber's voice, and I felt her mood deflate.

"You know, I never told you," she whispered, "that when I turned sixteen, the sweet sixteen … when Mom said, 'Blow out the candles. Ashley, you get the left side; Amber, you get the right side, and make a wish!' … the first thing that popped into my head—" Amber pulled the back of her hand across her face and sniffed again … "My only wish was that we would all be together forever, as a family. Us thirteen kids and Mom and Dad. I never swallowed my pride to call them that. And I never told anyone my wish. I was afraid of that silly superstition—about how if you said the wish out loud it won't come true. I was afraid that might be real. I didn't want anything to interfere with my dream."

Amber brushed her face.

"But, I can say it now. Because my wish has already been denied me." She was silent for a while. Then: "Goodnight, Ashley. Happy birthday."

With that, she turned and went back inside. I was left to reflect on all I had just witnessed.

The Journal of Amber Marie Gibson

October 8, Monday

Well, happy birthday to me. You would think that after 26 of these things, birthdays wouldn't be so stressful. But, nope—they still are. Except, this is the best I've had in a long time.

Chloe found out about my birthday a couple days ago. I told her not to breathe a word to the others, but she did anyway. They surprised me, and, I thought I would die from embarrassment. I just hate attention. But they only did four things: 1) Sing. That was excruciating. 2) Chloe got me a surfer's necklace. This was beautiful. 3) They all went in together to get me my very own surfboard. This one was my favorite. 4) Jordan invited me to their surf team. That one was the most unbelievable.

So, overall, it was 75% perfection, 25% embarrassment. I had a great time with them.

Today ... Teumessian killed 318 people at a political address in Massachusetts. The FBI couldn't get there in time because the building went into lockdown. Teumessian rigged the electronic locks so they could only be disabled from the inside.

I could have done something, I could have saved those people ... except, I didn't have my programs. I watched as the FBI discovered their bodies, and ... it will haunt me from now till forever, I know it.

The whole world now knows of this massacre. I'm so worried my emotions will give me away. I saw it all! How can I possibly keep up my act when this whole ordeal is tearing me up on the inside? I need to stay away from all of this as much as I can.

Also, I will get a list of the names of all who died and make Teumessian pay through the nose for each and every one of them.

<u>Days of Punishment Remaining</u>: 304

CHAPTER 20

The Salt Breeze Apartment Complex, Apt. 1407
Tuesday, November 13, 9:17 P.M.

Amber

My peaceful evening was shattered by an alert on the V0RT3X database. C3RB3RU$ was threatening an attack. Granted, this was something they had been doing often lately, and most times we swatted it away without any problem—but I still had to get to the stronghold to help, just in case. I didn't like going at night, but a girl's gotta do what a girl's gotta do—especially when that girl is a hacker.

Putting my drawing project on hold, I begrudgingly packed my computer gear, pulled my computer bag over my shoulder, and headed for the door. V0RT3X had been taking up most of my attention of late. I'd been distant around Chloe, Dylan, Matt, and Jordan—even aloof. But surely it wouldn't last much longer. I just had to take life one dilemma at a time. *Once I've assessed the situation, I can decide whether or not to come back and climb into bed. This master hacker needs her sleep. I can't keep doing this.*

Again? Where on earth is she going? I watched as a very tired-looking Amber began to slowly walk from the building. She glanced around, then continued carefully along her way, as if she didn't want to be seen. *Amber, you do realize I'm up here, right?*

A couple of weeks ago, I had noticed a strange tradition of Amber's. Every few days, she would sneak off, computer bag over her shoulder and purpose in her step, heading toward the older side of town. Evidently she had forgotten that I'm always out on the balcony in the evenings, either reading my Bible, thinking, or just simply existing. I like it out here.

On a couple of these occasions, I casually asked her what she had done the day before. She would coolly answer something like "not much" or "nothing whatsoever." It was strange. She always took the same path, but to where? *There isn't much in that direction. Keep going that way and town ends.* Curiosity and worry seeped into my mind. It was already dark. Amber was heading toward the sketchy side of the city. Judging by her gait, I decided she was exhausted. As of late, there were times when she seemed very distant, as if something was bothering her—as if something preoccupied her thoughts.

I'm not quite sure what got into me. Goaded on by concern and curiosity, I decided to go ask her where she was headed, hurrying so I wouldn't lose sight of her.

It may qualify as the worst mistake I've made yet.

This better be good. If it's just another false alarm, I will not be happy. Maybe they'll have it covered and won't need me. I gazed up at the black sky as I walked. *I wonder if Sonja will be there with Jason.* Of late, due to the rising tension between V0RT3X and C3RB3RU$, Sonja and Jason were staying home most nights. No matter what their family circumstance might be, I felt a bit better knowing they were safe.

The moon was on the rise and the wind brought a cool, salty-sticky sea breeze from over the water. But the usual humidity was missing. I felt a slight chill working beneath my skin. Shrugging my computer bag to the other shoulder, I started to untie my hoodie from my waist. That's when a tingling dagger found its way to the base of my spine—an electric shiver passed through my nerves, spreading across my back, and my hair stood on end.

I'm being followed. I can feel it.

When being tailed, the first rule to remember is this: do not look back. I decided my pursuer wasn't close yet. My eyes scanned the shadows. There was a corner up ahead. *I just have to turn it and disappear.* I continued my casual pace until I neared the edge of the building. Whoever was following me was getting closer, and fast! I rounded the corner and took off running, my feet hardly touching the ground before taking flight again.

As I ran, I almost thought I heard someone call my name. But I couldn't tell, not with the wind whipping past my face. Turning corner after corner, I left a complicated trail for my stalker to follow—if they could. For a bit, it seemed as if they were still pursuing me, but I doubted they could keep up. *Good luck. I was trained by the best.* Now I felt like laughing. *Catch me if you can. You have no idea who you're messing with.* After a while, I slipped into the shadow of an alley and listened. Silence. I had lost them.

It took a minute to catch my breath. Who could it have been? Could it have been someone from C3RB3RU$? I surely hoped not. If they'd figured out who I really was, I was in danger. Straightening, I pulled out my phone and opened the cyber tracking map. Within seconds, I'd pinpointed the stronghold. I wasn't too far away, just an extra five to ten minutes. Turning, I trekked back into the darkness.

For some strange reason, the moment I got close, Amber took off running as if death itself was on her tail. I tried to catch up, to tell her it was just me, but she was gone in moments. Wide-eyed, I stared into the darkness, baffled at what had just occurred. Why would she run? Where did she go? Was she expecting someone to follow her? How did she manage to shake me so fast? *What is going on?* Now I was really worried. Why was she scared?

Things were getting weird. All I wanted was to ask her where she was going and if she was OK. After witnessing her flee, I was convinced she wasn't. And now I looked around … and realized … *I'm lost.* I thought my internal map was complete, but apparently not. I had never been to this side of town before; everything looked unfamiliar. I wasn't sure which way was home. To make matters worse, my phone was dead. I could wander around all night. *Which way is home? Where did Amber go? Should I keep looking for her, or should I try to get back? Should I call her name? What do I do now?*

I huffed a little sigh of frustration and confusion. Too many questions. I decided to keep walking. Surely I would find a landmark I recognized. After awhile, I thought I heard the slightest noise in the distance. Curious, I moved toward it, and soon saw a faint glow from a window in one of the buildings. *What on earth … ?*

"Hey!"

Potential disaster averted. I congratulated myself. *That could have gone very badly, but I think I handled it well.* It had taken the full ten minutes to get to the stronghold, but I had decided to keep to the shadows, just in case the mysterious stalker somehow found me again. Since I had come at the building indirectly, I headed for a backside door. Focused on returning my phone to my bag, I entered the room, looked up, and made a resolution, right then and there: to never ignore, forget, or neglect Jordan for a long period of time again.

Because curiosity was going to get him killed.

There he was, in one of the chairs, surrounded by V0RT3X hackers, practically being interrogated. My eyes went wide. *No. You have got to be kidding me. How did he get here?!* Jordan looked quite scared, rattled, and exasperated as Sonja pounded him with questions.

I almost lost my breath. What was I going to do? I had to get closer, but if he saw me, I'd be done for! A tense moment of indecision passed. *Wait—my hoodie!* Dumping my computer bag in the corner, I knelt in the shadows as I put my hair up in a ponytail and ducked into my jacket, pulling the hood low over my face. Then I slowly made my way to the outskirts of the crowd around Jordan.

I couldn't intervene—yet. If I wasn't careful, my cover could be blown and it would be game over with no "try again" button. First, I would observe, then decide a course of action. My ears honed in on the debate between Sonja and poor Jordan, who looked as though he wished he hadn't gotten out of bed this morning.

" … with Cerberus, aren't you?" Sonja accused, using the most intimidating voice she could muster.

"What is Cerberus?" Jordan asked, looking afraid yet slightly intrigued. "Isn't that the three-headed dog from Greek mythology?"

"Don't play dumb with me. Yes, you may be stupid, but you know what I'm talking about! We were expecting a cyberattack, but we found a little spying rat instead! What is Cerberus planning?"

"I'm serious. I don't know! I've never heard about this group before. I'm not even supposed to be here."

"So, how did you find us?" Sonja pressed.

"I got lost," Jordan said simply, with the childlike honesty I had come to admire.

"Uh-huh. Likely story," Sonja scoffed, unimpressed. "Is that really the best you can think of? I came up with better lies when I was three. Dang, I would insult your intelligence, but I don't have the patience to explain the joke to you." I felt a flicker of anger at this. *Watch it, Sonja. Jordan's three times the person you'll ever be and twice as smart.*

"It's not a lie. I'm telling the truth," Jordan insisted, ignoring the rudeness. "I was looking for a friend. I was worried about her and I saw her heading this way. But I couldn't catch up and got lost."

This caused a bit of a stir. Whispers of "There's another one out there?" and "Could he be telling the truth?" could be heard. I felt like an absolute idiot. *Jordan was the one following me! I suppose, to him, my behavior has been strange, so he got worried. And like before, when he's concerned about someone, he's super persistent until he has some assurance they're OK.* I buried my face in my hands, cringing. *Good job, Amber,* I chided myself. *You can be so blind.* Ender, who had been quietly listening and pondering, stepped forward.

"What is your name?" he asked calmly.

"Jordan."

"Full name?" Jordan hesitated, looking as though he was about to refuse, until he caught a glimpse of Sonja's death glare. He seemed to gulp.

"Jordan Tyler West," he said in a rush, looking more and more frightened. Ender pointed at one of the bystanders; I realized it was Jason.

"Find him," Ender ordered. Jason nodded, pulled out his laptop, and started working furiously. Ender turned back to Jordan. "Let me ask again. Are you with Cerberus?"

"No." Jordan just shook his head.

"Are you with the police?"

"No."

"Are you with either Gregory Damon or James Brenton?"

"No. I'm nothing special," Jordan said. Sonja grabbed Ender's shoulder and spun him to face away from Jordan.

"What are you doing?" she hissed. "He's just gonna keep saying he's nobody. Take off the kid gloves, Ender. Come on! What's gotten into you?"

"I'm not convinced," Ender whispered. "He just might be who he says he is. I don't see the mark of a liar in his eyes. What if he's a civilian?" Sonja frowned and looked away, upset.

"Then he's landed himself in a mess that's bigger than he is, that's what." Jason came over and inserted himself into the discussion.

"I have him," he announced, handing the laptop to Ender, who, after scanning the screen, began to read.

"Jordan Tyler West, 27 years old, born in Santa Barbara. Parents Derick and Susanna West, a brother and a sister … grew up locally … " Jordan looked extremely alarmed that these hackers had his life story at their fingertips.

"You guys can do that?!" he exclaimed in horror. Ender didn't seem to hear him.

" … high school locally, West Mont College, then to Sta—" Something caught Ender's eye and he paused, intrigued. "Works at Ocean Front Rescue."

"Wasn't that place on the help list?" Sonja asked.

"Yeah," Jason affirmed. "Remember, it was Firestorm's pet project." At the mention of F1R3ST0RM, Jordan perked up.

"Wait, you're—this is—" Jordan looked around, a hint of excitement in his eyes. "This is Vortex, isn't it? And, Firestorm—is she here?" he asked hopefully. "Can you tell me her real name? I want to thank her."

I so wanted to go forward, to tell him it was me, that it had been me all along! But I couldn't. It was too dangerous. I couldn't even step up. Jordan could not be given any more hints than absolutely necessary. Ender shook his head.

"She hasn't given us her real name. And even if she had, I wouldn't tell you. And, no. I haven't seen her today." Jordan seemed to slump a bit.

Ender continued to scan the document, then sighed, frustrated. "He's telling the truth. He's just a civilian."

"Thank you," Jordan said, obviously relieved. "Now, can I please go home?" Sonja spun Ender around for another conference.

"Ender, this is bad. He's seen us. He's seen our base. We can't just let him loose. We have to do something!"

"Well, what do you suggest, Sonja?" Ender asked, frustration in his voice. Sonja scowled for a minute.

"For starters, we need to move," she said.

"Agreed." Ender nodded.

"And we can't let him follow us. He may not be with any of our enemies, but we don't know what he'll do with this information. He might follow us to our new location or alert the police to us."

"What if we keep him here until we're out of range?" Ender offered. Sonja nodded.

"Yeah. But how?" For a moment, the two just looked at each other. Then Sonja seemed to have an idea, because she tipped her head against her finger, tapping her chin, thinking hard.

"We could tie him up," she mused. Ender frowned a little, but they both turned to look at Jordan.

"But we can't just *leave* him," Ender argued weakly.

"Do you have a better idea?"

At this, my nerve broke. Sonja was about to say something to Jordan when I shoved my way through the crowd and stood between them. Behind me, I heard Jordan suck in a sharp breath of surprise. Ender snapped to attention.

"Who are you?" he demanded.

I held up my hand to calm him. After a low glance behind me, assuring that Jordan couldn't see, I slowly began to lift the edge of my hood. When recognition flashed across Sonja's, Ender's, and Jason's faces, I quickly held my finger to my lips to shush them, a wild look of urgency in my eyes. Ender raised his eyebrows, then nodded.

"Alright, then. I won't say anything. But would you mind explaining yourself?" *I can't say anything! Jordan will know it's me; think fast, Amber.*

I could sense Jordan leaning to the side, trying to get a glimpse of his mysterious defender. Sliding my phone out of my pocket and holding it close to my body so Jordan couldn't see it, I started hacking Ender's phone. Ender watched me inquisitively, then seemed irked when his phone dinged. He pulled it out and silently scanned my message, Sonja and Jason peeking over his shoulder.

* * *

Sorry about the phone. I can't let Jordan hear my voice, he knows the real me. I am the one he was looking for. He's not a threat at all. Please, you've got to believe me.

* * *

Ender appeared thoughtful, Sonja looked displeased, and Jason seemed to find this whole fiasco exciting. I waited nervously for the verdict.

"You're still relatively new," Ender said slowly. "I believe you, but—" He glanced at Sonja. "Sonja isn't convinced, and I doubt everyone else will be. Do you have any ideas?" Wracking my brain for a moment, I searched frantically for an alternative plan, but came up with nothing. I shook my head. Ender crossed his arms. "You're not making this any easier, you know." I nodded. "It's late, and no one wanted to be here tonight in the first place. So if you don't have any ideas, I'm going with the only one we have. I'm sorry." I looked back to my screen, and in a few seconds—*ding*— Ender's phone chirped again.

* * *

Fine. If you really can't think of any other way, I will stay behind and untie him when you are gone. You sure you don't have any ideas?

* * *

"No. None. Alright," Ender said, nodding. "Make sure to give us enough time."

From there, everything went downhill at an alarming rate. Ender explained the plan to poor Jordan, and after a few moments of numb terror, he submitted to the plan. Why must hackers be so paranoid? I did my best to stay out of sight. Leaning against the wall, I watched the entire painstaking process of ensuring Jordan's prisoner status. He was trying to be brave, but he just wasn't cut out for this type of tension. He was used to an ordinary, carefree, safe life. Despite his best efforts, as he held out his hands for Sonja to tie, I could see he was trembling. I cringed. *Oh Jordan, please forgive my savage friends. Their stupid paranoia is their worst flaw.*

After strapping one of his ankles to the chair to keep him from getting up and trying to run off, Sonja began to blindfold him! I sprang forward and grabbed her wrist, indignant at the thought of subjecting Jordan to more terror. Jordan glanced back and forth between us, in the middle of this fray, eyes wide with alarm. After a battle of wills, Sonja jerked from my grasp.

"You would do well to remember," she whispered threateningly, "that just because you've pulled some impressive stunts does not mean you have power here." She leaned in close, a dangerous fire in her eyes. "I am second in command," she said through gritted teeth. "And I will not risk the safety of this entire team for the temporary emotional state of a normal person!"

With that, she blindfolded Jordan, giving me a glaring smirk that dared me to contradict her. If I hadn't been worried about blowing my cover, I might actually have slapped her.

The only good thing that came from this whole disaster was watching Jason show Ender the "palace" on his GPS device. Ender was thoroughly impressed and appointed Jason to lead the way to the new safe house. We discretely fist-bumped as he passed me; Sonja gave me a funny look. I'd have to deal with her later. I watched as, once again, all of V0RT3X scrambled about to gather the tech, pack up, and leave without ever looking back—hopefully for the last time.

Once the building was empty and quiet, I straightened from my post at the wall and silently moved to stand in front of Jordan, staring at him sitting there blindfolded, trying to understand. *How do you manage to get yourself into trouble like this? You can be so oblivious. Yet ... all of this happened because you were trying to look out for me.* I shook my head, feeling torn. I wanted to tell him who and what I really was. I felt that out of all the people in the world, Jordan might not condemn me. But he must never discover the real Amber. *Never.*

What did I do wrong? I don't know. This is what I get for letting my curiosity get the better of me. But I still don't know where Amber is. What if she runs into these V0RT3X hackers? I'm worried about her. I shifted nervously. I was scared. Really scared. I couldn't help it. Listening carefully, I strained to hear any noise at all. Nothing. *Did that person leave with the others? Did they leave me here alone?*

I sat in silence, praying and fretting and fidgeting and regretting for what felt like hours, though it was probably only a few minutes. I didn't know whether to just cooperate with these people or try and make a break for it. Just as I was beginning to entertain the idea of escape, I heard a noise.

"Are you still there?" I called, my voice filling the empty building. There was a slight pause, in which I began to think I really was alone, and then two taps. "I assume that means yes ... two taps mean yes, one tap means no?" Two taps. "How long are you going to keep me here? You are going to let me go, right? Please tell me you won't just run off and leave me. I promise I'm not a threat to you. You will let me go, right?" Three taps. "That was ... that was more than two. Does that mean maybe?" One tap. "Does that mean I'm asking too many questions?" Two taps. "Oh. OK."

So I went through the questions, one by one. The mystery person patiently answered all they could, tapping three times when the question was unanswerable or if I asked anything other than yes or no questions. Honestly, I felt a little safer. Just a tiny bit.

Hang in there, Jordan. I just have to give Ender and the others a little bit longer. It had been half an hour since the last one stepped out. The time had passed quicker once Jordan started talking. Thankfully, he had begun to look less like he was on the brink of a panic attack.

It never ceases to amaze me how polite and kind he is, even with total strangers. He thanked me for standing up for him and not telling him to be quiet. I replied with a simple "yes" tap, hoping that would suffice for "you're welcome." After a while, it occurred to me that he could have found his way back if he had used the satellite map app on his phone. So why didn't he? Most times, he made sure to keep his phone with him. *I wonder …* Once more, I silently walked over to Jordan, observing. I could just barely see the edge of his phone sticking out of his pocket. I decided to take a bit of a risk and hack it. But I couldn't—it was dead.

Of course. He often forgot to charge it. I folded my arms and shook my head. To think that something so small could have been the difference between this mess and everyone being home right now seemed some kind of ironic, cosmic joke. Suddenly, an idea hit me. There was a way I could reveal some information to Jordan without blowing my cover. It might satisfy some of his curiosity. Coolly, I silently walked over to him and carefully slipped his phone from his pocket. Jordan tensed at this and seemed to bite his tongue to keep silent.

As I turned and walked back to my computer, he said, "You won't get anything off it. It's dead."

I smiled, tapped on a table three times, and left him to ponder what I meant. Booting up my laptop, I fished my charging cord from my bag and plugged in his phone. Thankfully, our phones took the same port. Noticing the slight drag in the programs, I amped his core processer, deleting any residual programs that were slowing the system. This way, it wouldn't die as fast; this was something he might find useful. Next, I pulled up a note-pad app, created a new memo, and started to type.

I wondered if I'd ever see that phone again. *And why would the hacker want it? And what does "too many questions" have to do with "my phone is dead"?* As I dangled over the inky black of the unknown, I could feel my grip on courage slipping. I couldn't do this much longer. It wouldn't be so bad if I could actually see and move. The same psychology of being trapped in a dark room applied here. I was trying to convince my brain that I was fine, that this was temporary, but it was threatening to go into panic mode.

I thought I heard someone approaching, then there was a slashing noise as the slight pressure around my ankle disappeared. The hacker was letting me loose! But then they grabbed my arm, hauled me up, and started walking; within seconds, I felt the night air on my skin. *Oh, or not, maybe I'm not free yet. Where … where are they taking me?*

Sending my mind into hyperdrive, I frantically tried to profile this person. Based on their stride, they were shorter than me, and rather lightweight. The hand gripping my shoulder was slightly small. To my surprise, as I listened to their breathing, I realized they were scared, too. At one point, the mystery person seemed to trip on something, stumbling a little, then quickly regained their footing. That was all I needed. It was a woman. She had gasped a little, a quiet yet distinctly feminine gasp. *Could … could it be … ?*

Suddenly, we stopped. Electric adrenaline shot into my veins, my breath caught, and I wondered if I would ever see the light of day. I felt her press something into my palm, then … *slash!* My wrists were free! I whipped my hands up to pull off the blindfold and whirled—but I was alone. She was gone. My eyes adjusted to the moonlight and I peered into the shadows for a long time. Nothing. Looking down, I realized the object in my hand was my phone. It was on, and the screen displayed these words:

I am sorry you were dragged into all of this. Do not worry, V0RT3X will not come after you. As long as you do not tell anyone about tonight or make a fuss, you will be safe. And, about Ocean Front Rescue, you are welcome. Your thanks is appreciated. Now go home and do not come looking for me or for V0RT3X. Goodbye Jordan.

~F1R3ST0RM

Slowly, I looked up, and—I couldn't believe it—I could see the apartments. F1R3ST0RM had led me home. Once again, she had come to the rescue, saved my hide. But why? I didn't … maybe … did I know her? *Why? Who? Who is F1R3ST0RM?*

Needless to say, I didn't ask Amber where she had been that night. I didn't read any more online accounts of how V0RT3X had saved organizations. I kept my head down. But I didn't stop pondering that one question.

Who is F1R3ST0RM?

CHAPTER 21

Ocean Front Rescue
Monday, December 3, 10:45 A.M.

Jordan

It was a relief that, since being kidnapped by hackers, nothing insane happened in the next few weeks. Except for the present, which was the closest thing to crazy I'd had in about a month—but this was a good crazy. The deep sea drone was coming back. It would be picked up by a boat around noon, and with it would be the proof we needed. Ocean Front was throwing itself into full throttle in hopes that, once the evidence was in, the information we had gathered would be enough to prove the existence of the new fault line.

Apart from Squeaker, Lexie was the only one I dared tell about the V0RT3X affair. Even though it took five pages front and back to recount the whole ordeal, I decided it was safer than emailing. *Nothing* electronic is safe. I am now aware of that alarming fact.

"That whole hacker business was crazy, wasn't it, buddy?"

Even though Squeaker didn't have a clue what I was saying, he performed one of the few tricks he knew in hopes that I would give him a fish; he nodded his head. I chuckled and tossed him the snack, then bribed him with another on the far side of a hoop. After some hesitation and squeaking, he filled the water with the fine vibrations of echolocation. He soon found the opening and swam through to claim his prize.

Squeaker was doing better. He wasn't being as anti-dolphin-social and had begun to try echolocation again. He didn't quite have it down yet, however. He'd barreled into me on a couple occasions, but as the saying goes, "it's the effort that counts."

Sophie came trotting—actually, *skipping* would be a better word—into my line of sight, her little silver turtle necklace bouncing up and down with her every step.

"Hey Jordan! All done with my chores!"

After almost slipping, she slowed and came to kneel at the edge of the tank, leaning forward as far as she could while holding her hand out to Squeaker, who forgot me and dashed for his new friend. He whistled excitedly, then proceeded to show off his new "trick" for getting attention: sneezing an underwater bubble ring. As with every other sea creature, Sophie had managed to bewitch Squeaker, winning his heart and trust, thus making her his third human friend. It was a shame she didn't have the know-how for rehabilitation; otherwise she would probably be helping with Squeaker, too.

"Oh, by the way, we're going with the team to get the hard drive from the drone!" Sophie chirped. *The negotiator strikes again!*

"How did you manage that? Who'd you convince this time?" I asked.

"Tristan again." I shook my head and chuckled.

"You're so persuasive. I'll bet if you asked him permission to adopt a pet pelican, he just might say yes."

She laughed. "I'll make sure to ask him some time. Thanks for the idea."

"You're not actually serious, right?" I felt slightly concerned she might try it.

Sophie shrugged. "Maybe," she mused, giving me a devilishly mischievous grin. "Maybe."

The expression "comedy is tragedy separated by time and space" is false, because it's been about a month since the fiasco at V0RT3X and it still isn't funny. In fact, the more I think about it, the angrier I feel. I haven't returned since that night; I decided it might be a good idea to stay away for a while so Jordan didn't catch on and figure everything out.

Anyway, I'm gathering my things, because I'm going back now. I have a bone to pick with Sonja.

She didn't have to be so harsh. Why was she so spiteful toward me? I thought we were on good terms. I shouldered my computer bag and headed for the door. *Even after she knew Jordan was a civilian, she still treated him like a spy! And she didn't have any regard for what I had to say. She totally ignored me.*

My mind went into autopilot as I turned down street after street, the sunny wind playing in my hair. I didn't bother to brush it out of my face. *"You would do well to remember that, just because you've pulled some impressive stunts does not mean you have power here ... I am second in command, and I will not risk the safety of this entire team for the temporary emotional state of a normal person!"* No matter how many times I played that part over in my head, it still stung, every single time. I thought I had found my place at VORT3X, and with Jason and Sonja. Apparently not.

I was trapped between two worlds. I was an actress, preforming for two different audiences. I couldn't let my act fall apart; I had to keep the charades separate. But the lines kept getting blurred. At the start of that night, my F1R3ST0RM mask had been on, fleeing from danger, sticking to the shadows, remaining levelheaded. But as time went on, as I defended Jordan like I did, standing up to Ender and Sonja, impulsively risking everything, the "Amber" mask had found its way out. But I can't be one person. It's dangerous. It's better if I keep my inner Jekyll and Hyde isolated. That way, no one gets hurt. But it was getting hard.

Even though I was being careful to seem cheerful and engaged around Chloe, Dylan, Matt, and Jordan, I was worried, and secretly wondering if I should pull away. The thought that I might be getting too emotionally attached to this place, these people, and this relatively carefree existence was tearing me up inside, shredding all my security. For some reason, I felt desperate to defend this tame life I had found, to hold up the fantasy that I could really belong here, that I might actually have found some friends who would never betray, judge, or leave me.

I was terrified of testing their love. What would happen if they knew who I really was? The thought of losing just one of them was a stab to my soul. And it could have ended that night. Jordan. If he had learned who I was ... *what if he got a glimpse of my face? What if he recognized something I was wearing? What if he heard me when I tripped? What if I hadn't gotten away fast enough when he turned?* If they had just let him go home, it wouldn't have been such a close call.

So, yes. I had a serious bone to pick with Sonja.

I had no problem getting to the new base. The fantastic setup and grandeur was lost on me as I strode into the main room, down the stairs to the server cove, and scanned the cavernous space for that girl. She was in the far corner, sitting sideways in a chair, computer on lap. Jason was beside her. Neither had noticed me yet. I headed straight for Sonja. Jason looked up and grinned.

"Storm! Good to see—"

"Sonja," I growled in a voice that commanded attention. "We need to talk."

"Talk about what?" She seemed to think for a moment. "That sorry excuse for a spy that stumbled into the stronghold? Are you still on that?" She glanced up in a bored fashion, calmly took in my fuming, then returned to her screen. "You sure are ticked. Been gathering courage to vent at me? No wonder you haven't shown your face around here lately." *She pushes all the wrong buttons.*

"No," I said through gritted teeth. "No. The reason I haven't been around is because that 'sorry excuse'—who has a name—is my neighbor! Do you have any idea how risky this has been for me? I told you he wasn't a threat. You tied him up! And blindfolded him! He didn't deserve any of that. You were a royal jerk. What is your problem?"

A tense Jason mumbled something that sounded like a sarcastic "welcome back," then made his escape before things got bloody. Sonja was now glaring at me steadily. There was also a look of irritation in her eyes. Perhaps I somehow hit one of her buttons for once.

"My 'problem' is that our base was breached," she said, dangerous and slow.

"By an innocent, oblivious civilian," I pointed out. "Keeping him there for so long only made things worse. He has an eidetic memory, Sonja. All he has to do is rewind the events and watch them all over again in his mind. He remembers *everything*." This was alarming for her, I could tell, and she sat up so quickly her laptop almost hit the floor. I didn't know whether to chuckle or snort in disgust. "Stop your fretting. Everyone's safe. I knew he wouldn't report anyone. Even if he was going to, he would have done it long ago." I went back to being furious with her. "I'm the one who was in danger. I took the risk of being the mediator. That was my choice. But if you had listened to me, I wouldn't have had to take all the other risks!" Sonja's glare deepened.

"Even if he's not some lame wannabe crime fighter—even if he is normal, like you say—that doesn't change anything. Normal is dangerous, so I treated him as such. People who aren't like us don't understand us.

They never will! They see us as a threat, Storm. Yes, some of our ways are unorthodox, but we're vigilantes. It's for the greater good. People like that Jordan character don't understand that. I don't trust him—and I'm not sure I trust you."

"Excuse me? *What?!*" I exclaimed. "What do you mean, you're 'not sure you trust me'? What's that supposed to mean? How deep does your stupid suspicion run?"

I began to realize that our argument was gaining attention. People were watching, holding their breath, waiting for the smackdown. As if I cared. I was beyond the point of no return, and I wasn't groveling or backtracking.

"It means what it sounds like, genius. You're sketchy, even for a hacker," Sonja said nastily, standing to face me.

"How so?" I challenged.

"You really want me to start the list?" Sonja scoffed. "Fine, then: your first contact with Vortex was to hack us, to screw with our systems. You won't tell us your real name. That's suspicious. I wonder what I would find if I looked the real 'you' up. You're a strong hacker, yet you say you were unattached until you joined us. I find that highly unlikely. Surely you're working for someone. You were conveniently absent when we caught your little friend, yet showed up just in time to interfere. Against my better judgment, you were the one left behind to let him go. For all I know you told him everything. You and this Jordan have managed to pull the wool over Ender's eyes, but I'm not easily convinced. Jordan said he was worried and came looking for you. But from what I've seen and heard—and by your own admission—you don't have many buddies and you suck at making new ones. And he didn't find you, he found V0RT3X. Explain that."

The answer came to me from the deep void of my subconscious. Before I could think deeply about whether it was a safe response, it came tumbling out.

"Jordan came looking for me because he is my friend. Which is why I stood up for him. I do that for my friends. They trust me. Maybe you would too. That is, if you were one of them."

The words were out of my mouth before I had time to calculate the cost. For a fleeting moment in time, I saw Sonja's mask crack. And I saw the real Sonja. I regretted every thought I had let enter and every word I said from the moment I woke today until now. Pain. My words truly hurt her. But the mask was quickly mended, the windows to her soul clouded with fake emotions, and she snorted.

"Alright. Whatever. If you won't talk, I'll find out the truth another way. You can't hide forever." And with that, she strode off. I watched her go, feeling sick to my stomach. Surely, the matter needed to be addressed, but … not like that. *What have I done?*

Soon, things settled down—except for my emotions. I couldn't get the horrid encounter from my mind.

I didn't even know if what I said to Sonja was true. Did Jordan and the others trust me? Should they? I felt sick at the thought. Probably not. I wasn't worthy of their trust; I betrayed it daily. I was a living lie. I tried to shake it off, to tell myself it didn't matter. *You're getting too attached, Amber.* My conscience seemed to be warning me. *Do you really think you can fit in here? Forever? No, it's only a foolish dream. You can't let yourself be loved. It's dangerous.* A thick, dull pain settled over me. *But … I want to be loved …* How many years had it been? How many years had it been since someone said, "I love you"? I thought for a moment. Three. Three years. Three long, lonely years.

My chronic trust issues made relating to people nearly impossible. I only had a few friends. I was lucky I had any. I could count them on my two hands and have fingers to spare. None of them had ever met the real me. They never could. Eric was the only one who ever knew—and he was dead because of it. So, I counted my blessings. Namely, my few companions. I made sure they were never put in danger or hurt because of me. But I might have just burned a bridge that could never be rebuilt. I was also scared. Sonja was too good. She had seen right through my disguise and deduced I was not what I seemed. For all I knew, she was on to me. *I've really messed up this time …*

"Cheer up, Storm. It's just Sonja. She'll get over it! Anyway, it was good for her overinflated ego. It needed a little deflating. Otherwise, it was going to burst," Jason said, nudging me, a tease in his grin. I decided I needed to work on hiding my emotions.

"I didn't mean to start a war, you know. I was just frustrated," I murmured quietly.

"Well, don't feel bad. I know what you're talking about. She deserves it sometimes."

I turned to Jason. "Why aren't you siding with your sister? I was pretty harsh. I'm the one who should be in the dog house." Jason went strangely still. "Jason?"

"I don't know," he said slowly. But I knew he was lying, and I gave him a look that said as much. He sighed. "Look, there are more than a few things she and I disagree on. We don't really see eye to eye anymore."

Jason seemed rather resolute not to say more, as if he was expecting me to try and torture an explanation from him. *Strange. What's up with that?* I quietly sighed and looked back to my computer, then up at the blinking pillar in the middle of the room—and felt saddened again. Memories of Eric's old hideout filled my mind. The intricate machinery, the tall servers, the core technology spreading like wild vines up the walls, into the halls, over the floor, and across the ceiling. We worked so hard on that place. It was hazardous, messy, strange, confusing—and perfect. It gave me a purpose to strive for in the midst of my gray existence.

I wonder what my life would be like … if he had never shown kindness to me. Actually, I don't think I would even be alive right now if he hadn't. Ashley and I drifted apart toward the end, so I was alone more often than not. At times he was my only friend, like a brother to me, and even better. I glanced at Jason, whose attention was furiously devoted to his screen, so I decided: it wasn't too late to redeem myself today. At least a little.

"I'll be back," I announced, then headed for the ground floor.

The main room was mostly empty, save for a few people here and there. I made my way to the enormous shelving units and found Jason's "apartment." It was wired up from corner to corner, like what I imagine the inside of a spaceship cockpit might look like. Unzipping the front compartment of his backpack, I grabbed his sack of marbles and slid back down the ladder. When I returned to the sublevel, I strode over to Jason and dropped the bag in his lap.

"Teach me?" I asked—though it came out as more of an order than a question.

"What?"

"Teach me how to play marbles. I never learned, and I'm pretty sure it's a lot more fun than sitting here hacking all day." A light sparked in Jason's eyes, but his face remained covered with surprised confusion. "Come on," I urged. "The world out there can survive without our help. It's been awhile since you've played with someone else, no?" I watched as his smile found its way out.

"It's been forever," he breathed, grinning with excitement. I felt my inner quiet side speak up. *Well, Amber,* it said. *Maybe you're not a purebred monster after all.*

I don't think I've ever looked at a hunk of metal and thought to myself: *Wow. It's so majestic.* The drone was finally back. It had been dragged into the hangar on what reminded me of a giant shopping cart and was being lifted out with a small crane.

Once it was secured to its platform, both tech teams bustled around it, hooking it up to hard drives and initiating unlock protocols. The port compartment popped open. Kirsty strode forward, pulled out a cord, turned, and held it out to Tristan. He looked unsure; she looked expectant, raising her eyebrows and smiling.

"Well, go on. This is what you've been waiting for, isn't it?" Tristan slowly took it.

"Thank you," he said, an excited light dancing in his eyes. "Kyle?" Kyle had our laptop out and on within seconds. His fingers flew as he created empty folders and new pathways for the data to travel across. "Download it as fast as possible," Tristan said. "We open the files when we get back, no sooner. It wouldn't be fair to the others." With that, he gave the end of the cord to Kyle, who promptly shoved it into the USB port.

Data flew across the screen. Everyone's eyes were fixed on this spastic display. It was like a fast-forwarded video. The visual burst only lasted about thirty seconds, after which a silent sigh seemed to pass among the others. I didn't notice everyone packing up. *Can it be ... ? Perhaps it's wrong.* I played it over in my head again, slowing it down to take in the details and check my calculations. Nothing changed. *I can't believe it. That was ... unexpected. Could it really be true?*

"Jordan?" My eyes snapped open. Had I zoned out?

"Yeah, Dylan?" I asked.

"You saw something, didn't you?" he whispered, voice instilled with excited wonder. "You saw the data! What was it? Is it right? Are we right?"

I shook my head. "I'm not telling."

"What? Come on!" Dylan begged. I shook my head again.

"No. Absolutely not. You'll know soon enough."

I would just have to suffer silently. I couldn't say anything. It didn't really matter, though; they would all see in time. Meanwhile, I would agonize over what I had glimpsed. Because, maybe I had seen wrong. Maybe I had only seen some of it. *I can't wait till we get back …*

Crack!

"Score! Double kill!" Jason laughed at my excitement as I scooped up two of his goldish-red marbles, proudly displaying the loot. "I think I'm getting it down!" I gave him a brave look. "Whatch'ya got, Jason? Come at me. Don't go easy!"

Jason grinned and reached for the fat shooter marble. He took careful aim, then launched it at the cluster of smaller marbles. *Crack!* Smugly, he took his time, gathering the seven teal, silver-swirled, and gray-speckled marbles—my marbles, my last marbles—that had been knocked from the ring.

"I believe that's called a septuple kill," he said, smirking.

I sighed despairingly. "This is hopeless." It had been awhile since my inner child came out. I hadn't cared about something as trivial as winning a game in ages. At that moment, it didn't feel unimportant. Because it wasn't really about me. It was about Jason. "Oh, you know what?" I frowned, mind churning with an internal debate. "Agh. Just set it up again. I'm going to win eventually!" Jason smiled and started to rearrange the marbles. I decided to test my luck. "By the way, what did you mean earlier: you and Sonja 'don't see eye to eye'? What did she say to you?" I was trying to stay casual. Jason sighed and shrugged.

"She thinks you're someone you're not," he answered.

"What does that mean?"

"I don't think I can tell you," he said slowly, as if each word was a land mine. Suddenly, he caught a glimpse of something behind me and froze. I perceived this and glanced back. *Sonja.*

"Come on, Jason. We're going." There was no emotion on her face or in her words.

"What? Come on, it's barely evening," he begged. "We've been staying here the past few days. Please. I don't wanna go home—"

"No. We leave. *Now.*"

Something inside Jason seemed to wither. I could feel it, as if he was radioactive with disappointment. He nodded sadly. I quietly helped him gather the marbles. He threw me a glance—apologetic, pleading, longing—then rose and followed Sonja. She turned and walked away without so much as looking at me. I watched them go, feeling like a failure. *How much damage did I do? I didn't mean to—*

"She sure is ticked off." That scared the daylights out of me. I hadn't even noticed Ender come up. He stood beside me, gazing after Sonja.

"Yeah." I glanced at him. "I'm sorry. I think I did it."

"I know," he said simply, making me feel even worse.

"Do you think she'll stay mad?"

"It's possible, but I doubt you did any real damage. Though she has been acting a little strange for a while. Probably just a phase." He turned to me. "I need your skills for a project. There's a new idea on how to freeze up Brenton's com system. The whole thing's theoretical, and I want to see if you can make it a reality. Cool? Got time?"

I nodded, feeling slightly down, but relieved I was being offered a purpose. "Yeah. I got time."

Seconds away … this changes everything, no matter the outcome. Any minute, my life will take a new turn. Everyone's will. So, what path will we end up on? Even though I had caught a glimpse of the data, it wasn't enough to be 100 percent certain. It was likely what I saw was right—but perhaps it wasn't.

"Jordan, just tell me!" Dylan wouldn't give up.

"No, you'll see it for yourself soon enough," I muttered halfheartedly, then turned to him, amused. "You are so impatient. I thought I was bad."

"Agh! No fair! Come on!" he exclaimed miserably. Sophie giggled at Dylan's exasperation, and he turned on her. "Come on, Soph, don't you want to know too?" he asked. "Help me wear him down!"

"Oh, I'm dying to know," she said matter-of-factly. "But I know I won't get anything out of him," she answered simply, then looked up at me and flashed a smile, as if to say, "you're welcome." I just smiled back.

Eventually, Kyle, who had been hard at work gathering all the files, exchanged words with Tristan, who started messing with the computer. Tristan didn't need to call anyone to attention, because he had everyone's the moment the projector booted up. All eyes were on the far wall. All sound stopped. Nothing else in the world mattered.

The light flickered and blazed to life, casting pictures and documents on the wall. There was a heartbeat in time—the deafening silence grew thick as mud—as everyone scanned the results. Slowly, one by one, new images and files replaced the old ones. The proof was irrefutable. There was no doubt, no room for possible error. The final pieces fell into place.

Finally, I could see the puzzle picture as a whole.

I wish it was Thursday. Or Saturday. I'm ready for the weekend. I desperately wanted something to take my mind off ... everything. Everything related to this day and to all the mistakes I had made. I had failed Sonja, burning bridges with raging, unquenchable fire. I had failed Jason, incapable of making his day a good one. I had failed Ender, falling through when he needed me. I had even failed myself and my expectations. I tried not to think about all my other failures in life. That was a one-way trip to depression and disaster. My past was best left buried, not left out in the open to be faced. I tried to forget, but memory can be a curse.

Twitching my feet nervously, I sat on a high stool by the granite counter in the apartment. Glancing down at the tiny clay figure in my hands, I frowned, then squished it. Out of all the creatures I had tried to make, none were worth keeping. More failures ... *Come on,* I scolded myself. *Stop. No more pity parties. Find something to occupy—* There was a knock at the door. For a moment, I just sat staring at it, stupidly. Someone was here for me?

After a quick glance around the room and at myself, I decided nothing was a true mess. I had decluttered the floor of circuitry earlier, and I was in an art-stained T-shirt and shorts, with a few paint pens and texture brushes sticking out of my pockets. All was OK. I hopped up, curiosity speeding my step, opened the door—and my day started to perk up a little.

"Jordan! Hi, um—" I managed to save the sentence with: " . . . what a pleasant surprise." He grinned, almost sheepishly.

"Hey, Amber. You're not in the middle of something, are you?"

You mean, apart from massacring figurines? "No, I'm not doing anything."

"Would you, uh ... " With one hand behind his head and the other jammed in his pocket, he looked comical. "Would you like ... to hang out a bit?" Jordan asked slowly, fearing rejection.

Though I kept a straight face on the outside, I smiled on the inside.

Betty wasn't here today. Mr. Talkative People Person was feeling a little lonely, apparently. I felt a smile break through.

"Yeah," I said with a laugh as quiet as a breath. "Come on in." All the nervous apprehension melted, and Jordan grinned.

I dropped the stack of sketchbooks, novels, DVD cases, and pencil pouches on the table, out of the way. Jordan sat at one end of the couch, and I was on the other. He politely asked all sorts of questions about my day, and I tried my best to answer them, making most of it up on the spot. After a while, though, I managed to get across to him that my day was nothing significant, and whatever he had to say would be ten times more interesting. So he talked. And talked. And talked. But I didn't really mind. He was so happy, like a child at the end of a wonderful day, ready to tell his tales and stories to anyone who would listen. So I listened.

Soon, my world didn't matter. I felt happy, hearing a happy account of a happy day from a happy person. It was contagious.

Jordan excitedly chattered about this and that, about little things that suddenly took on great importance. There was something other than small circumstances on his mind, though. The way he couldn't keep his attention on one thing, how his gaze occasionally flitted around the room, the tempo at which his feet were tapping, there was no question—he was seriously distracted. I felt a smile somewhere inside of me and chuckled. Jordan paused to give me an inquisitive glance, then his attention was drawn elsewhere, across the room.

"Jordan. Jordan." He looked back at me, his ever-present, absentminded grin shining. "Come on, Jordan. I know something's got you riled up. Just tell me." He seemed to fidget for a moment, trying to decide how to proceed.

"OK. So … " He thought for a moment. "You can keep a secret, right? At least for a little while?" *Ha! You have no idea how many secrets I keep!*

"I can keep a secret," I said, nodding. Jordan's smile returned.

"Alright," he said, eyes glittering with pure excitement. "A while back, I mentioned something about Ocean Front looking into the possibility of a new fault line opening up, remember? And you looked really confused, and it took six minutes to make it sound not-crazy?"

"Yeah," I answered, grinning. There was something quite amusing about the way he said that.

"Well—" All his nervous movement ceased. "First, we went to the Torres Center. It was months ago—there was a deep-sea drone, and it used sonar—

it was meant for algae or something, but … Tristan and the others, the data—" Jordan sighed in exasperation, in a "scrap that" kind of way, then finally got it out. "It's real! The fault line is there, and it traces out a new tectonic plate! Ocean Front was right, I was right—" His face went blank with surprise. "Wait a second, I was right … " After a second or two of a deer-in-the-headlights look, he beamed again. "It's real!" I found myself grinning too.

"Congratulations. That's huge! Wow, I … I don't know what to say," I admitted with a little laugh. Jordan laughed a little, too, and seemed about to say something when his face went from his glowing joy to curiosity, then awe. He was looking at me, but lower.

"You made that?" he asked in wonder, pointing. I glanced down.

I couldn't believe it. I had made something. A wolflike pup. Tiny, tawny, whitish. Straight out of my subconscious, a tiny Laelaps wolf pup. I've always known my fingers have a mind of their own, but this … Holding up my hand, I inspected the little wonder sitting on my palm, as did Jordan.

It was sitting up straight, as if someone had called its name. Its paws were big, in a puppyish way, and its tail curled partway around them. Tiny ears perched on top of its head, which was tipped slightly to one side, as if the creature was curious. The tiny nose and muzzle were smooth and symmetrical. Somehow I did all this without looking. After a moment of stunned silence, I made my decision. It didn't take too much thought.

I reached into my pocket and pulled out a brush and gray paint pen. Jordan watched in amazement as my hands flew, coating the tips of the brush's bristles with the pen, then patting the wolf just hard enough to leave tiny indents in the clay, along with the gray coloring. Grabbing a mechanical pencil from the floor, I started to carve in more details. I didn't know I could move so fast. It just … happened. Fur … tail, legs, ears, snout, ears. Color: honey-brown eyes, light-chestnut ear tips, gray paws, dark tail tip … texture. The whole process took only what seemed a matter of seconds.

I finished, pulled a little squirt bottle from my back pocket and sprayed the pup in one swift movement. I suppose I should have moved my hand a bit farther from Jordan, because he snuffed, like a miniature sneeze. *Oops.*

For a sluggish moment in time, I gazed at my creation. A feeling of happiness and serenity came with a smile—and then I just knew what I was to do with it. I held my hand out to Jordan.

My mind balked. Not only had I just witnessed an amazing display of artistic prowess at the speed of light, but now its maker was handing the creation to me? I admit, I just stared blankly at the wolf sitting in the palm of Amber's hand, unsure what to do.

"Take it," she said, smiling a little. Slowly, carefully, I took it. "Just leave it out overnight, or stick it in the oven at about 275 degrees for half an hour. The spray makes it harden faster and without cracking," she explained, putting her brush back in her pocket. Stunned for a moment, I shook my head.

"Amber, this is beautiful. But I can't take it. It's yours!"

"No," she said, also shaking her head. "I've made hundreds like this. I want you to have it. It's my way of saying thank you."

"Thank you? Thank me—for what?" I asked, glancing down at the wolf as if it held the answer.

When I looked back up at Amber, I realized she hadn't thought of why she was thanking me. But then a happy, full-faced smile made her eyes shine.

"Because you came to spend time with me."

Dear Lexie,

How did your geography exam go? Doesn't it feel great to have it finished? How was the youth group retreat? Did the twins Makayla and Markus tag along? If they did, did you get to sit with them on the car ride, or were you stuck in the back with the little kids? My guess is that none of you teens slept a wink, did you? Camp retreats are so much fun.

Poem challenge accepted! It took a while, but I came up with one. Don't laugh.

I found a baby shark's tooth while walking on the shore, and now I don't want to go swimming anymore. All those sharks darting around, leaving their teeth all over the ground—they've got enough to spare, so they just leave them there, in hopes of giving us humans a great big scare.

Now, if you find anything worse, please let me know, and I'll abandon the sea to live in the snow. But I can't think of anything worse than meeting a shark. Unless, that is, I met it in the dark.

I'm not sure that was worth the paper space! Oh well. Let me know if I have a future as a poet.

Squeaker is doing better! It's so much fun to work with him. My guess is that he'll be released within a handful of weeks! I'm gonna miss the little guy.

Ready for some crazy news? I hope you're sitting down for this.

The fault line IS there! The deep-sea drone came back today and the data confirms our hypothesis! As far as we know, no other organizations are pursuing this line of investigation. I don't really know what this means for Ocean Front as a whole, but good things are to come, I can feel it.

I wish you could have seen what I saw a while ago -- you would have loved it. This afternoon, I was chatting with Amber, and she somehow made a little clay wolf pup without even looking. I've never seen anything like it. It looks so real! And—she gave it to me, as her way of saying "thank you for spending time with me." If I had known she wanted someone to talk to, I would have stopped by more often. I guess she likes to listen.

I can't wait for your reply. Love and miss you!

~Jordan

CHAPTER 22

V0RT3X stronghold
Wednesday, December 19, 11:18 A.M.

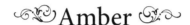

Amber

Sonja simply refused to pay me the time of day, yet she watched me like a hawk. Whenever I looked up, she was calmly staring at me with a stone-cold gaze. She didn't even have the presence of mind to look away when our eyes met. I suppose she didn't care. I always forced a smile regardless. I was trying to prove myself, to be considerate and as polite as I could, though she still rubbed me the wrong way.

Jason seemed to be ignoring the whole affair, as if thinking about it left a bad taste in his mouth. On a couple of occasions, he'd bravely stood up to Sonja; I seemed to be a source of discord between them. Whenever I was around, Jason seemed braver and Sonja seemed more iron-willed. I couldn't figure those two out for the life of me.

Speaking of Sonja the ninja … she's been watching me. Again. Meeting her eyes, I forced a smile. Again.

Why am I still trying? I doubt I can salvage a friendship, partnership, coworkership, relationship, or any other kind of "ship" with her. Maybe she's just trying to unnerve me as payback of sorts. If that's her goal, it's working—but I'm not letting it show. Maybe I simply shouldn't look up anymore. This seemed like a good fix even if it was temporary, so I turned back to my screen.

I hadn't really been focusing on contacting Brenton. I'd just been leaving that to the others. But, they were taking too long. I didn't blame them; few people can hack, and even fewer can hack things other than computers and phones. So, I was just gonna do it for them. I could have done it long ago. But I was trying to keep a low profile. I couldn't keep showing off. No one could know how powerful I really was.

I've hacked computers, phones, cameras, archives, lights, electrical grids, projectors, radios, stoplights, GPS systems, televisions, ATMs, vending machines, and subway controls. I've even hacked and reprogrammed the circuit boards of a microwave as a prank. But I haven't hacked a com system before. Better add it to the bucket list. *It won't be hard. I estimate this will only take … an hour. Let's see if I can do it in less than half.*

He turns right. Now dips, and … left! There! Through the cove—he sees the target. He takes a sharp turn around the corner—almost collides with an innocent bystander—oh! Is he going to make it? Yes! Score! I slammed the button on the stopwatch: 64 seconds. Squeaker came zooming to the edge of the tank and showed off his prize: the foam ring I had hidden among the columns of fake coral in the deep tank.

He had been getting better at "hide-and-seek-the-toy," and I sincerely hoped this was the final phase of his rehabilitation. Squeaker hadn't crashed for days. He was hanging out with the other dolphins. He was echolocating again. As far as I could tell, he was ready for release. Ready to go home.

"Good job, Squeaker! That was better," I praised, trying to wrestle the toy from him. "But let's try one more time, OK? Just for good measure." Squeaker suddenly let go. I fell back, landing hard on my butt. Squeaker splashed around, flicked his head back and forth, clicking and laughing at me. "Very funny, Squeaker. Hilarious," I muttered, feeling like a fool. Thank goodness no one was around. Even so, the fall hurt my pride more than anything. After the third time of *falling* for that trick, I should have learned.

After leading Squeaker through the gate to the side chamber, I closed the door and dove into the tank. Waves of echolocations hit me from all directions. Once the other dolphins were done inspecting this strange, finless, tail-less creature, they swam off, leaving me to hide the ring.

OK, I've already tried the cove and double arch … I thought I heard Squeaker whistling his unique call: *low, shrill-trill, down, shrill.* The sound waves were thick and warbled underwater. I wondered why he was calling, but decided to find out after I hid the ring. I couldn't hold my breath forever. *OK, not by the mini tunnel …* under the rock ridge! Yes, there. I wedged the foam into a small crevice and shot to the top, gasping for air.

"I was starting to worry you were sleeping with the fishes, you were under for so long." Startled, I whirled and found Marissa standing by the edge of the tank, a look of slight concern on her face. *So that was why Squeaker called.*

"Well, maybe I'm part fish." This was rewarded with a grin and head-shake from Marissa.

"Wouldn't surprise me," she mused. I finished pulling myself out of the tank.

"By the way, good timing," I said. "You've got to see this." Snatching the timer from the ground, I trotted over to the side tank. Squeaker clicked happily, swimming in a tight circle, impatiently waiting for me to open the gate. "Ready?" I whispered. Squeaker nodded his head vigorously; I laughed. "I keep forgetting you know that trick. Alright. Let's show Marissa what you can do."

With that, I unlatched the hinge. Squeaker was gone in an instant, fly-ing like a bolt of gray lightning, carving through the water as a bullet. I started the stopwatch, then joined Marissa at the edge of the tank to watch the action. Squeaker twisted and turned nimbly, shooting around corner after corner, methodically scouring the tank side to side, searching for the prize. When confronted with obstacles, he would cut out of the way just in the nick of time.

I shot a quick glance at Marissa. She was absolutely riveted, and the light in her eyes told me she was silently cheering our dolphin friend on.

Squeaker whistled shrilly, warning other members in the tank to move out of his way. His head turned back and forth, spraying sound waves all about, echolocating for all he was worth. It was almost as if Squeaker knew this was a test. Suddenly, he went straight down. Then, with a burst of water, Squeaker broke the surface, leaping high—in his mouth was the foam ring. I hit the stopwatch. When I saw the number, I smiled. Marissa leaned over to look.

"Fifty-seven seconds," she said, a grin creeping into her thoughtful expression. "That's about … a 70 percent improvement over the span of two days." She turned to me. "Would you say Squeaker is fully recovered? Is he almost ready for release?"

"I was hoping to ask you. You're the professional dolphin psychiatrist. I don't really know."

"Well, if you don't know, tell me what you think. Is Squeaker ready?"

I let my gaze drift to Squeaker, who was flipping the foam ring around in the air, chattering happily, as if recounting his conquest to the inanimate toy, singing out *low, shrill-trill, down, shrill* again and again, like a victory chant.

"I think … " *No, I feel it. I know.* "It's about time Squeaker got to go home. I think he's ready." Marissa smiled.

"Then we're both on the same page. It's time for the final test."

Done.

I sat back and inspected my work. It was almost disappointing: it had been so easy. I was hoping for a bit of a challenge. Not only had I hacked Brenton's com system, I had hacked the security cameras so I could know exactly where he was in the house at all times. The stage was set. The show could now begin. I glanced around the room. There was one problem: I couldn't possibly explain how I managed to hack the system so fast. If people started getting suspicious of me, it would all be over.

Doing nothing was dangerous, too. I couldn't sit here with footage from Brenton's estate on my screen. I had to pass the metaphorical hot potato, get rid of the bomb. And then, I knew. *Sonja. Give it to Sonja.* Another quick glance around the room proved that no one was watching me. Alright. Time to leave some bunny trails.

Stuffing the code and live feed into an enforced folder called "Brenton, A Gift for You, Take Credit for It," I put my plan into action. Carefully, with delicate precision, I started hacking V0RT3X computers one by one, dipping in and out of systems like a needle through fabric—the thread trailing behind me was the evidence, leaving a path wherever it went. Once I finished stringing computers like beads to the thread of the file's history, I singled out Sonja's laptop. In a few seconds, I had dashed in and out, leaving no trace—save for the new file sitting in the middle of her screen.

I didn't dare look, but out of the corner of my eye, I saw Sonja's head snap up. She turned to ask Jason something. He shook his head. She glanced around the room. To my horror, I sensed her gaze rest on me. After a solid chunk of time, she slowly returned to her screen. Within moments, her fingers were flying. Doubtless, she was scanning the folder for a Trojan Horse or some other nasty bug. By now, I had enabled the secondary camera in the corner of my screen and zoomed it in on Sonja. Eventually, she seemed to decide it was safe, because she stopped typing, reached for her mouse, and—*click*.

Her eyes went wide. She drew in a huge breath of surprise. She then used that breath to scare the living daylights out of everyone within ten feet of her.

"ENDER!!" she shrieked, jumping up and running off. It was so loud and sudden that Jason jumped—how I would imagine someone would jump if they sat on a thumbtack—and gave a little yelp of surprise.

Everyone looked up to see what the ruckus was about. After a hurried conversation with Ender, Sonja connected her computer to his and transferred the files. Ender's eyes grew wide as well. There was a stunned silence. Then a few keystrokes from Ender, and the main screen on the far wall displayed the long halls and grand rooms of Brenton's house.

"We're in," I heard Ender whisper. He turned to face the rest of the hackers. "Whoever did this, good work. Everyone get ready for the hack; you all know your places. Wait for my command. Until then, we wait."

Well, this was it: the final test. If Squeaker passed, he would be cleared for release. If he failed, it would be at least another month and a half till he could try again.

Squeaker fit into the "disoriented/disabled" category, so he would be doing the live fish test. It was similar to hide-and-go-seek-the-toy, but, unlike the game, these targets moved. The goal was to catch twelve fish within 75 seconds without crashing or getting distracted. Even though dolphins hunt in pods, solo hunting is still important.

All the other dolphins had been guided into the side tanks and Squeaker waited impatiently in the side chamber. A few people had gathered around, eager to see the outcome. Sophie and I sat by Squeaker, playing little games with him to keep him occupied. Soon, everything was in place and Marissa came over to join Sophie and me.

"Alright," she said. "It's almost time. Once the fish are in the tank, give me a heads-up countdown. You can open the gate and I'll start the stopwatch." We nodded and Marissa walked off. I turned to Squeaker.

"Hear that, buddy? You ready?" Squeaker thought for a moment, then decided to nod. Sophie giggled.

"I love it when he does that trick," she said.

"He just loves the attention," I said, pretending to direct the comment at Squeaker, who, oblivious to what I was saying, nodded again, making Sophie laugh even more.

"I'm gonna miss him," she said, stroking his side.

"Yeah. Me too," I whispered. Squeaker seemed to sense the subtle shift in my mood, because he looked at me and sang out that special call, as if doing so might reassure me. "Don't worry, Squeaker. You'll be seeing your friend again soon," I assured him.

"Jordan, look! It's time!" Sophie exclaimed.

Sure enough, Marissa was emptying a bucket of fat minnows into the tank. They momentarily scattered, then formed a small school, sticking close together. Everyone stopped their side conversations and waited for the action to start. Marissa and I made eye contact and she nodded. But as I reached for the latch—

"Sophie?" I asked.

"Yes?"

"Here. Would you like to do the honors?" She lit up. Nodding vigorously, she scrambled to the gate and waited. I knelt by Squeaker, who was chattering and splashing nervously. "This is your chance, Squeaker. You can do it." He froze, curiously watching my every move, as if each word I said was as important as the sun in the sky, or the water in the ocean, though he would never understand a thing I said. "All that stands between you and home is a few fish. Now, show 'em what you can do!"

"Ready," Sophie said. "Three, two, one, start!"

With that, she flung the gate open. For a millisecond, for a dumbfounding moment, Squeaker didn't move. Then, it was as if all his energy, focus, purpose, and willpower aligned right before our eyes. Because one moment he was there—the next he was gone. Squeaker shot forward. He was a sleek gray blur zooming through the water, like … a phantom, a shadow, a wisp of smoke, flying faster than light. His onset was so sudden that the fish didn't even see him coming. By the time the school scattered, he had already snapped up two.

In a flash, he turned tail and pursued a lone fish that had broken away from the group. It took a sharp turn around one of the coral pillars, but Squeaker was right behind it. A couple more seconds and it was over. Now the element of surprise was gone. The fish had dispersed. Some were regrouping. A couple had taken refuge among the rocks. But all were on guard now. Squeaker let out a shrill whistle, a call to war—then shot off.

Squeaker headed for a small cluster. At the last second, he turned and dashed between them and the decorated part of the tank, forcing them out into open water. Pouring on the speed, he swam circles around them, drawing the loops tighter, until he went straight through the center, grabbing two. The remaining fish scattered once again. Squeaker dove straight down after one, which brought his total to six. I checked my internal stopwatch. It had been around 32 seconds. If he kept up the pace, he could make it! *Come on, Squeaker! You can do it!*

Keeping low, Squeaker zoomed to the other side of the tank. He came up under another mini school and caught one. Almost all the minnows had hidden now. He started seeking. Methodically zipping through arcs and short tunnels, Squeaker flushed out three more minnows, bringing his total to ten. About twenty-five seconds remained.

Squeaker scared one out of hiding and chased it around a pillar, under a cove, and down to the bottom and back. It was a victory, but a costly one. Only fifteen seconds remained. He whistled, darting around the tank. Suddenly, he stopped and let out a loud, squealing squeak. Startled by this strange sound, a single minnow darted from a crevice. Squeaker shot after it. He was hot in pursuit, and with a final burst of speed, shot forward and grabbed it. Shouts of "Time!" rang out; Marissa smacked the stopwatch. After a moment, a smile spread across her face.

"One minute, nine seconds. Squeaker passed."

Cheers filled the air as my heart soared. Squeaker seemed to realize he had won, for he dove down, then came rocketing up, breaking the surface of the water with a mighty leap and triumphant whistle. After swimming some frenetic circles, he dashed over to Sophie and me, calling out every whistle-click combination imaginable.

"Hear that, Squeaker?" I said. "You're going home!" Squeaker contemplated this for a moment, sang out his call—*low, shrill-trill, down, shrill*—then nodded happily.

It was strange seeing V0RT3X like this. Everyone was still and silent, eyes glued to the main screen, watching Brenton's every move. Doubtless, I wasn't the only one whose fingers were itching to get to work, yet no one so much as touched their keyboard. Well, there was one exception.

Sonja would type like a maniac for a minute, then go completely still as she scanned her screen, devoting extreme concentration to her goal. After a moment, she would huff quietly in frustration, then type crazily once more, over and over. It was rather disconcerting.

I couldn't help but feel disappointed she didn't take credit for the hack. "Whoever did this, good work." *Whoever.* Not "Sonja." Ender said "whoever." *Why would she tell him it wasn't her when there was so much to gain?* I was lost in thought for a while, pondering her strange behavior, until Ender's call snapped me out of it.

"Get ready. This could be it."

Sure enough, Brenton was heading for the computer room, a folder under his arm and purpose in his step. He opened the door, closed it behind him, headed toward the desk ... and Ender started giving orders.

"This is it. Jason, make sure the scrambling program and camera are running well." Jason jumped up and got to work. "Firestorm, hack both the face cam and the screen share. Send the feed to the main screen. Once Brenton turns on the monitor, Sonja, I need you to send the virus email. Make sure it gets through. After that, stand by and take control of any problems that might arise. As long as I'm on that video chat, you're in charge." Sonja nodded and turned to her screen. "I need Aiden, Lenny, Mark, Daisy, and Firestorm as backup hackers. The rest of you know your places."

I woke my sleeping laptop. To my alarm, I noticed that my F1R3ST0RM programs were on alert. Something had spooked them. *I'll deal with that later.* I pretended to hack, clicking and typing away, but I was already in. After a convincing pause, I sent the footage to the screen; one side showed Brenton, the other showed his screen.

Within the minute, Brenton had turned on his computer. After a series of keystrokes from Sonja, the show began. On the other side of the camera, Brenton glanced at his computer. Confusion flitted across his face as a video chat popped up. He tried to close it. It remained the same. Out of the corner of my eye, I saw Jason pull on his headset, punch a few buttons, then motion to Ender ... *three, two, one* ... the camera blinked to life. Brenton sucked in a sharp gasp.

"Who are you?" he asked, a flicker of fear in his eyes. I pulled on my own headset to monitor the scrambling software as Ender began to speak.

"A friend," Ender replied simply. "I'm head of the vigilante hacking group known as Vortex. We've been trying to get in contact with you for a while. I'll cut to the chase. I'm here to help you."

"Help me? How?" Brenton asked.

"By returning what is rightfully yours." Ender paused, as if to ensure he had Brenton's full attention. "I want to help you reclaim the position of governor again. Because you didn't give it up; it was taken from you." Brenton's eyes went wide. "Correct me if I'm wrong, but you're being blackmailed by Gregory Damon, the political fraud currently holding your title."

Brenton sat back and thought about this strange turn of events. I noticed his arm move. An alert popped up on my screen. Brenton had tried to unlock his phone. But, thanks to my hacking, it wasn't functional, just like his com, mouse, keyboard, Bluetooth earpiece, alarm system, and electric locks. Ender must have seen the data on the screen, because he smiled.

"Sir, there's no use trying to contact the authorities. In fact, there's no way to contact anyone outside of your house at this moment. There is no satellite connection and no Wi-Fi. The electric locks in the doors have been engaged; no one can come in and you can't walk out. It's just you and me." The color drained from Brenton's face, and Ender continued. "You are bound by the law, and thus you cannot officially associate with us, I understand that. But think of me as Robin Hood. I'll help you with or without your blessing. Now, you can give me information to make things easier on our side, or we can continue to fight for you in the dark." There was a long silence. The gears were turning in Brenton's head; I could almost see the internal war raging in his mind.

"How do I know I can trust you?" he asked slowly. "How do I know you're not working for somebody, perhaps Damon himself?"

"In time I can find a way to prove it to you, but for now, you're just going to have to trust me. The longer this call is open, the more dangerous it is for my team. I will not push my luck much further. All we need to help is a bit of information, a starting point. How much you give is up to you." Eventually, after another long pause, Brenton spoke.

"What do you want to know?"

Ender smiled. "What is Damon using to blackmail you? I don't mean the situation. I mean: what is his evidence? What 'proof' does he have?" Brenton understood.

"Files. A while back, files went missing from my database. Very important files. They contained a wide variety of dangerous documents, such as personal records and history on … ”

I stopped listening. In that moment, I realized Sonja was staring right at me. She had been typing like a madwoman on her computer for the past couple minutes, but now she turned her attention to me. I didn't dare meet her gaze. *Why is she watching me like that? What is going on?*

"Can you get me the file names?" I heard Ender say, and I forced my mind to refocus. Brenton nodded.

"If I can use my computer again, I can find the empty spot in the archives." Ender glanced over at me. We made eye contact.

"I'll have one of my hackers search for it. Talk me through how to find it," Ender insisted. Brenton consented. A minute later, we had found the gap in the files. "We'll track down the documents and return them to you," Ender assured. "If any copies have been made, I will have them deleted. We'll provide some dirt on Damon and hand that over to you along with the files. Then you can present your case against him. We'll handle all the loose ends."

"I suppose … thanks is in order," Brenton admitted.

"Not necessary," Ender insisted, shaking his head. "Your service for this state is thanks enough. I will check back in with you from time to time. If you have any news for us, just type it into a document entitled 74D7Y5." Ender paused to allow Brenton to write down the code. "Don't tell anyone about this. If you do, I cannot guarantee my team will be able to help." A slow nod from Brenton caused Ender to smile. "I look forward to restoring things to the way they were. You have our respect, sir. Thank you for trusting us, at least a little. I'll prove that trust soon enough." Jason cut the feed, the video feed went black, and I pulled out of the hack. Ender pushed his hood off, stood, and grinned.

"We did it," he breathed, his smile widening. "Well done, all of you. Well done."

In just nine days, on Friday the 28th, Squeaker would be going home. It would be the final release before New Year's. I couldn't help but feel a little sad. Yes, I was ecstatic Squeaker was ready for release, but I was sad to see him go.

Marissa, Sophie, and I spent the remainder of the day by Squeaker's tank, playing little games with him and praising his hard work. Whenever he would get excited, he would sing out the mysterious name over and over, as if he knew he would soon see this important friend again.

Soon, Squeaker, soon. You'll be home again with your friends. Don't forget us.

Everyone was celebrating, in small ways or big. People chatted in little groups, some sat and hacked each other, and the younger ones ran around, playing a variety of games, basically underfoot. But I didn't mind. In fact, hardly noticed. All that mattered was me, Jason, and his marbles. We talked for a while, then played in almost utter silence, just enjoying the game. He seemed tired but content. There was a long stretch of peace.

At one point, something caught Jason's eye—something behind me—and he hesitated. I glanced over my shoulder. Sonja stood in the doorway, as quiet as a ninja. Who knows how long she had been watching us. Her stance was comfortable. It seemed to me that the spite had drained out of her. For a moment, none of us knew what to do. I decided to try redeeming myself, one more time.

"Come play marbles with us, Sonja."

I wasn't expecting her to take me up on it. I was expecting her to snort and stalk off, muttering something about how childish we were. But to my total surprise, she walked over, sat between Jason and me, snatched up the shooter marble, and knocked Jason's four remaining marbles from the ring before I could blink. Jason sighed, and after gathering the rogue marbles, started setting up a new game. Sonja sat back, pleased with her work. Then, without any explanation, she spoke.

"I thought you were a spy, Storm," she said quietly. My brain balked.

"Wait, what? You think I'm a spy? I'm not a spy! What makes you think that?"

Sonja regarded me calmly. "No, I don't 'think' you're a spy. I 'thought' you were a spy."

"Oh." I seemed to run out of words. "What made you change your mind?"

"I searched your computer."

"What?! You hacked me?"

She shook her head. "I didn't have to. Our laptops were already communicating because you're the one that hacked Brenton. You sent the live feed to my computer, but your computer was still the host. I just traced it back."

Right there, I thought I would have a heart attack. *She really did get into my computer! What did she see? How much does she know? No, no, no! I don't want to go, I don't want to have to leave this place! Please ...*

"You hacked Brenton?" Jason asked in awe. I nodded numbly.

Sonja continued. "I searched for the keyword C3RB3RU$, I searched for references to any of their crimes, emails to other hackers, contact with other organizations, and suspicious apps. Nothing. The only non-hacking programs on your laptop are art or music related. There is nothing that links you to Cerberus, or anyone else for that matter. You really are unattached." I had to fight to keep from sighing in deep relief. My F1R3ST0RM programs hid most of my data after all.

I had programmed my computer in such a way that if it was ever hacked or infected, it would hide all references to Laelaps, Teumessian, Edge, the FBI, and anything else that could put me in a dangerous position. The data was still there. It was just buried deep in the circuitry, waiting for me to dig it back out. Slowly, I nodded.

"It's just like I said. I don't really have any connections," I lied. "Why did you think I was a spy?" Sonja picked up a stray marble and fingered it as she talked.

"You're just downright suspicious. I guess it's something in your personality, or ... mine. From the start, I found your introduction to Vortex a little strange. For a hacker with such skills to be unattached seemed too far-fetched. A couple weeks after you arrived, I noticed some money disappear from our overall account. I didn't think anything of it until about a month later; I picked up on a connection running between Vortex and a signature Cerberus signal." Jason suddenly sat bolt upright.

"You didn't tell me that part!" he exclaimed.

I turned to him. "Jason, you knew about all this?" I asked.

"Yeah. I told her you weren't a spy," he muttered, directing the comment at Sonja in an I-told-you-so sort of way.

"Well," Sonja mumbled, "can you blame me?"

I shook my head. "Honestly, no, I can't," I said, then thought for a moment, realization dawning. "But just because I'm not a spy ... doesn't mean there isn't one." Jason huffed a sigh and I turned to him. He put his head down, slowly shaking it back and forth.

"I don't think there is a traitor among us. Honestly, I trust almost everyone here like family. We shouldn't be so suspicious of each other."

"Look at the evidence, Jason," Sonja said. "I know what you mean, how you feel. But we need to think about this logically."

"Have you shared your suspicions with Ender yet?" I asked.

"No," Sonja said. "I don't want him to start investigating. If we're not careful, the little Cerberus rat might get spooked and do something drastic. They're killers. We're not. For the most part, the best hand-to-hand fighters we have only took karate in the third grade or something lame like that." *You should see me in action*, I thought. "If Cerberus attacked our base, we would fall," Sonja said.

"Then what are you going to do?" I asked.

Sonja sighed. "I don't really know. I guess I'll just take things one step at a time, watch for signs and clues. Whoever it is will slip up eventually." She turned toward me and frowned. "Don't breathe a word to anyone."

"I won't. I'll keep my eyes and ears open, though." *She's entrusting me with this information.*

Sonja seemed satisfied with this and turned to Jason. "We're going home tonight, just as a precaution. Even though things went well with Brenton, I don't want to take any chances." Jason nodded, packed up the marbles, and stood, a disappointed look in his eyes. "Try to keep out of trouble, Storm. Glad you're not a spy, and sorry I thought so," Sonja said, looking back over her shoulder as she and Jason started off.

"Sonja, wait." Sonja turned. "I'm sorry too. About what I said to you a couple weeks ago." A tiny, soft flake of emotion escaped, and for a moment, the right corner of Sonja's lips turned up in a smile. Then she hid it away again.

"We're square again?" she asked.

I nodded. "Square and fair."

E ... A ... D ...G ... B ... E ... done. I pulled my fingers across the guitar strings and smiled.

"Still in tune," I announced happily.

"It's always in tune," Samuel said, chuckling. "I don't know why you always check. I bet you practice before practice. That's what it is."

"Wouldn't surprise me," Cassie agreed. Lia, who was sitting on the piano bench beside Cassie, nodded and smiled.

"Forgive me for enjoying music so much. I didn't know it was a crime," I said, chuckling.

Every Wednesday night there was a prayer meeting at church. A couple years back, I stopped going to the main gathering to help with the youth group. I love children. I love to work with them, talk with them, sing with them, play with them, be with them! And if it hadn't been for the youth leaders at this very church years ago, I never would have come to Jesus. I wouldn't be here now. So, if even one of these kids heard the gospel while they were under this roof, if even just one came to Christ, I could want nothing more.

Samuel, Cassie, Lia, and I made up the praise team for our church's youth group. Cassie is the lead singer, Lia the pianist, and Samuel and I the guitarists.

Cassie's spunk is the fuel that gives us an energy boost when we need it. She's never afraid to speak her mind, yet seems to have her finger on the pulse of everyone's emotions. I cannot think of a time when she's hurt anybody's feelings.

Lia is a timid girl with a sweet, thoughtful personality. She's shy more often than not, yet secure in who she is. She's unshakable in her trusting love for others. I doubt she's ever thought a judgmental thing about another human being.

Samuel is a gentle soul. He also has a quiet and patient demeanor, and wisdom beyond his years. He and I have been friends longer than the others. He went to the same high school Dylan, Chloe, and I went to.

Also, Samuel is in love with Chloe. He's loved her since the day he met her. But as I said: he's a quiet, gentle soul. He doesn't speak unless spoken to. Especially if it's around Chloe.

She passed, chatting with the other leaders. He watched her go, a quiet sigh summing up his mood.

"Go over," I whispered, nudging him.

"What? No, Jordan. Not now."

"If not now, when? You need a bit of a push, so I'm pushing you. Do me a favor and take the fall!"

"I'm not sure I'm brave enough," he muttered, frowning slightly. I shook my head.

"You're brave enough. You're gonna have to talk to her eventually. Carrying her books for her back in ninth grade isn't exactly a confession of love. You gotta give her more to go on than that. She won't know you care until you tell her." Samuel frowned again.

"I don't know. Maybe it's just me, but I feel like she has a well-hidden crush of her own?" I thought on this for a moment.

"I know Chloe pretty well and I'm practically positive she's not seeing anyone. You're just nervous. No more excuses."

"Hey Jordan! Sam!" Cassie called. "What are you two going on about over there?" Samuel froze, but I came up with a save.

"We're discussing the strange ways of the human heart and mind."

"Well, you can debate psychology later. Lia and I are ready to run through the songs for tonight," she said.

"Alright." I turned to Samuel. "Try talking to her later. Just walk up and say hi. You know Chloe. There's a good chance she'll take it from there."

"OK. Maybe," he said, smiling a bit despite himself.

I sat around a little longer, but soon remembered that, other than Jason, Sonja, and a few of the younger kids, I didn't have any real friends at V0RT3X. So, after that depressing realization, I packed up my computer and left without a word to anyone. Even after I got back to the apartment, I was feeling an intense lack of purpose. It was too early to go to bed, but it was a little too late to do much else. It had been a full day, yet it felt like something was missing, as if I had skipped dinner or forgotten to check my email or missed something else entirely routine.

Thinking through my day, I wondered what was different, and realized: *Oh, I didn't see Jordan today. I was at V0RT3X when he got off work.* Jordan had been dropping by more often, and to be honest, this introvert was actually enjoying it. True, it wasn't necessarily a daily thing, and I'd been gone before, but tonight it was weighing on my mind. Perhaps he was on the balcony. I went out to check. Not only was he not there, I noticed the lights weren't on. Now that I thought about it, I realized Jordan was gone most Wednesday nights. No, wait—every Wednesday night. Normally, this discovery wouldn't have held much importance. But I was curious. *Where are you, Jordan?*

After a moment of thought, I pulled out my phone and started to hack his. It didn't take long. He actually wasn't very far, only about seven or so blocks away. Suddenly, I had an inexplicable need to know. Before I could think twice, my feet were on the move.

It wasn't long before the building was in sight. I approached from the back and couldn't get a fix on where I was. A glance at my screen showed the point of entry closest to Jordan's phone was a side door. I likely wouldn't be in his line of sight. I slipped in before I could convince myself otherwise. The first sensation that met me was music. I took a quick glance around, slightly confused by my surroundings.

I was at the back of a medium-sized room. Rows of chairs swept across the center of the floor; almost all of them had occupants standing in front of them. It would seem that most everyone was a child, mostly high schoolers and middle schoolers, with a couple adults scattered here and there. The lights were slightly dimmed, drawing my attention to a bright screen toward the front, words projected on the surface, reminding me of the music that filled the air. I was about to focus in on the lyrics when I spotted Jordan.

He was at the front of the room on a slightly raised platform along with two girls and another guy. The foremost girl seemed to be leading the singing. Her big, brown doe eyes were shining, and her super curly beige hair was shoulder length and bobbed with her as she bounced on her toes in time with the music. The second girl sat at an electric piano, a calm smile on her face as her fingers flew across the keys. Her long, straight black hair, dark eyes, and skin spoke of Asian ancestry. The third member, the guy, played a guitar like Jordan, though his seemed slightly different. Bright, grayish-blue eyes shone, and light brown caramel hair bobbed as he sang alongside Jordan.

Jordan seemed to be radiating light and joy in their purest, most concentrated forms. For him, I don't think the rest of the world existed in that moment. My ears picked through the sounds. I've heard Jordan play guitar before, but I've never heard him sing. It was warm and beautiful. Then I started listening to the words.

Marana tha! Come, oh Lord;
your children want to know You more.
We gather here to bless Your name,
our hearts will never be the same!
For I sing of a love that's greater than me,

love that broke the curse and set me free.
Abounding, amazing, unending grace!
I count the days till I see His face.
Marana tha! Come, oh Lord;
your children want to know You more.
We gather here to bless Your name,
our hearts will never be the same!
It's finally over, the fight is done.
It is finished, and the war is won ...

Oh, how cute. I had stumbled into a church. Carefully, quietly, I turned and slipped back out the door, feeling almost sad, almost angry, and, almost envious of the people who had won the love of their beloved God. I had only gone a few steps from the door when the clouds opened up. Cold, fat raindrops splashed on my head, urging me to return to the dry indoors—back to the church. But I refused. I wanted nothing to do with this. I didn't want to be anywhere near the God who had shredded my life so mercilessly. Thunder boomed. I looked up at the sky and glared.

"You just can't leave me be, can you?" I asked angrily, heavy with hurt. "You've taken *everything* from me, and that's not enough! You're always trying to remind me. I've seen what you allow to happen to those who love you. I want nothing to do with it. Stop imposing such guilt and sorrow on me. Just leave me my fragile memories ... "

A thousand conversations suddenly exploded through my mind: of my family, of Ashley—dear Ashley—trying to explain God's love to me. For minute after long minute, the noise dragged on, a storm raging in my mind and the world around me. Then the images came. The images that haunt me. The images that make me question the all-inclusive "love" I've heard about all my life.

Because, where—in deep piles of ash and dark puddles of blood—does one find love?

THE JOURNAL OF
AMBER MARIE GIBSON

December 19, Wednesday

It's been a crazy day. First, VoRT3X successfully contacted ex-governor James Brenton. Sounds like he's not going to raise the alarm on us yet. We know what we're looking for, so it's all downhill from here. I'd say Brenton will be back in power within a month.

All of this is thanks to yours truly. I sincerely hope these hackers don't catch on to me. I did it anonymously, yet "The Ninja" figured out I'm the one who did it. (I won't give real hackers' names here. Sorry cops.)

Ninja used the connection between our computers to trace it all back to me. She apparently thought I was a spy from C3RB3RU$ and searched my computer. But my programs hid all reference to my real work, so I remain safe. Problem is, that means there might be a real spy at VoRT3X. Ninja, "Marbles," and I are going to try and figure out who it is. If this is what it looks like, we could be in hot, deep water.

"Aether" doesn't know about all of this, and Ninja says it should stay that way for now. To be honest, I feel bad about hiding things like this. Aether is the leader, after all. Is this considered mutiny? Even though Ninja is 2nd in command, I don't want to get in trouble with Aether. This might be a very bad idea.

A memory weighs heavily on my mind: Jessica was blinded by desperation and lies, so she sold me out. I wonder ... what about the spy at VoRT3X? What would cause them to sell out *their own team? Do they fully realize what they're doing? Also … what does "mar-rah-nah-the" mean?*

<u>Days of Punishment Remaining</u>: 232

CHAPTER 23

Santa Barbara, The Flying Turtle
Thursday, January 24, 10:47 A.M.

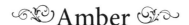 Amber

Christmas came and went like a dream. It didn't feel very Christmassy. Probably because the outside thermometer boasted a whopping 60 degrees. Since Chloe and Dylan were with their mom and Matt was out of town with his family, the only other friends I had left were either at V0RT3X or one floor below my apartment. Needless to say, Jordan was the only qualified companion. It would seem that he felt the same way. I didn't mean to crash his Christmas, and I hope I didn't ruin it, but I spent most of the day with him. I was just going to chill alone at home, but Jordan interjected other plans. He didn't have anyone to talk to, and I didn't really have anything to do … so he came and found me.

I knew Christmas is especially important to Christians, so I decided to hold up my end of the deal I'd made the day I got grounded: I would hear Jordan out. Delighted, he talked for a while; thus, I was subjected to the retelling of the Christmas story all over again. Oddly, I didn't mind much. Perhaps it was because it had been so long. Perhaps it was because it reminded me of my family. Either way, it left me thinking.

Things had fallen back into a safe, predictable pattern. I spent most of my time at V0RT3X, hanging with my friends, surfing, drawing, or doing something else relatively tame. Especially on Thursdays. I get about as excited about Thursdays as typical people do about Fridays. It's my "Be a Normal Person Day."

This week, thankfully, Chloe had chosen the Flying Turtle as our meeting place. In other words, I had a chance to get coffee before we hit the waves. On top of that, the fun was starting earlier than normal. Jordan and Dylan had today and tomorrow off, Chloe could get time off on a whim, Matt did most of his work from home, and I was a hacker. *Life is good.*

But I've also hit a bad night spell. I almost got through two entire months without one of these phases. It's been eleven days since I last slept well. Between Brenton's return to the governorship, searching for the spy at V0RT3X, fighting off C3RB3RU$ attacks, fretting over my grounding, hiding my true colors from the others, suffering from haunting memories, and the ceaseless nightmares ... Needless to say, I'd been a little less harsh on myself, which was why I was showing up at The Flying Turtle early: I needed caffeine to start kicking in in advance.

The lovely, warm scents met me at the door. I made my decision, got my order, and looked for a cozy spot to sit. But my mind hitched as it caught on a familiar face. Matt. Matt was early, too. He typed something into his laptop, clicked a few buttons, then sighed and sat back. I made my way over to him.

"Hey, Matt." He glanced up, a faint smile painting his face.

"Hi, Amber. Why are you here so early?"

I held up my coffee cup. "Needed a head start on the energy boost. How about you?"

"Well, I was in the area, and I knew this was where we'd be meeting today. Thought I'd try and fix a client's system in my spare time." He pointed at his laptop. "You'd be surprised how good the Wi-Fi is here," he added jokingly. As if to protest, the computer beeped. Matt glanced at the screen and sighed, muttering under his breath; he typed away once more. I leaned over to get a better look.

"What do you do, exactly? I knew you're with that tech firm, but this almost looks like code testing. Are you a programmer?"

Matt shrugged. "Sort of. My official label is system analyst, but that's almost meaningless. What I really do is, well ... at times, a little bit of everything. Basically, when a system goes squirrelly, I link my computer to the client's over a cyber connection. I figure out exactly what's wrong, find the source of the problem, and shut it down." He frowned at his screen. "This one's had me stumped for days."

I inspected the scrolling data on the screen. Something seemed vaguely familiar, as if I'd solved this puzzle before. Suddenly, little lights started going off in my head, and before I could stop myself ...

"Matt, can I try?"

"Sure, have at it. Doubt you could do any damage. But—" I had stepped to his side, taken a seat, and spun the laptop in front of me. My fingers were already flying. "I thought you were a graphics ... designer ... whoa." Matt leaned closer, watching in awe as I typed command after command, divide and conquer, bit by piece by line.

I knew what the problem was. It was a type of virus I liked to call a shifter bug. It doesn't move unless you do. When you catch one piece of the code and set it right, another piece changes. One thing triggers another. Its weakness is its perfect randomness. There is actually a pattern by which it modifies the code. Extremely complex though it may be, it is a pattern nonetheless. Once I found it, I could flip it, push the dominoes the other way, and send the damage back to base to destroy its core. After a minute of intense programming and a small amount of what might border on hacking, I hit home and the virus disintegrated. I sat back, feeling good about my work—until I noticed the look of disbelief on Matt's face.

"How did you ... ?"

"I, uh," I stammered, realizing my foolish error. "I used to be ... " I sighed. "I'm a bit of a computer geek. Programmer, beta tester, and the like," I muttered, then awkwardly gestured at the laptop. "Those shifter bugs are a real pain in the neck." *Please, buy it. Please buy it, please ...* Matt stared at me wide-eyed.

"That was amazing. No offense, but you chose the wrong career path."

I forced an innocent smile. "No offense taken." My mind grasped frantically at tiny straws for a safe conversation topic. "So, how did you know your calling was to be a system analyst?" To my surprise, Matt chuckled a bit.

"For the longest time, I didn't know. I didn't even know what I was going to study when I first got to college. I only liked tech and numbers. Believe it or not, Jordan helped me figure it all out."

"You went to college with Jordan? You went to West Mont, too?" I asked, intrigued.

"No. Stanford." I almost choked on my coffee.

"Stanford University!? OK, I knew you two were smart, but—Stanford!" Matt looked bashful. "But ... I thought Jordan went to West Mont."

"Oh, he did. But he went to Stanford to finish parts of his degree. It was only for a couple of years."

"Still," I insisted, "why doesn't he ever mention it? Lots of people don't even dare dream of getting in there."

"You know how much he hates attention," Matt pointed out. *True.* "Anyway, Jordan and I were roommates." Matt noticed the surprise on my face and laughed. "Yeah. Roommates. I don't exactly know how we got paired. At first, he got on my nerves, he was such a chatterbox." Matt smiled. "But then I started listening. It wasn't long before we were friends. Best one I've ever had. He led me to Christ. I had been thinking about coming to Santa Barbara for a while, and it sounds crazy, but I followed Jordan back. Decided he was the first friend worth keeping."

I nodded slowly. "I know what you mean. He annoyed me half to death when I first got here, yet somehow managed to endear himself to me anyway. Kind, patient, fun—" I grinned. "He's got sunshine coming out his ears. He's always so happy." Matt seemed to almost choke. Whatever I said cracked him up. "What are you laughing at?" I asked. Matt caught his breath.

"The mental picture that brings up!" For a moment, I didn't understand. Then I saw it for myself and started laughing. *Sunshine coming out his ears!* We laughed so hard we didn't even notice the others come in.

"What are you two laughing at?" I looked up, and through tears of laughter, saw Chloe, Dylan, and Jordan looking at us curiously. Our answers clashed midair.

"Nothing," I said.

"The joke of the century," Matt replied. He and I made eye contact. Matt pretended to zip his lips shut, and we burst into laughter again.

Eventually, Matt and Amber stopped laughing. I was dying to know what they were talking about, but they wouldn't say. We all chatted for a while. Chloe recounted the hilarious firing and almost instant rehiring of a coworker. I talked about Squeaker's release, how happy he was to be free, and how teary-eyed Sophie got. Dylan and I finally told the others about the whole funding ordeal at Ocean Front, about how everything almost hit the floor, how the V0RT3X hackers saved us, and how Brenton was governor again. Then we all talked about the scandals with Damon and the huge legal firefight over it.

Over the next half hour or so, I noticed Amber tapping her fingers to some silent tune in her head, even quietly humming occasionally. It was only in tiny bits and pieces, but I felt I should recognize it. It seemed hauntingly familiar. *There she goes again. That tune, I know it. But I can't place it. Ah, think Jordan, think …* I turned up with nothing. *Never mind, I'll figure it out later.* I tried to focus on what Matt was saying.

"… should have seen it. Amber's a cyber genius!" At this, Amber first went white, then blushed profusely.

"It was just some geeky thing I learned to do in high school. It's nothing, really."

"Seriously, Amber, it was amazing," Matt said. "I'll bet none of those hackers dare come after you. It'd sure come as a blow to their ego when you beat them at their own game." Amber must have been totally embarrassed about the whole thing, because she didn't laugh like the rest of us.

Soon, we were ready to hit the beach. Competitions were about two months away, and the excitement was growing steadily—as was the need to practice. As we split up to retrieve our boards, I heard it again as Amber passed me—she was quietly humming that same uncannily familiar tune. *I really do know that tune. But from where?*

That was such a close call. I knew Matt was just teasing, but the conversation had been too close to home for comfort. *Come on, Amber. Keep a low profile, will you?* I silently scolded myself while waiting for waves with the others. The whole event must have rattled my subconscious, because I was absentmindedly typing on my surfboard as if it were a keyboard.

For I sing of a love that's greater than me … love that broke the curse and set me— I stopped.

I couldn't get that strange song out of my head. I still didn't know what "mar-rah-nah-the" meant. (I had tried to look it up, but must have spelled it horribly wrong, because autocorrect changed it to "manta ray.") I frowned, mind churning, and my fingers started flying again, typing out the lyrics to the song, spelling the strange word differently each time.

Chloe came up beside me. "Whatch'ya thinking about, Amber? You have that serious look on your face, that look you get when you're thinking hard," she teased. I glanced over at her and an idea came to me. *Oh, just ask. She might know.* After a moment of internal debate, I nodded slowly.

"Do you, by any chance … know what 'mar-rah-nah-the' means?" I asked.

Chloe seemed surprised. "Marana tha. It was an expression used by early Christians, meaning 'Come, Lord.' Paul says it at the end of the letter of First Corinthians." Chloe looked extremely interested in this new development and watched me closely. I then realized I had just landed myself in a very uncomfortable conversation … when something behind Chloe caught my attention. My heart almost stopped. Apparently, my fear was evident.

"Amber? Why are you looking at me like—" I pointed beyond Chloe, trying to keep my arm and voice from quivering.

"A fin. I just saw a fin. Big, gray, sleek. Heading this way, fast." My mouth had gone dry, and I tried to swallow. "Shark. I think it was a shark."

We all felt it. Something moved in the water, like a cloud passing over the sun and casting a shadow, except … beneath the surface. Beneath us. Everyone scrambled on top of their boards, trying to keep their feet out of the water.

"What was that?" Dylan asked, eyes wide with alarm.

"Shark," I whispered, losing grip on the fear as it spilled into my voice. "I saw a fin." Jordan slowly reached forward, placing his hand ever so lightly on top of the water, as if he could feel the shark beneath the ripples. He tipped his head to one side.

"Um, guys, I don't—" Suddenly, in a flash, Jordan's tether jerked and went taut. An instant later—he was gone. Something had pulled him under. For a terrible heartbeat in time, no one could move. Panic welled up inside me, yet I was frozen. Chloe opened her mouth to scream, when … Jordan broke the surface. "It's OK! It's OK!" He was actually laughing. He glanced down and his grin widened. Something was circling him under the water. Jordan patted the water with his hand, and up shot … a *dolphin*. Dylan lit up.

"No way!" he breathed as he carefully slipped into the water and swam closer. "Squeaker?" Dylan asked in awe. Jordan beamed.

"It's Squeaker!"

"He came back! Why?" Dylan asked, gently stroking the top of the dolphin's head. Jordan shrugged. He was beaming, and didn't seem to have words. Chloe slipped off her board and went over beside Dylan.

"It's not afraid of us?" she whispered, as if worried she might spook it.

"Seems any friend of the animal whisperer is a friend of Squeaker's," Dylan said.

"Who's the animal whisperer?" I asked, slowly lowering myself into the water to join Chloe. But the moment I asked, I knew. *Jordan.* Sure enough, Jordan had a sheepish look on his face.

"Me. It's just a silly nickname Dylan came up with." Squeaker seemed to notice the rest of us. He swam over to Matt—who had moved beside Jordan—and began circling him.

"What's he doing?" Matt asked.

"He's just checking you out," Jordan explained, smiling. "That's how he decides if he likes you or not."

A moment later, Squeaker returned to the surface, clicked and whistled a few times, then briefly rubbed his nose against Matt's chest. Squeaker next zoomed over to Chloe. After circling her, he popped up and waited expectantly. After a nudge from Dylan, she slowly reached forward and petted Squeaker on the head. Both mammals were delighted. Soon Squeaker came over to me, looping tight circles from my feet to my stomach. Surely I should be elated to be this close to a dolphin out in nature, but for some reason ... I felt rather nervous. Squeaker seemed to read this unusual reaction, watching me curiously.

"Just hold out your hand, Amber," Jordan gently encouraged.

Carefully, slowly, I reached forward. Squeaker whistled, startling me and making me jump a bit, thus causing me to withdraw a little. But Squeaker closed the distance and pushed his head up under my hand.

"He likes you," Jordan said, smiling. At the sound of his voice, Squeaker turned and swam for Jordan, clicking happily all the way. "Make some new friends, buddy?" To my complete surprise, Squeaker nodded. Jordan laughed. "I don't have any fish. But good trick." Squeaker launched into a long monologue of squeaks, squeals, clicks, and whistles, then jerked his head toward open ocean. Suddenly, Chloe gasped.

"Look!" There, not far away, were more dolphins.

"He found his pod," Dylan whispered. Squeaker turned his attention back to Jordan, looked him right in the eye, and whistled: *low, shrill-trill, down, shrill.*

"You found your friend?" Jordan asked, excited. Squeaker looked at him a moment longer, then called it again. Suddenly, I realized.

"It's you." All eyes turned to me. "I think Squeaker's saying your name."

Before Jordan could process this, Squeaker nuzzled up against him—*low, shrill-trill, down, shrill*—and then turn and swam toward his pod. We all watched him go, awed at everything we had just witnessed. There was a long silence.

"Goodbye, Squeaker," Jordan whispered, a bittersweet joy in his eyes.

The day's surprises weren't over. When I got home, I had a message from Chloe.

New Message: Chloe

Chloe
Jordan, Amber asked me what "Marana tha" was this afternoon.

Jordan
She did?! Where did she hear it?

Chloe
I don't know. I thought you might.

Jordan
Nope, not a clue. Oh! She's been humming a tune all afternoon -- that's it! That song! Did she come to Wednesday night prayer meeting?

Chloe
Not that I know of. I didn't see her … ?

Jordan
Neither did I.

Chloe
This is all really odd. I have to go, but if you figure it out, text me, OK?

Jordan
Will do.

I put down my phone, pondered this unusual turn of events and, despite the strangeness of it all, came away with one thought: *I haven't been praying for her like I should.* I decided it was time to change that.

CHAPTER 24

Ocean Front Rescue
Thursday, March 7, 11:15 A.M.

Jordan

Weeks flowed calmly by, slipping away like a creek in a still autumn forest. It was almost as if change itself swam away when Squeaker did. Every day was like the last: semi-predictable, yet not too tame. Finally, at long last, all was as it should be.

Ocean Front was constantly abuzz. Thankfully, though, it didn't affect me much. With all sorts of people from the scientific community stopping by daily, publicity was skyrocketing, and Ocean Front was better off than ever. I was glad no one had noticed me. I didn't want to get dragged back into the chaos; I was perfectly happy with routine. But today was a little boring.

"Hey, Jordan." Dylan dropped into the chair next to mine. "What's up?"

I shrugged. "Not much. Waiting for Sophie to finish her chores and wishing for some excitement. How about you?"

Dylan sighed. "I'm bored. There are too many smart, efficient people working this shift today, you know? I can't find much to do."

That made me chuckle a bit. "Yeah. I know what you mean. I'm glad most of the original employees are back, don't get me wrong, but—" I never got to finish that sentence.

"Jordan! Jordan! *Jordan!*" I looked up to see Sophie barreling down the corridor toward us, almost slipping as she came to a skidding halt.

"What is it?" I noticed she was soaked. *This doesn't look good.* Sophie shut her eyes tight in a cringe.

"I messed up. I messed up big time."

Another computer cleared. I nudged Sonja. She leaned over, inspected my screen, and shrugged. After scanning the room, she typed something. A message popped up on our secure chat page. *"Try Mariah. I'll mark Jackson off the list."* I nodded and returned to my laptop.

We had been searching for the spy for more than a month. Nothing. Sonja kept an eye on the others and alerted me of any suspects. I would hack them, search for dangerous keywords or strange activity, and report back to Sonja. Of course, no one noticed they'd been hacked. I'm better than that.

Last week, there had been a glitch in the database; the main system was frozen for one minute and twelve seconds. When it unfroze, more than four hundred dollars was missing from the database. Also, the connection between V0RT3X and C3RB3RU$ was gone. We had to find the spy, soon. Sonja said that if anything more happened, she would share her suspicions with Ender. Things were getting real.

My fingers started flying as I singled out Mariah's computer when a blur of teal caught my eye. I stopped for a split-second to admire the colors. Hacking with nail polish is really distracting.

Chloe had convinced me to go shopping with her Saturday. She said it'd be the perfect time to help me find a good wet suit for competitions. For lack of something better to do, I agreed. But Chloe's definition of shopping was totally different from mine. For her, it had nothing to do with food, art supplies, or new earbuds. For her, shopping included things like getting a manicure/pedicure, having our hair done in a new style, looking for cute outfits, shoe shopping, makeup, accessories—the list went on and on. It would seem she enjoyed all of it; she tried stuff on just for fun. I was so out of my comfort zone. But—Heaven forbid I admit it out loud—*it was fun.* I even found something I liked. A lacy green dress. Yes, a dress. I scolded myself afterward; it wasn't practical. But … it was pretty. I chided myself. *Focus, Amber, focus.*

I cannot believe I was wishing for some action a minute ago. I take it all back. This is a disaster. The deep tank was full of animals. Nothing unusual there. But there was more than one kind of animal. Now we have a problem.

"Sophie, what did you do?!" Dylan asked in shock. I stared in disbelief at the dolphins and seals frolicking side by side in the water. Sophie gave a stressed, sad sigh.

"I was supposed to measure the pH in the dolphin tank and check it against the tank's data board. I was waiting for the meter thing to read when one of the dolphins came and splashed me and I dropped the meter. I tried to reach it before it sank, but I almost lost my balance and grabbed the gate to keep from falling in. I accidently grabbed the latch ... " She trailed off. I leaned over and peered into the water. Sure enough, at the bottom of the tank sat the pH reader, a big blue "8.1" on its screen.

"Well, pH is good," I muttered. Sophie buried her head in her hands.

"I'm so sorry. I'm so, so sorry! I didn't mean to mess things up ... "

"It's alright, Sophie," I assured her. "It was just an accident, and thankfully dolphins aren't hostile to seals and vice versa."

"What do we do?" she asked. "Not all of the dolphins answer to the whistle yet! They all eat fish, so we can't bribe them with food—some of them might not even be hungry!"

"Seals eat crustaceans, dolphins don't," Dylan pointed out.

I nodded. "That's a starting point." My mind churned. "And some of the dolphins do answer to the sliding whistle. The seals might answer to the silent whistle, I'm not sure." An idea formed. I shot a teasing glance at Dylan. "You still want something to do?"

I sat back, sighing in frustration. Mariah wasn't the spy. This was absolutely pointless. We needed more to go on than just hunches. I decided I might as well go find Sonja and tell her it was time for plan B—whatever that was.

As I scanned the room for my ninja friend, I noticed something of interest. Jason was up on his perch in the shelving unit, computer on his lap and headset on his head—nothing unusual there—but as I watched, he held a notebook up to the camera and looked a bit sheepish. There was a giant heart drawn on the page, the words "MISSING YOU" in the middle, along with packed lines of illegible writing down the side.

Oh, my goodness. Jason ... has a crush? This was an intriguing turn of events. I crept over to the bottom of the ladder and quietly scaled it. Slowing near Jason's platform, I peeked over the edge. Sure enough, on the other side of the screen was a girl. She knelt, legs tucked daintily beneath her, in front of her computer, sketching away on a notepad of her own.

Her short, choppy, raven black hair had dark green patches dyed in it. Not many girls can pull that style off, but she was an exception. Her mini, plaid skirt and leggings reminded me of school uniforms, but she looked about Jason's age. Surely she had graduated. All this gave me the impression she was either an anime enthusiast, an artsy rebel, or perhaps she simply didn't know how to match clothes. She picked up her notepad. Before she could get it flipped around, she saw me and her eyes went wide. Jason quickly followed the girl's line of sight.

"Storm!" Jason shrieked, mortified, slamming a button on his computer. The video chat went down. "How long have you been here?!"

"Was that your girlfriend?" I asked, climbing onto the platform, ignoring his question. "She's adorable." Jason looked like he was going to shrivel up and die; he had gone white, but now was blushing redder and brighter than the crimson heart I had seen on the notebook. He was stuttering, incoherent. It was kind of cute.

"It's … well … um … she's just … It's, we—"

"Don't worry, Jason. I won't tell Sonja, if that's what you're worried about." For a moment, he just stared at me, horrified. Then he breathed a huge sigh of relief.

"OK, thanks. Alright, yeah. Please. She'd kill me … just, don't tell her. It wouldn't go well." He was still stumbling clumsily over words. Suddenly, Sonja popped up from the ladder.

"Hey, geeks," she said. "Whatch'ya talking about? Don't tell who *what*?" Jason looked stricken, but I quickly filled in some gaps.

"Don't tell Mariah how bad her security system is. She brags about it so much, but it's actually nothing more than a flimsy wall of children's building blocks." I casually nudged the open notebook into the corner with my foot as I spoke.

"I take it she's clean?" Sonja asked. I nodded. "Another dead end. Dang it. I'm ready to peg someone. Keep trying, Storm. We'll find them eventually. I started a list on our secure chat. I'll take the odd, you take the even." Sonja started to leave, then gave Jason a funny look. "What's wrong with you? You look like you swallowed a lobster." Jason shrugged, trying to hide his nervousness.

"Rage-quit my game a minute ago," he murmured. After a moment of extreme scrutiny, Sonja muttered "nerd" and dropped down the ladder. I leaned over the edge and watched her strut off.

"Gaming. Good save, Jason," I smiled.

Things were actually going pretty well. First we opened the dolphin enclosure and tried the whistle. A few responded and we shut them in the tank; same tactic with the seals. Now to wrangle up the remaining critters.

Dylan and Sophie were coaxing the seals along, one by one, with crustaceans in the long nets. I stood by the dolphin enclosure, trying to mimic the dolphins' names with the slider whistle, bribing them with fish as they got closer. It was slow going, but it was working. The trick was getting the gates open and shut fast enough.

"No! Get back here!" Sophie scrambled along the edge of the tank after a seal, waving her food net around. It barked and continued to tease her, swimming around and around the tank, just out of her reach. Dylan and I couldn't help but laugh.

"Hey, Dylan!" I called. "You bored anymore?"

"Nope," he said. "This is actually kinda fun. Slightly hard, but fun."

"Very hard!" Sophie corrected as she ran by, making us laugh more. Out of the corner of my eye, I saw Tristan enter the room.

"Jordan," he said. "A quick word?"

"Sure," I replied, walking over to him, hoping I could keep Sophie out of hot water. "Hey, Tristan. Look, the tank … it was an accident, and—"

"The tank?" Tristan asked, puzzled, leaning to the side for another look. A moment later, he smiled. "Oh, yes. I see." He shook his head and chuckled. "That's not why I'm here. I'm here, because … well, it would seem that everyone has forgotten that it was your idea that we look into the fault line. It's been a while, and no one has given you any recognition. It doesn't seem quite fair. Should I remind them?"

I thought about this for a moment, then looked back at Sophie and Dylan. Sophie had caught up with the seal and was pleading with it to return to its tank; Dylan was offering a crab to a tentative pup. True, things could go from boring to crazy without warning, but I didn't want anything to change, to jeopardize life the way it was now. A smile spread across my face.

"I couldn't be happier than I am. Thank you, Tristan. Both for remembering and giving me a chance at recognition. But, no. I'd rather remain forgotten." Tristan smiled and nodded.

"Alright, then. Let me know if you change your mind." He started to walk off, then turned. "Good luck wrangling up the animals."

"Thanks," I said, smiling. "I think we're going to need it."

It had been a full day of hacking. I crossed two more names off the list, as did Sonja. I couldn't get Jason to tell me much about his secret girlfriend. I didn't exactly blame him; at least he wasn't mad at me. I had to hand it to him; Sonja didn't have a clue! Looks like ninja runs in their family.

But now it was time to return to my other life. Surfing competitions were coming up. I was excited—but also terrified. Despite all the assurance that I wouldn't bring the team down, I felt the pressure I had put on myself to excel. I needed to practice with the others, not just on my own. *I especially need to work on the 360s, like kick-flips.* I was pinning my hair up in a messy bun as I thought on this. *They're so hard. I need to get to the point where I don't end up with a mouthful of ocean ...* Soon I was ready and headed out to wait for the others.

Can't wait! Can't wait! It's such a lovely day. Dylan, Sophie, and I had managed to sort out the animals in time; feeding remained on schedule. I had sensed it myself and heard it from Tristan: no one seemed to remember my involvement with the fault line business. Life had gone back to normal. The sun was shining, the sea was calling, and it was almost time to meet up with the others.

OK, I think I'm ready. Just have to grab my board. My phone started ringing. The moment I saw the caller ID, my heart took to the sky. It was too good to be true! *Lexie? Could it really be?* I didn't know I could answer a call so fast.

"Jordan?" a quiet voice asked.

"Lexie! Oh my goodness, Lexie! It's so good to hear your voice! Have Mom and Dad finally relented?" Something on the other line stopped me cold. "Lexie? Are you ... crying?" She was softly weeping.

"I'm so sorry, Jordan, I don't have long at all, but … they're … they're …" Lexie sobbed. "Mom and Dad are getting a divorce." It was like someone hit the light switch and my bright mood was plunged into pitch-blackness. I felt gut-punched, heart-wrenched, choked. But Lexie wasn't done with the bad news. "They got in a long debate with Hunter. He's really mad they didn't say something sooner, and he just stormed out! I tried to message him, but he's not responding. I'm worried about him. He was in a terrible state. That was over an hour ago; I only got away just now. They're fighting again, and I'm scared … Jordan, I—" she went silent, listening. On the other end of the line, I could now hear the angry, raised voices … coming nearer. "I have to go!" The line went dead.

For a moment, nothing happened. The seagulls didn't call. The breeze didn't blow. The sun didn't shine. The waves didn't crash. I don't think my heart was beating. Everything just … stopped.

My head was swimming. The conversation pounded from side to side, hammering loudly. But I felt detached, as if I was looking at all this from afar, like watching storm clouds gather around the peak of a mountain. I sank onto my couch, numbly dropping my phone on my coffee table, and fell into the hurricane raging inside my mind.

After an immeasurable stretch of silent chaos, distantly, I noticed my phone light up. Seeing it wasn't Lexie, it didn't seem to be part of my world anymore, so I chose to block it out. *I'll wake up soon, right?* Time dragged on. I don't know how long I sat there, waiting for the nightmare to end, waiting for my alarm clock to go off, for the sun to fall on my eyes and wake me up …

"Hey, Jordan! You there? You aren't answering your phone. We're starting to get worried. Is everything alright?"

Amber? "Oh, hi Amber," I called out, still feeling disconnected from reality, wondering where this strange, sad dream was headed. "My phone?" I glanced down and saw that I had five unread messages and three missed calls. "Oh! Right. Um, yeah. I'm fine."

A pause. "You hesitated. You're not fine, Jordan. Open this door. What's going on?"

A moment later, Jordan opened the door. He stood looking at me, no words, almost no expression—only slight curiosity and confusion. His ever present smile was missing. Yet, the thing that surprised me most was the vast, spacy emptiness behind his eyes. I couldn't believe what I was seeing. This looked like only a shell of the Jordan I knew.

"Jordan, what's going on?" To my complete surprise, he slowly melted and sank to the ground, sitting, silent tears sliding down his cheeks. There was shocked silence.

"I got a call from Lexie ... My parents are getting divorced."

My heart tripped and took a plunge. Even though this news meant nothing to me, his pain made it universally important—and personal. Seeing Jordan without joy was like ... the sun without shine. It darkened the room. It was wrong, all wrong.

I didn't know what to say. So I sat across from him. I'd never ever seen Jordan sad before, let alone crying. It wrenched my heart. I had to do something. *Comfort him! Somehow!* Slowly, awkwardly, I reached forward and placed my hand on top of his head. A sob escaped his lips, and he wept.

"I'm sorry," he whispered.

"Don't be," I whispered back.

CHAPTER 25

The beach across the road from The Salt Breeze Apartment Complex
Saturday, March 30, 1:37 P.M.

Amber

Already, Jordan was doing better. It had only been a couple of weeks since Lexie's distressing call, and he was still rather down from time to time, but Jordan stubbornly refused to let the news defeat him. He seemed to be able to pull strength from thin air. This always amazed me.

Apparently, all this wasn't a total surprise. Trouble had been brewing for years. It still came as a shock. He and Lexie were communicating more; that certainly was a great comfort to him. It seemed Jordan was focusing on surfing to distract himself from it all. His feisty determination was scary at times, and I dearly hoped the approach of the competitions was a big part of his state of mind. If all that energy came entirely from the divorce … well, I worried about him.

We all surfed every spare minute. Competitions were in less than a month. It was like cramming for a presentation. Practice, practice, more practice. But it was beginning to pay off; I began to feel like we had a decent chance.

Then everything changed, and our goals took on a new perspective.

A wave had just carried me to shore. I was going to take a break with the others. Jordan was still out there, waiting for the perfect wave. I looked up to watch him. He had finally found the right one, apparently, successfully pulling off two tricks. But the show was cut short: he lost his footing and tumbled. The wave carried his board straight at him … the last thing I saw before the wave crashed and Jordan went under was his head jerking back like he had been slapped. I froze. A long second passed. Nothing. Another second. Nothing. My heart dropped and my blood turned to ice. *He's not coming up—he's not coming up!* I sprang into action. Throwing my board into the water, I started to paddle out to where I last saw Jordan.

"Amber, what are you doing? Dry land is this way!" Matt called out, laughing.

"Jordan's not coming up!" I yelled over my shoulder. *"Help!"*

Soon I heard Matt jump in behind me, but I was way ahead of him. By the time I reached Jordan's board, the tether was hanging straight down. *Follow the tether. Find Jordan.* Filling my lungs as full as possible, I dove in.

My eyes were open wide, searching for any sign of Jordan. The sun rays didn't penetrate farther than a foot down, and there was nothing but dark, murky green water clouding my vision; the salt made my eyes sting like acid. With one hand tracing down the tether and the other stretched out before me, I was bound to find him. The question was, could I find him in time? Some strange, sharp pang of panic filled me at the thought of Jordan … drowning. *Please! Please, I've got to find him!*

A shadowy form began to appear in front of me. Jordan. It appeared he was no longer holding his breath and not struggling at all. I wrapped one arm around his chest and pulled on the tether with the other. Kicking with all my might, I pulled him to the surface and lugged him onto his surfboard. He exhaled seawater and gave a weak cough. All was still.

"Jordan?" I whispered in horror. Was he even breathing? I was about to despair when I heard a soft moan.

Thank goodness, he's alive. I have to get him to shore, and fast, or he might not be alive for long. Scrambling onto my board, I pulled his alongside mine and started paddling. It was slow going, though, because I had to hold onto the nose of his surfboard, so I only had one free hand.

I felt it coming. The water was changing. Less than one hundred feet away, a wave was forming. There was no way I could outswim it. Matt was too far away to help. It would break before long. I glanced behind me. It was right on top of us. Seconds remained. Betting everything on the chance Jordan was semiconscious, I cried out.

"Jordan! Hold your breath!" I leaped from my board.

Landing on top of Jordan, I wrapped my arms and legs around his board, pinning him to it, and flipped into a "turtle roll." The wave pounded the underside of the board, sending a shock wave through my body. I felt my own tether jolt my ankle as the current jerked my board away. Time itself seemed to slow, and I felt the bubbles brushing against me, kissing my face as they floated up toward the surface like glowing pearls, escaping the dark depths that longed to swallow them. Moments later, the wave had passed and I flipped the board back over. Jordan gasped for air. *He heard me.*

We reached Matt soon after. A silent agreement passed between us. Jordan was priority. Panic could come later. He came alongside and helped pull Jordan's board along; we quickly made it to shore. Dylan was frozen in shock. Chloe was flipping out. She was breathing way too fast, and great big tears were rolling down her cheeks.

"Is J-Jordan gonna—" She let out a sob. " ... die?" I put the board down and grabbed her shoulders.

"Chloe, calm down," I ordered. "I don't think he's going to die, he's just really hurt. You're no use to him if you're out of control." Her panicked breathing slowed a little and she nodded. "Good. Now, I need you to go get my phone from my bag, and toss my car keys to Dylan while you're over there. Call 911 and give them the directions to the Salt Breeze Apartments. Stay on the phone with them until you can see the flashing lights." She stared at me for a moment, a look of terror in her eyes, then she spun and ran toward my bag. I turned to Dylan, snapping him out of his shock. "Take my keys and run across the street to the apartments. Press the alarm button on the remote key until you find my car. Drive it across the sand if you have to. Just get it over here."

Dylan too stared at me for a moment, but was jolted out of his surprise once more as Chloe hurled my keys his way. He caught them and was gone in moments. Ripping my surfboard tether off, I jogged over to Matt, who looked a little scared himself, and Jordan—well, Jordan was down for the count.

"Do you know where it hit him?" I asked Matt. He nodded and gently pulled back the hair plastered against Jordan's face. Usually, I can steel myself against this sort of thing, but I couldn't help but cringe. It was black, purple, and looked extremely painful. I touched his forehead softly, but even that made him moan. "I'm sorry, Jordan," I whispered. And then, there was hope again.

Jordan opened his eyes and looked right at me—no, past me. *Through* me. Like I was made out of glass. *Oh no.* I slowly waved my hand in front of him. Nothing. He muttered something that sounded like "Amber" and

"Matt," his eyes rolled back in his head, and he was out again. Matt shot me an alarmed look.

"Was that good or bad?" he asked, worried. I shook my head.

"Both. He's semiconscious, but his eyes didn't track our movement. His brain isn't registering the images he sees. I think … " I hesitated. *Somehow, I know. This isn't the first time I've seen this, but where? Oh. Ashley—that time when she fell from the tree … she—oh no.* "I think he might have a concussion of some sort. Mild at best, severe at worst." Matt's face turned a few shades whiter.

"What does that mean for Jordan?" he asked.

I racked my brain. "His vision could get messed up. He might lose hand-eye coordination. And … amnesia. Any number of memories could vanish. I don't know, it all depends."

"Depends on what?"

"How bad it is, and how fast we can get him help," I answered.

Jordan murmured something again. He seemed agitated, as if our conversation was disturbing his little nap. He tensed, opened his eyes again, looked through me, and then … saw me. He looked between me and Matt for a moment, blinking. Matt noticed.

"Jordan! Can you hear us?" he asked hopefully. Jordan looked slightly confused, as if this were a silly question.

"Of course … I can hear you." Something didn't sound quite right, but this was still an improvement. Suddenly, he shut his eyes tightly, cringing. Slowly, he raised his hands to his head and clutched it as if it were going to crack and fall apart. When he opened his eyes, he seemed to be having difficulty seeing us again. "What happened?" Jordan groaned.

Something definitely didn't sound right. His words sounded slightly slurred, and he occasionally put the emphasis on the wrong syllables. Matt glanced at me, as if he wanted my permission to explain. I gave him a puzzled look, then nodded.

"You hit your head. You almost drowned," Matt explained gently. Jordan squinted at us in disbelief, trying to decide if he liked this story or not.

"I'm fine," Jordan insisted. To my shock, he started to get up. Well, tried to. We didn't let him. Matt and I pushed him back down.

"No, Jordan! You're not fine, you're not going anywhere, and stop being such a child!" I scolded him like a mother hen. Jordan was none too pleased with this. After frowning at us, he closed his eyes, as if to shut us out and pout—just like a child. He didn't seem to have any intention of ever opening them again. I freaked out. "Jordan, don't go back to sleep! Keep talking! Tell me about—" I tried to think of the right subject. *Remember what they did for Ashley. Go far back.* "Lexie!" I had his attention once more.

"What'd you want to know?"

Stay awake. "Anything and everything! Just tell me all about her. I don't want to forget." *I don't want you to forget.* Even though he didn't open his eyes, Jordan's frown softened into a small smile.

"Well … her birthday's in 79 days, she'll be eighteen. She loves art and music, and … she's really good at both of them. She adores her cello; she's had it since she was six. She hates geography, her favorite subject's science, her favorite color is lilac purple. Her middle name is Christina."

"What about Hunter?" I asked. Jordan actually chuckled.

"Hunter's an enigma. Thinks he's the king of England. He refuses to grow up; still lives at home. I think he really liked being an only child; he tried to sell me when I was three, but all's forgiven. I'd sell me if I was him," Jordan said, a grin pulling at his lips. "He was aloof more often than not. Even so, I thought he was so cool. My big brother, my hero! Wanted to be just like him when I grew up." He pondered this for a moment. "I miss him."

I steered Jordan from subject to subject, careful to hit as many important things as possible. The longer he talked, the more his speech improved. Matt was watching me with a look of awed astonishment, but I had to block that out for now.

" … Sophie's a sweetheart. She talks so much! Sometimes it's all she can do to keep from chattering. She's so smart, it blows my mind." I was going to see if I could get Jordan to elaborate on more subjects, but Dylan chose that moment to come careening over the dunes. Jordan opened his eyes. "OK, what is going on? Can I please get up now?"

Until then, no one seemed to have noticed our predicament, but now a few heads were turning. Thankfully, everyone kept their distance. I glanced over at Chloe. She seemed to have collected herself a little but was still scared to death. I wanted to reach out and reassure her that everything would be alright, to tell her this was a minor setback. I wanted to tell her we'd all be out surfing tomorrow like nothing had happened. But there was a good chance that would be a big lie. It probably wasn't a super serious concussion, but it certainly wasn't minor. I didn't know enough about this kind of thing to be sure. Dylan jumped out of the car and raced the short distance to me.

"Now what?" he asked.

I hesitated. "I ... I don't—" A distant flash of red and blue caught my eye. Chloe had seen it too. She hung up on the emergency respondent and ran to me.

"They're here." With trembling hands, she handed me my phone. I looked into her eyes, her sky blue eyes overflowing with tears and fear, and gave the best smile I could muster. That seemed to encourage her a bit.

"Who is here? What exactly is going on? This is ridiculous! Stop playing around, I'm fine! Let me get up!"

How I temporarily forgot about Jordan, I'm not sure. The results were almost disastrous: he began to sit up again. I forced him back down, muttered an apology under my breath, and managed to touch his forehead rather gently despite all his squirming. I might as well have shot him. He gave a short, pained gasp, shut his eyes tightly, grabbed his head, and trembled a little.

"I'm sorry, Jordan, but I had to do that. You have to listen to me. You are not fine. A couple minutes ago, you came inches from death. Do not try to get up again. Promise me you will let us help you, OK?"

After a moment of painful thought, he gave a little nod. *Good.* I stood, took a shaky breath and let it out silently. When I looked up, I found everyone was watching me, waiting. Finally, it came to me.

"OK, Dylan, gather our stuff and stash it somewhere out of sight. We won't be back for a while. Chloe, if you feel up to it, I need you to explain the situation to the respondents." She nodded. "Good. Matt, help me drag Jordan's board further inland. Once everything's done, everyone meet at my car."

For a moment, no one moved. Then they all scattered to their tasks. I watched them go, then glanced back at Jordan. He was watching me, blinking against the light. He searched my eyes for a moment and then closed his tightly again. He didn't have to say it for me to know. I saw it in his face. He was scared. *Hang in there, Jordan ...* Matt and I started pulling his board, the motion making Jordan cringe.

"Try to keep still, Jordan, especially from the shoulders up," I encouraged. "I know the light hurts, so don't open your eyes. I'll explain. We called for an ambulance, and once we're closer to the sand dunes, the emergency respondants will take it from there. No way under the sun will they allow us to tag along for the ride to the ER, but we'll be close behind, OK?"

It would seem Jordan was about to nod, but then remembered my warning, and whispered what must have been "OK," though it simply sounded like a weak "K." Soon, the exchange was made—stretcher for surfboard—and Chloe, Dylan, Matt, and I climbed into my car. We drove in almost complete silence, broken only by Chloe's occasional sniffles, Dylan's directions, or quiet gasps from the others whenever I displayed my frightening lack of driving skills. At the ER, I parked and we all jumped out, rushing in.

After some inquiries at the receptionist's desk, we discovered Jordan was still getting checked out, but it would seem he was going to be OK. Indescribable relief washed over us. Soon we were all seated together in a waiting room, shaken yet grateful. As the adrenaline dropped, it began to sink in. *Jordan ... could have ... died.* I felt tears stinging the back of my eyes. I shoved them away, defiantly denying their presence. I had to stay strong and keep the mask on until I was alone. Matt caught my attention.

"How?" he asked, bewildered. I knew what he meant. How did I know what to do, and how did I do it? All eyes were on me, waiting for an explanation. I dropped my gaze, watching my hands clasp tighter in my lap.

"When I was little," I began, quiet and slow, "my sister and I were climbing a big oak tree that stood in front of our house." *It was my fault ...* "We were messing around, and she lost her grip and fell ... she got a major concussion. I remember it so clearly, because I had been so scared she was going to die."

And with that, though no one saw it, a single, hot, fat tear escaped from behind my mask and slipped down my cheek. *I thought you were going to die ...*

CHAPTER 26

Santa Barbara, Silver Bay Memorial Hospital
Saturday, March 30, 4:13 P.M.

⸙Amber⸙

We sat in the waiting room for what felt like eternity. Eventually, the wait ended, and the last bits of anxiety melted away. Hearing the doors open, I looked up. To my complete surprise, there was Jordan, walking out, followed closely by a nurse, a knowing, patient smile on her face. I stared at him. Apart from the patch on his forehead, he seemed perfectly fine! We all stood and Jordan noticed us. Donning a wide grin, he came trotting over, and that's when I figured it out. Whatever the doctors had given him had left him tipsy. The best part was, Jordan didn't seem to know it. *This is funny, but poor Jordan ... well, at least he's keeping his big mouth shut.*

I spoke too soon. "Hellooo!" Jordan exclaimed happily, a lopsided grin plastered on his face. "I'm back! Oh! Have you guys gotten a lollipop? There's a great big jar of them over there!" he said, pointing enthusiastically. "They're super pretty, really colorful. I bet they're super good!"

Everyone's jaw dropped. Matt looked astonished and amused. Dylan turned away, holding his sides and shaking with silent, hysterical laughter. Chloe clapped both her hands tightly over her mouth, as if moving one finger would result in a fatal breach in the dam. And I face palmed, burying both my cringe and grin in my hands, trying to keep a straight face. *Oh, my goodness. This is too much ... Don't laugh, don't laugh ...* And then Chloe lost it. A single giggle slipped past her barricade and she gave up the fight. Jordan watched her, puzzled.

"Why are you laughing?" he asked, confused.

"Jordan! Oh, my goodness, I—I'm sorry! I couldn't—" She started

297

laughing again.

"It's OK," the nurse assured us. "He won't remember any of this."

"What?" I asked, intrigued at this piece of information. The nurse glanced at Jordan, who was staring wide- and starry-eyed into space, observing some imaginary wonder. His inner child was on a sugar high.

"He'll wake up tomorrow morning and won't have a clue about what went on today. Especially the past few hours."

"He has an eidetic memory. Are you sure?" I pressed.

A smile and a nod. "He won't remember a thing."

"Nothing?" Dylan, who had partially collected himself, asked. The nurse gave an *um-hmm* of affirmation. "Huh," Dylan muttered, a mischievous grin creeping across his face. Chloe poked him in the ribs.

"I don't know what's going through that sneaky little head of yours, but whatever it is, don't you dare!"

"Come on, Chloe!" Dylan exclaimed. "This is your one chance to ask him anything! This stuff is like truth serum." With that, Dylan turned to Jordan, looked him in the eyes, and asked, "What is your deepest, darkest, most laughable secret?" None of us wasted a moment in smacking Dylan upside the head.

"Dylan! How could you?!" I shrieked.

"Jordan got my wild card the other day. Now it's my turn to get his! You guys don't have to stick around, but I am."

"Dylan," Chloe scolded, "this is not called a wild card, this is called being a jerk!" The nurse's eyebrows went up, an amused look on her face, but she remained silent.

"Jordan," Matt said slowly, "don't answer that question."

I had been so focused on punishing Dylan that I hadn't noticed Jordan. He was thinking, long and hard, considering his options. *Oh no.* No matter what we said or did, he wouldn't snap out of it. Finally, he looked up.

"Is anyone else hungry? I'm hungry. For some reason … is it just me, or does pineapple sound really good?" Dylan and Jordan were the only two not laughing.

"Ah, that was perfect," I gasped, pulling my hand across my face, wiping away tears of laughter. "You just got wrecked, Dylan."

"It's what you get for being such a little devil," Chloe chided.

Dylan just moaned.

"For Jordan's sake, we must never speak of this again," Matt said. We all agreed. The nurse, who was still chuckling, held up a paper bag.

"Here are his meds. Everything you need to know is on the labels, though I wouldn't trust him with them for a day or two." When no one moved, I hesitantly took the bag.

"He can go home?" I asked.

The nurse nodded. "Yes. He's fine, just very distractible. Suffered a grade 3 concussion, but it would appear no brain damage. It isn't unheard of, yet still considered lucky. No spinal injuries, but he did endure a pretty serious jolt, so it'll probably hurt to move for a while. Keep a close eye on him for a few days. Make sure the headaches don't get worse, that he doesn't lose coordination, and don't let him sleep endlessly, though he'll want to. He can sleep for the rest of the day, but wake him in the morning."

"Sleep for the rest of the day?" Matt asked.

"Um-hmm. He'll probably crash in about half an hour." At this, for some reason, Matt, Dylan, and Chloe groaned. I gave them a puzzled look.

"He sleeps like a *rock*. Absolutely impossible to wake up," Dylan explained. "Once he's out, he's out, no way around it."

Needless to say, we all hurried to get out of there. I dropped Matt, and then Dylan and Chloe, off at their homes and headed back for the apartments. There was no doubt about it; Jordan was losing energy. Fast. By the time I parked, it had been about half an hour. I sighed and glanced at the back seat. Jordan's eyelids were about two-thirds closed. When he noticed me, he grinned and mumbled, "Home sweet home" with about as much coherency as a three-year old.

I had to steady Jordan; I was worried he would fall dead over, fast asleep. I could practically see the bubbles floating up and popping around his head. Apparently, he could too; he was poking at some invisible thing just out of his reach. We didn't make it halfway across the lobby without disaster.

"Good gracious! What in heaven's name ... ?"

"He's fine, Betty, he's fine," I muttered, hurrying along.

"Hi Betty!" Jordan exclaimed dopily. Betty, for once, couldn't find anything to say.

"Just a concussion. He's fine," I said. Miraculously—I couldn't believe my luck—the front desk phone started to ring. After a moment of stunned stillness, Betty hurried for it, and we escaped to the elevator.

Alas, this day wasn't finished with the cruel tricks: I didn't have Jordan's key card. I had a hunch he kept the spare around his door or down on the ground level, perhaps near where the water hose was. Moving Jordan to lean on the wall, I searched frantically around his door. Nothing.

"Jordan, where's the key card?" Jordan stared at me blankly, fighting to keep his eyes open. After a moment, I decided it was pointless. "Alright then, fine!" Turning to the door and pulling out my phone, I pressed it against the electric lock. "I am seriously counting on you not remembering anything," I muttered. Jordan watched in awe as I hacked the lock, fingers flying across my screen, until the little click of a lock disabling rang out. I turned to see Jordan, wide-eyed, staring at me.

"How'd you do that?" he asked slowly.

"Jordan, look at me," I ordered. He tried to focus. "Forget what you just saw, OK? I know you can. Do not remember." With that, I nudged the door open with my foot and urged Jordan forward. "No, this way," I said, steering him toward the bed.

"I'm not sleepy," he slurred.

"Oh, yes you are," I insisted, gently pushing him onward. "In bed. Now. Go to sleep." He reluctantly obeyed.

"But, I'm … not … " He never finished that sentence. Smiling, I pulled a blanket up over him; he was down for the count.

I found his main keycard on the bedside table, stuck it in my pocket, pulled the plug from his alarm clock, and drew the curtains shut. After a bit more snooping, I slipped out. Closing the door, I put my back to it and slid to the floor, wondering what I had gotten myself into.

I sighed and began assessing my emotional state. I was surprised at what I was feeling. Exasperation, exhaustion, slight annoyance. But mostly … pity? No. Sympathy, care, affection … a wish to protect this … child. This child I had grown so fond of. *Fondness. That's it. And you are such a child, Jordan. Don't ever scare me like that again.*

When I got back to my room, I flopped onto my bed and stared at the ceiling. *I'm alone now. I can let go.* Hesitantly, I let my mask fall off. And I cried.

It felt good to finally let it out. All the fear I had felt slid down my face in the form of tears. Eventually, I grew still. I lay there, unmoving. Hours later, I fell asleep.

CHAPTER 27

Salt Breeze Apartment Complex, Apt. 1307
Sunday, March 31, 9:45 A.M.

ᶜᵉᵂ Amber ᵂᵉᵂ

Now I know what the others were moaning about. Is Jordan a heavy sleeper? Yes. Yes he is. And this wasn't regular sleep. It was drugged sleep. He was in the exact same position he had been in when he hit the pillow the day before. At first, when I saw him, I had a miniature panic attack; I thought he was dead.

"Jordan. Jordan!" I whispered loudly. "Wake up!" I might as well have been talking to a tree. *"Jordan! Wake up!"* I hissed, louder. Still nothing.

I remembered how stiff and miserable Ashley had been when she woke up after her concussion. No way was I going to shake Jordan and risk causing pain, and the same went for slapping. Any loud noises would annoy the people in surrounding apartments, and Jordan would be sound and light sensitive.

Oh sure, there were plenty of nonconventional, creative ways I could break his hibernation, but most of them would still be a rude wake-up call. I could think of 101 efficient ways to wake him. But the answer was a simple one. Jordan was breathing through his nose. So I pinched it. He was so deeply asleep that he wouldn't be able to subconsciously start breathing through his mouth. *Wait for it ...* Sure enough, within ten seconds, his eyes snapped open and he gasped for air. *Thanks, Ashley.* Jordan blinked at me for a moment, blank confusion painting his face. I smiled.

"Good morning, sleepyhead," I said softly. "Feeling any better?" He was silent for a long time.

"How did you ... why ... ?" Suddenly, he grew alarmed. "Why can't I remember?" This was a somewhat disturbing statement.

"What can't you remember?" I asked, a hint of anxiety in my voice. Jordan slowly sat up, slid his legs over the edge, and looked up at me, still blinking, a bewildered, slightly scared haze about him.

"Yesterday. No wait—I remember yesterday, just not all of it. There's a huge gap." *That's probably a good thing.* Jordan dropped his gaze, closed his eyes, and was still for a moment. I waited patiently. "What happened?" he asked quietly.

"You got a concussion, Jordan. You don't remember?" He stared at me in shock, then slowly shook his head, cringing at the motion.

"Surfing's the last thing I remember," he said hesitantly. "There are little bits and pieces after that, but they don't make much sense."

"It's alright. There's bound to be some gaps," I said gently. "You were out for a while." Jordan thought for a moment.

"Exactly how 'out' was I?" I didn't mean to, but I chuckled, causing Jordan to shoot me an alarmed look.

"Oh, you were *out*. I know because you didn't worry about my driving." Jordan nodded slowly, probably counting his blessings and shoveling this information into the gap in his memory like filling a pit with sand. He was pondering his next question.

"OK, that answers why my head hurts. But why does my rib cage hurt?" I stared at him blankly for a second, then felt my cheeks go from rosy to roasted. *The turtle roll.*

"I don't know," I muttered, turning toward the kitchen.

That was one memory hole Jordan was just going to have to live with. Hearing how he got sandwiched between a surfboard and a girl while trapped in a catnap wasn't exactly going to help his already slightly damaged ego, and it certainly wouldn't help mine. Anyway, he didn't need to know that I was the one who saved him. I don't know why, but I didn't really want him to find out. I wasn't a hero.

Pulling prop number one out of my little box on the counter, I turned and swiftly tossed it.

"Catch," I said.

Jordan reached up and caught it. "A flashlight?" he asked. I stepped forward, took it from his hands, turned it on its lowest strength, and shined it in his face. The sudden light caused him to cringe and jerk back, shutting his eyes tightly.

"No, Jordan. Hold still for just a minute."

Hesitantly, he opened his eyes, blinking against the light. I glanced back and forth between his big green eyes, frowning, carefully searching for any sign of trouble. Jordan seemed rather scared and surprised at how intent I was. After a moment, I clicked off the light and covered his left eye.

"How many fingers am I holding up?"

"Four. Now one. Two." I covered his right eye. "Five. Well, four if you don't count the thumb. One. Three." I let out a huge sigh of relief and sat down beside him, sending him deeper into confusion.

"You're OK. Everything's alright." I looked at Jordan and scowled. "Don't ever scare me like that again, you hear?" Jordan nodded, wide-eyed and surprised.

"I won't." He paused. "You know none of this was on purpose, right?"

"Yeah. I know."

We sat there a minute. It was really strange, seeing Amber ... flustered? *Is that what this is? But why? Why would she be flustered?* Amber suddenly stood, walked to the kitchenette, and busied herself. I sat, stunned, frozen, trying to figure it all out.

How did I get a concussion? Why do my ribs hurt? What is this faint memory of Matt, Dylan, and Chloe all looking to Amber to lead? I think Chloe was crying. Was she scared? I don't remember much from there. Who are the people I didn't recognize? Doctors? Did I go to the hospital? I glanced at my wrist. *Hospital wristband. Yep, I went to the hospital. Why do some of the memories make no sense? They're all scrambled. Amber opening the door with ... what? How did she get in here, anyway? And what is this sense that I was underwater? Was I drowning? I don't remember.*

A fragmented memory suddenly streaked by; I grabbed it. Shattered, distorted, but a memory nonetheless. It was of Amber, talking to me. But when? *She asked me to do something. But what?* I strained my mind as hard as I could, and a thin thread of conversation began to return. *"Jordan ... look at ... forget you just saw ... I know ... remember—"*

It felt as though someone hit me with a baseball bat. My breath caught and I grabbed my head. It felt like someone had pointed a gun between my eyes, paused for dramatic effect, then pulled the trigger out of spite. There were bombs going off in my skull. I sensed motion and carefully opened my eyes. Amber stood in front of me, holding out her hand and a glass of water, looking concerned.

"You OK?" she asked. I slowly shook my head. She handed me a glass and dumped two pills into my hand. "These will help." She retrieved something from the counter. "As will this." Amber placed a mug and a plate beside me. "Breakfast," she explained. "Coffee's decaf. Sorry, no caffeine for a while. Most of the food is from your fridge or cupboards. Except—" she pulled out a plastic container. "Pineapple."

"Pineapple?" I just stared at it.

"Pineapple," she affirmed. "You like it, right?"

"Yeah. Love it."

"Great," she said, smiling slightly. Amber's phone chirped. She frowned, pulled it out of her pocket, scanned the message, and stood. "Chloe, Dylan, and Matt will probably pop in in a couple of hours to make sure you're OK. Try not to get up unless you have to, and you know how to reach me if you need anything." With that, she headed for the door.

"Amber?" I asked. She turned. A thousand questions threw themselves around in my head, making it throb. A billion comments fought toward the forefront of my mind, making it hard to focus. I pushed it all away.

"Thank you," I said. A tiny smile grew across her face. She nodded and left.

I had to check in at VORT3X. Sonja had messaged me—quite cryptically. "The storm must come. Water's rising. First strike, will fall." Now, Sonja smelling trouble was nothing unusual. But for her to get past her pride to hack me and say so was meaningful. She wanted me there. Apart from Jason and Ender, I seemed to be the only other person she partially trusted. And for some reason, she was speaking in riddles. I knew my plan: *just get in and out. Assess the danger, smooth some ruffled feathers, and leave. I have to get back to babysitting Jordan.*

All my plans for a quick exit melted the moment I walked through the VORT3X door.

Scrambled images flickered across the big screen, as did shifting lines of data and code. Chaos ruled as everyone ran around, calling out to each other, frantically typing at their computers. My eyes went wide. Sonja had been serious! I scanned the room. *There!* Sonja and Ender. I pushed through to get to them.

"Sonja!" I called out. She looked up, and just for a moment, I thought I could see relief in her eyes.

"Storm, you're here. Good."

"What's going on?" I asked.

"Cerberus," Ender said grimly. "Somehow, they infected the mainframe. Not only is the virus deleting files and such, it's deleting base code. Six computers have already crashed, probably permanently. Anyone connected to the Vortex system is in danger."

"You didn't think to mention that, Sonja?!" I exclaimed as I hastily booted up my computer in hopes of disconnecting before it was too late.

My protection programs had detected the bug, though, and were already fighting it off. I was safe for now. As my legion of A.I.'s banded together to fight this threat, they returned with information they had snagged. I began to read the stats.

"The program's name is 'grim_reaper.' Cerberus certainly has a taste for the underworld and the dramatic. It's a self-modifying virus—'bomb' might be a bit more accurate term. It targets protection programs, then hijacks controls, and vandalizes at random." I found something of interest. "It's not just destroying. It's stealing." Ender's eyes went wide with alarm.

"Cerberus is stealing our information? They're going to sell us out to the police!"

"No," I muttered, mind churning. "No. This is good!" That earned some *are-you-crazy?* looks, which I ignored. Cerberus had made a fatal error. I could destroy them. "I can beat them at their own game," I said, typing away, booting up all my programs in preparation for war. "They've made a mistake."

"What mistake?!" Sonja demanded, exasperated. "Spit it out!"

I turned to her. "The host for this virus—the launcher program—is Cerberus's mainframe. Not a dedicated computer. The mainframe."

"It's sending information directly back to their database?" Ender asked. I could see some light bulbs going off in his head. I nodded.

"Yes. Straight back to HQ. I have an idea. I can fix this. But under one condition."

Ender shot me a look. "What condition?"

"That no one but the three of us and Jason know that I'm the one who did it and how," I insisted. Ender and Sonja exchanged confused looks, then Sonja shrugged.

"It's cool with me, Ender. She's legit."

Ender nodded. "Agreed."

"Alright. We need everyone working together, doing exactly as I say. I need two-thirds of all the hackers building spyware. It can be scrappy; all it has to do is copy a single line of data and return it to a central point in … an estimated 750 milliseconds. How big is Cerberus's hacker legion, would you say?"

Ender thought for a moment. "I'd say … anywhere from sixty to ninety."

"Alright. I need the rest of our hackers except five to be ready to destroy. The five will be you two, Jason, me, and … one other person you completely trust. We will keep the program from falling apart. I'll take the lead. Once the programmers are done with the malware, they'll join the fight." I did some quick calculations in my head. "The programmers have seven minutes, starting now."

Ender hastily called for attention in the midst of the clamor and gave orders. While the two-thirds hammered out code, I got Sonja to rally the remaining hackers and fire up their programs. Meanwhile, I awoke the hibernating, special section in F1R3ST0RM. I never thought I'd use it again. It was almost sacred. It was the force that joined Eric's computer to mine, mine to his. Our hacking powers were one and the same. That's why people thought WH1RLW1ND was one person. One hacker, one computer, one mind. But it was two.

"Time's up," I said as Ender returned to our inner circle. "Who's the fifth?"

"Lenny. I trust him. He's been here about as long as I have."

I nodded. "Good. Here's what I need. On my command, tell everyone to start hacking the connection that appears on their screen. Once they're in, they will just have to trust me. They need to wait for fifteen seconds before they so much as touch a key on their keyboards. I won't let them fall. At twenty seconds, they can start defending their computers. At thirty seconds, destroy everything within their grasp and get out."

Ender hesitated, then nodded. "Alright." After another pause, he wrangled for attention amid the noise. "Alright everyone! Listen up!" Jason, who had been in an intense conversation with Sonja, came over to me.

"Storm, what on earth are you doing? Sonja says you can fix all this. How?"

"I have a program that can protect our hackers and sell Cerberus out. All their data and files will soon belong to us, and their hacker stats to the police." Jason nodded, chewing on this idea, weighing his trust, then set up his computer by Sonja's.

"I'm in," he said, determination in his voice and a light in his eyes. "I'll take the main defensive?"

I nodded. Turning to my computer, I launched F1R3ST0RM, saddled up, and soared into the cyber realm. *Don't fail me now.* I ducked through system after system, recruiting soldiers for my war, tying them all together, making them one. Gathering the spy programs, I distributed them inside the hacker's computers: their ammo. The path to the source of the virus appeared on the screens of the computers that I hacked, a seal of their allegiance. Soon, forty-six hackers later, I singled out Ender's computer and sent a single-word: *Done.*

And just like that, the battle had begun.

Notifications exploded on my screen, reporting successful infiltration of the enemy's base. The moment a computer made it in, it released its spies. A progress bar appeared on the side of my screen, showing how much of C3RB3RU$'s database had been copied.

Ten seconds remain.

Ender's, Sonja's, Jason's, and Lenny's fingers flew, swatting off counterattacks. It didn't slip my attention that Jason was typing almost twice as fast as the others. Looks like F1R3ST0RM had more holes than I was expecting.

Five seconds remain.

Data was pouring into my files like the torrents of a raging river. Enabling my sorter A.I., I watched as it scrambled to piece everything together and categorize it into files.

Three … two … one!

The next five seconds passed in a blur as the burden was shifted to the other four protectors while my computer was driven to its knees as the final burst of data hit the circuit boards. The progress bar took to the clouds … Then my computer recovered and I jumped into the fray as the clock ran down, hitting twenty seconds. All across the room, a clicking, ticking, clacking clamor rose as the hackers began typing away, defending their computers. Distantly, out of the corner of my eye, I saw a flash of deep blue. A laptop had gone down.

Now for the best, most fun part: delete everything. Diving into the fray, I began to add my powers to the destruction, setting off chain reactions, mini viruses, and bombs, electricity bursts, and blackouts. I could practically see C3RB3RU$'s servers crackling, popping as I hit them with waves of energy. A warning popped up in the corner of my screen. Time to pull out. With one last pulse of electricity, I commanded a drop. Across the room, all the laptop screens went black. I waited for the file transfers: the goodies to us, the incriminating data to the police. Then, a reboot of all the computers.

It was over. The war was won.

I spent the next few hours reading, thinking, battling back headaches, and questioning my shaky memories of the events of the previous day. Everything seemed surreal. Not being able to remember was a terrible, odd experience, and I tried desperately to fill the hole in my internal timeline—to no avail.

I'm bored. Bored, bored, bored. I couldn't read anymore; it was giving me a headache. Just looking at my computer screen made my head hurt, let alone watching or listening to anything. *This is going to be a long day.* So I literally had to sit, holding my breath, waiting for something to change. Eventually, Matt, Dylan, and Chloe showed up. I couldn't have been happier to see them.

"Jordan! I'm so glad you're OK!" Chloe exclaimed, tackling me with a hug.

"Yeah." *Ouch.* "I'm fine. Not entirely sure why I wouldn't be, though." Dylan, who had been acting rather strange, gave me a funny look.

"You smacked your head and almost drowned, silly. That's why."

So I was underwater ... "Was it really that bad?" I asked, having a hard time swallowing this new information. More glances from the others. Suddenly, I realized I might be able to get the full story. "Well, I don't remember," I said simply.

"Wait. You don't remember any of it?" Matt asked.

"Bits and pieces, but not much. How about you remind me?" They looked at each other, exchanging glances of varying degrees of surprise.

"Well, we were all out surfing ... "

Jason's computer was the one that went down. I felt so bad. I had been the one to let him take the defensive. But after some intense programming and cyber side-stepping, I managed to bring it back from the brink. It would be glitchy for a while, but at least it wasn't displaying the blue screen of death anymore. Sonja and I told Ender about the spy. He agreed that the current circumstance was proof enough. How else could the mainframe have been infected so quickly? We had to keep our eyes open. Surely something drastic was bound to happen now that C3RB3RU$'s hackers had fallen.

I hurried home. I didn't want anyone to find out I had been the host computer, that they had all been hacking as one as a legion under my name. C3RB3RU$ now knew about F1R3ST0RM. They saw my hacking name, my handle, my tie to V0RT3X. But it didn't matter much, because all their hackers would soon be behind bars. The police already had arrest warrants on all eighty-one of them. Probably, they had already scattered. But it was only a matter of time before they were caught.

After gathering my frayed nerves, I headed down a floor to check on Jordan. The moment I stepped through the door, everyone looked up. Yes, everyone. Chloe, Dylan, and Matt were here. Just as I was about to say hello, I noticed Jordan's expression. Wide-eyed amazement, shock, and … gratitude?

"You … saved me?" Jordan asked, looking straight at me. *They told him.* A quick, tiny, sad smile flashed across my face. Jordan thought about this for a moment, then smiled. "Thank you, Amber," he said quietly. I nodded, slowly came forward, and slid into the chair beside Chloe, fighting the urge to withdraw. *I didn't want him to know. I'm no hero.*

"It was nothing," I muttered, then dodged a retort by frowning at Jordan. "You're officially grounded for scaring us like that, by the way." I felt a bit better as my apprehension melted away in the laughter that followed.

CHAPTER 28

Somewhere near The Salt Breeze Apartment Complex
Saturday, May 4, 1:10 P.M.

Jordan

Time passed slower than a sleepy turtle creeping down a sticky tar road. Turns out, Amber was partially serious about me being grounded. It was a whole week before she let me leave the apartment, let alone go to Ocean Front, church, or the beach! If it weren't for the headaches, I would have banged my head against a wall or gone into hibernation for a year or wore a circle in the carpet—all out of pure, brain-numbing boredom. I think I looked insanity in the eye, smiled, and willingly shook its hand at least twice.

But I wasn't lonely 24/7. People dropped by to keep me company. I was reminded just how many good friends I have, especially Matt, Dylan, Chloe, and Amber. Matt, Dylan, and Chloe stopped by on a whim, and Amber would bring stacks of books from the library, movies, snacks, and games. Sometimes she would just come hang out and sit and chat, or simply listen to me talk instead. It meant a lot.

There was a great deal of debate on whether we should still enter the surfing competitions. I didn't see what all the fuss was about. I was fine. Well, would be. Ultimately, I managed to convince them that if I was still down and out a couple of weeks before the competitions, we could back out. But if I was totally recovered, they better be ready to cram in some practice, because I was not giving up.

The day of competition had come. I was ready. I waited with Amber for the others at the rendezvous point.

"Are you sure you're fine?"

"Yes."

"Positive?"

"Yes!"

"Does your head hurt at all?"

"No."

"What about when I do this?" Amber challenged, suddenly shooting forward and poking my forehead.

"Um, yeah, you just stabbed me in the face with your finger," I said. Amber sighed in exasperation and appeared to be about to grill me with more questions. "Amber," I cut her off, chuckling. "I'm fine. Just because you got to be my mother for a day—OK, more like a week—doesn't mean you get to fuss over me like one." Amber frowned, blushing.

"I just want to be sure. And be very, very careful!"

"I will," I muttered, trying to pacify her. "Anyway," I teased, "if something does go wrong, I trust you'll haul me out before I drown, scold me until I wake up, and then punish me accordingly."

"Jordan! Don't joke around, it's not funny! I'm serious!" Amber exclaimed. I saluted in mock solemnity.

"Yes ma'am, Mother Amber!" At this, Amber sighed, blushing and frowning in slight annoyance, yet fighting to keep from grinning.

Eventually, the others showed up, sparing me from Jordan's jokes. I knew he was just trying to put my mind at ease. It did help a bit, but I couldn't stop being nervous—for both of us! Jordan didn't seem concerned at all, just excited. Apparently, almost drowning hadn't really scared him. The fact that this was a once-a-year contest didn't seem to hold much weight for him either. I couldn't help being afraid. Last time Jordan tried crazy tricks, he almost died. Also, this was my first surfing competition. Two very good reasons to be on edge.

My nerves hit the sky when I first glimpsed the sea. The first sensation that met me when the five of us came over the pale gold sand dunes was numbed amazement—and then dread. The waves were huge jade giants, towering high, stretching to grab the afternoon sun, then falling, crashing to the sand, roaring with rage, sending spray high, then rearing their foamy green heads to try and touch the sky once more. We froze, awed and intimidated, watching these monsters for a moment.

"Whoa," Matt whispered, voicing what we all felt. I tossed a pleading glance at Jordan, hoping he would now take my warning seriously. He seemed a little more down to earth, yet still undaunted.

"Come on. We got this, just … " Jordan smirked. "Just don't look down." That lightened the mood a bit, and we headed for the beach, feeling braver.

So, this is a surfing competition. In all, there were eight teams, each waiting patiently in little huddles, eyeing the other contenders. What I assumed to be the judge box stood farther inland on platforms. Thankfully, it wasn't a particularly official event, just a local tradition of sorts—though "local" seemed to be a bit narrow of a term. A medium-sized crowd had gathered to watch the fun.

The contest was split into quarters. Each segment was half an hour long. For the first half, points could only be earned, not lost. Scoring was based on the difficulty of the trick or length of the ride. At the halfway mark, the four teams in last place would be eliminated and the judges would start deducting points for errors.

No pressure.

"Chloe," I whispered. "I'm nervous."

"Don't be. I know its super cliché, but just have fun. Don't worry. It gets better once you actually start."

"Alright. I'll try." *Excuse me while I barf butterflies; there are too many in my stomach.*

Soon the rules were read, the teams announced, and it began. It was a battle to get past the impact zone. The closest I'd ever been to waves this big was the other side of my computer screen. I cannot express how terrifying it is to have the sun temporarily blocked out by a wall of water overhead, then to feel it go *boom* behind me as I dive under it. Absolutely terrifying. For the first ten minutes, it was go-go-go nonstop. I bailed on my first wave, wiped out on my second. It was like being thrown off a building and somehow landing in an underwater washing machine. But on my third wave, I pulled off a 360, and my confidence started rising.

I wasn't really focusing on the other surfers, but I did occasionally hear a few terms I'd never heard before. I figured out "Barney" and "Kook" were insults of sorts, and I had a feeling "choka" was slang for "awesome," but I couldn't figure out why a couple of the guys kept calling me Gidget. They called both Chloe and me *wahine*, which is Hawaiian for a female surfer, but I'd never heard "Gidget" before. I asked Chloe when I got the chance.

Apparently, there was a really old movie from the 1960s about a small-fry surfer girl nicknamed Gidget—short for "girl midget." How flattering; people noticed I was a runt.

There wasn't much idly sitting in wait for waves during the second quarter. Things were picking up, if that was even possible. At one point, I witnessed a harsh wipeout and felt a twinge of fear for my friends. It was getting dangerous. Once I looked around, I noticed the numbers seemed to be thinning. This was disconcerting. I tried to catch a glimpse of the others whenever I got the chance. There: Matt. And Dylan. Jordan. Chloe. We were all still in.

When the horn was blown for the halfway point and we all scrambled to shore, I realized one of the teams was missing. Upon checking, we discovered they had to pull out. One of their members had been dragged under by a current and taken to the hospital. Also, two other teams were down to four members instead of five. This was getting serious. *Please, Chloe, Dylan, Matt … Jordan. Please be careful.*

Team White Water made it past the halfway mark, sliding through rather comfortably in third place and in a tight battle for second. It was kind of sad to see the last four teams when the scores were called out. I wished they could keep going. But I wouldn't trade places with them.

I was a little concerned for the others. Chloe had a scary wipeout and was lagging behind a bit. Dylan had been force-fed a mouthful of sand. Matt and Amber had both gotten caught inside the curl of a wave. And I wasn't going to say anything, but I'd had a pretty bad wipeout too—and had a thrumming headache because of it. Other teams were having trouble as well. Within fifteen minutes of being back on the waves, three more surfers had to be pulled from the water, a board was snapped in half, and another team quit.

At the time of the final quarter, for some reason, the halftime horn blew. Someone figured out that meant "come to shore," and we all scurried for the beach, trying to stay clear of the angry waves on our way in. There was a lot of activity in the judging booth. After a minute, someone picked up the mic and gave an explanation.

"The three remaining teams are too uneven, which is going to be a disadvantage to some. The scores are close; it's anyone's game. The judges have decided: each team must pick one member to finish the contest." We quickly huddled.

"Everyone doing alright?" I asked, getting weary nods in reply.

"I'll survive. You?" Dylan asked.

"I'm fine," I said, feeling bad about lying. "Who should go on?" We all glanced at each other. I was about to nominate Dylan, based on skill and energy levels—when they all looked at me.

"You should, Jordan." My brain balked.

"What, me? But why?"

"Well," Amber started, "I'm definitely not the best candidate."

"Same here," Matt said.

"I'm sore," Chloe added.

"And I'm exhausted," Dylan said. "Anyway, you have the best skills of all of us, Jordan." For once, I didn't know what to say. *They really think I should do it?*

"But, I—"

"Just say yes, Jordan."

"Alright."

It was so nerve-wracking watching Jordan surf those waves. Chloe and I often covered our eyes, scared to see the outcome. Part of me hadn't wanted to send him back out there. But I also knew he was our best chance, and he loved surfing more than the rest of us. Points were pouring in, yet the scores remained close. As time ran down, the more impressive the tricks became—and the more dangerous the wipeouts. Each of the three surfers were pounded at least twice. Jordan was neck and neck with the surfer from team Rip Tide, the two battling for first place. Each trick changed the ranking. Back and forth: first, second, first, second, first, second …

Minutes remained. A set of huge waves came raking through the lineup. The other two surfers caught one. But Jordan waited. Then I saw why. An enormous wave was forming. *Oh no. No. That's suicide, Jordan. Don't take it!* He took it. The drop-in alone was enough to make my heart stop. Angling his board down the line, Jordan started weaving a bit, but stayed in the center of the monster.

"He's going for a barrel ride? In that wave?!" Dylan gawked.

"I can't watch," Chloe moaned, covering her eyes.

"I can't not watch," I muttered. My eyes were glued to Jordan, as if looking away would spell his doom.

The wave was closing. He was going to be trapped inside! A wave that big could easily kill him. The impact alone was enough to crush him, let alone the ton of water following. I lost sight of Jordan as the opening tightened like the loop on a noose. For a terrible second, nothing happened. The hole was closing …

Then, just as the wave collapsed, Jordan came shooting out from the explosion of sea spray like an arrow from a bow. Speeding up the remaining crest, he gathered all the momentum possible and did a full 360 kickflip, landed perfectly, then ended with a slash over the edge of the wave, as if the stunt wasn't daring enough already.

I was on my feet in a moment, laughing and cheering with the others. There was still half a minute on the clock, but it was over. There was no question. We had won. Jordan popped out of the water and, despite the distance, I could see the huge grin on his face. When he saw us jumping around and shouting, he smiled wider and punched the air in victory.

I could practically hear him say it: "I told you I'd be OK … "

The Journal of
Amber Marie Gibson

May 4, Saturday

GO TEAM WHITE WATER!!!

Today was surfing competitions, and we won first place! It was fantastic!

There were eight teams in the first half and three in the last part. From the very start, the waves were enormous. I was so scared at first that I messed up my first two waves. But it got better as time went on.

Since people were getting hurt and pulling out, the teams were uneven by the end. So the judges had each team choose one member to continue. We chose Jordan, and he was amazing! Right at the end, he almost got caught inside a monstrous wave, but made it out at the last second, and did a kick-flip and a slash! He's crazy good ... and just plain crazy.

I pulled off my first perfect shove-it, and cross-stepped eleven steps without falling! Chloe apparently nailed some 360s, and Dylan and Matt both got a few special high scores from the judges ... and Jordan did all the above.

After it was all said and done, we had victory ice cream and recounted our daredevil tales while strolling down the boardwalk. I could have stayed there with Chloe, Dylan, Matt, and Jordan forever.

Also, I learned new surfing terms: 1) Barney and Kook refer to bad/beginner/try-hard surfers. 2) Choka means awesome/epic. 3) Gidget (which is my new nickname in the group) is a reference to an old movie about a "girl midget" surfer. I kind of like it. Fits me.

This is definitely one of the best days I've ever had. If I could do it over again, I would. Not so I could change it, but so I could do it over again exactly like it went today. Nothing could be better. It was perfect.

CHAPTER 29

Santa Barbara, V0RT3X's stronghold
Tuesday, June 25, 8:43 P.M.

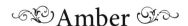 Amber

It's been almost three months since I brought C3RB3RU$'s hackers down. Still, the spy among us was nowhere to be found. Yet, now and then, money disappeared, or a connection would form between us and the enemy, only to crumble into oblivion before we could trace it. The traitor was still here. Ender had agreed that the existence of the spy shouldn't be announced. Sonja and I continued to search in secrecy; we didn't even set up in the same spot anymore, in case someone got suspicious. I was beginning to question everything we thought we knew for certain, but I still came up with nothing. Surely we were missing an important clue. It was maddening.

A message popped up on my screen from Sonja.

> Ender needs my help, be back in a bit.
> Let me know if you find anything.

I glanced across the room, caught her eye, and nodded. After exchanging words with Jason, she stood and strutted off. Just as I returned to my screen, I sensed movement. Jason was packing up, closing his laptop, and sliding it into his bag, grinning all the way. As I watched, he trotted for the giant shelves, scaled the ladder, returned with his freak GPS device, and headed for the door. Unfortunately for Jason, I sat between him and freedom, though he didn't seem to realize I had noticed. Just as he passed by, I reached out and snagged him by the back of his shirt.

"Just where do you think you're going?" I asked, slightly teasing, slightly serious.

"Out," he said distractedly.

"You do realize the sun has gone down, right?"

"Ahh, so what?!" Jason exclaimed, exasperated. "Let me go. I have somewhere I've gotta be." Considering the fact he had his GPS thing, I figured he wanted to go exploring. But it was getting late; I wasn't going to let him wander around alone.

"You can't just go off on your own after dark," I pressed, the unspoken *I'm coming with you* making itself clear.

"No," he insisted, scowling at me. Just as he opened his mouth to argue some more, his attention was drawn across the room and he faltered. Sonja had returned, deep in conversation with Ender. Jason sighed in annoyance, looking miserable. "Fine."

Jason seemed thoroughly annoyed that I had tagged along. I just kept a few steps behind him, keeping an eye out for trouble. I wasn't exactly expecting trouble, but better safe than sorry. Anyway, I was thankful for an excuse to take a break from hacking. I couldn't bear sitting around all day, staring at my computer screen for hours.

The farther we went, it began to dawn on me that Jason might actually have a specific destination. He kept glancing down at his GPS thingamajig, then making slight changes to his route. It was almost like he was tracking something. After a while, we neared the old docks. Jason seemed on edge. He pocketed his gadget and glanced around nervously. Then, as we rounded a corner, he froze. There, kneeling on the ground, wrists cuffed to a lamppost, was a girl, about his age.

"Maggie!" Jason cried out and started to run for her, but I lunged for him, managing to grab his shirt and yank him back, clapping my free hand over his mouth.

The girl jerked her head up; I realized she was gagged. The dim streetlight illuminated her face. It was the girl from the video chat! She scanned the darkness. Her gaze landed on Jason and me. She shook her head wildly, her muffled shrieks sending a desperate message: *Run.*

"It's a trap!" I hissed in Jason's ear. He started to tremble, and to my surprise, I felt a single tear slip over my hand. Suddenly, I sensed a presence somewhere behind us, something nearing quickly, quietly. I had no choice. I turned and started backing away, dragging Jason with me. I couldn't see anything. It was too dark …

The girl was scrambling, trying to get on her feet, crying and calling out. Jason wasn't helping matters. He was struggling, fighting to break free of my grip, desperate to reach her.

We entered a surrounding, artificial circle of light. The moment we did—we were surrounded. Tough-looking thugs stepped out from the darkness, hedging us in. I glanced around, searching for an escape. There was none. Panic closed over me, like water filling a sinking ship, and I started drowning in fear. *This is bad.* Someone approached from behind, chuckling. I whirled, simultaneously holding Jason behind me, trying to shield him from whatever menace was coming our way. To my surprise, Jason offered no resistance. A man stepped from the shadows into the pool of light.

"Well, whatta we got here?" he mused, a dangerous light in his eyes. The moment Jason heard the man's voice, he pressed himself closer to me, his chest rising and falling at an alarming rate.

"Who are you?" I demanded. He smiled a pearly white grin, a gold-capped tooth catching the light.

"That's for me to know, and you … to not find out." His gaze drifted behind me. "Though, I am very interested in who you and your little friend are." Now Jason was the one doing the clutching. He gripped me so hard it hurt. *He's scared. He's legitimately scared!* "Step forward, small fry."

"Don't," I whispered to Jason. The mystery man smiled again, then started slinking to my left. I turned, never taking my eyes off him. Then, too late, I realized he was heading for Maggie. He reached forward and grabbed a handful of her hair, making her cry out.

"Come out, or your freak girlfriend gets hurt." To my horror, Jason wrestled free from my grasp and stepped from behind me with no more than a moment's hesitation. "There we go. See? That wasn't so hard, was it?" the man asked, dropping Maggie.

"Jason," I whispered, "what's going on?"

"Cerberus," he breathed, confirming my fear. This had to be the leader of C3RB3RU$. Slowly, I took a step forward.

"What do you want? If you're looking for a victim, you can have me; just let these two go," I said. "They're just kids." I had no intention of giving myself up, but I had to protect Jason.

"Storm, no!" Jason hissed. Suddenly, the leader perked up.

"What did the boy just call you?" he asked, ignoring my offer. The color drained from Jason's face. "He just called you Storm, didn't he?" I suppose he took my silence as a yes. "Firestorm!" he exclaimed. "The one who defeated all my hackers, put them behind bars. What a night! A turncoat, a rogue informant, and a master hacker, all in the palm of my hand!" He looked me in the eyes, a chilling, evil, glaring smile filling his face. "I've wanted to meet you, Firestorm. I have so much I want to … repay you for." I hardly heard him. It all fell into place. Slowly, I turned to face Jason.

"You're the spy, aren't you?" I whispered, a numb sense of shock settling over me.

"Storm, I can explain," he said, a desperate tone in his voice. "Please. It's not what it seems—"

"You're helping *murderers!*" I shouted. Jason flinched like he'd been slapped.

"Sorry to break up the party," the leader cut in. "But I do believe we have something to settle." He grabbed Maggie again, but this time, he held a knife to her neck. "The boy comes with me, or she dies." He nodded, and some of the thugs grabbed Jason, dragging him over to the leader. I was frozen. Jason looked desperate.

"Storm, listen to me, I'm not—" Suddenly, there was a blur of motion behind him, a horrible *whack!* sound . . . Jason fell forward, clutching his head.

Though my body remained frozen, my mind turned back on and took in everything at once. Jason's gasps for air. Maggie's muffled screams. The thugs waiting impatiently, gathering around me. The leader hauled Jason up by the shirt collar and began to walk off. Then he paused.

"Firestorm's all yours, boys. Teach her a lesson and hand her over to me when you're done. She can be in her birthday suit, half dead, and missing some limbs when you bring her to me. As long as she's conscious enough to suffer her last moments at my hands, have all the fun you want." With that horrifying order, he turned and continued to drag Jason off. The thugs started to close in on me. I still couldn't move.

The first one approached me, sneering taunts of "hey, girly-girly." His intentions were dark. I was momentarily petrified. I felt strangled, terrified, buried under a mountain of doom. A thud and a stifled cry drew my attention past my attacker. Jason was on the ground and the leader was standing over him, laughing. *He … hit Jason.* Rage clouded my vision.

They were going to rape me, beat the daylights out of Jason, slit Maggie's throat, and toss the three of us into the ocean. Our bodies would never be found. *What am I going to do? . . . I'm going to fight.*

Now my terror was merely a mask, one I kept on for my attackers. As the creep began to slip my sleeve down, the long-buried instincts kicked in—and my mask of fear fell off. With speed like lightning, I made my move. Grabbing his wrist, I twisted it back over his shoulder. A surprised, pained shriek rang out and I heard a crack. He hit the ground. My heel made contact with the back of his head and he was out. *One down, about ten to go.* The others were stunned to silence, stupid, blank looks of shock on their faces; apparently, they didn't expect this pint-sized girl to fight back. I felt a dangerous smile pulling at my lips.

"You wanna play? Come on. Let's play. Winner gets her," I taunted, pointing at Maggie.

After a moment, they snapped out of their surprise. One came at me with speed, his fist aimed at my face. I dodged it, letting him overshoot. Bringing my elbow down hard between his shoulder blades, I watched as he dropped like a stone, smacking his head on the pavement. *Two down.* In one fluid motion, I swung a punch of my own at the creep coming at me from the side, then launched straight into a side kick, pegging another.

Quickly, I leaned back; a dented wooden bat bent the air in front of my face. Using my momentum, I kicked up, knocking the weapon off its course, making its wielder stumble. Temporarily landing on my back, I rolled away as the beam pounded the ground where I had been seconds before. Grabbing it, I twisted just right and managed to bring the attacker down with it, cranium to concrete. To my dismay, the bat was stuck underneath him. With no time to wrestle with the unconscious brute for the weapon, I sprang to my feet and continued to fight unaided.

Time seemed to be glitching around, going from superspeed to slow motion and back. My heartbeat pounded in my ears. I felt electric adrenaline filling every fiber of my being. This was real.

. . . I never understood why Edge forced me to go through what I called FBI Boot Camp. He tried to cram-teach me everything, from defusing a bomb to picking a safe drop spot to how to fight. I never landed a blow on him. It always made me furious. I always ended up on the ground, his boot on my back, my face on the mat, a ringing in my ears. "Again," he'd say. "Come on, hit me already. Fight, Amber, fight!" Somehow, maybe . . .

perhaps he somehow knew it'd save my life one day.

. . . *Move!* The air warped as a fist flew inches from my face. I kicked my foot out, tripping my attacker. Out of the corner of my eye, I saw one of them reach for something inside his coat. I raced toward him at full sprint. At the last possible second, I hit the ground and slid as a silent, metal sphere of death sliced the air. Leaping up, I started to wrestle with him for the gun. I heard the *click* of the weapon being cocked. Grabbing his hands, I jerked them straight up as the gun fired into the night sky.

Out of the corner of my eye, I saw one of them head toward Maggie and reach for her. She thrashed, terrified, trying to get away, then raised her leg and delivered a strong kick to his face. He crumpled back, then turned a hate-filled glare on her, slowly crawling closer, making her squirm in fear. *No! He'll kill her!* Returning my attention to my attacker, I pushed him as hard as I could without letting go, then jerked him back toward me, straight into my foot, knocking the air from his lungs. The gun was ripped loose. Whirling, I took a split-second to aim, then pulled the trigger. There was a shriek; the thug had fallen flat, holding his leg—and Maggie remained out of his reach.

"Stay away from her!" I yelled, firing the gun into the ground inches from his head to prove my point.

I fumbled with the silencer, desperately trying to get it off. After ducking and whacking someone in the face with the gun, I managed to unscrew the nozzle. Aiming the gun straight up, I pulled the trigger over and over, until it was out of ammo. *Much more efficient than calling 911. Help is on the way.*

Suddenly, my legs were knocked from under me and I crashed to the ground. The all-too-familiar ringing filled my ears. I'd smacked my head. Hands grabbed my ankle and I felt someone scramble up my body, trying to pin me down. The one with the gun. I never knocked him out! I struggled, trying to break away. His hands groped for my neck. Then I remembered what I was holding. I swung the gun at him as forcefully as I could. It didn't do much damage, but it was all I needed. It stunned him just long enough for me to roll, putting me on top. I grabbed his head and slammed it down. He was out.

Tossing the gun aside, I turned to face my remaining attackers. There were only three left. After a fistfight, one was down. The next one proved tougher. He seemed to know better than to let his momentum take him anywhere near me. After dodging most of my punches, he threw one of his own. My head was still fuzzy, and I didn't move fast enough. It glanced off my shoulder. I almost lost my balance. Then a desperate idea came to me: I let myself fall.

The moment he started to reach for me, I gathered the last scraps of my strength and launched myself at him, barely avoiding his grasp. Wrapping one arm around his neck, my momentum carried me around until I ended on his back. I jammed my finger into the pressure point by his ear and held on for dear life. It was like riding a bull. Within a few seconds, his thrashing stopped and he hit the ground, down for the count.

I stood, scanning the darkness for the last one. *Where did he … ? I don't see—* Suddenly, searing, raw agony slashed across my back from my shoulder, crawling and ripping like a bolt of lightning. Distantly, I heard a scream. It took me a moment to realize it was my scream. I dropped to my knees, gasping in pain. Out of the corner of my eye, I saw red blossom on my sleeve. Shakily, I turned to see a blood-stained knife, raised above my attacker's head.

Wham!

Shock covered the thug's face and he slumped forward, the dagger clattering harmlessly to the ground. After a second, he fell flat. Jason stood over him, knees knocking, clutching an old pipe in his quivering hands. My eyes flicked behind him. Despite the spots and stars obscuring my vision, I got a glance at the leader, unconscious on the ground, shards of a shattered bottle around his head. Maggie was gone, and in her place lay empty handcuffs and gag. I turned my attention back to Jason. He was trembling uncontrollably, his breathing ragged, his eyes wide and empty, like the onset of a panic attack.

"Jason?! Talk to me. What's wrong?"

"Storm … *help—*" He collapsed. I lunged, catching him just before his head hit pavement.

Dread filled me as I lowered Jason and rolled him over. He was thoroughly banged up. After running my hand over his chest, I decided he didn't have any broken ribs. There were no obvious wounds on his neck or shoulders. Then I remembered. Carefully, I lifted his head and gently ran my fingers through his hair. I looked at my hand. Wet and red.

"Hang in there, Jason. Please, hang in there … "

Sirens. My gunshot call for help had reached the police. For a moment,

I thought the nightmare was over. But then I realized: *we can't let the police find us.* No matter what I said, we'd all end up in prison. I quickly evaluated the situation. Based on Jason's breathing pattern, he hadn't gone into shock yet. His heartbeat was relatively normal considering the circumstance—it was only slightly fast. He wasn't in immediate danger of bleeding out. Once again, I found myself silently thanking Edge for my training.

The combination of pain, the adrenaline drop, and the emotional panic must have flipped his internal power switch, I thought. As if to validate my assessment, Jason flinched and moaned quietly. He was going to be OK.

"Hang on, Jason. I'm going to get you out of here," I whispered.

Grabbing the dagger, I sliced off the hem of my shirt and did my best to wrap it around Jason's head. After a short struggle, I managed to get him onto my back, piggyback style. He was surprisingly light. I gritted my teeth against the pain in my shoulder. I would have to deal with that later. Once the adrenaline wore off, I wouldn't be able to protect myself, let alone Jason. As I stood, Jason muttered something that sounded distantly like "Storm," and though he didn't lift his head, slowly, weakly, he wrapped his arms around my neck.

"Hang on, Jason. Hang on."

A little too late, I realized something of near cosmic importance: *Sonja is going to murder me.*

Sure enough, she all but lost her mind the moment she caught sight of us.

"Jason! Oh my … " The color drained from her face. "Holy— Storm, *what the heck happened?!*" Everyone looked up; several came running.

"Cerberus," I answered, trying to ignore her and focus on the important things. Ender sprinted to a stop beside me and helped lower Jason to the ground. "He talked to me a bit on the way here; he's semiconscious. He's going to be alright. The bleeding's stopped. It's mainly his head. He didn't go into shock. He's just a little disoriented." Sonja looked dangerously close to losing it.

"Storm, I swear, if—"

"Sonja?" All noise ceased, and all attention turned to Jason. Slowly, he opened his eyes. "I'm OK. Storm … saved me. Please, just—just don't get mad." For a moment, as relief washed over her features, I thought I could see tears in Sonja's eyes.

"You stupid boy. You stupid, stupid boy, you could have been killed.

Don't ever scare me like that again, you hear? You stupid, pigheaded child, I almost lost you," she scolded over and over again, insulting in the most endearing way possible while stroking the hair from his face. Then Ender noticed the blood slowly trickling down my arm and off my fingertips.

"Storm, you're hurt," he said. I tried to shrug, but ended up cringing.

"It's nothing. Really."

"No, it's not," Ender murmured. Without asking permission, he stepped behind me, pushed my sleeve off my shoulder, and peeked down the back of my shirt. I thought I would die.

"Ender!!!" I shrieked, mortified.

"Sorry. Do hold still," he muttered, gently inspecting the gash. Someone must have brought a first aid box, because he started mopping up the blood with a sheet of gauze. I tried to focus on anything but the intense pain now radiating across my entire back. "What happened?" he asked.

Jason caught my gaze. I could see it in his face. He was silently pleading with me. My brain churned, and I made my decision.

"Jason picked up on a stray signal. Sonja was busy, so he asked me if I could come with him to check it out." I bit back a cry as Ender started cleaning the wound. "Too dangerous to go alone. It was a trap. Cerberus was waiting for us. There was a fight; we got separated. The cops showed up. We got out before they arrived. I think the attackers were all still unconscious." I glanced at Jason. "And thanks to Jason, the ring leader was also down for the count. Probably all apprehended."

He appeared overwhelmed with gratitude as he gave a silent, shaky sigh of relief. I threw him a quick glance. I was letting him off the hook for now. But later, when all the ruckus died down, I was going to demand an explanation. All around, people were praising Jason, amazed that he— the youngest hacker—had defeated their enemy. For a split-second, Jason caught my eye, and though his lips didn't move, he smiled.

We were both fussed over for the next half hour, then things started to settle down a bit. Ender made me promise I'd check myself into an urgent care or hospital within the next few hours, though I had no intention of doing any such thing. I eventually managed to corner Jason once Sonja had stopped puppy-guarding him.

"Care to explain … *spy?*" I asked sternly, though it was clearly a demand, not a question. Jason was silent for a long time, as if carefully selecting each word he would use.

"I'm not a traitor," he said slowly.

"And I'm almost willing to believe you. But not quite. I need some convincing."

Once again, Jason was lost in thought. After glancing around, he nodded. "Alright. Follow me."

With that, he headed toward the back of the building, typing away at his GPS device the whole way. He started down one of the halls, then side-stepped into one of the dark, unfinished rooms. Dropping the GPS onto an old table, he walked to the window along the far wall and pushed up hard on the edges. To my surprise, it creaked open; apparently, it hadn't been welded shut like the others. Jason pulled a small flashlight from his pocket and flicked it, sending a beam of light streaking into the night.

After a few seconds, I caught a glimpse of a hooded figure emerging from the darkness of a nearby building, hurrying toward the open window. Before I could say a word in warning, Jason reached out and helped the living shadow through the opening. The moment the mysterious person's feet touched the ground, she threw her arms around Jason. He immediately returned the affection.

"It's OK. We're safe now," he soothed. "Are you OK?"

A nod. "I'm fine," a small voice whispered. "What about you? You were hurt!" I shifted, unsure what all this meant. The person seemed to sense my presence and gasped, whirling to try and hide behind Jason. He chuckled a little.

"It's alright. She's a friend," he said, gently pulling the person back around to face me, wrapping his arm endearingly around the shy one's shoulders. I couldn't see anything past the deep hood—until Jason started lifting it. A girl emerged from the shadow of the fabric. "Maggie, meet Storm. Storm, Maggie." Sure enough, it was the green-and-black-haired girl I had seen cuffed to the lamppost earlier that night—and from Jason's video screen months before. We stared at each other. Jason smiled.

"OK. Yeah. You were right, Storm. She's my girlfriend. But … she's also my spy." Jason's smile seemed to spread to Maggie; she grinned a little at this.

"Spies? What exactly have you two been doing?" I asked, unable to take my eyes from this strange girl. "And tell me plain: who've you been double-crossing? Vortex or Cerberus?"

"Cerberus," Jason said, snapping my focus back to him. "We've been collecting info and giving it to Ender anonymously. We're both loyal to Vortex."

I'd had a feeling Jason was on our side, if not for the sake of doing what was right, then for the sake of his sister. I felt there had to be some logical explanation for all of this, but even so, hearing him say it out loud was a huge relief.

"Then what about the money and the virus?" I pressed.

"We had nothing to do with the virus," Jason insisted. "But, yes. I did take money. It was to save a life."

"My mom has cancer," Maggie explained, and Jason gave her a little squeeze of comfort. "Jason said he'd help me scrape up the money to get her treatments. Now she actually stands a chance," she said, hopeful determination in her face. I nodded—saddened, overwhelmed, trying to swallow all of this without chewing. It was just so much to take in.

"I wish her the best of luck," I said quietly. More questions pelted my brain. "But why all the secrecy? Why not just tell us what you were doing?"

"Sonja," Jason answered, shrugging. "She'd never go along with it all. She would sooner tie me to a tree than let me be a spy." Maggie giggled, lifting her mood into a smile.

He has a point. "But why do it? And how long?" I asked, feeling more and more amazed.

"Maggie and I've been hackers for Vortex since middle school," Jason said. "But Cerberus just kept getting stronger. Eventually, Sonja became second in command, and I heard about all the damage Cerberus was actually doing. That's when Maggie and I started scheming. We thought, if someone from Vortex infiltrated Cerberus, we could finally have the upper hand. And who would suspect a kid?"

"I left Vortex about … two and a half years ago to go join Cerberus," Maggie said. "Jason wanted to be the one to go be a spy, but couldn't for obvious reasons." Things were starting to make sense when my mind tripped on something else.

"But Maggie, if you've been a hacker at Cerberus, how come you didn't get caught when I brought their database down?" She grinned and looked at Jason.

"I was protecting her," Jason said, smiling. "That's why my computer crashed. There wasn't enough time to contact her and tell her to escape, so I just did my best to cover her system." For a moment, I stared at him in shock. *He's craftier than I gave him credit for.*

"Then what went wrong?" I asked. Jason shrugged, glancing at Maggie for explanation.

"I entered Cerberus under a fake identity," Maggie explained. "I hacked the archives and edited some information on a Kim Abrams, a dead hacker with the same general description as me. Somehow, they figured out Kim was dead and that I was lying to them. They followed me to our rendezvous point and set me up as bait." She looked at Jason. "Now what do we do? I don't think I can get back in … "

"Of course not. It's over, Mag. The war is won."

"It's over?" she asked, wide-eyed with disbelief. "We really won?"

"It's over," Jason confirmed, smiling.

Maggie looked as if she might burst into tears as she threw her arms around Jason once more. Part of me was ecstatic this story had a happy ending. But part of me was troubled. I started pacing, cringing at the thrumming pain creeping across my shoulder.

"Jason, you have to tell Sonja," I said.

"What? Why? It's done now!" he exclaimed, exasperated.

"She deserves to know," I insisted. "I'm not sure she will be as freaked out as you think. She might even be proud of you once she cools down. Yes, she'll probably be a little upset, but think of how steaming mad she will be if she finds out on her own."

"Storm, no. This is a bad idea—"

"I'm not debating this with you. Either you tell her or I do." That caught Jason off guard.

"You're not serious," he said slowly, evidently hoping I was somehow joking.

"Oh, I'm dead serious. Look, if she tries to kill you, I'll step in. But I can't continue on with life as if none of this happened! You've got to tell her. Tonight."

Maggie looked concerned, watching Jason for a reaction. He was quiet, thinking hard.

Finally, after a long, agonizing wait … "Fine," he sighed. "I'll tell her."

A few minutes later, I watched from a safe distance as Jason walked up to Sonja, Maggie trailing a step behind him. Though I couldn't hear what was being said, I could see well enough. Sonja's face went from raw red to death white to bruised purple and back again; shock and rage and horror covered her expressions. But she remained still, silent.

Jason finished and braced for the inevitable explosion. Indeed, I was worried I had been wrong about how she would react. Sonja was unmoving, rigid with shock, her fists clenched tightly at her sides, a flashing fire in her eyes, staring at him in disbelief. There was a tense pause. Then, suddenly, she took a quick step, pulled Jason forward, and embraced him tightly. After a moment of stunned stillness, Jason slowly returned the hug. I smiled. I could leave in peace. Grabbing my computer bag, I slipped out the side door and headed for home.

By the time I got back, it was nearly three in the morning. I was beginning to regret my decision to not go to an urgent care or hospital; my shoulder was ablaze with pain. *Suck it up,* I scolded myself. *You can handle this. All that matters is that everyone's safe now.*

I peeled my ruined, blood-soaked shirt off and dropped it in the shower. I'd scrub it best I could, then throw it away later. After some twisting and turning in front of the mirror, I managed to patch up the bandage Ender had fixed me up with. The gash was about seven inches long, across the back of my shoulders. I was lucky the blade hadn't hit my neck. Since I didn't feel like fighting with a shirt, I simply pulled my jacket on and flopped onto my bed. My mind was swimming with all that had transpired in the past few hours.

Life can finally settle down. Things are the way they should be. I'll be fine in a couple of days. No surfing for a day or two, though … I don't want to be shark bait.

I smiled at that thought and eventually drifted off to sleep.

CHAPTER 30

The Salt Breeze Apartment Complex, Apt. 1407
Friday, August 9, 12:10 A.M.

༺Amber༻

The dark, silent peace was shattered. My eyes snapped open. For a moment, I wasn't sure what had woken me. But there it was again—*my phone?* I didn't know why I bothered to put it on vibrate every night. It woke me up anyway. I stared at it dumbly as it jittered across the side table. My first jumbled thought was that I had forgotten something; perhaps I had left my bag or sketchbook when I was hanging out with Chloe, Dylan, Matt, and Jordan that evening, and one of them was calling to tell me. Or perhaps Jason, Sonja, or Ender were hacking me. Maybe someone on the other side of the world had dialed the wrong number by mistake—then I realized how late it was.

Who in their right mind would call anyone this time of night? I wondered foggily, then realized I was about to miss the call. Without bothering to look at the ID, I snatched up the phone and swiped the accept button on the last ring.

"Hello?" I mumbled.

"You're alive. Good. What the heck, Amber? Don't tell me you were *asleep*?!"

"Why shouldn't I be?" I muttered, my tired brain trying to figure out who I was speaking to and why they were so riled up and rude.

"Because I was expecting you to call the moment the clock struck midnight. That's why." *Hold up. Edge?*

"Edge? But why are you—" Suddenly, my heart tripped. Slowly, I pulled the phone from my ear and looked at the date. August 9.

Distantly, I heard Edge call my name impatiently. My head was swimming. *It's over. My punishment … is over?* I couldn't believe it. A smile started crawling up my face, though I didn't feel it. *I did it. I can return to hacking! I survived the year!* Something stopped me cold.

Survived?

Hadn't I done more than that? Had I *lived*, perhaps? Had I laughed? Had I been truly happy? Or had it all been a dream? I had a chance to return to my real life, to be Laelaps again! I could go back to reality. Then … why did the dream seem so precious all of a sudden? Memories from the past year flooded to the surface. Jordan. Chloe. Dylan. Matt. The firefly festival. Joining V0RT3X. Surfing. The surprise birthday party. Christmas. Playing marbles with Jason. Settling my differences with Sonja. Squeaker the dolphin. Surfing competitions. Smiling and laughing with my friends …

Perhaps … I'm different now? Suddenly, I shook my head, scattering these foolish thoughts. *I am Laelaps. Master hacker, friend of the FBI, enemy of Teumessian, fighting to avenge those I've lost. And I'm finally back.*

"I'm still here. Talk to me. What have I missed? Get me up to speed." I could practically feel Edge's dangerous smile on the other side of the line.

"Welcome back. Teumessian noticed Laelaps was out of commission and they've grown bolder. The long absence of an adversary has left them king of the hill. I'll admit: it's been rather difficult to hold them back without you."

As Edge talked, I ran around the apartment, booting up my computer, grabbing coffee, clearing the desktop, and pulling on my headset, feeding the call through it. Kneeling, I slid Cyra from beneath my desk. I was trembling. I could hardly contain my ecstasy. Gathering my nerve, I pressed the power button. Cyra whirred to life and my computer displayed the launch data for my Laelaps programs. I almost laughed out loud.

"Sector nine has a new branch, and that's the point of focus for now. Got it?" Edge finished. I grinned.

"Got it. Time to knock Teumessian's crown off." Sliding into the chair, I shut all else from my mind and prepared for battle. "Cyra, activate hacking program Laelaps."

```
>Launch in 3 …
    >2 …
    >1 …
>Launch complete.
```

That night, Teumessian suffered a vast loss. They didn't know what hit them. Oh, I was back. My power had been restored. My fury had been caged long enough. They would pay. I let loose the wolf—the wild, dangerous, blood-lusting killer. I released the hunter dog—the precise, methodic, shadow-clad tracker. I was Laelaps once more.

But what I didn't see ...

```
>Error_
>Error_
>//Router missing
>Error_
>Initiating protocol 35_2174
>Searching for closest network...
>Network found
>Connecting to "J_surfs.net" (Not Secure, Protected)
>Deciphering log on...
>Connected
```

THE JOURNAL OF
AMBER MARIE GIBSON

August 9, Friday

At long last, my punishment is over. I am Laelaps once more.

Being away for so long must have done something to my brain. I actually forgot today was my day of freedom until Mr. Ice-E called me earlier this morning. Well, I say "morning," but it's still pitch-black outside. But I don't think I'll be sleeping anytime soon.

There is much to do. Sector nine has a new branch and is guarded by a strong A.I. Until my programs adapt, they won't be able to fight it off very well and I will be vulnerable. I've already started working on the code, though, so it won't be long before I can read this new enemy like a book. The hole in sector three was patched, so there will be no more slipping in that way. But there's a promising hitch in sector two -- I need to investigate it closer. Cyra is back and doing well. I plan to upgrade some of the command capabilities tomorrow.

Just now, I stole enough information to ruin four attacks Teumessian planned to carry out within the month. They have suffered a huge loss. As Edge said, they have been king of the hill for long enough. I just knocked their crown flying.

Even if I forgot about today, it doesn't matter now. Because I'll never forget again. I'm back. And I'll never let anything stand between me and Teumessian's defeat.

CHAPTER 31

The Salt Breeze Apartment Complex, Apt. 1407
Saturday, August 24, 2 A.M.

ᥰᥱᥰ Amber ᥰᥱᥰ

Before I was grounded, I was living the dream—everything I ever wanted. When that life was put on hold, I entered a daydream. From the start, deep down, I knew it couldn't last. Now I've been called to return to my old life. I was still living a dream, but it was a different kind. At first … it was a living nightmare.

I missed my friends, I missed surfing, drawing, reading, sleeping, being normal! But I had no choice. There was no going back. The only thing left to do was bury the past and press on. So that's just what I did. Once I let go, the ache faded and I was happy once more. Why shouldn't I be? Nothing stood between me and my destiny. Life was simple. Rest wasn't essential. I hardly ever had to leave the apartment. My side art jobs were dropped. I stopped responding to group texts. All these trivial things fell away, leaving me to focus on the only thing that mattered: defeating Teumessian.

So, yes. I was perfectly happy again. All was as it should be.

Just not tonight.

Insomnia was plucking the strings of my mind, wiring it up and making my heart race. I couldn't settle. But the more I tossed and turned, the more agitated I felt. Finally, something within me snapped. *Forget it. I'm not sleeping anytime soon.* Swinging my legs over the edge of the bed, I escaped my linen prison and headed for the balcony.

Cool air met me at the door. It was a lovely, peaceful night. The darkness lay over the face of the buildings, covering the street and turning the sea into a rolling mass of black velvet. The moon was dim, throwing a hazy glow here and there. My eyes slowly swept the view, taking in the stillness.

Wait—there, on the beach. *A person?* Yes, there was a single person sitting on the sand, head tilted back, watching, patiently waiting for something. I glanced up. There was nothing but empty, starry sky. Looking back at the shore and its lone occupant, I felt strangely compelled to join them.

Normally, I would have let it be and gone back to admiring the night. But it was almost as if someone nudged me onward, whispering to me to investigate. I must have been far more tired than I thought, because I was halfway across the street before I realized I was moving. The closer I got, the clearer the person became, until …

"Oh, hi Jordan."

I almost jumped out of my skin.

"Ahhh!" I turned. "Oh, Amber." My heart slowed again. "Wow. I didn't even hear you coming. What are you doing up so late?"

"Couldn't sleep," she said, shrugging. "What about you?" Grinning, I shot a quick glance back at the sky.

"There's a meteor shower tonight, in about—" I checked my watch. "In about four minutes. Wanna stay?" Amber smiled faintly, and in answer, she sat down beside me. I was glad to see her again. Lately, she had been strangely absent.

"We've all missed you the past two Thursdays," I said.

"Yeah, been pretty busy," she murmured quietly, smiling. "I, uh, kinda got my old job back. They decided they needed me."

"Really?!" I sat bolt upright to look at her. "That's fantastic!"

"Um-hmm," Amber muttered. "Yeah. It's great." Due to her level of enthusiasm, I couldn't figure out whether she was talking to me … or herself. Suddenly, a rift of bright light briefly tore open the darkness as a meteor flashed across the night sky.

"There's one!" I exclaimed, pointing excitedly, though it was already gone. *Thank you, Lord, for my friends.* Instead of wishing on a star, I thank the Lord for my blessings. It's amazing to step back and realize how many I have.

"I've never seen one before now," Amber said. I could hear the smile in her voice. "It's really pretty."

"They really are," I agreed. Another one streaked across the horizon. *Thank you for my family, especially Lexie.* "I'm surprised more people aren't out to watch the show." Two more. *Thank you for saving me, and for the hope you give.* I glanced at Amber. "Did you ever want to be an astronaut when you were a kid?"

"Yes," she admitted, grinning. "Right up until the fateful day I realized I was shrimp-sized and would never qualify for a mission to Mars." Amber shook her head with a short, pitiful laugh. "I was devastated. But then I discovered chemistry and decided I wanted to be the next Dimitri Mendeleev and discover the secrets of quantum mechanics and the elements."

"That's ambitious," I said, chuckling. "Were you good at it, or did you just enjoy blowing things up?" Now Amber was laughing too.

"Both, I guess. I've been reading adult books since before I could reach the top shelf." Another flash of light. Then two more! *Thank you for Sophie, for my little home by the sea, and for the sea itself.*

"Yeah, same here. Hunter showed me his old school books about the planets, and all I wanted for a few years was to go see them in person," I said. "I did the Styrofoam solar system thing for the science project two years in a row." We both chuckled at this, then watched the shooting stars in silence for a while, sand at our backs, faces turned toward the sky.

Thank you for the kids in the youth group at church. Thank you for Betty's kindness over the years. Thank you for Ocean Front Rescue and saving it in such a miraculous way. Thank you for my memory. Thank you for bringing Amber to Santa Barbara. Thank you for music and color; the world would be dull without them. Thank you for books, too. Thank you for helping and protecting us at surfing competitions. Thank you for this meteor shower!

"What do you think is out there? Beyond the stars, beyond the edge of the universe?" I asked, my mind swimming with wonder. To my utmost surprise, Amber hesitated—just briefly—then answered.

"Eternity. Heaven ... God." *Did I hear her right?* Numbly, I turned and stared at her in shock. She noticed and chuckled, in a sad sort of way. "You thought that I didn't think there is a God. No, there is. I know He's real."

I managed to recover my senses. "You've never wanted to talk about God. What ... what do you believe about Him?" Amber frowned, as if she hadn't thought of why she was bringing this up now, and devoted a good deal of thought to her answer. Eventually, she let out a little sigh.

"I guess something along the lines of, 'All have sinned, and fallen short of the glory of God,' from Romans 3:23. Also, 'For the wages of sin is death, but the gift of God is eternal life through Jesus Christ our Lord.' That was from, like, Romans 6:23, I think. Then, 'Believe on the Lord Jesus Christ, and you will be saved.' That's Acts 16:31. After all that, it goes something like … " I couldn't believe what I was hearing. *She's right on the brink! A step away!* Amber was still talking. "… And, 'If I go and prepare a place for you, I will come again and receive you to myself, that where I am, there you may be also.' That's from John 14:3."

"Amber, what is stopping you? You know the truth! Why haven't you accepted it?"

Amber thought about this, calmly selecting her answer. "Because I don't believe God is good. He can't be. Look around, Jordan. The world … it's a terrible place. People are living in fear, suffering, dying, and doing terrible things to each other. Why doesn't He just stop it? Actually, why did He let it happen in the first place? No, I just can't believe God is good." She announced bitterly.

"Oh, Amber. But He is good!" I exclaimed, my heart going out to this poor, broken, lost soul. "Yes, the world is a dark place, I agree with you totally, but God didn't make it that way. To be honest, half the bad stuff that happens—well, we bring it on ourselves, some way or another, wouldn't you say?"

"I guess so," she muttered, eyes following another meteor.

Thank you, Lord, for this opportunity. I pressed on. "You said it yourself: humans are fallen. We're wicked at heart. So it's not really God's fault we're this way. We chose it."

"But, shouldn't He just … fix it? And what about the terrorists dropping bombs on innocent people, or the communists starving citizens into obedience, or cancer, natural disasters, child abuse, and wars? I guess it is our fault, but why doesn't He do something?"

"He did do something," I pointed out. "He sent Jesus."

"But Jesus promised He would save the world. It's still messed up," she said sadly.

"He didn't save the world, He is *saving* the world, one person at a time. With His help, it's the job of the saved ones to make a difference. The world isn't *all* bad, you know." Amber nodded slowly, chewing on this new perspective. "And while He was on this earth, Jesus did make a difference. He healed thousands, helped the poor, taught the masses to honor God and live at peace with one another. He even gave His life to save us, to take our punishment. Then He rose again to show the penalty of death had been paid in full. Amber, if you believe even half of what you just told me, then surely you see what I mean."

There was silence. A long silence. Then a thought hit me. "God's promise to mankind is not that He will protect us from hardship, but that He will be with us through it. If, that is, we accept the free invitation to be His child."

A white, blazing star darted across the sky. *Thank you, Lord. Thank you.*

Honestly, I didn't feel preached at. The whole thing felt more like a conversation than a sermon. My mind was churning. I'd always had the impression that Jesus was supposed to have done all the work. He was supposed to pound out all the kinks and leave a perfect society. But His followers actually suffered because of Him. People hated them. So I'd always felt that He sort of made things worse. But people do hate those who do what is right, those who repress the wickedness in the world.

What if what Jordan said was true? It was. *Was it?* I knew it myself. I'll admit, the verses I'd memorized in AWANA all those long years ago with Ashley ... they hadn't made sense at first. They seemed to be some sort of weird, non-rhyming religious poems of sorts. But as I went on with my life, I began to understand what they meant.

Yes. Mankind has fallen. Even the best people are selfish and wicked; they only think about themselves, and the good they do is corrupted. Their only purpose is to gratify themselves, not the people they are "helping." We are absolutely depraved. I felt it in myself and tried to fight it, to make up for all the wrong I had done.

I had proof enough that God was real. From all the studying I had done, I had come to the conclusion myself: this world couldn't just happen. Someone or something had to have made it. If someone took the pieces of a clock—the screws, the hands, the glass, the gears, and the battery—and put them in a bag and shook it, they'd never end up with a clock. Even if all the right ingredients for the universe were thrown together, there was no way, even in a million years, that they could produce life. It was just too complex. You can't get something from nothing. No matter how long you have. Start with nothing, and you get nothing.

So, I had evidence there was a God.

Also, I saw the change in Ashley when she got saved. It was frighteningly strange. Foreign. She'd always been good to me, but I had seen a whole new level of kindness from her. It was just … love, in its strongest, most selfless, most genuine, purest form. It didn't make sense. No way could that have come from Ashley. She really did change when she decided to follow Jesus. She'd begged me to as well.

Never before had I thought of Christians as God's "children," or "change-bringers." I thought they were just goody two-shoes. Ashley once said that God was growing Christians to be more like Him, showing them how to love like He loves. So, if Christians really were reflections—yes, reflections of sorts—of God … if Ashley, my siblings, my parents, Jordan, Chloe, Dylan, and Matt were any indication of what God was like … perhaps … *Could Jordan be right? Is God good?*

I stared at the sky for what felt like half of eternity, mind racing, my thoughts warring, my heart pounding, my logic and heart screaming at each other. The meteors continued to streak by, but I wasn't making wishes anymore. My head couldn't produce anything other than questions.

Eventually, the shooting stars faded and I realized I was watching an empty sky. Turning, I looked over at Jordan. He had fallen asleep. What he had said kept me wide awake, though. *You've all but convinced me …*

I awoke to Amber kneeling over me, shaking my shoulders hard and calling my name. When she realized I was awake, she sat back, sighing, a deep, empty void beyond her eyes.

"The meteor shower is over," she said quietly. "I'm going home. What you say might be true, it might not. But I'm not deciding tonight." The recent events clicked into place in my mind and I sat up.

"Tomorrow isn't promised us," I said slowly, concerned. "Why put it off?" Amber gazed at me sadly for a moment.

"Because … I just need time to think. I'm not ready."

With that, she stood and walked off without looking back. I too stood, watching her go. I don't actually "wish upon a star," but as that last speck of light fell and faded from the sky, I whispered a single wish into the cool night air.

"I wish … I wish Amber would come to Christ."

With that, it was over. The sky went black, and the world went back to sleep.

CHAPTER 32

The Salt Breeze Apartment Complex, Apt. 1307
Monday, August 26, 1:57 A.M.

Jordan

I woke with a start. Never before had I been so wide awake so fast. The moment my brain registered the awful noise, I clapped my hands over my ears and rolled off the side of my bed. *Make it stop, make it stop, make it stop!* If I had to rate the shrillness, I would say about 4,000 Hz. In other words, worse than nails on a chalkboard. And it was reverberating all around me.

I shoved myself upright and looked around, feeling as scared as a puppy in a thunderstorm. Where on earth was this dreadful sound coming from? My eyes widened in horror when I noticed embers flying from my door. My tired head couldn't make sense of it. *Well, that's not normal. Why are there fireworks … no, sparks! What's going on?* Then it hit me. I had seen it on TV once on a crime show. Someone was sawing through the dead bolt. This was a break-in.

What is protocol for this kind of situation? No one teaches this type of thing in school or college—or anywhere for that matter. I was more astounded than afraid, actually, and feeling rather annoyed at having my door chopped up in the middle of the night. But I started being afraid when the door swung open and three armed intruders rushed in. They were yelling at me in some foreign tongue and waving guns around. They were interested in me and me alone. They weren't here to steal. They were here to kill me. I scrambled backward, trying to get as far away as possible.

The night was a pleasant one, so I had left the balcony door wide open. It would buy me a few seconds. But ultimately, my brains were probably going to end up all over the walls no matter what I did. What was the point?

Where was I going to go, over the side? The phrase "choose your poison" came to mind, and I realized there was nowhere to run, nowhere to hide. No escape.

I was cornered. My attackers seemed to revel in it. They took their time, slowly advancing toward me, snickering at my terror. I couldn't back up anymore; the balcony railing was already digging into my spine. If I leaned back any farther, I would go over the edge. I glanced over my shoulder at the ground far below. The nose of the gun came up and pointed at me.

This is it. I don't know why, but I'm going to die tonight. I wasn't afraid to die, but I didn't exactly want to. There was sadness at the prospect of leaving my friends and family behind, and the disappointment that so many hopes and dreams would forever remain incomplete. Worse yet, I had the dreadful sense that this wasn't the end. It was the beginning ... of something worse. Something much worse.

It happened so fast ... so fast.

There was a scrambling sound above my head, then I felt the air in front of me bend and warp as a figure sailed over my head, landing between me and the intruders. *Amber!* She leaped up and flung her arms out in attempt to shield me with her body.

"*No—!*" A muffled thunderclap cut her cry short. *Bang!* They ... they shot her.

The impact made her lose her balance, launching her back, straight into my arms—and beyond. *Oh no. No, no, no! Help!* My brain screamed what my voice could not as we fell backward over the railing. Just before we went into free-fall, I grabbed Amber's arm. *I can't let her die.*

My mind went into hyperdrive. I reached for something—anything!— that would keep us from going *splat.* Lightning fast, my hand closed around my surfboard tether. The sudden halt sent searing pain spiking down my shoulder. Our lifeline wouldn't last much longer, and Amber's hand began to slip from mine. Her breaths were coming in short gasps. Seconds. She would fall ... Above us, I could hear the gunmen rush back inside, chattering furiously at each other. Evidently, they believed their prey had fallen and was dead.

I could feel the tether beginning to fray. Twangy vibrations were pinging down the line at an alarming rate. A desperate idea came to me. I swung once, and back, one more time—and then let go. We sailed through the air and dropped onto the balcony below. I rolled and tumbled for a few feet, but

Amber was like a rag doll. She collapsed in a misshapen, crumpled heap. I sprang up and pulled her against the wall. Beyond her quivering, she wasn't moving at all.

"*Amber!* Please, answer me!" After a frightfully long pause, her eyes fluttered, half open. She struggled to focus on me.

"J-Jordan ... ?" As recognition sank in, a tiny, broken smile flickered across her lips, ending in a grimace. "I'm ... so sorry," she whispered. Her voice was so weak ... Grabbing her trembling hands, I pressed them against her bleeding abdomen.

"Don't move. Hold your hands here, don't let go. I'm gonna get you out of here, OK?"

Turning to the glass doors, I quickly scanned for any sign of life. *Vacant. Good.* I slammed into the glass with all my might. It shattered into a trillion shards, twinkling briefly like icy stars as they rained down around me. The glinting spikes dug into my hands and knees as I hit the floor, but I ignored the pain as I scrambled to my feet and turned to scoop up Amber. She had lost consciousness. Her hands had fallen away, and she was losing blood fast. Too fast.

Time slowed. I didn't feel pain in my shoulder. I didn't feel the glass slashing my feet. I didn't feel the warm blood seeping into my shirt. I didn't feel the movement of the elevator. All I felt was Amber slipping away. She felt weightless. Cold. All I heard were her sporadic, shallow gasps for air. *I'm losing her.*

Not waiting for the elevator doors to fully open, I slipped past and raced to the front desk, gingerly laying Amber atop it. With one hand I desperately tried to stop the bleeding; the other hand grabbed the phone behind the desk and dialed 911.

"This is 911. What is your emergency?"

"Send an ambulance and police to the Salt Breeze Apartments, Driftwood Avenue. There's been a shooting, thirteenth floor. Someone's been shot ... she's losing blood fast. We're in the lobby. Hurry! Please!"

"OK. Remain calm, and don't hang up the pho—" Suddenly, there was a click and the line went dead. Horror-stricken, my heart stuttered as hope was snuffed out like a candle flame. The Internet cable had been cut. Dropping the useless hunk of plastic and circuitry, I turned all my attention to Amber.

I applied all the pressure I could without inadvertently snapping her ribs. Was it even doing any good? There was blood everywhere, and there was more coming. There wasn't much I could do. *Stay with me ... please, you can't die ...* A life without Amber would be terrible, but an eternity without her—just the thought of it sent unspeakable horror to my heart. *No! She can't die! Please don't take her, Lord! Please, give her another chance, more time. She needs more time!* I hadn't noticed the tears rolling down my cheeks until one landed on the wooden surface beside Amber. *Please ...*

I could hear the sirens.

"Hang in there. Don't give in, Amber. *Fight it!* Don't die on me!" I begged, though I was pretty sure she couldn't hear me anymore. She needed real, professional help. It was her only chance. Time would be the judge as to whether she lived or died. Every second was precious, yet I let a few more slip away so the emergency vehicles could get closer.

3 ... 2 ... 1 ... now!

Slipping one arm under her knees and the other under her shoulders, I sprinted for the door. She was totally limp, no movement in the least. I had lost her.

I felt like someone was tearing my heart from me when the emergency respondents took Amber from my arms. For a few seconds, I was frozen where I stood, watching them rush her away. Some of the respondents were fussing over me, but I couldn't have cared less. Breaking away, I battled my way to the back of the ambulance and demanded to come along. I wasn't going to leave her side. At first, they tried to dissuade me, then seemed to think better of it. Not only did they let me ride, I even got one of those ridiculous orange squares of fabric called a shock blanket. I couldn't tell if it helped or not.

It hurt to see Amber like this. Closing my eyes, I willed all of it to simply vanish, but to no avail. She looked like death itself. Her crimson-smudged, snowy-white face was almost lost under the oversized oxygen mask. Her rosy pink lips were slowly turning a bluish-gray, like the sea right before a hurricane. There was already a long needle jammed into her left wrist like a tiny dagger. Numbly, I remembered she was scared of needles. Her heartbeat was out of control. The medics were running all over the place. Never in my worst nightmares ... yes, that's what this was.

A living nightmare.

CHAPTER 33

Santa Barbara, Silver Bay Memorial Hospital
Monday, August 26, 2:39 A.M.

Jordan

I don't remember much from there. It was all a mess—one big, terrible blur. It could have been an hour. It could have been a minute. I don't really know. The doors finally swung open and everyone rushed out. I tried to stay with Amber as long as I could, but as they passed through another set of doors, a nurse held me back.

"She's going into surgery. You can't go any further," she said kindly. Nodding slowly, I collapsed onto the closest chair, buried my head in my hands, and tried to pull myself together. Feeling a hand on my shoulder, I looked up. "I'm sorry, but apart from the young lady, you are the only other person involved in this whole affair, so I need to ask you some questions. We have not been able to identify her and we need to contact her family. Do you know who she is? Who are you? Are you related?" Silent for a few seconds, I met her eyes. Then, though my voice sounded a bit shaky, I blew her away.

"Her name is Amber Marie Gibson. She's twenty-six years old. About five-foot-five, sandy-brown hair, amber eyes. She was born in New Carrollton, Maryland. No, we're not related. No one is; she doesn't have any family left. I believe she was orphaned when she was little and her siblings died a long time ago. You're better off contacting her friends. My name is Jordan West. She's one of my closest friends. I know her better than anyone, I guess." The nurse was scribbling on her clipboard like crazy. It took a moment, but she soon regained her composure.

"OK," she said, a hint of surprise still in her voice. "What of her other friends? Can you get us in touch with them?" I quietly listed off Matt's, Dylan's, and Chloe's numbers. After jotting this down, the nurse scanned her notes, then turned to me. "Thank you for all of this. I will contact her friends, and in the meantime, you need medical attention yourself."

For a moment, I couldn't fathom why she would say such a thing; apparently my face said as much. The adrenaline was blocking any pain signals, so I had forgotten that I probably did need some help. That and the bloody shirt only made things worse. She seemed to pick up on my reluctance to cooperate.

"You need to let us help you. Go get patched up. If anything changes, I will inform you personally. OK?" I considered this proposition, then finally gave in.

Apparently, I had a partially dislocated shoulder, a serious gouge on one side of my hand from skidding across the balcony, some deep cuts and shards of glass in my feet, and I had entered a degree of shock. All that, yet I didn't feel a thing. After the doctors were satisfied, they found a clean T-shirt for me. My old one was beyond saving, and after some intense scrubbing, my shorts were acceptable for the time being.

I was sent to a room to wait until Amber came out of surgery. The moment I opened the door, I was promptly tackled. Once I recovered from my surprise, I found Chloe clinging to me, sobbing. Slowly, I wrapped my arms around her in an attempt to impart some small scrap of courage, though I doubted I had any to spare. I looked up. Matt and Dylan were here too. No one was talking. Everyone looked scared.

"What happened?" Dylan asked quietly.

At least I'm not wearing those blood-soaked clothes. Still, how am I going to explain this? I was about to attempt an answer when I realized the question wasn't directed at anyone in particular. Matt was shaking his head, saying he got a call that Amber was gravely injured and that he should probably prepare for the worst. Dylan and Chloe had similar stories. They turned to me. It felt like an icy shadow had descended. A chill ran down my spine. I couldn't tell them.

All this time, I had been shrugging off little things here and there. All the "coincidences" had slowly piled around my feet—and now they were up to my neck. The puzzle pieces were falling into place, and what I saw told me this was huge. Bigger than me. Bigger than Amber. Bigger than all of us put together. *This isn't my secret to give away. It belongs to Amber. Play it cool, Jordan. Careful.* I hated the thought of lying to my best friends. But I didn't have much of a choice.

"I got the same call." That seemed to be all they needed to hear. *Please forgive me. Perhaps someday I can tell you everything. But not without Amber's consent.*

In the following hours, we all began to fall apart in our own way. Matt sat staring into space, a deadened look of horror on his face. Dylan looked like he wanted to run away and never look back, but he was trapped under poor Chloe; she was clinging to him, stuck halfway between sleep and hysteria. And I was agonizing over the inevitable. The chances of Amber surviving were slim. There was no sugarcoating it. I didn't see how she could possibly survive.

As far as I could tell, the bullet had hit within half an inch of the edge of her rib cage, probably hitting a vital organ. She lost too much blood. She was barely breathing. Judging by her erratic heartbeat, I realized she had gone into extreme shock.

Lord, please spare her. Please … how am I supposed to live with myself if she dies? That night on the beach, two days ago—that was it. She had never been so open before. That was my chance and I blew it. What did I miss? What did I not say? Oh, if only our places could be exchanged! Why did she intervene? Why? It doesn't make sense. Why would she sacrifice herself for me? She can't die. She just can't …

After a while, I began to worry that she had died and the doctors were simply afraid to tell us. It had been more than two hours. I decided I would go find out what was going on if nothing happened within thirty minutes. But I didn't have to. Before long, the door opened. A grim-looking doctor peeked in and cleared his throat. Chloe practically jumped out of her skin. Slowly, Matt stood.

"Is … is Amber …" *Is Amber alive?* Despite the long suspense, I didn't want an answer anymore. I was petrified. The doctor looked at each of us in turn. He seemed to be searching for the right words.

"Miss Gibson is alive, but we don't know for how long. Currently, her condition is somewhat stable, but that could dissolve at any time. I'm here to take you to her."

These words were so profound that I almost wept. Amber was alive! I was relieved she survived surgery, but it sounded like she was standing on the edge of a knife. *Thank you, Lord. But Amber still needs a miracle. Please spare her. Please.*

We were led down hall after hall. I stared at the gleaming tiles passing under my feet, wondering if Amber still looked like she danced with death. I was a little concerned about how the others would react to seeing her in such a state. Last I saw her, it was bad enough. Now? Surely it couldn't get worse, right? Chloe could have a mental breakdown or something. I shot a silent glance at her. She was actually holding up pretty well, considering she had been called to the hospital at 3:30 A.M. because one of her best friends was on the grim reaper's doorstep. But judging from the way she was twisting her ring around, I decided she was about to snap.

Eventually, we came to Amber's room. Nothing could have prepared us for this. I didn't think she could possibly look more lifeless. There were so many tubes and cords attached to her, branching out every which way; she seemed more plastic and machine than human. The doctors had cleaned the blood off her face and hands, but she looked like a marble statue: white and unmoving. The light blue smock, the way her arms had been laid at her sides, the expression on her face—it was like she was ready for viewing at a funeral. The silence was deafening.

"She is going to die, isn't she?" Slowly, all eyes turned to Chloe. She said it so evenly, more like a statement than a question, as if she was resigned to the awful fate. The doctor seemed unsure what to say to this.

"We don't know. She might survive, she might die. But, either way … she probably won't ever wake up." He paused to let the dust and ash settle after that bombshell. "She's in a very deep coma. Very deep. Her brain has gone into hyper-sleep, a last resort self-preservation instinct. I'm sorry."

I was so numb. Any minute now, the ground would drop out from beneath me. The walls would cave in. The sky would fall. Anything and everything could happen, all at once—except for this. *I didn't save her. I failed. She'll sleep forever. Death will come, sooner or later, and it's all my fault …* The doctor seemed to be saying something, perhaps explaining some useless term, attempting to calm Chloe, or maybe even declaring Amber's estimated date of death. But I didn't hear him, or the door opening beside me.

Distantly, I heard someone whisper my name. The nurse I had met earlier was motioning to me. I glanced at the others. Only Matt had noticed, and he watched me with a puzzled expression. Hesitantly, I slipped out the door and followed the nurse. She seemed jumpy and wrung her hands nervously.

"I have to make this quick. Don't tell anyone what I'm about to tell you, OK? This is actually considered confidential medical information, but I think you should know." She took a deep breath, as if she was about to plunge into nine feet of water. Until this point, she hadn't met my gaze. Now she looked straight into my eyes and took the plunge. "Miss Gibson should be dead. Technically, she was dead."

Seeing my shocked expression, she hurried on.

"Halfway through surgery, her heart rate suddenly spiked, then stopped completely. She flatlined for seven minutes. Brain crawled to a stop—no pulse, not breathing. She was declared legally dead. But she started breathing on her own, her heart started beating again, and her brain came back to life. Nothing like this has ever happened before. Despite what the doctors are saying, I doubt she's dying anytime soon. I think she'll wake up eventually; no one cheats death like that." She paused, letting it all sink in. "I thought you should know. Remember, you don't know this. I never told you, right?"

I had to remind my vocal cords how to work.

"Right."

With that, she hurried off. My brain was choking on this amazing information. Cheat death? No, she didn't cheat death. It wasn't luck, happenstance, or a freak phenomenon. God had given Amber another chance. *A miracle …*

The expression "it felt like a load of bricks was lifted off my shoulders" simply does not cut it. Not only had the weight of the universe been lifted off my chest, I felt like I could jump off a cliff and fall up instead of down. The tears made a grand comeback, but I was beaming. *Amber is going to live, and she will wake up. I know it! Thank you, Lord, thank you!* I rubbed my face, trying to get rid of the tears and wipe the smile off my face. I couldn't tell the others—not yet. And I definitely couldn't walk back in there with a grin as big as the sun.

Quietly, I glided back in as if I had never left. Due to the way we had entered the room and where everybody was standing, Matt was still the only one who knew I had left. He was watching me steadily, and when I finally met his gaze, he mouthed: "What was that?" I shook my head and shrugged. *That wasn't very convincing.* I got the feeling this was going to come back to bite me. I looked back down at the floor and decided it would be a good idea to keep my mouth shut, at least for now.

I wasn't quite sure what I missed. Our pessimistic little raincloud of a doctor had just finished saying something and everyone's mood seemed to have dropped once again. There was a long silence. Then he simply walked out. Dylan finally spoke.

"What do we do now?" Chloe dropped into a chair and gazed at him miserably.

"We don't do anything. We just … wait," she said. *Wait for Amber to die.* No one said anything for a while.

"Is there any hope?" Matt had voiced the question we were all thinking. Two answers clashed midair.

"Not really."

"Of course."

I flinched. *What happened to keeping my mouth shut?* Chloe's bitter response cut like a knife. Apparently, I was alone in my opinion. I had just gained everyone's attention, though, and everyone seemed to demand an explanation.

"It will turn out OK in the end. Amber will wake up, I'm sure of it." Well, I thought that was the right thing to say. But … bad timing.

"Haven't you been listening, Jordan? She's not going to wake up. She's going to *die!*" Chloe yelled. Angry tears started streaming down her face. She looked ready to punch something, maybe me. No one offered defense on either side of the argument.

"No, I think she will wake up," I insisted. "Amber's a fighter. God has kept her alive. I don't see why He would preserve her life this long and then just let her waste away. Coming this close to death snaps things into perspective. This might be what it takes to get her to listen to the truth. And there is *always* hope. We can't give up yet."

Chloe glared daggers a few more seconds, then stopped. She looked back at Amber, and after a while, declared that she was going home. Dylan nodded sadly and Matt got up to leave as well. Apparently, I had failed again. No one seemed encouraged in the least. *I can't be conspicuous. I'll go with them partway and then circle back. Amber can't be left alone; she's still in danger.* Slowly, I stood and began to follow.

Pretty soon we split ways, each going down a different wing in this white-walled maze of a hospital. Stepping around a corner, I waited a few seconds before heading back the way we had come. When I saw the door to Amber's room, I felt like I was in the clear. I hadn't run into any of the others. No one had tried to stop me. I hadn't gotten lost. I opened the door, took two steps, looked up—and stopped in my tracks. *Matt.* He glanced up from his watch.

"Twenty-seven seconds. Record time. You sure do move fast," he said flatly.

"What?"

"I timed how long it was from here to where I left the group. I'm guessing you split pretty soon afterwards, or you ran." He straightened from his post at the wall. "I had a hunch you would come back. You have a lot of explaining to do."

"How did you—what? Why are you here again?" I feared I already knew why. He wasn't here for Amber. He was here to confront me.

"You were there, weren't you?" Matt asked, calm and serious.

"I was where? What do you mean?" *I was there when Amber got shot.* Matt strode forward, grabbed my wrist, and held it up. I cringed. The patch on my hand. He had seen it.

"I'm going to ask you again, and you know what I mean. You were there, weren't you? You didn't get a call; no one had to tell you that Amber was dying. You already knew because you were there. Your hand and those socks on your feet tell me you were injured too, which explains why you were the last one in that waiting room, even though you live right around the corner from here. You got here long before we did. How did the hospital get Chloe's, Dylan's, and my phone number? Well, obviously someone told them, and it couldn't have been Amber. It was you. You seemed fidgety when you told us you got the call. That nurse singled you out. Now, all I want to know is this: why did you lie to us, what did that nurse want, and *what happened* tonight that landed both you and Amber in the hospital?" For a moment, everything was dead still, including my heart. I'd never felt more trapped in my life. Matt was good. Too good.

"Matt," I started shakily. "I can't tell you. You're putting me in a really difficult position here. I'm trying to protect Amber, Chloe, Dylan, and you all at the same time. I know it looks bad, but please just let this go. These are not my secrets to give away." Matt looked incredulous.

"How could I possibly just 'let this go'? This is huge!" Something changed in Matt's expression. I got the feeling he was about to have me squirming and begging for mercy. "And another thing: why were you and

Amber together at such a late hour? I know this isn't an issue of immorality, and I know you weren't the one who shot her, but I also know you don't lie. This 'looks bad'? No, Jordan. This looks horrific. You better tell me."

I was caught. Matt had me backed into a corner. If I told him, I could put both Matt and Amber in danger. If I didn't tell him, he would alert Dylan and Chloe, and they too would demand to know what was going on. Then I would be putting all of us in danger. It hurt that he was questioning my integrity in this situation—but he was right. I had lied.

For a moment, the only sound was the sluggish, burdened beeping of Amber's heart monitor. Which reminded me she was alive. That she would make it. That I didn't have to worry. My panicked thoughts cleared enough for me to look at things logically.

What is the worst that can happen? Amber's real identity could be compromised. OK, so how do I get around that? Make sure Matt either doesn't know, or won't tell anyone. I didn't want Matt to complicate things, but out of all the possible options … this was the least complicated.

"I can't tell you much," I started slowly. "I shouldn't say anything. But, if you promise me that what is said in this room stays in this room, I will do my best to explain."

"You can't expect me to blindly agree to something like that. What if you told me you shot her? I would have to tell, and I am not going to lie like you did."

OK, that was low. "You know me better than that, Matt! I didn't shoot Amber. I did lie, though, and I'm sorry for that. But I didn't have much of a choice! What was I supposed to say? Please, forgive me for lying. But I cannot and will not explain anything until I know you won't tell anyone."

"OK. Start talking," he said, nodding resolutely.

"I need more than that, Matt. You have no idea how risky this is. I'm serious." Matt sighed a little in exasperation.

"Alright. I promise. I won't say a thing."

I stared into his eyes, trying to decide how much I could entrust him with. *If only you knew what you are getting yourself into.* Turning, I glanced at Amber, hanging to life by a thread. *Please forgive me.* Sighing, I took the plunge.

"Amber got shot trying to protect me." The accusations and frustration drained right out of Matt's face. He wasn't expecting that.

"What!? You were the target?" he asked in shock.

"Yes and no. Yes, the gun was aimed at me. No, I don't think I was the intended victim. They got her anyway, though."

"You think they were sent to kill Amber?"

"Yes."

"Why, what has she done? Who are these people?"

"I can't tell you. Amber doesn't even know that I know about all this." Matt looked like he wanted to ask more, but he tried a different avenue.

"How are you so sure she is going to wake up?"

"Well, that's where that nurse comes in. I can't tell you exactly what she said. All I can say is, Amber being alive right now is a miracle to the highest degree. She is going to live, trust me on this, but she's still in danger. From what I have seen, these people will do anything to get rid of her."

"Surely someone can't just waltz in here and murder her. The police will probably place surveillance on this room," Matt pointed out. Suddenly, my mind clicked. *Oh no. I didn't think of that …*

"I haven't even been questioned yet," I breathed, more to myself than to Matt, the doom sinking in. "It won't be long, though, and I have no idea how I'm going to explain all this." Matt seemed to find my predicament rather absurd.

"It's simple, Jordan! Just tell them everything! This is the Santa Barbara police we're talking about. I'm sure they can handle it." I shook my head, trying to pull my full attention back to Matt.

"No. It's not simple. If they discover the magnitude of this, there will be a huge fuss and things will get out of hand. The police are out of their league. There is a higher power at work here." *Like, the FBI.*

Matt's brain was churning; I could practically see the gears turning. I didn't blame him. It was a lot to take in. Perhaps he was beginning to regret his stubbornness—maybe it was dawning on him that he was now in danger as well.

"You better keep your promise, Matt. You absolutely cannot breathe a word to anyone, not even to Amber. Don't ever ask her about this. Maybe someday I can tell you more, but that's all you are getting from me tonight," I insisted. Matt nodded slowly. With that, I plopped into the chair closest to Amber and crossed my arms. Before I could retreat into my mind, though, Matt butted in again.

"What are you doing here, anyway?"

"Amber can't be left alone. I don't know when, if ever, there will be someone guarding the room. Her life is still on the line. If her attackers track her down, she'll die for sure this time. My place is probably crawling with cops. I can't exactly go back; here is as good as anywhere else—probably safer, too. And if Amber wakes up alone in a strange place, in pain and confused, she might do something drastic, like try and escape." Matt thought for a moment. "Are you seriously going to stay here all night?"

"Probably," I said, shrugging.

"I'll keep you company if you want," Matt offered. I gave him the best smile I could muster.

"Thank you, Matt. But it's OK. You can go home. It's late. You should get some sleep."

"Same goes for you," he pointed out.

"Me?" I chuckled. "No. Not a chance. I may never sleep again."

CHAPTER 34

V0RT3X's stronghold
Friday, September 13, 9:21 P.M.

⚬❀⚬Sonja⚬❀⚬

"Sonja?" Jason whined. I huffed a sigh and looked up from my computer.

"What?"

"I need help. I think I broke it," he said, sliding his laptop toward me while simultaneously wilting onto the tabletop. "I give up." Reluctantly, I grabbed it from him and scanned the screen.

"Oh," I snorted. "You're programming an A.I.? And you're asking me for help? Ha! You are on your own, little bro. Go pester Storm. She's good with these things."

"But she's not here again," Jason pointed out miserably. "I haven't seen her for about a month." I stopped typing to think about this for a moment. *Come to think of it, he's right. Storm has been gone for an unusually long time* ... I'd noticed her absence a couple of days ago, but I hadn't realized it had been a month.

"Well, I can't do squat for your program," I muttered, trying to brush Jason off. "Go try someone else."

After a moment's hesitation, he picked up his computer and wandered off, looking rather disappointed. I actually might have helped him—if it wasn't for this strange feeling that blossomed in my mind: the feeling that something wasn't right.

Storm was constantly dropping by V0RT3X. I'd labeled her perfectly from the start: a typical geeky, antisocial introvert with little life to speak of beyond her screen and keyboard. And whenever she did disappear for a time, she would always tell Jason or me, saying she'd only be gone for a short while, as if her return would be the highlight of the week. Like I said: geek.

Entering the mainframe, I searched for any activity from Storm's computer. Nothing. She hadn't hacked under the V0RT3X system for thirty-two days. She hadn't even checked in. I frowned. *That's way out of character for her. She checks in almost daily. I've seen her on the database at three in the morning.*

Leaning back, I tilted my chair onto two legs, then daringly onto one, pondering this new information. Normally, the absence of a fellow hacker meant nothing to me. But ever since C3RB3RU$ fell, I'd been a little more wary of strange occurrences. If one of the punks that attacked Storm and Jason were to get a message to their wretched friends, bad things could happen. I'd been watching over Jason carefully. It was possible someone might come after him. But Storm was there that night too. *What if they went after her?* Suddenly, I felt sick. Something was wrong. Even if Storm wasn't in danger, there was no doubt in my mind this absence was unplanned and unwelcome. If all was peachy, she would have been here in the last few weeks, or at least messaged someone.

I let my chair fall back to the floor with a bang, earning a few confused, temporary glances. Storm was missing; I had a bad feeling about this. Eventually, I decided: to heck with it all. I was gonna look her up. If she didn't want me snooping, she'd have to stop me herself. I smiled at that. It was finally time to hunt the real "Storm" down.

Time to lay out what I knew: she was a master hacker. She was kinda short. She was an introvert, lived alone—a thought hit me. *That Jordan guy! She said he was her neighbor! Oh, Sonja, you're a genius ...* Grinning, I started searching.

It didn't take long. Soon, I had pinpointed Jordan's exact residence. "Salt Breeze Apartments." Pulling up the residential list, I eliminated everyone who wasn't within a two-room radius of him. That left only four girls listed, and only two were single. *Haley Kate Maddison* or *Amber Marie Gibson.* It didn't take much thought. *Amber ...* Fits. I pictured her pretty little face. There was no question how she got her name. So, Firestorm's real name was Amber. Good to know. I had all I needed. Now I turned to the deeper recesses of the cyber world. *I will find the real "you," Amber. I've been dying to know what you've been hiding.*

After half an hour of searching, I had turned up ... nothing. A big, fat nothing. *What on earth? This chick doesn't even have a social media account. I couldn't find anything on her. It was like she didn't exist. Go further. Keep looking.*

This time, I enabled my scout A.I. Within ten minutes, it returned.

```
>File found
<File.Retrieve
>Retrieving...
>Error_
>//RESTRICTED INFORMATION
```

Huh? I tried again. Same thing. *OK, what the heck? Restricted freaking information?! What on earth? Who is she?!* I was done searching. Time to hack. Isolating the source of the file, I sent my programs to steal a copy of the data cache and decipher the code to open them.

Suddenly, a second, minor reference popped up. I glanced at it. *What's this?* Clicking on it, I scanned the stats. *Check-in information? Where is this from ...?* I was about to hack the system when I noticed the tangled web of alarm triggers surrounding it. Hacking this alone was somewhat risky. Instead, I decided to track it. Once I got closer, I might be able to access the same Wi-Fi it was on, thus side-stepping a chunk of the tripwires. There was no telling why Amber had been put into these protected archives—but I was going to find out. Sliding my computer into my bag, I slung it over my shoulder, stood, and headed for the towering shelves.

"Jason?" I called up. He poked his head over the edge.

"Yeah?"

"I'm leaving for a while. Stay here and out of trouble, or, I swear, I will ground you till Christmas!" Jason threw his hands up.

"Alright, alright! Yeesh," he exclaimed, frowning. Satisfied, I hurried off. *Today of all days, I hope that boy just behaves.*

The moment I was out the door I pulled out my phone and synced it to my laptop; I then turned my tracker onto the protected computer with the mysterious archives. Surprisingly, it wasn't super far away. It would only take about fifteen minutes by foot. I decided to take the walk, thus giving my computer more time to steal that file. I followed my phone down street after street. Eventually, I looked up and saw the destination. My confidence stumbled. A hospital. I froze for a moment, staring at it. *This can't be right ...*

For a second, I hesitated. Perhaps I should head back. Suddenly, I shook those thoughts away. *No. I'm not leaving till I find out whether Amber is here or not.* Gathering my wits, I casually sauntered into the lobby. Sliding into one of the chairs in the lounge, I pulled out my computer and started hacking. Once more, I found the information on Amber. But this time, I hacked the secure Wi-Fi, focused in on the laptop, and had it split wide open in no time. *Room 3W-104. Got it.* Part of me didn't believe this was legit. It felt like a ruse, just like everything else I thought I knew about this mysterious girl. But I was still going to check it out.

Now to get past security. I didn't want anyone asking me questions. I couldn't afford it. Calmly, I stared at my computer, thinking hard. I had to make a diversion, then slip past the front desk. A plan formed in my mind and I hacked into the overall utility system. *Bingo.* The front doors were activated by motion, yes—but they could also be controlled manually. Grinning, I set them off. I heard them slide open behind me. I flicked the cyber switch a few times for good measure, then, when they were partially open, sent them into a loop. Open, shut. Open, shut. Open, shut ...

Sure enough, in the reflection of a darkened window in front of me, I saw the lady at the front desk get up to inspect this strange occurrence. Silently, I stood and slipped past the befuddled nurse, who was staring at the doors as if they were possessed.

I kept my head down, noiselessly making my way down the still hall. Whenever I came to a security camera, I recycled empty footage through its lens until I was out of range. I was a shadow, a phantom, passing among the pristine walls and doors and halls, hunting my target.

Eventually, I came to the room. It was long past visiting hours, so I used my phone to hack the electronic lock. I was expecting it to be empty. I was expecting it to be a trap, or a joke, or a dead end. But as I stepped in, I froze. My blood ran cold and time came to a grinding halt. This wasn't a mistake. She was there. Amber was there. Unconscious, white as bone, still as stone. She looked dead. For a terrible moment, I thought she was. But then I heard the unnaturally slow beeping of the heart monitor. Blood bag, IV, oxygen mask, tubes ...

Dying.

Everything within me grew still. This was not supposed to be happening. This couldn't be true. It seemed like a storybook, with a chapter squeezed in at the end as a cruel joke. *"And then she died. No happily ever after."* Storm ... Amber ... whoever she was—we weren't really friends. But she was the closest thing I had to one. I'd never realized it before. Before all this could sink in, I heard a gasp and something crashed to the ground behind me.

"Who are you?" a frightened female voice demanded. *Think fast.* I didn't dare turn. Throwing a low glance at the speaker, I quickly assessed my options. I had to get out of here; no questions asked. The nurse stepped boldly toward me. "How did you get in here? Who are you?"

Slowly, without taking my eyes off Amber, I took a few steps back. Just as the nurse began to reach forward, I spun, ducked, side-stepped, dodged the fallen tray, and sprinted for the door. Calls of "Stop!" rang out behind me, but I was long gone. I raced down the halls, turning corners on a dime, hiding my face from the security cameras. The walls and doors and halls flew past. The bright white lights flashed by, searing spots into my vision.

Bursting through a side exit door, I ran until I was well out of sight. Flattening myself against a building, I peeked back. No one pursued me. Everything began to sink in. *No … She can't really … she's dying. She's actually dying!* I buried my face in my hands, mind swimming. *Why? She was fine just a month ago … Who did this? Why?! What's going on?*

From within my bag, a ding rang out, piercing the silence. For a moment, I simply stared at it. Then, letting out a trembling sigh, shakily, I drew my computer out and flicked open the screen.

The file had been decrypted. Sliding to the ground, I caught my breath and started reading.

CHAPTER 35

Silver Bay Memorial Hospital
Wednesday, September 18, 5:35 P.M.

Jordan

Those first few days passed so slowly. In our hearts, they were cold, bleak days. It was hard to find the strength to get up and face them. Even though my hope kept me going, seeing the others without any was killing me inside.

Whenever I passed Dylan at Ocean Front, he was silent. He didn't make his usual jokes or even smile. Chloe had uttered a grand total of eleven words in three days, including text messages, and Matt was avoiding me like the plague. I didn't blame him.

The moment I finished a day at Ocean Front, I would race to the hospital to guard Amber. I had somehow managed to bluff my way through the police inquiries. But the answers I gave resulted in no added security. The incident had been labeled a robbery gone wrong, yet I couldn't get any information. For all I knew, the attackers were still out there, hunting their prey. It felt as though Amber's fate remained in my hands.

Never before had I thought my life was anything out of the ordinary. But now I wondered what crazy path I had stumbled onto. I spent long hours rewinding the events of the past year, and now I saw it. I saw everything. All the signs, slip-ups, and circumstances surrounding Amber that had led to my suspicions, to the fears I refused to realize. Until now.

Amber was a top-notch master hacker under the name F1R3ST0RM. I had a feeling she had ties to the FBI, yet she didn't have their blanket of protection. Her "job" was hacking. For some reason, a little more than a year ago, she lost that job. Once she got it back, her enemies tracked her down, somehow mistaking me for her—perhaps by the mere one-floor difference in our apartment numbers. Amber had been living as a fugitive, fighting and fleeing this hostile group for years, running for her life whenever they got too close. I think they killed her family and others she loved. She was afraid to make friends or let anyone close to her. She had been heroically braving this burden alone, just to protect people like Chloe and Dylan, like Matt. People like me.

Teresa, the nurse who had confided in me that night, seemed to realize something serious was going on; not once did she try to stop me or send me home. I think I earned her trust. In doing so, I also ended up inadvertently overhearing details of what happened that night. It really was a miracle Amber was alive . . .

The bullet had glanced off the edge of her ribs, cracking one, causing it to slow down considerably. Her liver was hit, but it only began to collapse during surgery, so most of the damage was prevented. The reason she stopped breathing was because she went into shock. Without air, her heart slowed to a crawl. If it hadn't, she would have bled out. Six minutes without oxygen is pushing the limit of life. Amber survived at least twelve. The doctors assumed that was when she went into hyper-sleep, yet as far as the scans showed, she had suffered no brain damage: a complete miracle.

But there wasn't any explanation for why her heart rate spiked before, well, she died. Then came back. My mind was still stuck on that part. Surely she would see that God is good when she woke up. She had to. But she was certainly taking her time returning to the real world.

The days continued in a bleak routine. But then, finally ... something happened. Most of the doctors didn't give it a second thought, but a few took interest. Amber escaped a layer of her coma. Now her heartbeat maintained a slightly faster pace and her brain activity increased.

To my surprise, Matt was the first to act on this turn of events. He sent a link to a scientific report page on the group chat. After some searching, he discovered that, though it was true few people ever wake up from these types of comas, there were ways to increase their chances. Anything that stimulates well-established memories, like familiar voices, scents, sensations, or even favorite music will bring them closer to reality. It was then that I saw the first spark of hope in the others.

When I reached the hospital the next day, I was met at the door with a sense that something was different. *There's a new ... smell? Wait, I know that scent. That's … but that doesn't make sense. Chloe's not here.* I knew that smell: nail polish. *Nail polish?*

Dropping my bag in a chair, I went over to Amber. Her nails were a bright teal, more blue than green: her favorite color. There was a beautiful bracelet of woven ribbons around her wrist, and a little flower tucked in a braided section of her hair. On the table beside the bed was a music disc. The meaning of it all sank in. *Chloe came back. She came! She has hope Amber will wake up—she hasn't given up!*

The following days brought evidence that Dylan and Matt had come too. Little things. Surfboard wax, the kind that smells like candy. Books. Amber's favorite movie, which I found in the television's DVD player. Flowers. A sound stick of the ocean, plugged into a timer in a circuit, a gadget I assume Matt had rigged. A small jar of paint. Music.

I did my share as well. I knew that, somehow, Amber could hear me. So I talked to her, about everything, like always, except—I felt free to tell her anything. I guessed that she wouldn't remember.

I told her how I got saved that evening at vacation Bible school, both Dylan and I; how we witnessed to Chloe that night and how the three of us became so close. I recounted how I felt when I heard I was going to be a big brother, and what it was like growing up with Hunter and Lexie, and about my Mom and Dad. Then I told about how Chloe, Dylan, Lexie, and I would sneak out at night when we were little to go exploring along the shore. I tried to describe the joy of hearing Lexie declare her love for the Lord. I told Amber how sad I was when they left, how deep it hurt.

I talked about my original feelings of distress when I first ran into her, making her drop all her groceries, and how Betty had scolded me for it. I described how scared I was when I had stumbled into V0RT3X, and how relieved I was when the mysterious F1R3ST0RM stepped forward to defend me. I confessed what it was really like to hear that my parents were getting divorced. I admitted how surprised I was when I found out Amber was the one who had saved me from drowning. I told her how hard I was praying that night on the beach, under the meteors flying through the sky.

I admitted how terrified I had been when I thought she would die. I asked her how long she had been running … whether she fought alone … if she knew I had figured it all out. And if she cared. I wondered if she would be angry, happy, sad, or scared when I told her. I even rehearsed what I was going to say.

I hadn't been avoiding the others, but it was like we were playing tag. I never seemed to run into them, until, eventually, all our paths collided outside Amber's room. At first, no one spoke. We simply stood staring at each other. We hadn't really talked since that first night. There was a tense pause. Then Chloe took a swift step forward and embraced me. Before I realized what was happening, it was one big group hug. A silent sigh of relief seemed to sum up our mood.

"So," Dylan asked quietly, "what do we do now?"

"We wait," Chloe whispered. "We wait for Amber to wake up."

And thus, hope was restored.

More than a week had passed since that day, and we'd all shown up regularly, determined to bring Amber back. It would only be a matter of time. *Only a matter of time.* I liked the sound of that. Just as I caught sight of Amber's door, Teresa turned the corner in front of me.

"Jordan!"

"Hi, Teresa," I said, smiling a little.

"I've been meaning to tell you, but … Friday night, someone got into Miss Gibson's room!" My brain balked.

"What?!" I exclaimed in horror. Teresa shot a glance at the open door, as if to remind me to keep quiet. "What on earth? Who?!" I whispered.

"I don't know," she admitted. "She got away before I could get a good look at her. She slipped right by me—like some sort of ninja! None of the security cameras caught her coming in, and when she ran, she covered her face and turned away." Relief washed over me. *"She"? OK, oh, thank God. That likely means it wasn't one of Amber's attackers; I think they were all male.* Teresa thought for a moment, searching for any useful information. "She seemed about Miss Gibson's age. She had a nondescript black computer bag over her shoulder, and her hair was short. And crimson. Security couldn't determine anything else."

"Wait. Crimson?" I asked. Teresa nodded. My mind churned. I couldn't know for sure, but … *that sounds like that girl at V0RT3X.* Nodding slowly, I tucked this information away to review later. "Alright. If you would, please let me know if this mystery girl comes back, but I don't think she's an immediate threat." A puzzling thought hit me. "If I may ask, Teresa, why do you trust me? You've confided in me at least three times. Why?" At this, Teresa smiled slightly.

"Because I remember you." She chuckled at my confused expression.

"You've been here a lot. Not as a patient, but as a visitor, for so many people, more than once. I can see you risked a lot to protect Miss Gibson—you saved her life. Even your friends seem trustworthy. Never before have I seen such loyalty like the loyalty you all have for her. It's enough to trust you." She smiled.

Any opportunity to respond or express my gratitude was cut off.

"Amber?" Teresa and I spun at the sound of Chloe's voice. "Amber! She's … I think she's waking up!" Everyone dropped what they were doing and scrambled to her bedside.

"Chloe, what happened?" Matt asked excitedly.

"She moved! Like, she jerked a tiny bit. And her breathing changed."

Sure enough, Amber's once slow, even breathing sounded a bit faster, not as patterned. She seemed to tense, then the heart monitor started to pick up. Her breathing continued to quicken …

"Amber?" Matt asked hopefully.

She started to shiver a bit. Her lips moved silently. My heart tripped. Something was wrong. The bright hope I had felt moments before began to melt. The light fled the room. Something wasn't right. Now, after three or four breaths, Amber would give a quiet gasp, desperately grabbing at air. Her face changed, her expression going from peace to slight discomfort. Her lips moved, again without sound. This time, though, I realized what she said. My soul froze.

"*Help.*"

"Amber, can you hear me? Amber?" Chloe begged. For a moment, all was still. Then a single tear slipped down Amber's cheek, and she whispered:

"Help me … "

In less than ten seconds, everything changed.

Amber trembled like a leaf, shaking uncontrollably. Pain and fear spread across her face, like a crack crawling over glass. She flicked her head from side to side, tears pouring like driving rain in a storm.

"What's happening?" Chloe stumbled back, her eyes wide with horror. "What's going on?"

Suddenly, Amber cried out, this time with surprising volume and strength. The fast beeping of the monitor filled the room. She seemed to draw her shoulders up tensely for a moment, then her entire body jerked as she cried out again.

Matt lunged forward and tried to hold her down. "Someone go for help! Get the doctor!" Teresa was gone in an instant.

Chloe was crying now, clinging to Dylan, who was in shock. Amber's heart rate soared. She gasped, went rigid, and lurched again. A blossoming spot of bright red appeared on her gown. She had opened one of her stitches.

"Jordan—"

Matt didn't need to finish. I closed the distance and pushed down on Amber's petite frame, trying desperately to restrain her spastic movements. She was surprisingly strong, and it was hard to control her. It was like she was fighting for her life. *What's happening?! Dear Lord, please help! She's going to injure herself even more! I don't know what to do!*

Teresa burst through the door with three doctors behind her. They bustled around Amber, trying to figure out what was causing this horrifying display. It was as if I stepped back from space and time to take everything in: the rushing of the doctors, the tears streaming down Amber's face, the desperate gasps for air, her trembling body—the heart monitor. It was going faster, faster … faster! Suddenly, I remembered. *"Halfway through surgery, her heart rate suddenly spiked, then stopped completely. She flatlined …"* The lines spiked, almost hitting the top of the screen.

"Amber!!!"

The moment my voice filled the room, all went still—including Amber's heart. Time stopped as the monitor wailed its mournful cry. Then Amber slowly exhaled, her muscles went limp, and the sluggish beeping started again. Medics hurriedly wheeled her bed out, past Matt, Dylan, Chloe, and me. We huddled together, horrorstruck, not daring to move for a while. To my surprise, within a few minutes, a concerned, kind-faced doctor came in and gestured for us to sit. For a moment, no one spoke.

"What was that?" Matt finally asked, shakily. The doctor adjusted his glasses, considering how to answer.

"A dream," he said gently.

"Don't you mean 'nightmare'?" Dylan asked.

A nod. "Actually, 'nightmare-induced panic attack' would be more accurate. There is actually a good side to all this, believe it or not: Miss Gibson is coming closer to waking up. Her brain has escaped to a shallower level of dormancy. But the bad news is she is trapped in her current state. Trapped in a delirious dream world." There was a pause. "Did she have insomnia as a child? Sleepwalking, night terrors, or the like?"

"We don't know much about her childhood," I said quietly.

"Well, did she suffer some kind of extreme trauma that you know of?" he pressed. I froze. *I think so ...*

Matt seemed to notice my sudden silence and spoke up. "We don't know much about her life before she came here a year ago." The doctor sat back, nodded slowly, pondering this information.

"Alright. Not that it would make a huge difference, but if you think of anything, please let us know." He stood. "You're welcome to stay, but it will probably be an hour or so till Miss Gibson is returned to her room."

"I think we'll go," Dylan gently suggested. Chloe turned her big, teary eyes on him, as if to ask, *But why?*

Dylan watched Chloe steadily for a moment. I could practically hear their telepathic debate. Finally, Chloe nodded, sadly. Dylan threw Matt and me a farewell glance on his way out with Chloe. The doctor waited a moment, as if expecting Matt and me to leave also, but we both stared at the floor, unmoving. A moment later, he left. Matt turned to me.

"Amber's known suffering before, hasn't she?" he asked, a burden in his voice.

"Yeah. I think so," I said quietly, feeling horrible.

"It has something to do with whoever attacked her, doesn't it?"

"Maybe, maybe not," I muttered. Matt sat back, thinking, then carefully tested the waters.

"I've been thinking ... That night, you said, 'a higher power is at work here.' Does Amber ... work undercover for the FBI?" My lack of an answer and slightly choked expression apparently spoke volumes. A grim, tiny smile tugged at Matt's lips. "I'll take your silence as a yes."

"Matt! Don't think too hard about all this! You're gonna get yourself in trouble!" I buried my face in my hands, wondering just how bad things could possibly get.

"It's alright, Jordan! I've had suspicions of my own. I mean, come on, she deleted an advanced virus from a computer she'd only looked at for twenty seconds. She acts like she's hiding things on a regular basis. And graphics designers don't have four layers of password protection on their laptops."

I lifted my head. "You noticed that too?"

"Yeah." Matt waited for a moment, then opened his mouth to say something more. But I didn't let him.

"No more questions," I insisted.

Matt shrugged. "Alright." Standing, he glanced at me. "You OK?" he asked, concerned.

"Yeah. I'm fine. I'll go home eventually, I guess."

After a pause, Matt nodded sadly and left. I waited a moment, then let out a heavy sigh. *"Eventually" is a loose term. I can't let Amber suffer through another nightmare. I just can't.* I looked around the room. *I bet Teresa would let me stay late if I asked.*

In light of recent events, Teresa agreed it would be fine. Once that was settled, I found the doctor who had talked with us earlier and told him I believed it was very likely Amber had been through significant trauma before. He thanked me, and I went back to wait.

After about an hour, Amber was returned to her room, just as predicted. For a long time, I paced, then sat, then paced again. A few times—though I couldn't be sure—Amber seemed to begin to dream again; she would start to quiver. I simply talked to her until it stopped. This went on for hours. The sun set and the hospital officially closed to visitors. I was getting tired.

Stay awake. Don't drop your guard. Keep going. I glanced at Amber. *I should be the one lying there. I owe it to her to keep her safe. Why would she intervene ... why?*

I paced the room awhile longer, but eventually, I reluctantly allowed myself to melt into one of the chairs. The thought of going to sleep and leaving Amber to a nightmare weighed heavily on me. Turning, I gazed at her. What should I do? As if in response, she started shaking again, a single tear slipping down her cheek as the heart monitor started picking up a bit.

"Amber, it's alright! I'm still here! Don't worry, it's going to be OK," I insisted, trying to pour all the comfort I could into my words. Then an idea dawned on me. *I don't sleep as deeply as I used to, and she always quivers before she cries ...*

Slowly, I stood, pulled the chair closer to the bed, tried to get comfortable—as comfortable as one can in a chair—reached out, and gently held on to Amber's wrist. Sure enough, I could feel her fragile pulse. A few minutes later, she started quivering.

"Don't worry. I'm not going anywhere. Please wake up, Amber, please. Here, I'll keep talking if you want. That seems to help." Of course, no response. "You really scared us today, you know? But don't worry ... "

I talked for a long time, and Amber sank into what seemed to be a dreamless sleep. Eventually, I did too. Though I often awoke to trembling or fast-paced beeping, it didn't matter. All that mattered was the fact that I could stop it.

"Don't worry. I'm not going anywhere … "

CHAPTER 36

Silver Bay Memorial Hospital
Saturday, September 21, 4:18 A.M.

Amber

Wake up. Something's … wrong. Slowly, I opened my eyes. Blinding white light filled my vision. I shut my eyes again. Waking from what seemed like an eternal sleep had left me disoriented. *It hurts. Don't wanna … No. Wake up. Come, on, wake—*

I took a deep breath, trying to wake my brain, and almost cried out. The light wasn't the only thing that hurt. Pain signals hurled themselves into my brain faster than lightning, careening off each other and piling up in one big mess. I thought my nervous system would collapse.

Swallowing back the pained cry, I forced my eyes back open. The agony was unreal. My stomach, both internally and externally, felt like it had been scrubbed with a wire brush. I was painfully aware of every tingling, icy nerve in my body, and my throat felt like a cat's scratching post. A dull, stabbing pain in my arm made me turn my head. *What—an oxygen mask?* I pulled it off with my sore left hand, then noticed the needle marks and IV tubes. *Where … where am I? Why am I in so much pain … What happened?*

Allowing my head to fall back onto the pillow, I stared at the ceiling. It soon grew blurry as tears filled my eyes. *Why can't I remember? What's happened?* A feeling of isolation clawed at my mind. I could feel that I was drugged. Heavily. But why? It wasn't doing a very good job of blocking the pain, so I wasn't sure that was its purpose. I was starting to panic. Fear seeped into my very soul. It was too quiet. *I have to get out of here. Wherever "here" is.*

I shifted slightly, trying to wake up, when I realized my right hand wasn't cold. Something was loosely intertwined between my fingers, keeping them warm. It was … comforting. This was one sensation I didn't want to go away, so I stayed as still as a stone. I chose to simply exist, focusing all my attention on this safe feeling.

The longer I lay there, the more the pain seemed to subside. I decided whatever medicine was coming through the IV was starting to circulate; I was grateful I hadn't yielded to my initial impulse to rip it out. I also decided the source of the pain was just below my rib cage. But why? I must have stared at the ceiling for at least an hour. Or a minute. I couldn't tell. Before long, I realized the bright, silver glow was moonlight, floating in through the window and landing on my pillow. I watched it for a while. It was serenely beautiful.

Eventually, I could sense sound again. It wasn't as quiet as I had thought, though everything sounded a little fuzzy at first, as if I was underwater. A low, slow beeping, the rattling whoosh of the air vents, and the ticking of a clock whispered to me. Before long, I became aware of another presence in the room. I could hear quiet, rhythmic breathing. *I'm not alone.* That simple revelation filled me with both joyous relief and sheer terror. *I'm not alone.* Someone is here. Concentrating hard, I finally decided whoever it was … was to my right.

Gradually, little by little, I turned my head toward the sound, afraid of what I might find. I stared at the scene before me, trying to make it compute. My brain couldn't absorb it.

A chair was pulled up beside my bed, and in it was … Jordan, tightly curled into an uncomfortable-looking heap. His head lay on the armrest and he was sleeping peacefully. He was reaching out … toward me. My eyes traced up his arm to find he was holding my hand. *Remember …*

It all came back in an overwhelming rush. Waking to the angry yells in Arabic. Swinging down from my balcony. The gunshot. Falling. Jordan slamming into the glass. The last memory flashed before my eyes and faded away. Jordan carrying me to safety. It all finally sunk in. *Jordan … saved me.*

My vision grew blurry again. I bit my lip so hard I almost drew blood. But it wasn't enough. I couldn't hold back the tears this time. Silently, they slid down my cheeks and dripped on the bright white sheets around me. I cried quietly, trying to hold it together. Soon I was quivering, unable to stop sobbing. *Jordan … saved me. He saved me. I'm alive …*

"Amber?"

I couldn't contain it anymore. Pretty soon I was all-out weeping. Jordan sprang from the chair and was by my side in moments. "Please don't cry! Are you in pain? Do you want me to call the nurse? Should I—"

All the fear and hurt, the broken hopes and discarded dreams that had been chained around my shattered heart, had been banished by the one standing beside me. He had saved my life, and as if that wasn't enough, here he was, by my side, sleeping in a tiny chair just so he could keep watch over me. So I wouldn't be alone. I could bite back the pain because there was nothing in the world I wanted more in that moment. Shoving the bedrail down, I reached out as far as I could and wrapped my arms around him.

It had been four years since my last real hug. It might take that long for me to let go. There was a stunned silence, broken only by my pathetic whimpering.

"You"—*sniff*—"saved my"—*hic*—"life! Please for"—*hic*—"give me! This is all my fault. I'm so sorry. And you were"—*HIC!*—"hurt, all becau—" He pulled me in close and held me.

"I'm fine. It's OK. It's over now."

I felt myself growing lightheaded. Darkness ate at the edges of my vision. My grip loosened and my cries got weaker. My weeping was making me gasp for air and the pain was astronomical, but I couldn't stop. To my dismay, I felt Jordan begin to let go. *Please don't leave …* He picked up my discarded oxygen mask and gently held it to my tear-stained face.

"It's alright. You're safe now. Calm down. You're gonna pass out. Stay with me, Amber. Please."

He sat on the edge of the bed and enveloped me in a warm embrace. He comforted me, wiping away my tears, quietly reassuring me. *I … trust him.* If only this could last forever. I didn't want to return to the insecure lifestyle I was fated to live, to the uncertainty and the fear, the loneliness. Never in my life had I felt so valued, hopeful, serene. So … loved. Like I mattered. Like I wasn't just part of an equation, or a pawn in a war. *This is what it feels like to belong. I will cherish this moment forever …*

The next thing I knew, it was morning, I was back under the sheets, and the oxygen mask was gone. The sun was shining and I felt a little more alive. The air conditioning had been turned down; it wasn't so cold anymore. Something was missing, though. *I don't hear Jordan.*

"Welcome back to the world of the living."

Turning my head, there sat Jordan, a faint smile on his face. I couldn't decide whether to laugh, cry, or just roll back over.

"Amber?" I looked up and realized Chloe, Dylan, and Matt were here, too. "Amber!" Chloe exclaimed. She leaped from her chair and was beside me in a split-second. Throwing her arms around me, through tears, she whispered, "You came back."

Slowly, slightly stunned—mostly overwhelmed—I returned the hug. Over her shoulder, I caught glances of Dylan and Matt, impatiently waiting for a turn to welcome me back. Beyond them: Jordan. Our eyes locked for a moment. He held his finger to his lips, then pretended to zip them shut, shaking his head slightly. *Jordan hasn't said anything?* Unbelievable gratitude filled my soul, but any opportunities for tears were interrupted by embraces from the others. I didn't want to let go—even though the hugs hurt a bit.

There were various versions of "Welcome back, Amber," and "I'm so glad you're alright."

And, then suddenly: "You scared us! What happened?" Dylan asked. Apparently, my blank, wide-eyed, deer-in-the-headlights face was obvious. Chloe noticed.

"Don't answer that," she quickly said. "It's fine. How are you?"

I gazed at each of them in turn, my heart brimming with happiness. I tried to form the right words.

"I'm … " I swallowed, trying to bury the tears and make my voice work. "I'm … alive?" That brought grins all around.

I wasn't quite sure what to say next. *"I thought I was going to die and never see you all again"* wasn't really a good conversation-starter. Also, "Getting shot hurts like you wouldn't believe"—uh, that was a bad one, too. I felt conspicuous, fidgety. Had I disrupted their lives? How badly did I scare them? Did I look as fragile as I felt? I was in the dark. I didn't know what had transpired while I was unconscious. *Oh, my goodness. How long has it been?*

"How … long have I … ?" The others exchanged looks. I noticed. "What's today's date?"

"The twenty-first of September," Jordan said gently. "It's been about a month." Even though this information hit me like an icy snowball to the face, the blow seemed softer than it should have been. It didn't seem real, but neither did it seem crazy.

"Oh," I whispered. "Oh, my goodness. That's—"

"A long nap?" Dylan teased. Mortified, Chloe gasped and swatted him. A small smile broke through my numb shock.

"Yeah," I chuckled quietly. "A very long nap."

"You're lucky you woke up at all. Only a handful of people ever wake up from those kinds of comas," Matt said. Then he smiled. "The doctors are having fits. They've never seen anything like this. You're a living miracle."

A living miracle. Hearing all this stole the very air from my lungs. Miracle never seemed the right word to describe my existence. Perhaps mistake or curse, but ... *miracle?* I didn't know what to say. Then, as if to emphasize Matt's point, a nurse stuck her head in the room, her eyes widening and lighting up at the sight of me.

"Hello, Miss Gibson," she said, smiling. "My name is Teresa. It's nice to finally meet you. I heard you were awake. How are you feeling?" I wasn't in the mood for wracking my mind for a good, descriptive word meaning *ouch*, so I just shrugged.

"Alright, I suppose." Her smile broadened a bit.

"I'm glad to hear that. Some of the doctors want to check you out to make sure you're OK."

"That's doctor-speak for 'get out,'" Dylan said with an impish grin.

Chloe leaned over to hug me again. "We'll be back, Amber. I'm so glad you're OK."

"Thank you, Chloe," I whispered, trying once again to refrain from crying like a little girl.

As the four of them got up to leave, Jordan caught my eye. The look in his gaze: I couldn't unpack it all. Relief, joy, thankfulness, concern ... tender, hopeful, endearing, understanding. Then, with no warning, he grinned and winked. I almost laughed out loud.

CHAPTER 37

The Salt Breeze Apartment Complex, Apt. 1407
Wednesday, September 25, 1:07 P.M.

Jordan

It was time to find out the truth. It was time to ask Amber what was going on. It'd been a couple of days since she woke up, and it seemed all was well. Yet I was still worried this might end in disaster or that I would seriously freak her out. Then again, I really didn't have a clue how she'd react.

I planned it all out: take the day off at Ocean Front, then notify Lia, Cassie, and Samuel ahead of time that I wouldn't be at church that evening. Matt, Dylan, and Chloe would be at work till the afternoon, then head for youth group. So, unless that mysterious redhead showed up, I would likely be Amber's only visitor that day. Even so, it seemed like a good idea to wait till Matt, Dylan, and Chloe were on their way to church—just in case. I spent my morning scrounging up a "peace offering" of sorts. In other words, finding a way to get Amber's computer and sketchbook to her so she wouldn't get bored.

The mission proved to be less than tame from the start. I had to go to Betty for the master key, and she could be about as persistent as a hungry young seal at feeding time—and fussed almost twice as much. Still, she let me have the key. Like everyone else, she still didn't know much about the shooting. But, ultimately, she let me go.

Outside Amber's door, I hesitated. I half-expected an assassin to be in there, or even a trap to spring. But after deciding I was being truly ridiculous and breathing a quick prayer, I slid the card in the lock and stepped into her apartment.

Heavy stillness hung in the air like that of an undisturbed attic. The apartment that was once so alive and welcoming seemed dim and color-less without its occupant. Things just weren't right. *Just find her sketchbook and computer. Focus.* Shaking off the lonely feeling seeping from the walls, I started to search. I headed for her little study room. Surely her laptop would be in there.

Sure enough, sitting on the desktop was Amber's computer. I'd seen it often, but now that I had a close look at it, I could see tiny marks and strange lines along the sides. *Is that … solder metal?* Along the screen, beside the keys, on the lid, underneath the base, everywhere! The entire laptop had been heavily modified. It seemed as though she'd torn the whole thing apart and put it back together again on a whim. *Why am I surprised? I know who she is now. Why wouldn't she amp her computer?* With that conclusion out of the way, I ducked under the desk to unplug it—and came face to face with a mechanical monster.

I shrieked, and I may or may not have smacked my head on the under-side of the desk. It looked like a bomb! Whatever it was, it turned on when I got close. Lights blinked and a quiet hum resonated from its core. I scram-bled back, worried it might explode, then noticed Amber's laptop light up. Slowly, I stood, rubbing my head, and watched as words filled the screen.

```
[11:15:27 INFO]: Initiate Cyber Net Launcher Version 3.7.18
     [11:15:33 INFO]: Checking surrounding networks
     [11:15:34 INFO]: Launching Cyber Net Launcher
          [11:15:34 INFO]: Searching for routers
       [11:15:37 INFO]: 34 of 35 routers functional.
      [11:15:37 INFO]: Connecting to "J_surfs.net"
                 (Not Secure, Protected)
         [11:15:38 INFO]: Deciphering log on...
   [11:15:40] Connected. 35 of 35 routers functional.
      [11:15:40 INFO]: Launching Central Network
    [11:28:43 INFO]: Central Network is functional
       [11:29:50 INFO]: Initiation complete
                          ~
   >"Hello. I am Cyra, an AI created by Laelaps."
                 Awaiting input_
```

All this was gibberish to me, but I did recognize my network name. I couldn't make sense of it. Why was it connecting to my Wi-Fi? Who was "Cyra" and "Laelaps"? *Wait, is Cyra the bomb under the desk? And if it is, that means Laelaps is Amber! But I thought she was F1R3ST0RM. So who or what is Laelaps?*

Fascinating though all this was, I wasn't going to let this A.I. keep me from my mission. Soon, I figured out how to close the program, and thankfully, Amber's computer shut down normally. Pulling the plug, I packed it into her bag and headed back for the main room.

My first guess was that her sketchbook would be on the coffee table by the couch, alongside about twelve jars, each overflowing with colored pencils and tubes of paint. But neither it nor the jars were there. Perhaps on the kitchen counter? Nope. *What about the bedside table?* I sighed. I'd wanted to be in and out, but things weren't going as well as I had hoped. I certainly didn't want to pry, but I wasn't leaving without that sketchbook.

Poking my head around the corner of the main bedroom, I headed for the side table and continued searching for that sketchbook. Once again, it was nowhere to be found, though I noticed Amber's phone—a nice bonus—and slid it into the computer bag. Tentatively, I checked the drawer. Nothing. Sighing in frustration, I stepped back, frowning, when I heard the tiniest sound behind me. I whirled.

Due to the way I entered the room, I hadn't noticed the dresser. Now, my surprised reflection stared at me, gaping at its surroundings. All around the mirror, the wall was covered in paper. Newspaper clippings, magazine articles, printouts, pictures, and long strips of paper covered in cramped lines of writing, all fluttering from tiny bits of tape.

The sound I had heard was the quivering of one such strip, caught by cool wisps of air slipping from the overhead vent. Hesitantly, I held the paper still and began to read. It was a long list of names and dates. They were grouped beneath underlined titles, like "Massachusetts Address," and "The Miami Massacre," or "The 42nd Ambassador Scandal," and even "Attempt on Washington." I recognized a few. These events had been in the news.

I looked across the wall. It was like a bird's wing, layered with hundreds of paper feathers. Awestruck at how many of recent history's darkest hours had found their way to Amber's giant scrapbook, I stepped back to take it all in. And that's when I saw it. On top of the dresser lay her open sketchbook; pencils held the pages down as the fringes occasionally fluttered in the artificial breeze.

A young man smiled softly up at me from the paper, appearing as realistic as my reflection in the mirror, a testimony to Amber's flawless artistic skill. My guess was that he was in his early to mid-twenties. Everything about him seemed … kaleidoscopic, if that was possible. His eyes were speckled storm gray, chestnut brown, jade, bright gold, and flecked with tiny shards of sky blue—like shattered stained glass in a collage of shining colors. His slightly messy hair was auburn yet brown yet dirty blond all at the same time. Even the headphones around his neck were composed of every shade of blue and green under the sun, just like his mahogany red-orange sweatshirt. Mischievous laughter could be seen in his expression, and I couldn't help but smile as well. Oh, there—at the bottom corner of the page: "Eric."

My gaze was drawn to three photographs on the opposite page. The first was a cutout from a yearbook; the name read: "Jessica Santoro." Shoulder length, blackish-brown hair was held back by a creative, colorful ribbon headband. Chocolate eyes and a naive smile made her seem innocent. She too seemed to be in her early twenties.

The second picture was an older photograph of a large group of children. I did a quick headcount. Thirteen children and two adults. *Wait. Amber? But, no—there's two?* I looked closer and realized they were different; Amber was on the right. A memory popped into my head. *"Happy birthday, Ashley … What's it feel like to turn twenty-six?"* I inspected the second girl with new interest. She must be Amber's twin, Ashley. They weren't quite identical, just remarkably similar.

I'd always gotten the vibe that Amber hated her past, that she didn't want to even think about it. Yet these people, whoever they were to Amber, seemed quite lovable. As I turned to the third and final paper memory—and realized it wasn't a photograph—I realized why Amber was the way she was. Everything fell into place.

Overtop chaotic splashes of deep color, scrawled in angry, bold letters:

TEUMESSIAN TOOK THEM FROM ME.
REMEMBER THAT. AVENGE THOSE
THEY'VE TAKEN,
DON'T LET THEM TAKE ANY MORE.

I'm so sick and tired of feeling … sick and tired.

The doctors were done poking and prodding me for the day, impressed with how fast I was healing. But I was still feeling like I'd been run through with a sword. Whenever I was left alone, I had nothing to do but think, leaving me with regrets, warring thoughts, or horrible memories. The nightmares had surfaced in my mind, making me afraid to sleep. They had been so real ...

It felt like I would be stuck here forever. I just wanted to go home. But what would be waiting for me? I wasn't sure I was safe here anymore. I didn't know what to do. I wished ... I wished ... Actually, I didn't know what I wished. I frowned at the far wall. *I don't like this.* A sound snapped me out of my dilemma. I looked up—and felt a little better.

"Oh, hi Jordan!" I said, more enthusiastically than I meant at first. He smiled, but in a sad sort of way.

"Hey, Amber. How are you feeling today?" he asked, sitting in the closest chair to me.

"Alright, I suppose."

A strange, rather awkward silence ensued. My mind was telling me something was wrong. *Wait—it's Wednesday! Why is Jordan here? And—* my heart stumbled a little—*that looks like ... my computer bag. It couldn't be ... could it?*

"Why are you here? Isn't there, um ... you're usually gone Wednesdays," I muttered incoherently. Jordan shifted, looking unsure how to proceed, then slowly slipped the bag strap over his head and handed it over. It was mine.

"Thought you might want this," he muttered quietly. He then held out my sketchbook. There, sticking from among the pages, I could see the edges of the photos. Distantly, I heard the heart monitor speed up and felt the blood drain from my hands and face. *He saw it. He saw everything. Oh, my goodness. He saw everything!* "Amber," Jordan said carefully, fidgeting with each word. "Look, I've ... I've kept your secrets. Please, don't keep so many from me. There have been hints from the moment we met till now—you're not who you say you are. Someone tried to kill me, but I have a pretty strong hunch they were sent to kill you. And they almost did. Please, please tell me what's really going on. No lies. Just tell me the truth this time. Please."

Deep down, I'd known this was coming. There was no way Jordan would simply ignore what had happened. But I hadn't really thought about what to say. My mind started desperately spinning an elaborate tale, thinking up a good lie, when I realized the truth.

I can't do this anymore.

Though it would likely be my undoing, I wanted to tell him. I hated lying to Jordan. I hated lying, period. It had destroyed my life. Honestly, I didn't have a clue where my future was headed anymore, except that I probably wouldn't be around much longer—whether by death or relocation, I wasn't sure. But Jordan deserved to know.

"Alright," I said, sighing sadly. "But what I am about to tell you: I swear, you can't tell a single soul. If you do, it will be your demise. And mine. Lots of people could die. Promise me you won't ever tell anyone, Jordan. Please." Surprisingly, this didn't seem to faze him.

"I promise. You have my word," he said with a solemn nod.

My soul begged me to refuse, but I couldn't. My heart warned he would hate me. My mind retorted that it didn't matter. And I didn't blame him. He deserved to know the truth. After all that had happened, I owed him at least that. Another sigh escaped my lips.

"I'm sorry, Jordan. You're right. Almost everything you think you know about me is laced with a lie," I whispered miserably. "I won't ask you to forgive me for that. I only ask that you hear me out." Taking a deep breath, I took the plunge. "Where should I start?"

"The beginning, I suppose," Jordan said.

I nodded. *No turning back now.* "Remember when I first told you I have twelve siblings, and that most of them were adopted?"

"Yes."

"Well, 'most of us' were adopted would have been a more accurate statement," I said, a small smile breaking through.

"You were adopted?" Jordan asked. I nodded.

"My family was in a car wreck when I was twelve." I pushed my sleeve up a bit. "You asked about this once before and I didn't answer: that's what this strange scar on my arm is from. Something pinned me. I don't know how my sister, Ashley, got me out. All I really remember is her dragging me away from the wreck as it burst into flames. My parents were dead before the car stopped spinning. We didn't have any close relatives that were willing to take us. So we spent two years in the foster system."

"I'm so sorry, Amber." Jordan paused and seemed to think for a minute. "Wow, that sounded so lame. But, I really do mean it!" he exclaimed earnestly.

"It's OK. Thank you, Jordan. I know you're being sincere. My parents weren't around much anyway. They were always busy fighting or working. It was only ever Ashley and I."

"What happened? Who adopted you two?"

"Mr. and Mrs. Gibson were retired missionaries. By the time they took Ashley and me, they had already adopted eleven other children." I shook my head and gave a short chuckle. "Life was ... interesting, to say the least. Every year, we took a group picture, the whole family together." I pulled the photo from my sketchbook, handing it to him. He looked at it for a while, searching each face, then handed it to me.

"What are their names?" he asked gently. I smiled at the sweet memory.

"Well, from left to right, Ashley, then me, Katlyn, Akoni, Johnathan, Khari, Liesel, Zachary, Cameron, Baisil, Elizaveta, Aida, and Tongo." Now Jordan was smiling too and I continued with my story. "When Ashley and I started high school, Mr. and Mrs. Gibson gave us each our own laptop. It was probably the defining moment of my life. It wasn't long before I became ... " I stopped, feeling distraught. I could hardly bring myself to tell Jordan.

"A hacker?" he prompted.

"What?" I'm afraid the stress and disbelief showed on my face.

"You're Firestorm," Jordan said simply, then chuckled softly when my jaw dropped. *How did he figure it out?* "Let me guess, you're wondering how I figured it all out." I could only nod; shock had finished stealing my voice. Jordan smiled. "I only just now finished putting together the pieces, though I've known for a while and had my suspicions even longer. That night I stumbled into Vortex, I found it strange that you went to such lengths to make sure I never saw your face or heard your voice. Your fellow hackers had no fear of me knowing who they were, so I couldn't help but wonder if you were someone I might recognize. I figured out you were a girl, and when you untied me and escorted me across town, in your haste you forgot that—" Jordan tapped his nose. " ... That everyone has a unique aura, a scent. You always smell faintly of strawberries and paint. Also, you have a really weird computer, and there's a bomb named Cyra under your desk."

He was finished with his little speech. I was so stunned that my mind went completely blank for a moment. After a dumbfounded pause, I found my voice.

"I'm sorry my savage friends tied you up. They overreacted," I muttered. Jordan grinned.

"Well, my prison guard was polite enough. No worries." An unbidden giggle escaped my lips. *Despite all this, Jordan is still making me smile ...* "You and your friends have done a lot of good, Amber. The world needs white hat hackers like you. Don't worry! I think it's amazing." At this, I couldn't help it. I laughed. It wasn't out of happiness, though.

"Oh, Jordan. You make me sound so selfless and courageous! I'm not." I chuckled sadly when I saw his confused expression. "No, I'm not a hero. On the contrary, I'm a wanted criminal." Jordan seemed to falter at this, unsure whether to believe me. "When I started hacking, I was infamous. I destroyed millions of dollars—perhaps billions. But it wasn't traced to me till years later."

Honestly, I was expecting Jordan to be a bit more shaken at all this. He didn't seem shocked, though, just a little surprised. I pressed on, a sinking feeling in my gut.

"Ashley and I survived high school. College flew by. Eventually, I got a job as a member of an I.T. support team. Ashley sorted and cataloged data from police investigations. But she got herself into a dangerous situation. One of her colleagues was stealing confidential data. In order to gather evidence against him, she took an incriminating USB stick. Fearing he was on to her, she asked me to turn it in. It was safe that way. But I refused. In fact, I laughed inside at her predicament. I didn't want to go anywhere near the police. I agreed to hold on to it, just to pacify her. I put it in my laptop bag and, honestly, forgot about it."

Jordan was listening in absolute stillness, as if he somehow knew my life's story was nearing its collapse.

"About a week passed. Nothing happened. It seemed Ashley was in the clear, and she had plans to try to turn it in soon." I stopped. I didn't want to go on, to unearth what I had buried for so long. But I had to. "It was late, probably around 3 A.M. I was walking back from work. When I got home, I saw some men hunched over something on the ground. They didn't see me, so I hid—like a coward—behind a building across the street. They were speaking loud enough to be heard, but I couldn't understand what they were saying. It was Arabic. There was a shout and they all made a break for it."

I couldn't go on. I couldn't share the nightmares I had relived so vividly just days before. Tears were streaming down my face, but I just stared ahead, not bothering to wipe them away. I took a deep breath and continued.

"There was an earsplitting bang, searing heat, and the sensation of being thrown like a rag doll. What I saw … killed me inside, even though I lived. My home was in flames—mostly blown apart. Everyone was inside … all dead. I don't know why, but … I ran."

Slowly, I flipped open my sketchbook, careful to hold it away from the tears dripping down my cheeks.

"Apart from my family, the only other person I trusted was Eric, a hacker like me. He taught me a lot, and … he was probably the only friend I ever had." Distantly, I realized what I was doing and quickly stopped. I hoped Jordan hadn't noticed me rubbing my wrists; the scars that were no longer there. *Keep going.* "He saved my life," I whispered, my aching heart begging for a break. But I couldn't stop now. "He hid me for months. We hacked the site on the memory stick and found Teumessian: a huge system of crime. A well-organized terrorist group. That's why my laptop's whacky. I 'upgraded' it. I set up my systems, modified my computer, and attacked. Teumessian must have thought they were safe with Ashley out of the way. The last thing they saw after I drained the information from their screens was one word. My new hacking name: Laelaps."

"Why 'Teumessian'? And 'Laelaps'? What does it mean?" Jordan asked, carefully sounding out the strange words.

"In Greek mythology, there was a fox named Teumessian. It had been given a special fate: it would never be caught by man or beast. There was also a magical dog named Laelaps. It was fated to always hit its target. Laelaps was sent to catch Teumessian; this was the first paradox. The mythology states that Zeus was so confused that, in desperation to end the enigma, he turned both dog and fox to stone and threw them into the sky. Canis Major is Laelaps and Canis Minor is Teumessian."

Surprisingly, the history lesson wasn't lost on Jordan. He seemed to get it. Maybe he had heard it before. He nodded sadly. I returned to my story.

"Shortly after we hacked Teumessian, the FBI found me. Their sensors had picked up on the connection from my computer to the Teumessian database. The signature Wi-Fi led them straight to me. How a messed-up teen from nowhere discovered and hacked Teumessian baffled them. I begged them to let me join their team of hackers. They quickly managed to pin my criminal past to me, though, so they couldn't officially associate with me—unless it was to send me to prison. So they brought in a special agent: Edge. He's the only person in the FBI who can have contact with me."

I frowned. *How to describe Edge? ... Never thought about that before.*

"He's like my 'handler,' I guess, keeping me in line and giving me orders. About 10 percent of the time I enjoy the view of him wrapped around my little finger, but the other 90 percent is spent under his boot."

Jordan chuckled a tiny bit, and I gained a shred of courage at the sound. But then, my heart fell. Once again, one of the deepest regrets and most haunting nightmares of my life ... was the next chapter in my story.

"Teumessian tracked me down. They must have found me the same way the FBI did. They ... Eric ... I was—" I sighed, a bitter tear slipping down my cheek. "Eric hid me, then gave himself up to save me. They shot him, right in front of my very eyes, though they didn't know I was there." I tried to swallow a sob. "I watched him die," I whispered, then pressed on, trudging toward the dark end. "I had nowhere to go. So I took a risk and tracked down Jessica, an old school friend of mine. Apparently, she was deep in debt, but put me up anyway. I told her everything, thinking she'd understand and that I could trust her. She contacted Teumessian—probably for money. I learned of her plans, knocked her unconscious, and escaped, but Teumessian showed up before the FBI could. They killed her. It was all my fault. I've been running ever since. North Carolina to Georgia. Georgia to Texas. Texas to Colorado. And now to California."

I couldn't read Jordan's expression through my tear-blurred vision. Perhaps that was a good thing. *Finish. End it.* Taking a deep, shaky breath, I began the final sprint.

"When I was still in Colorado, Teumessian began to show interest in the government-funded Project Plutonium. When I arrived in California, Edge ordered me not to hack until he decided I was safe here. But I launched Cyra, my A.I. program that monitors the data going in and out of Teumessian. It picked up on some alarming news about Teumessian's destructive intentions. I warned Edge of the impending doom and hacked solo. My actions saved lives. Still, I was put on probation for a year for directly disobeying orders. That was when I told you I had lost my job. About a month ago, I was allowed to return to hacking with the FBI. My best guess is that one of my networks went down mid-hack, and Cyra, in desperation to fill the quota of required routers, jumped onto your Wi-Fi.

It's not modified to be invisible like mine. So Teumessian came straight to you."

Until this point in the story, I hadn't met Jordan's gaze. Now I looked right at him, blurry though he was.

"I am so … so sorry. You are right; they were sent to kill me. But Teumessian's never actually seen me, so they have no way of knowing you are not Laelaps. I am. I'll admit, for a second, I knew that, if Teumessian killed you, they'd think they had finally won and I could go free. But I couldn't bear seeing Chloe, Dylan, or Matt ever again knowing it was my fault that you died. And I couldn't live with myself."

There was a long, heavy silence. Doubtless Jordan was choking on all this, ruing the day our paths collided and questioning his attempt to save my life. I almost wish he had failed. It would have been justice if I'd died.

"That night of the meteor shower," I started slowly, my voice quivering, "you asked me, 'Why wait?' Well, if God is good—then He certainly doesn't want anything to do with me. He's made that perfectly clear. God obliterated everything that ever mattered to me, all at once, in a display of blazing fireworks before my very eyes. He made me watch helplessly as the life drained out of my best friend. Because of me, a college girl's life was cut woefully short. Their memory lives only as long as I do. Yes, I am alive, but I wouldn't say I'm truly living. Now you know my story. Can you find any evidence, anywhere in my life, that God loves me? I can't. Because I'm too far gone."

Hot tears were streaming down my face, and I gritted my teeth to keep from sobbing. Jordan wasn't answering. *It's no less than I deserve. I've destroyed lives, stolen millions, selfishly endangered everyone around me. If only I could do it all over again … I wish I had died when I got shot. I wish I'd never come here. I wish I hadn't run to Jessica for help. I wish I'd never met Eric. I wish I'd never been adopted. I wish I'd never been born …*

"No," Jordan said very slowly. "No, you're not too far gone."

I sobbed in exasperation. "Why can't you see?! My whole life, I've been nothing but a curse!" I exclaimed, longing for this miserable existence of mine to end.

"I see a different story," he said simply. That stopped me.

"What?" Another sob escaped. "What do you mean?"

Jordan went silent again. Then, very quietly, he spoke.

"You know the truth. There's nothing more I can say to help you understand. But you can still see the proof. Look back over your life. Search for the times when you should have been discovered, hurt, or killed—but escaped against all odds. Go back and find everything." Jordan slowly got up, coming toward me. "Because I'd say God's intervened a lot for someone you believe He doesn't love." With that, he slipped his hand behind my head, gently kissed my forehead, threw me a tender, saddened look of compassion and care, and then … left. Just like that.

His words hung in the air. His act of kindness stung my heart. His gaze split my soul. I'd expected him to condemn me, judge me, hate me! I feared he would be angry, disgusted—perhaps he'd even tell the others to stay away. But, he hadn't.

I sat frozen for hours, staring at the door, tears streaming down my face like rain on a window. Outside, night had fallen. Eventually, the lights dimmed. Forcing myself to lie down, I stared out the window, my mind screaming like a rushing train. Torrents of memories washed about my mind.

We were almost aborted. … I shouldn't have been born. The wreck. Ashley never lost consciousness—she got me out.

"Hang on, Amber. I'm going to get us out of here!"

That family we stayed with, they tried to hurt me. But … we escaped. Then, Mr. and Mrs. Gibson almost passed us over. But we went to them. Eric hid me when R0GU3C0D3 fell. I was held late at work that night … I could have been killed too. Eric came back to the safe house hours early. If he hadn't, I'd have died.

"You say God hates you. I'm not convinced. Somehow, your radial arteries are intact. The skin on either side of them is absolutely raw. It's a miracle you didn't cut them. If you had, I don't think you would have survived … "

Edge came. He was willing to give me a chance at being part of the FBI. If he hadn't made that allowance, I'd have been thrown in jail. Eric gave his life to save mine; Teumessian almost found me. I escaped the flames. I heard Jessica's plan, confronted her, and fled before they came. Edge told me to go into hiding.

"Somehow, Teumessian got here before we did. They were still here all along …"

I lived on the run for so long, yet no one hurt me. I escaped in Colorado. I didn't get caught when I hacked during Project Plutonium. I didn't get injured in competitions. I wasn't killed the night C3RB3RU$ attacked Jason and I.

I survived getting shot. I woke up.

Guilt bombarded my mind. The ranks clashed; the war began. I watched the moon rise, my mind shredding itself with doubt, teetering on the edge.

I deserve to die ... But I'm alive ... All have sinned, and fallen short ... I have the blood of at least seventeen people on my head ... Edge protected me ... The gift of God is eternal life ... I am a guilty, vile, wretched criminal ... Eric deemed my life worth saving ... For God so loved the world, He gave His only Son ... I'm a liar ... But Jordan hasn't judged me ... Believe on the Lord Jesus Christ, and you will be saved.

I couldn't be loved ... But I am loved ... but I'm too far gone ... or am I?

On and on and on the storm raged, until I couldn't take it anymore. *Enough! I've made my decision!* Suddenly, it all ceased, and I immediately plummeted like a stone into a deep, dreamless sleep.

CHAPTER 38

Ocean Front Rescue
Thursday, September 26, 5:10 P.M.

Jordan

"Hey Jordan! Wait!" I turned to find Dylan trotting toward me. "You OK today? You're really quiet. It's kinda scary."

"I'm fine," I said halfheartedly. "Just tired." Dylan seemed to be deciding whether to buy this story.

"Alright, just checking. Chloe thought we should all hang with Amber later, have a tiny celebration. It's her first Thursday back. Think you'll come?"

"Yeah. I'll be there." *Long before the rest of you.*

Dylan grinned. "See you then." He jogged off, evidently convinced all was well.

But it wasn't.

I'd hardly slept the night before. All day, I'd been distracted, unable to get Amber's story from my thoughts. It replayed itself over and over in my mind, haunting my dreams and my every waking moment. My heart broke for her. She knew the truth, yet she just wouldn't accept it. I longed for her to see that she was loved. She wasn't too far gone. Every ounce of me wished I could take all the horrible pain away. The tears. The nightmares, the guilt, the past itself! But I couldn't. Only God could.

To be honest, I wasn't sure what to say when I went back. Would she be angry? Sad? Scared? How would she interact with Matt, Dylan, and Chloe from here on? Did she fear I'd say something to them? The entire way to the hospital, these questions pounded my head. But no answers were popping up. I couldn't feel my feet as I walked down the corridors. Eventually,

I came to a stop in front of her room's open door. Still, I didn't know what to say or what awaited me. I swallowed my questions and stepped inside.

Amber was sitting up, calmly gazing out the window, hands folded contentedly in her lap. She heard me enter and turned; my heart skipped a beat. I saw something in her face. Something I'd never seen there before. It was inexpressible. Peace beyond measure, a hint of joy, a gentle light. Her faint smile didn't seem to come from happiness. It was something deeper than that. Something much deeper.

Could it be?

Slowly, not daring to believe what I was seeing, not daring to hope, I numbly let my bag strap slip from my hand and took a hesitant step closer. Amber held my gaze steadily, her serene smile growing a little. I opened my mouth to say something, but I didn't have any words, so I shut it again. That brought a quick chuckle from Amber.

"Hello, Jordan," she said softly, a laughing, happy smile filling her face, making the gold flecks in her eyes dance. Distantly, I felt my feet moving closer.

"You're … Did … ?" I couldn't bring myself to ask. It was too good to be true. Amber simply searched my face for a moment, and I could have sworn I saw tears in her eyes. After a long, breath-holding moment, she spoke the sweetest words I'd ever heard.

"Yes," she whispered, joy filling her voice. "I got saved."

For a moment, time stopped. Overwhelming joy and amazement washed over Jordan. His face lit up like the sun, he closed the distance—and smothered me in a hug. I couldn't hold the happy tears and laughter in any longer.

"Ow, Jordan. *Ow!* Too tight!" I exclaimed, giggling despite the pain.

"Sorry!" He apologized and loosened his grip. Within moments, though, it was just as firm as before. "You really mean it? Truly?"

"Yes," I replied. "Yes, I mean it." Jordan held me at arm's length, searching my eyes, his brimming with tears.

"You have no idea how long I've prayed for you. Oh, Amber … " Once again, I was enveloped in a bear-sized embrace. I too wrapped my arms around him, happy for the first time in my life. Truly happy.

I was free. The chains that had bound my heart and hands had been broken. My guilt, my past, my fears, and my failures had been washed away—all placed in the palms of Jesus. He took them away, remembering them no more. What had I been waiting for? All my life, all I had to do was simply *ask* Him to forgive me and *believe* that He had risen, that He was faithful, that He was in control. Simple as that. God *was* good. I *was* loved. I was *never* too far. *The cross of Jesus is enough.*

"Have you told Matt, Dylan, and Chloe? You gotta tell them! You should tell them. We've got to get them over here!" Jordan exclaimed excitedly, then started pulling out his phone.

"No, wait. I wanna tell them in person. Is there a way to get them to come without giving it away?" I asked hopefully.

"They're already planning on coming in the next few hours," Jordan said, nodding enthusiastically. Then he sighed impatiently, like a school kid waiting for the lunch bell to ring. "But that's so long to wait," he pointed out miserably. I couldn't help but laugh.

"You're not the one with the surprise to tell, yet I think you're just as excited as I am." That got Jordan beaming again.

"How could I not be? One of my best friends in the whole wide world got saved!"

That caught me off guard a bit.

"You think of me as a best friend?" I asked tentatively.

Jordan seemed surprised at this. He nodded. "Yes, I do. Don't you know it?"

I sat back a bit, delighted with this information, pondering how to respond, and eventually settled on my response.

"I didn't consider myself so lucky."

CHAPTER 39

Silver Bay Memorial Hospital
Saturday, October 5, 6:27 P.M.

Jordan

Over the course of the next week, I could see Amber changing. She smiled more, laughed more, loved more. Every spare moment was devoted to her new Bible, and she was constantly asking deep and insightful questions. Timid though she may be, she'd already boldly witnessed to three nurses. She was surprisingly strong in her faith for such a new believer.

I'll never forget watching Matt, Dylan, and Chloe that day, as they walked into the room and saw what I had seen: the bright hope in Amber's eyes. And hearing what I'd heard: Amber was a Christian. They'd been overjoyed. What a happy Thursday that had been! I don't think there's been a happier one. That made me think. *Perhaps today could go down in history, too.*

"Is something special going on today, Jordan?" Amber asked, looking up from her sketching, putting my thoughts on hold.

"Hmm? What makes you ask that?" I asked. She glanced out the window.

"There are a lot of people out and about near the boardwalk, and there are more lights down there than normal."

"Ah, keen observation, my dear Watson," I teased, winning a smile from her. "Yeah, tonight's the Firefly Festival." Amber appeared confused.

"But, I thought that was last month?"

"Nope," I said, shaking my head. "The date changes every year. It was bumped back a bit because of conflicting events." Amber looked out the window again, anticipation in her expression.

"Oh. I wonder if I could see it from here," she mused, peering intently out the window. She sighed, and quietly murmured, "I wish I could go." Closing my book, I sat back and thought for a moment.

"Why are the doctors still keeping you? You seem fine."

"Well, I'm almost entirely healed," Amber explained, casually returning to her drawing. "They might release me within a couple of days. The X-rays say all is well—except for a small chip of metal in my arm. It's just a little souvenir from the car wreck when I was little, but since it's not doing any damage, they're not gonna take it out. My rib's mended and the stitches are gone. But I'm still recovering my strength. I can't stand for long before getting dizzy."

"Oh," I answered, a bit distraught.

It didn't seem fair that Amber was stuck here like this. I dearly hoped she'd be home before her birthday, at least. For about five minutes, I agonized in silence, and then an idea began to form in my head. Suddenly, the details fell into place and I sprang up, catching Amber off guard. She gave me an inquisitive look.

"I have a plan! Stay here; I'll be back!" I exclaimed, hurrying for the door—and then realized how stupid that was. *"Stay here."* I turned to see Amber, an amused grin on her face, trying not to laugh. I sighed, feeling silly. "Just … never mind. I'll be back."

I couldn't help but wonder what Jordan meant by "I have a plan." It wasn't too unusual for him to be sitting calmly and quietly one second and then suddenly bounce up chattering about a fantastic idea the next. But an idea about what, exactly? *The last thing we were talking about was the Firefly Festival. What could he have in mind?* About ten minutes later, a jubilant Jordan returned, Teresa in tow—with a wheelchair.

"You still wanna go to the festival, Amber?" he asked. Blushing, I nodded as Teresa offered me a hand, helping me into the chair and handing me my hoodie. "Good," Jordan said, "because I just got permission to take you on a field trip!"

Teresa turned to him. "Remember, I'm making a bit of an exception for you. Be back before ten, not a minute later—I'll be checking this room on the dot. Come back sooner if it gets chilly out there or if Miss Gibson starts feeling tired," she ordered. After a convincing grin from Jordan, she nodded once and left. Jordan turned to me.

"Ready to get out of here?" he asked.

"More ready than you'll ever know," I breathed, itching to feel the sun on my skin and smell the sea again.

Though I felt awkward and antsy in the ridiculous wheelchair, rolling out those doors felt like a tiny taste of Heaven. Freedom! No white walls and hospital smell for a few hours! I could have kissed the pavement or hugged the nearest tree—if I had been feeling up to it.

Jordan continued around the side of the building, then stopped once we were a short distance from the front, gazing over his shoulder as if he expected we'd be followed. Before I could ask why we had stopped, he hurried around to the front of the chair and knelt, his back to me.

"Come on. Let's go!"

"What?"

"Get on!" Jordan said, suddenly twisting, grabbing my wrists, pulling them over his shoulders, lifting me into a piggyback ride, slipping his arms beneath my knees, and standing. "Onwards!" he exclaimed. Without further explanation, he started walking.

"Jordan!" I gasped, "What are you doing?!"

"I know you don't want that thing, that you'll worry about 'being a burden' or something like that."

"Aren't I more of a burden now?"

"Nope," Jordan said, throwing a smile my way. "You're light as a feather. Don't worry! I wouldn't do it if I didn't think I could." He glanced at me. "You don't mind, right?"

I had no idea how to respond. Had he read my thoughts? I hate wheelchairs! I always feel so conspicuous in them, yet I'd never said anything. And he was right; I did wonder if I'd be a burden.

Blushing yet grinning, I muttered: "So long as you don't drop me."

I knew he wouldn't.

Amber seemed so happy. The others were ecstatic to see her out. They feared I'd kidnapped her and was going to get arrested. I convinced them it was all perfectly legal, to stop worrying, and just have a good time. It didn't take much persuading.

Matt and I took turns carrying Amber. Dylan tried a couple of times, but he only lasted about fifteen minutes each time. She would constantly tap my shoulder and quietly ask, for the hundredth time, if I was sure she wasn't too heavy or being a bother. I assured her, for the hundredth time, that she was not.

We walked up and down the boardwalk, chatting and looking at all the fun stands and booths that had been brought out for the evening. Games were played, dares were accepted, jokes were told. The skies cooperated beautifully; the only clouds to be seen were soft, fluffy, and few. The slight breeze never brought a chill.

About halfway through the night, I realized this was Amber's first night of freedom since she got saved. And it happened to fall on the Firefly Festival. No doubt about it: God had planned this specially for her. I knew He wouldn't have it any other way.

Everything went by in a blur. Everything felt perfect. Jordan and Matt took such good care of me; even dear Dylan tried a few times. Not once did my feet touch the ground.

Before long, we staked out a spot to watch the show. Perhaps the sky had been a bit darker, or the lights had been a bit brighter. Maybe the balloons had been more vivid, or the moon dimmer—whatever it was, the show was even more brilliant than I remembered.

A new section had been added. I decided to call it "snowy." Clusters of soft white were mingled with dots of bright gray and a touch of light blue, all swirling in the slight sea breeze. It reminded me of Maryland, of the days when Ashley and I sat at the window watching snowflakes flutter down, telling stories and playing games. Though I hated cold, I did love the snow and being with my sis. *Ashley! I'll ... She's ...* Somehow, I hadn't realized it till that moment. *I'll see her again! I'll be with her—and my family! I'll see them all again! I'll be with them in Heaven someday.*

It took every ounce of self-control and courage I had to keep from crying. I'd never been so happy. Fixing my eyes with new rapture on the glowing lights, I felt my smile widen. *This is one of the best days of my life.* As that thought hit me, as if to agree, the rainbow colors of the finale surged up, lighting the sky and sea. For as long as I live, I'll never forget that night.

The walk back to the hospital was a peaceful one. Amber chatted a while, then went quiet. Doubtless, she was shutting her eyes tight, concentrating on the fading image of the lights like she'd done last year.

Everything had gone perfectly; the only hitch in my plan was that the wheelchair was gone. I'd had a bad feeling this might happen. It had been close enough to the door that someone likely took it back in. Shaking my head, I continued on, deciding the worst trouble I could get into was a lecture. If I got a tongue-lashing from Teresa, so be it. She couldn't possibly be worse than Betty.

Miraculously, the lady at the front desk merely glanced at me, then returned to her work. I balked. Did she somehow miss the fact that I had a patient clinging to my shoulders and it was past visiting hours? Apparently. All the way to Amber's room, no one paid us any mind. *There's no way this is normal. Thank you, Lord. Looks like I'm not getting into trouble tonight after all.*

I nudged Amber's door open with my foot and slipped in. To my surprise, Amber didn't move. She didn't even say anything. I tried to get a glance at her, but from the way her head was tipped, I couldn't. Gently, I turned and lowered her to the bed. Then I realized: she had fallen asleep. Amber murmured something, shifted, and opened her eyes partway.

"Are we back?" she muttered groggily.

"Yeah. I didn't know you were so tired. Why didn't you say something?"

"I didn't want you to take me back early and miss something, and I wanted every minute I could have with you guys." She tried to hide a yawn, failed miserably, then turned a faint smile on me. "Thank you, Jordan. Thank you so much for everything." As she spoke, her eyelids slowly fell, and her words trailed off. She was out again.

I smiled. *Sleep well, sweet Amber.* Pulling the sheets up over her, I lightly patted her head—causing the corners of her lips to twitch up briefly. I slipped out and headed for home.

CHAPTER 40

The Salt Breeze Apartment Complex, Apt. 1407
Thursday, October 10, 8:48 P.M.

Amber

Within a couple of days, the doctors released me. I cannot express how wonderful it was to walk through my door and see my home once more, to wash off the harsh hospital smell, to sleep in my own bed, to wake up to sunshine and the sound of the waves, to walk the shore—to be free.

The only stressful thing was the fact I was still Laelaps.

My assessment had been correct; a router was down and Cyra had connected to Jordan's Wi-Fi. I soon had that fixed. Next, I took the papers down from the wall, storing them in a notebook. I didn't want to always be thinking about Teumessian. I wouldn't let them control my life like that.

Try though I might, I couldn't get in contact with Edge. It was disconcerting. Also, the shooting had literally ceased to exist. No matter how many archives I hacked, no matter how far I looked, there was no account of the attack, the assailants, the investigation—or even of me. I had been erased from the hospital records.

I couldn't figure out if that was good or bad.

There was no telling whether the hitmen had been caught. Jordan was exceedingly worried about my safety and I about his; we stuck together. Why wasn't there any information? What if they got away? Would they come back? If so, who would they target, and when? It was unnerving, and the topic of many discussions between us.

"But, is it safe?" Jordan pressed. "Surely someone who already has access to the archives could help."

"Until I get a reply from Edge, I can't call in aid from the FBI," I explained, distraught and frustrated at how in the dark I was. "For now, it's still up to me to find out what's going on." I dug in my bag, searching for my door key.

"What if you get, ah, cyber-trapped? Would the police help if they knew who you were? If push comes to shove, perhaps you could confide in one of them."

"I don't know," I muttered, sliding the card into the lock. "But push *hasn't* come to shove yet. There has to be another way. I don't want to endanger anyone." I nudged the door open.

"Good point … maybe—"

My blood ran cold. "Hush!" I exclaimed, cutting Jordan off. He looked confused. "Listen," I shushed. He went still.

"I don't hear anything," he whispered. "Why are we being quiet?"

"There was a noise," I breathed, scanning the room. There: my notebook had been on the side table when I left; now it was on the counter. "Someone's here."

"*What?!*" Jordan whisper-shrieked. Dropping my key into my bag and quietly dropping the bag to the ground, I silently slid out of my flip-flops, pulled my handgun from my waistband, and unlocked the safety. This was too much for Jordan.

"Amber, since when do you have a *gun*?!"

I held up four fingers—*four days*—then slowly, noiselessly, began to creep forward. Jordan grabbed my wrist and started pulling me back. "No, Amber! This is where we run or call the police!" he whispered desperately, a pleading look in his eyes. I pulled out of his grasp and kept going.

Silently, my bare feet padded across the carpet, my ears peeled for the slightest sound. Muffled though it may be, I heard it. *Click.* It came from around the corner near the hall. My heart was pounding. My hands were shaking. But I had to do this.

I neared the turn. Taking a soundless, shaky breath—*one, two, three*—I whirled around the corner, yanking my gun up. I came face to face with the barrel of another handgun. Beyond it was a hooded figure, shrouded in shadow, standing with a sure stance, matching my own. *Wait … could it be—*

The standoff was shattered as, out of nowhere, Jordan suddenly sprang forward, smacked the gun—hard—straight up, away from me, and somehow got between us. In an instant, before I could blink, there was a flurry of motion. Jordan was pinned against the wall, an arm across his neck and a gun to his forehead. I found my voice.

"Edge! *No!!!*"

I couldn't move. I couldn't breathe. My head was spinning from being slammed into the wall. My ears were ringing. There was a gun at my head.

"Edge! *No!!!*" Amber cried out. "He was only protecting me! Let him go!"

Edge? I searched the deep darkness beneath the hood. Even if stars and spots hadn't been dancing in my vision, I doubt I could have seen the man's face. There was a horribly long, painful pause. The pressure on my throat decreased ever so slightly—and he suddenly let go.

I stumbled forward, gasping for air, trying to regain my balance. Everything was blurring into darkness. Distantly, I felt Amber pull me back against the wall just as I collapsed and slid down it. Inky black pulsed in front of my eyes, then gradually faded. Eventually, I managed to settle my gaze on Amber's concerned face, then beyond at the shadow-shrouded figure, standing just out of reach, watching in silence. A chill ran down my spine.

"Are you OK?" Amber asked, her voice laced with worry. I nodded. Amber, kneeling beside me, now stood, hit the light switch, and turned to the intruder. "What are you doing here, Edge?" He remained silent as he calmly turned his attention from Amber to me, as if to say, *"He's still here, you know."* Amber frowned. "He's a friend, Edge. He can't be bought or sold. He already knows everything." After pondering this for a moment, Edge pushed his hood back. My eyes went wide.

His skin was pale as marble. In stark contrast, his hair was blacker than a raven's feathers, so much so it appeared to absorb the light; perhaps it was spun from darkness itself. His irises were the lightest blue I've ever seen. No, not blue—white, almost. They looked like the eyes of a Husky dog, like arctic ice. And sharp as ice, too. His slightly displeased, emotionless gaze was potent enough to slice my soul in half, making me want to squirm.

"He knows everything. How?" Even his voice was cold and sharp. Amber, though, didn't seem phased.

"I told him," she stated simply. "The rest is not important. Now, what are you doing here?"

Edge turned and scrutinized me for a moment, as if I was an annoying, burdensome child. He seemed to be wishing I would spontaneously combust. When I didn't, he frowned slightly, then turned back to Amber.

"I came to finish cleaning up your mess and make sure you don't do anything else foolish," he said, throwing me another quick glance. Amber noticed and seemed to bite back her frustration.

"I made my decision and took a risk. It was the right choice," she said carefully.

"You've never had good judgement, Amber," Edge pointed out. Slowly, I stood, frowning. I didn't like this guy talking smack to Amber. She didn't deserve it. But Edge continued to ignore me. "I had to take your name out of hospital archives. And police databases. Do you have any idea how hard it is to keep people quiet about a shooting?"

"Hard. I know. Thank you, Edge," Amber said quietly. Edge seemed rather intrigued that she was taking this lecture in such a calm way.

"What happened to your sass?" he murmured, searching her face with a hard gaze. Amber smiled faintly, but before she could say anything, Edge pressed on. "I'll be heading for Seattle, Washington in a few days. Before I leave California ... " Edge stopped and frowned at me again, then, turned back to Amber. "سمعت انا السجين على استعداد يتكلم في مقابل حياته وحماية الشرطة، وقلو حصلت على إذن لتحقيق."

Amber looked concerned.

"سجين، واحد؟ ولكن، كان هناك ثالثة. فعل الاثنين من هروب الآخرين؟" Amber asked.

"عندما أدركوا ان هناك ليس مفر، انتحروا، ولكن تم القبض على ثالث. ويقول هنا فرع عن الأربعة الكبار." Edge replied, shaking his head.

"كيف؟! الأربعة الكبار يعرف عن هنا؟" Amber gasped.

"Can someone please speak English?" I asked, earning another glare from Edge, who turned back to Amber.

"انا لا أعرف، ولكنني سوف اكتشف ذلك. قريبا، سوف يتم تحولهله. في اشهر. أظن على القل بضعة. الآن، انت في امان هنا، على القل بضعة. عندما اتصل بكي ... تتبعيني كن على استعداد للتحرك. خطط، كني على استعداد اتصل بكي ... عندما اتصل بكي استكوني أكثر امنا هناك!" Amber thought about this for a moment, then nodded slowly.

"OK. Will do," she affirmed, resolutely, looking disquieted yet overjoyed.

Eventually, I managed to boot Edge out of my apartment. I didn't want to know how he got in. Though he brought good news, he also brought some cold, harsh reality, too. I couldn't bear the thought of what I knew was coming.

"What was that all about? Was that Arabic? You know Arabic?" Jordan asked once he was sure Edge was gone.

"Yes, that was Arabic. And … two of the attackers are dead. They committed suicide when they realized they were cornered. But the third was captured, and he's willing to talk," I said slowly, staring at the door, half expecting Edge to pop back in and start scolding me. He didn't. Grinning slightly, I turned to Jordan. "Also, for at least a few months, we're safe."

THE JOURNAL OF AMBER MARIE GIBSON

October 10, Thursday

This is likely going to be the longest, craziest, most important entry I've ever made. I haven't written for a long time because I've been both unconscious and busy, so I have a lot to catch up on.

First, I made a foolish mistake. When I returned to hacking, one of the routers went down and I missed the error messages. Cyra, desperate to fill the quota, initiated protocol 35_2174; in other words, "jump on to the nearest Wi-Fi network and make it function as a router." It hijacked Jordan's network. I didn't discover this until it was too late. Teumessian found the unprotected signal and tracked it down. They went after Jordan. I intervened and got shot. I can testify that it is hands-down-and-hats-off the most painful thing I have ever endured. I almost died. But Jordan saved my life. From there, there is a huge gap, because I was in a coma for about a month.

When I finally woke up, it wasn't long before I had to give Jordan an explanation as to what was going on. I haven't told anyone the truth about me in years. I was expecting him to reject me once he knew who I was and what I had done -- but he didn't. My life changed forever that night. Before all this went down, there was a meteor shower, and for the first time in my life, I wondered if God might really be good. And now ... I am convinced of it.

God IS good. It's true. Every day I discover more in His Word, and I can't get enough. I never will. He had planned every second of my life before time began. From the moment I was born, He was there, counting down the days till I finally gave in to mercy. Without Jesus, I am nothing. But He loves me, and His love is all that I need.

Please, whoever you are, if you're reading this, I beg you to hear my testimony. This is the only true peace and love you'll ever find.

I have let go of my grief. Yes, I will miss those I have lost deeply for as long as I live. But, no -- none of them would want me to grieve for them like this. Especially Ashley. She is singing with angels, walking streets of gold with our Mom and Dad, sitting on the lap of her Savior, hanging on His every word. She's probably looking down at me right now, wondering when I will hurry up and come join her. And honestly, I'm not afraid to die anymore. (The apostle Paul said perfectly what I feel, in Philippians I think, and it goes something like this.) "For to me, to live is Christ and to die is gain ... I am torn: I desire to depart and be with Christ, which is better by far; but it is more necessary that I remain."

So, my work is not done. It's only been a couple days since I was released from the hospital, and tonight Mr. Ice-E. showed up in my apartment. He says two out of the three attackers are dead. They committed suicide once they realized there was no escape. But the third is willing to talk in exchange for protection. Soon, E. will find out what he has to say and relay the information to me. In the meantime, I am safe for a couple of months. I don't know what the future holds, only that it will not be easy. Hard decisions lie ahead. I can only hope and pray I will choose the right path.

CHAPTER 41

V0RT3X's stronghold
Tuesday, October 15, 10:07 P.M.

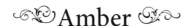Amber

The next few days passed in a blur. While I agonized over what Edge had told me and what I would do, I also reveled in the good news: Jordan and I were safe. It was unlikely Teumessian would send another hit team, and unless they heard about what happened, they would have no reason to believe things had gone awry; their target had successfully been eliminated at the cost of a few expendables. Edge predicted they wouldn't catch on for a couple of months. So I had that long to figure out how to defeat my enemy.

But I wouldn't let that consume my thoughts. I had a new life now. In all honesty, I didn't quite care about winning the war like I used to. Fear no longer chained me—and revenge wasn't important. All that mattered now was ending the threat. And if I failed … well, someone else would take my place. Simple as that. Meanwhile, I was going to live. I hung out with Chloe, Dylan, Matt, and Jordan whenever I could. I started drawing again. Sleeping. Programming. Even surfing. Everything I loved was returned to me.

I even went to church with the others on Sunday morning. It was so amazing because, for the first time in my life, no one had to force me. I wanted to go. It made sense. It was real and personal. Practically everyone was friendly, evidently elated at the arrival of a new Christian. I made so many good friends—and then I remembered my old ones.

It had been a long time since I went to V0RT3X. A very long time. I'd thought about them, but now—today—I knew I needed to go back.

I was happily greeted by Jason, Maggie, Keri, Ender, and some of the others. Even Sonja seemed glad to see me. All day, I hacked and programmed, helped Jason with an A.I., taught Maggie how to hack electricity, played games with Keri, and debated battle plans with Ender. Sonja was strangely distant, though. But that was alright. She seemed busy.

So much had piled up to discuss, hack, and program since I was gone that I didn't finish until ten at night. *Wow, I actually spent all day here. It was good to see everyone again,* I reminisced as I shut down my laptop. *I'm so glad Maggie's found her place here once more. Next time there's a youth group event, I've gotta invite her and Jason.* I stopped packing up to think about that for a moment. *Wouldn't it be amazing if they got saved?* Smiling, I continued with my task. *And Keri's enjoying seventh grade after all. I knew she would. Also, it was nice to talk with Daisy for the first time. Perhaps I've found another friend.*

I shouldered my computer bag, thinking over these happy things, said farewell to my companions, and started for the side exit. There I encountered Sonja. She was leaning against the doorframe, inspecting her nails, a disinterested air about her. I smiled at her as I got closer, but she didn't look up. Maybe she was tired. I just looked down and kept walking. But as I began to step through the door, she stuck out her arm, barring my way.

"What happened, Storm?" she asked, not even lifting her head.

"You mean why I haven't been around?" I asked. She didn't respond. "Like I said, I just got too busy with the outside world. That's all." She was still blocking the door, but now she looked up at me.

"We both know that's a lie." My heart tripped. I felt fidgety. *What does she mean? What does she know?* Had I slipped up and contradicted myself? Sonja straightened and regarded me square on. "You've been out of commission, that's why. Wounded in action." She pointed an imaginary gun at me and pulled the trigger. "Someone shot you, and I want to know who." I started to panic. *How could she know that?!*

"What? Come on, Sonja, that's ridiculous—"

"I believe it was right around here," she interrupted, suddenly punching me in the gut. It wasn't particularly hard, but she might as well have run into me with a car. I doubled up, searing pain flooding my senses. "Whoops, my bad," she said flatly. "Have I proven my point yet, or do I need to hit you again?"

"Alright!" I gasped. "Please, don't do that again. That really, really hurt.

That was dirty, Sonja." I finally caught my breath. "How did you know I got shot?"

She ignored my question. "Who's trying to kill you? Was it someone from Cerberus?"

"No, Cerberus isn't after me."

"Then who is? I can't bash skulls until I know who I'm after."

"Sonja, no. They're in custody. Don't poke your nose into this, please. It's fine. How did you know I got shot?"

Still, I was denied answers. "I had a hunch you were hiding stuff from day one. But this—you're in deep. Tell me how, why, who's involved. What exactly is going on?" One eyebrow went up. "I would like to know more, but I can jog your memory to get you started if need be."

"Sonja ... " I pleaded. She launched into her findings.

"I looked you up. Firestorm. You're not from here. You were quite infamous in Maryland, weren't you? There was another hacker, you were a team. WH1RLW1ND. What happened to the other? And why did you leave?" Shakily, I righted myself and looked into her eyes. *Sonja, no ... not you too ...*

"Sonja, please. Just stop," I begged, holding up my hand to keep her from continuing. "I've already had someone do this to me recently. I won't go through it again. I can't tell you. This will only make things more dangerous—for you, Jason, and everyone here. I hid my past because I don't want to endanger anyone. People have died over this information, Sonja. You have to stop. Please."

Sonja tipped her head to one side, thinking hard. Then she sighed, her shoulders fell, and she stepped out of the way. As if to say: *"Your loss."* After a moment's hesitation, I hurried for the door.

"Don't you want to see how much I know ... Amber?" I froze and slowly turned. She smiled sadly. "Amber Marie Gibson. You work for the FBI. Presumed dead in Maryland. You dropped off the map. I'm sorry about your family and friend. He was the other hacker, wasn't he? Oh, what was his name ... Aaron? Evan?"

"Eric. Eric Everhartt," I whispered. She smirked triumphantly, like she'd just won Major League Gamer of the Year.

"I knew his name. I just wanted confirmation that he was part of Whirlwind. Looks like I was right." *I can't believe I just fell for that. This might be very bad for me.* "The FBI handled the investigation of his death:

a street kid found shot. Nothing special or unusual, except for the fact that he was a master hacker. After he died, there were no more reports of WH1RLW1ND hacks. Before that, the mysterious explosion that presumably killed fifteen people: the Gibson family."

Sonja paused, frowning, as if realizing this might be a delicate subject for me. "Look, I don't know who's chasing you, but they're out for blood. I'm sure you've already figured that out. I also know that someone in your position isn't allowed to talk. But you can trust me, Amber. I already have your secrets, so there's nothing to hide. I'm on your side. No more lying, OK?" I gazed at her for a moment, feeling shocked, and yet—despite everything—somehow strangely comforted.

"OK," I agreed softly.

CHAPTER 42

The Salt Breeze Apartment Complex, Apt. 1407
Tuesday, October 22, 12:00 A.M.

Amber

I woke to the buzzing of my phone alarm. Midnight. Rolling out of bed with the silence of a panther, I pulled on my black hoodie and gloves, grabbed my lock pick and flashlight from my bedside drawer, and crept out the door. If anyone saw me, they would probably call the cops on account of a shady character prowling around. I'd finally decided what I needed to do. It would be the first step in a long, hard decision—but it was the right thing to do. *Focus. Don't get caught. Don't be sloppy. Don't panic. Keep calm. Because this is for Jordan.*

Opening the door to the stairwell a slit, I squeezed through and jogged the long pathway toward disaster. My tired legs tempted me to slide down the handrail, but I knew better. Reaching the bottom, I peeked around the corner to confirm the lobby was empty. It was, and I hurried on. Keeping my head down, I crept toward the mail drop box in the wall beside the front desk.

Kneeling on the ground beside the slot in the wall, I stared at the sheet of metal standing between me and my target. *Dear Lord,* I prayed silently, *you know this is for a good cause. I promise I'll try to stop breaking into things after tonight. But please, don't let anyone pass by. I don't want to go to prison. Please help me find the right letter in time. I've got to do this!* I slid my lock pick out of my pocket and got to work.

It was a stubborn lock. Before long, I started to freak out. Why wouldn't it disengage? It wasn't an electric lock, so why wasn't my pic working? Just as I was about to give up, I heard the lovely, crisp *click* of a lock bar sliding away. Pulling open the hatch, I stared at the endless mounds of envelopes. I was not anticipating there would be this much mail.

Clicking on my flashlight, I started digging. There were so many letters. How would I find the right one? I grabbed a handful and started flicking through them. I searched through pile after pile. Then, on my eighth stack, I found it. *No, no, no … Wait, yes! Yes! Thank you, God! This is it! Jordan's letter to Lexie!* I stuck the rest of the mail back in the bin, locked it, and sprinted back upstairs.

When I got back to my room, I ditched my dark clothes and laid a blank envelope beside Jordan's. Picking up my pen, I copied the address and got started. As I wrote, and the letter grew, a smile spread across my face. *This just might work.* Putting the pen down, I massaged my wrist and inspected my handiwork. Lexie would be getting two letters this week. One from Jordan.

And one from me.

Hello Lexie.

My name is Amber Gibson. You don't know me, but I know your brother, Jordan. He's my neighbor, and one of my best friends. What I'm about to say, well, please hear me out. I have a proposition for you. Now, I know you are starting college later this year and might not have much time, so I don't know if this will work out. But I am willing to try.

I'll get right to it.

Long and short of it: if you want to come and can find an empty spot in your schedule, I would like to fly you out here for a visit. You decide when you want to come, how long you want to stay, and when you want to leave. I will take care of all the arrangements.

Please consider my offer. I insist on paying for this, it would be an honor. Jordan misses you very dearly, and though we've never met, I feel like I know you, he talks about you so much.

Though I will never be able to properly thank him for all he has done for me, I will never stop trying. I think this is a good place to start. Nothing compares to seeing him happy.

Don't mention this to Jordan. If it works out, I really want it to be a total surprise. And if it doesn't work, I don't want to let him down. Please think about it. I hope to hear from you soon!

~ Amber

I added my phone number and email address, slid the letter into an envelope, and sealed it. No longer in my spy attire, I could head downstairs normally. After all, I wasn't doing anything illegal. *Me? Steal mail? No, never.* I returned Jordan's original letter to the mail box along with mine.

Now to wait and see how, or if, Lexie would respond.

CHAPTER 43

The Salt Breeze Apartment Complex, Apt. 1407
Thursday, October 31, 4:25 P.M.

⟨Amber⟩

This was it. This was the day. All my planning had finally payed off: Lexie was coming. She was arriving today. Once my letter had been sent, it wasn't long before I had a reply. We had been messaging each other back and forth for about a week, and I couldn't believe how perfectly things fell into place.

Apparently, Lexie hadn't chosen a college yet; none of the ones in Las Vegas fit her. And for a long time, she had been secretly considering moving back home to Santa Barbara, but felt she needed a clear sign from the Lord to take such a huge step. She had excitedly accepted my invitation, though she did fight a little over the matter of who would pay. I won. Anyway, I'd only need to get her a one-way ticket. Because if things worked out, she wouldn't be staying for a visit. She was here for keeps. I paved the way from her front porch in Las Vegas to the airport to the doors of the apartment. Now the only thing left to do was wait.

Ding! My pointless, tight laps across the carpet came to an abrupt stop as I yanked my phone from my pocket.

New Message: Lexie

Lexie
I'm on the ground and already caught a cab! Based on the route it's taking, I'll be arriving in about 20 minutes.

Amber

Great! I'll think of something to keep Jordan in his apartment. Welcome home!

Lexie

Thank you so much Amber!!! I'm so excited, I can barely wait to see Jordan and meet you!

Amber

Same here. See you soon. ☺

Slowly, deep in thought, I slid my phone back in my pocket. This was good and bad. She would be here soon. But I had miscalculated. Twenty minutes? I had been counting on a maximum of fifteen. Jordan liked to show up at the rendezvous point slightly early on Thursdays. How was I supposed to keep him in his apartment?

Somehow, I had to occupy his attention so he'd lose track of time. But how? I found a solution as my gaze landed on the checkers and chess box in the corner. *Chess, that's it!* I didn't know how to play. Checkers, yes. Chess? No. I never dedicated enough time to learning it. But Jordan knew how to play. He'd even tried to explain it during my miserable stay in the hospital, but reluctantly eventually gave up and just played checkers with me.

Since I was running out of time, I decided to go with it. Grabbing the box, I scrambled downstairs. At Jordan's door, I breathed a quick prayer that I hadn't already missed him, and then knocked. After a heart-wringing wait, he opened. *Thank God.* A grin spread across Jordan's face.

"Amber! Hey, what's—" Noticing the box, he stopped and gave me a puzzled look. I held it up.

"Teach me chess?" I asked hopefully. Jordan stared at it.

"Really?" he asked, almost hesitantly. Perhaps he was remembering the headaches from the last time he tried explaining it to me. I nodded.

"Really. I bet it's actually quite fun. And it seems like a good day to learn, you know," I said, a bit lamely. Jordan thought for a second more, then smiled a mile wide.

"Yeah! This'll be fun!"

Soon I was suffering through the wooden world of kings and queens, rooks and bishops, knights and pawns. Chess is ridiculously complicated.

There are so many terms, maneuvers, and rules. I had to wrack my brain to try to retain it all. But Jordan seemed to be enthralled with the complexity of it. To him, it was a challenge worth meeting.

"So I move the push pin-looking thing—this one—the, ah … "

"Pawn?"

"Yes, pawn. I move it … " I strained my brain for the answer. "I can move it … diagonal? No—straight. Straight! Right?" Jordan grinned, nodding enthusiastically.

"Right!" I really should have had that part down by now. "The pawn can move diagonal to capture, but has to go straight to move normally." I fought to hide my despairing sigh.

Jordan seemed about to say something more, when … there was a knock at the door.

I shot a confused glance at Amber as I stood. I got a strange feeling her shrug was slightly forced. *Who on earth could it be?* Curious, I headed for the door, my mind running through the options. Twisting the handle and pulling … my breath caught. My heart skipped a beat. My eyes went wide, unable to believe what they were seeing. My Lexie. My little sister. My dear Lexie. She was right there, looking back at me. For a moment, neither of us moved. Suddenly, she stepped forward and threw her arms around me.

"Jordan!" she exclaimed, hugging me tight. I hardly felt it. I was stunned. Lexie sensed this and slowly pulled back a bit, her happy gaze faltering. "Jordan? Don't you recognize me? It's me, Lexie!"

"Lexie," I whispered, staring at her. If I moved, she might disappear. I hardly dared breathe. *Is this real?* Slowly, I reached forward, almost trembling, and carefully touched her cheek. Solid, soft, warm. *Real.* "Lexie?" I whispered again. Tears filled my eyes and her image began to blur. *It's not a dream. It's not a dream!* "Lexie!" I cried, pulling her close, hugging her for all I was worth, tears slipping down my cheeks. "Of course I recognize you! Oh my goodness, you're real!" She giggled that happy, sweet giggle I had missed for so many years.

"Of course I'm real!" she said. I peeled her off me and held her at arm's length.

"Look at you. You're all grown up." She'd grown at least a foot since I'd seen her last. Her once super-long, medium caramel hair was now shoulder-short and had darkened to an ashy, auburn brown. The baby-ish, sky-bright blue eyes had also darkened, morphing into a deep, rich azure, making her look wise beyond her years. Her smile—oh, her smile! My precious, beautiful, amazing little sister … wasn't so little anymore. I embraced her again, my heart brimming with happiness. "I've missed you so much."

Quietly, I stood, smiling. Jordan's joy was so strong I could feel it radi-ating from across the room. Over his shoulder, Lexie caught my eye and smiled, mouthing, *"Thank you."* Jordan seemed to remember I was here.

"Oh, Amber!" he exclaimed excitedly, starting hurriedly toward me, then stopping, scurrying back, this time bringing Lexie with him. "Amber, it's Lexie!"

"Lexie?" I asked innocently, smiling. "As in, *the* Lexie?" I turned my smile on her. "I've heard so much about you. I'm glad we finally get to meet." To my horror, Lexie didn't respond. She had been grinning, but now she just stared at me, a confused and amazed look on her face. Jordan too found this strange and glanced at her. She shook her head.

"Amber, I can't pretend anymore," Lexie said. "You weren't seriously going to keep it secret, were you?" Reluctantly, I let out the sigh I had been holding, feeling foolish.

"Well, I was going to try," I muttered.

"Lexie," Jordan asked, "what are you talking about? What's going on?"

Turning, she grinned at him. "This is all Amber's doing." Sadly, she didn't give Jordan enough time to absorb this bombshell before hurtling on. "She wrote me with the idea, flew me here, and planned out the whole surprise. For some reason, I don't think she was planning on ever telling you, which doesn't seem quite fair, but I guess you found out anyway."

Wide-eyed, Jordan stared at me. Disbelief, amazement, and over-whelming gratitude painted his face. It became one of those rare occasions when Jordan West couldn't seem to find any words.

"Surprise!" I muttered weakly, forcing a smile and fighting a cringe. But I knew … *in the end, this will only make things harder.* Thankfully, Lexie managed to redeem the moment.

"Does everyone still hang out on Thursdays?" she asked hopefully. Jordan snapped out of his daze.

"Oh wow, yes. In less than ten minutes!" he exclaimed, then paused for a second, thinking hard. "I have an idea, but we've got to hurry." Jordan turned to me. "Chess is going to have to wait. I'm really sorry."

"I'm not," I admitted, chuckling.

Soon we were all scrambling out the door, Lexie chattering excitedly the whole way. I could see she and her brother got the same jabber gene. Just as we stepped into the hall, Lexie three happy steps ahead, Jordan suddenly pulled me into a quick embrace.

"Thank you, Amber. Thank you so much," he whispered.

"Don't even mention it," I whispered back, feeling like a hypocrite.

Because, if Jordan knew what I was really doing, he wouldn't be thanking me. *Just enjoy it while it lasts.*

We had to hurry to meet the others on time—and to keep up with Lexie. I had to keep pinching myself to make sure I wasn't dreaming. As the three of us neared the pier, my plan started to unfold. Amber and I walked side by side, with Lexie behind us trying to stay out of sight. It was my turn to orchestrate a surprise. Soon, I caught sight of Matt, Dylan, and Chloe. Dylan saw us.

"Hey, you two! We were wondering if you'd ever show up. You're late!"

I glanced at my watch. "Only a few minutes. And anyway, I couldn't just leave this little stranger on my doorstep," I said, grinning, as Amber and I stepped apart, revealing Lexie behind us. For a moment, there was shocked silence.

"*Lexie?!*" Chloe gasped, then ran forward to tackle her in a bear-sized embrace. Dylan lit up and joined Chloe, all three ecstatic to finally be reunited. Matt came over, grinning.

"So, you're Lex—" Lexie detached herself from the Lynn twins and threw her arms around him.

"I've heard so much about you, Matt," she said, and once again became the center of a giant group hug.

Needless to say, that was the start of one of the best nights I'd ever had.

CHAPTER 44

The Salt Breeze Apartment Complex, Apt. 1307
Monday, November 4, 4:10 P.M.

Jordan

Well, this is odd. My little sis is … missing? I'd gotten off Ocean Front early, bounded back to the apartment, happily exclaiming "I'm home!" … but no answer. Lexie was nowhere to be found. I noticed her meticulous list of schools was still on the table, just like I'd seen that morning. Her cello was on its stand in her room. Her laptop was still plugged in by the bookshelf and her flip-flops were by the door. But no Lexie. The only things that were different was that her pencil pouch and sketchbook weren't on the counter anymore. But she couldn't have gone far; her shoes were still here. After a minute more of searching, I decided to text her. No reply.

I wasn't exactly worried. Lexie was a big girl now. But it was still unusual. I decided I should check Amber; I had been hoping to talk with her anyway. As I neared Amber's apartment, I caught a faint hint of music. It was soft, but it grew more distinct as I got closer. It was only when I came to Amber's open door that I realized it was coming from inside. Curious, I continued on.

Well, the music was louder than I originally thought. I didn't get Amber's attention until I walked around the corner—straight into the biggest mess I'd ever seen. My mind was so shocked it took a moment to slow down and take everything in in all its chaotic glory.

A plastic tarp had been spread from one end of the room to the other. On it was a huge canvas, partly covered by intricate designs in colors ranging across the spectrum. There was paint everywhere. One end of the canvas had been pinned up on the wall, and Amber stood by it, fine-tipped paint pen in one hand and her reference sketchbook in the other.

There were brushes and pencils sticking out of her pockets. Her art-stained shirt—which read "Earth without Art is just Eh"—had at least twelve new splatters, each a different color. Paint spanned from her fingers to her elbows; there was even some on her face. Her hair was up in a bun, but wisps had escaped and were now psychedelically colored, fluttering in the breeze from the open balcony doors. She turned, saw me, her eyes lit up, and she smiled—suddenly, the sun didn't seem that brilliant. *Wow. She's ... beautiful. Even when covered in paint.*

Hello. Where'd that thought come from?

"Hey Jordan!" I distantly heard Lexie call. I forced myself to glance over toward her voice. I found her on the other end of the canvas in a similar state of disaster while sitting amidst the bright swirls and lines. She giggled. "You OK?"

"What?" I asked, bewildered.

Lexie giggled again. "You got that look on your face, the look you get when you're really, really shocked or amazed," she said, clearly amused. Scrambling to gather my wits, I slowly nodded and saved myself by declaring, "What a mess ... " while scanning the room once again, making sure to look thoroughly dumbfounded.

Amber laughed. "If you think this is bad, you should have seen my college dorm room before the final exam week. Anyway, I'm sure the spots will come out of the carpet with some scrubbing. Well ... I think," she muttered, frowning at a spot to her right with new scrutiny.

Out of the corner of my eye, I noticed Lexie hop off the canvas, leaving purple spots in her wake as she tiptoed over to the little speaker to turn the music down a bit, only to realize, too late, that her fingers were still covered in paint. I heard her mutter a quiet "oops." She proceeded to try and wipe off the nob with the hem of her shirt, but this only made things worse. Suddenly, she spun around excitedly.

"Oh, Jordan! Has the mail come yet?"

I nodded, chuckling. "Yes, Lex, you have four pounds of snail mail. As usual. You'd think people would just stick with email these days. Exactly how many colleges are vying for your attention?" She promptly grabbed a paint cloth and hastily started rubbing the paint off her feet.

"A lot," she answered, hopping about, trying to get safely away from the mess, "but I sent out some inquiries and I'm expecting a reply today or tomorrow. The rest won't matter. And oh, Amber! Thank you! You're the best! I gotta go!" And with that, she was gone, barreling down the hall. Smiling, Amber came to stand by me, sighing happily. I glanced at her.

"You've bewitched my little sister, you know." Something in my tone must have amused her, because she chuckled.

"What, are you jealous?" she asked, grinning.

I was grinning too. "Be more specific: jealous of her being under your spell, or just part of your fan club?" *I'm think I'm already both.* I blinked. *Wait, what?*

"Lexie's great. I'm really glad I got to meet her," Amber said, shaking her head and chuckling, then turning to me. "So, what's up?"

"Pardon?" I managed to ask, still confused about my crazy thoughts.

"Well, you didn't exactly drop by for tea," she said, smiling faintly. "Or did you?"

"Ah, no. Oh! Right! I was hoping to catch you without Lex around. How's hacking going? Is Teumessian losing ground yet? Has Edge found out anything that will help in the fight?" I asked hopefully. Amber's mood seemed to falter a little.

"The third attacker, the one who was captured, gave information in exchange for his safety, just like he promised. Honestly, it doesn't change much, though it is extremely important. Any intel we can gather on the Big Four is essential."

"What is the Big Four?" I asked.

"The FBI's goal—and my mission—is to take down the Big Four: the leaders of the four divisions collectively known as Teumessian. In basic terms, they are broken down into hackers, thieves, spies, and mafia. They work together with equally shared power and control," Amber said calmly, as if she had simplified and reviewed this in her mind a thousand times. "Together, they are strong. But if the Four fall, Teumessian as a whole will disintegrate."

"Then, what of the information? You said it was essential, yet doesn't change anything. How does something important fail to make a difference?"

"I suppose I should be more grateful," Amber admitted. "In time, it might win the war. But it doesn't do any immediate good. Apparently, the leaders don't communicate through the main database; they have a private network that branches off from it, on which they can discuss their plans. The good thing is that it places them in the same cyber location when they call in. It could be used to trace them straight back to base. Problem is, unless they are currently using it, the line is invisible. And the FBI doesn't know when Teumessian will open it or how to locate it." Amber shook her head. "I can't predict when or where they'll strike next, let alone when they'll communicate or how to find the line. Without exact dates and cyber guidance, it's next to useless."

I nodded slowly. To be honest, I felt disappointed too. Ever since I'd heard the attacker was willing to talk, I'd been praying it would be the final piece of the puzzle and Amber would be able to defeat Teumessian. But apparently it wasn't over yet. Turning, I gave Amber the most encouraging smile I could.

"Don't give up. Like you said, in time, it might win the war. It'll be soon, I'm sure of it," I insisted. Amber tried to smile, but ended up with a sad, sideways grimace instead.

"Yeah. Soon."

Jordan chatted with me a while longer, but eventually I found myself alone again. I tried to busy myself, but I knew I needed to stop procrastinating. Sadly, I sat at the counter, pulled up the minimized tab on my laptop, and got to work. It was one of the hardest things I've done in years. Just as I finished … too late—I heard something behind me. Whirling, I found Lexie disconnecting her phone from the stereo system. She looked up and grinned.

"Hey, Amber! Sorry, forgot my phone. I—" Her eyes landed on my computer and went wide. I slammed the "X" in the upper corner of the web page. But it was too late. She had seen it. "Amber? What … what are you doing?" Lexie's voice was quivering, confusion filling her face.

I stood. "Lexie, listen," I said gently. "Before you make any assumptions, I need you to do something for me."

"What?"

"I need you to give me your word of honor that you won't tell anyone about what you saw, or what I'm about to say until it's all over. Anyone. Especially Jordan."

I could see Lexie considering this. "But … what if—" She saw my pleading gaze. "I guess … alright."

"Promise?" I pressed.

"Promise," Lexie agreed, though hesitantly. My calm, collected act melted and I sank back onto the chair, fighting the welling emotions inside of me.

"Oh, Lexie. I wish you hadn't seen that."

I sat flicking through the mound of mail on the table, sorting college propaganda into one pile and everything else into another, wondering once more why people don't just stick to email. I was happy for Lexie. She was so excited, eager to start the next chapter in her life, to live on a campus, take her classes, and grow up.

It was going to be bittersweet when she did eventually choose where to go. It'd taken years for me to get used to a quiet house. I knew deep down I'd have to get used to it again soon. But I was so grateful for this time I did have with her.

It was wonderful to wake up to the sound of cello music from somewhere across the apartment, to listen to her talk about a book she was reading, to hear her sing, or even to be routinely asked, "What's for dinner?" I finally had my sister back, if even just for a time. *I wouldn't trade these days for anything.*

The sound of the door announced Lexie's return.

"Welcome back, Lex!" I exclaimed as she came around the corner. "I have your mountain of mail. I don't even recognize some of these places. They're so far away. Your grades must be way better than you give yourself credit for."

"Mm-hmm, thanks Jordan. What's for dinner tonight?" she muttered distractedly. I was about to answer when I noticed a sad, faraway look in her eyes.

"Is everything OK?" I asked, concerned. Lexie wouldn't meet my gaze.

"I'm fine. I think I'll look through the letters later. I'm just … tired."

Lexie wandered down the hall, into her room, and shut the door, leaving me wondering what could possibly be wrong.

CHAPTER 45

The Salt Breeze Apartment Complex, Apt. 1307
Thursday, November 7, 10:48 P.M.

 Jordan

I lay staring at the ceiling, wondering what had awakened me. A minute ago, I had been running around on the sea floor, surrounded by glowing gold fish while talking with an octopus named Jim. Dreams are so weird.

Now I was back in reality. Everything was still, silent. The moonbeams poured in from outside, but that wasn't what had woken me. I had a slight recollection of a noise. A *clunk*. Laying stone-still, I strained my ears for the tiniest sound for about three minutes, but didn't hear anything more. Perhaps it was a car passing by or someone returning home late to a nearby apartment. I could have just imagined it.

Rolling over, I tried to get settled again. That's when I saw it. There, on the balcony, was a medium-sized conch shell. I gazed at it confusedly. *I didn't put that there. What is it doing on the balcony? I don't think I've seen that one before. It's ... blue? Am I still dreaming?* Sleep could wait. It wasn't every day a blue conch shell magically appeared on the balcony. I crept out of bed, carefully slid the door open, and slipped out.

Well, it wasn't naturally blue. On closer inspection, the subtle strokes of a paint brush could be seen, and tiny silver and emerald fish had been added. I decided Amber must have painted it. Maybe it fell off her balcony and somehow landed on mine. But when I picked it up, I discovered a small, sealed plastic bag inside the curve of the shell. In the bag there was a folded piece of paper, a single word written on the front.

Jordan

What? This is for me? Carefully, I slid the bag from the shell and pulled out the paper. I flipped it over, but there was no other explanation. As I began to unfold it, I discovered it was a handwritten note from Amber, in her distinct, elegant cursive. *Why write me a note? Why not wait until morning?* But as I read, my hands started shaking. I felt like I couldn't breathe. The more I read, the more I wished I had found it earlier. It might already be too late.

Dear Jordan,

It is already in order. I will be out of Santa Barbara by morning. If you somehow find this before then, please don't try to find or stop me. I have to do this. I'm putting you in danger. I have reprogrammed my phone, so don't try to contact me. I don't know who will answer your call. Forgive me for leaving like this, but I think it is the kindest way to go. Goodbyes are so hard ... if possible, I want my last memory of you to be when you are smiling.

If the others ask where I went, you can honestly say you don't know. Why? I only said that I must. When? Not sure. Chloe will not understand, please look out for her for me. And don't let anyone feel like they are to blame for me leaving, especially you. This is not your fault, Jordan. I would have to leave eventually no matter the circumstances. I've never stayed in one place this long before, so, I am happy for the time I did get.

I'm running early in hopes of drawing Teumessian away from you. If I hack from another state and purposely get caught mid-attack, they will know I'm no longer in California and come looking. Teumessian will always chase me, but I won't let them catch up. And even if they do ... I'm not afraid of death anymore.

You have given me a new life. I will remember your every kindness, from helping carry my groceries to saving my life and guiding me to Christ. Whether or not you decide to forget me, that's your choice.

If I survive, if this war is won, I'll come back. I'll find you, but, don't count on it. If things go ill for me, I will see you again in Heaven one day. Whichever comes first, I don't care. I will see you again, and I hold on to that. Until then, I will miss you dearly.

I owe you everything, Jordan. Everything. Thank you. Please don't grieve me if I never return, we both know where I will be.

Goodbye, Jordan.

~ Amber

Amber was leaving. She was fleeing early. She was going to get caught on purpose, risk everything, just to lure Teumessian away from me. I dashed back inside. She couldn't leave. Not yet. I couldn't let her. I had to try! There was no way she was still in her apartment. There was no point in checking. I would only waste precious time. Somehow, I had to figure out where she was headed. Where would she go? There was nothing but ocean to the west, and she wouldn't double back, so that left north or south. *Flights! I could see what flights are leaving tonight. But what time frame am I working with? And where? Where!?*

As I passed Lexie's door, I heard something. *Is she ... crying?* I knocked. The crying intensified and got a little louder. Pushing the door open, I found Lexie sitting on the edge of her bed, weeping bitterly. Then it hit me. Amber was the one who flew Lexie out. She had talked to Lexie privately a few days ago, and Lexie had become progressively more troubled ever since. But she wouldn't tell me what it was about. Amber planned to leave after Lexie arrived to distract me from her departure ... so I wouldn't be suddenly left alone.

"You knew?" I whispered in shock. Lexie tried to answer, but couldn't seem to form the words, so she just nodded miserably. "Amber made you promise, didn't she?"

"Yes. Oh, Jordan, I am so sorry!" She sucked in a deep breath and tried to hold it, but she couldn't stop the tears. I pulled her into a hug, desperate to comfort her. She held on so tight it hurt.

"It's OK. You did the right thing. You kept your word. Please don't cry."

"Why is she leaving? I begged her to stay, but she wouldn't!"

"I'm sorry, Lex. If Amber didn't tell you, I can't either. You're not the only one who has made promises. I'm going to try and bring her back. Do you know where she's planning on going?" Lexie shook her head miserably.

"She wouldn't tell me. All I saw was the flight confirmation page on her computer." My heart sank.

"Did she say *anything*? Surely there was some sort of hint." Lexie shook her head again. "Think, Lexie, think! There's got to be something. Please!" For a moment, Lexie stopped sniffling, then pulled her hand across her tear-stained face.

"Well ... she said she had to. That she didn't want to. And ... that a friend had a place for her. And— " That last bit caught my attention.

"A friend?" I asked. *A friend? But, Amber's unattached except for— wait. Could it be?* "Lex, what exactly did she say about this friend?" Lexie thought hard for a moment.

"She said, 'An old friend has a place for me in case I should need it.'" An old friend! *Edge!*

"Oh, my goodness," I breathed, scrambling up. "I'll be back, Lex. Give me a second. I have an idea!"

Racing back to my room, I grabbed my phone and hastily pulled up the translate app. I had a wild idea. But I had a hunch it was the key to finding her. Tapping the mic button, I wracked my brain for the conversation I had heard a month before—the Arabic conversation between Edge and Amber—and somehow managed to mimic the strange sounds. I doubted I'd ever take my memory for granted again. After some autocorrecting, the words came together in a coherent message:

"I heard the prisoner is willing to talk in exchange for his life and police protection, and I've got permission to interrogate him."

"Prisoner? Single? But there were three. Did the other two escape?"

"When they realized there was no escape, two committed suicide. But the third one was captured. He says he knows about the Big Four."

"He knows about the Big Four?! How?"

"I don't know, but I'll find out. Soon, he'll be transferred to a more secure facility. For now, you're safe here, for at least a couple months. In the meantime, make plans. Be ready to move. Once I contact you ... follow me to Seattle. You'll be safer there."

Seattle! That's it! I had to get to my computer. Dashing for the book cave, I almost collided with Lexie, who had moved into the hall. Confusion, fear, and hope filled her face. Grabbing her hand, I pulled her along with me and answered her unspoken question.

"Seattle. Amber's going to Seattle."

Sprinting into the book cave, I flung my laptop open and spammed the mouse, trying to wake it up. *Come on, come on! Time is slipping away!* Finally, it was up, and a few keystrokes later, I found the web page of the nearest airport. Peering over my shoulder, Lexie nodded excitedly.

"That's it! That's the format I saw on Amber's screen. She's going to that one."

Within seconds, I found it: Seattle, WA. Gate A22. Departure 11:30 P.M. I glanced at the corner of the screen. It was 10:56. Thirty-four minutes remained. Jumping up, I shot down the hall, grabbed my jacket, and yanked on shoes; I didn't worry about socks. I just couldn't seem to move fast enough.

"Jordan, wait!" Lexie called, scrambling to catch up with me. "What should I do? Should I come with you?"

"No," I answered over my shoulder. "Stay here. Stay here and pray I can get there in time."

The drive to the airport was one of the most heart-wrenching experiences of my life. I may or may not have broken a few traffic laws. As I flew down the dark roads through the misty night, memories of Amber lit up in my mind. Memories of her smile, her laugh, of *Amber* ... from the day I ran into her till that very night, when she was waving goodbye to Matt, Dylan, and Chloe as she walked home with Lex and I ...

I saw her across from me at the Flying Turtle and crying on the beach the day she "lost her job." I saw her gazing up at the sky during the Firefly Festival. I remembered when she almost ran me over with her surfboard when she first started to surf. The way she blushed so brightly during her surprise birthday party, and how much she had loved it. When she, as F1R3ST0RM, stood between me and all of V0RT3X. I could see the little clay wolf-pup on the palm of her hand as she held it out as a gift. Her gentle words when my parents got divorced. Waking up to her concerned face the morning after my concussion. The night of the meteor shower. When she leapt between me and death, taking a bullet, willing to trade her life for mine. I could still feel her clinging to me in the hospital when she finally woke up. The light in her eyes when she got saved. The day I stole her away from the hospital. Her painting with Lex. Her bidding me goodnight as she turned and headed for her apartment ... *No, I can't lose her! Not yet, not now! Please, God, don't let her go!*

By the time I reached the airport, it was 11:12. I dashed through the doors, searching desperately for the terminals. Seeing the gateway, I hurried forward—only to be held back by security.

"Ticket?" a checkpoint officer asked.

"No, I'm not here for a flight. I've got to find someone!" I hurriedly explained, craning my neck to see if I could pick out the way to go once I cleared this woman.

"You can't go any further without a ticket or a formal accompaniment form," she said calmly, as if she dealt with desperate people like me daily. My heart plummeted. Amber was slipping away.

"Please! There isn't much time, I have to find—" I was cut off by a loud, blaring *beep* from the walkie-talkie-like device clipped to the woman's belt. Frowning, she pulled it out to inspect it. After a moment, she returned her attention to me.

"I need to see to this." She pointed at a bench against the wall. "If you will wait over there, I'll be with you shortly."

Miserably, I trudged to the bench and plopped down, watching her fuss over her device. Amazingly—due to the time of night, I'm sure—she was the only officer at the checkpoint. And then, without warning, she walked away. For a moment, my brain balked. I couldn't move. Suddenly, I was on my feet. I had come this far. I'd already broken a few laws. And I was not leaving until I convinced Amber to stay or watched her plane lift off. Before I knew what I was doing, I threw anything metal I had through the side metal detector, jumped through the gate, grabbed my stuff, and sprinted on, toward the terminals.

I flew past gate after gate. It was 11:19. Unless I found her before the passengers boarded, I wouldn't find her at all. Something caught my eye. I came to a skidding stop. There, A22. I'd found the gate! Scanning the rows and rows of people, I searched frantically for Amber. She wasn't there. I searched the seats again. Nothing. Despair began to well up inside me. Perhaps I had the wrong flight. Maybe the wrong airport. She might already be gone.

Suddenly, my gaze was inexplicably drawn to my left. There, in the shadow of a corner, sitting with back against the wall, computer bag over shoulder, chin on arms and arms around knees, hood on head, head down: *Amber.* Overwhelming relief washed over me. Carefully, I made my way over to her. When she didn't sense my presence and look up, I crouched to my knees, reached forward, and gently pushed the hood back. She gasped, jerked her head up—and tears filled her eyes.

"Amber?" I asked softly. She broke. Sobbing, she buried her face in her hands, weeping bitterly.

"No ... " she breathed, tears streaking her cheeks, "No, Jordan ... Please. Please just go home. Just go home and forget me. It's so much harder this way, and there's no way around it ... "

Distantly, I realized a few heads were turning. *This is drawing too much attention.* After a few worried glances around, I quietly encouraged Amber to stay quiet, then drew her up and pulled her aside into a tiny souvenir shop. Taking cover among the stands and racks, I gently pried her hands away from her face and tried to get her to look at me.

"Amber, please don't do this. Please," I begged. She sobbed.

"I have to leave. I'm putting you in danger. I can't bear the thought of you getting hurt because of me, or worse ... "

"But I haven't gotten hurt, and I'm not in danger. At least not yet," I pointed out. "You still have time, Amber. Don't cut that time short."

"But there's no point," she whispered. "There's no way I can defeat Teumessian before they strike again. What choice do I have but to flee? I've come this far ... why put it off?" And with this, she buried her face in her hands once more.

I couldn't believe she couldn't see it. No, actually—I couldn't believe I hadn't seen it, until now. Slowly, I wrapped my arms around her and pulled her head down to rest on my chest, hugging her as tight as I dared.

"Why put it off?" I asked quietly. "Because ... " *I think I've fallen in love with you ...* "I think there is still a chance."

Amber gave a quick, sad laugh. "Not a big one!" she exclaimed miserably.

"But there is one," I insisted. "And you have just as much chance defeating Teumessian here—in Santa Barbara, California, the Salt Breeze Apartments, as my neighbor—than anywhere else in the world. So please don't go, Amber. Please don't go."

As I spoke, Amber's quivering intensified, and now she was crying again. From the gate, the order to board came over the speakers. When she heard it, Amber turned to look back, then searched my eyes, her own full of sorrow. There was a heartbeat in time. Then she pulled from my grasp, threw her arms around me, and buried her face in my chest, staining my shirt with a new batch of hot tears.

That's when she whispered it: "I'll stay."

Jordan held me for a long time. And I cried. Eventually, I heard the plane take off; it carried at least half my troubles with it. A couple minutes later, Jordan, who had been tenderly holding me and gently swaying back and forth, suddenly went still. I could practically feel him frowning.

"Oh. I hope you didn't have anything particularly important on that plane," he murmured, eliciting a quick giggle from me.

"It's not a problem. I can have it sent back by tomorrow morning. I have to travel light; most of my stuff is still at the apartment." Reluctantly, I pulled back from Jordan's embrace, opened my mouth to say something— and my gaze landed on what was right in front of my nose. I dissolved into laughter. "What on earth … are you wearing?" I managed to ask. Confusion flitted across Jordan's face. He glanced down, then blushed.

"Pajamas," he muttered, looking so very bashful. I think if a hole had opened in the ground, he'd have gladly jumped in. Inside his jacket was a black T-shirt, a bold white arrow pointed up, with the caption "World's Worst Morning Person" underneath. His shorts were the most ridiculous orange plaid I'd ever seen. "Yes," he muttered miserably, "I came looking for you in my pajamas."

"Chin up, Jordan. They're adorable," I assured him through giggles. He perked up a bit at that.

"Oh, alright then. In that case, I'll wear them more often." Once again, I dissolved into laughter. Jordan turned a warm smile on me. "Even so," he said, "please don't run away in the middle of the night again. Don't ever run away again, period." I nodded slowly, rubbing the last of the tears from my face, but then more started falling—whether from relief or despair, I don't know. I shut my eyes tight, trying to stop this childish behavior. To my surprise, I felt Jordan's fingers brush against my cheeks, then gently lift my chin. "Hey, look at me. Do me a favor?" he asked.

I opened my eyes. "What?"

"Promise me you'll stop crying soon, then we'll walk out those doors, put tonight behind us, and never talk about it again," he said, a kind smile in his eyes. A shaky breath later, I sniffed and nodded.

"OK. I'm ready to go home," I whispered, determined to pull myself together. A minute later, all was well. Just as we started to leave, Jordan suddenly stopped, a slightly strangled look on his face. "What is it?" I asked.

"I can't just walk out. I'm not sure, but I think I might have security looking for me." Apparently, my face displayed more surprise than I meant to show, because he quickly waved his hands as if to calm me. "Or maybe they think I just went home."

"What did you do?"

"I snuck past a checkpoint." Once again, I found myself chuckling; I didn't know Jordan was capable of something so brash.

Soon I had it fixed, though. Hacking into the airport's systems, I searched for any security alerts. There weren't any. But just for good measure, I fabricated a pass and inserted it into the database. Then, together, we slipped away and headed for home.

The drive back was spent mostly in silence, and since I was no longer speeding and because of the rain, it took the full twenty minutes. I didn't mind. I almost wished it was longer. Amber gazed out the window, tiredly watching the world drift by. As the streetlights flashed by, her face would briefly light up, then go dark again, searing her peaceful expression into my mind.

I couldn't quite tell what she felt about all this. Was she glad she hadn't gone? Was she regretting her decision? Was she scared? Happy? Sad? I couldn't figure it out. Perhaps she was simply exhausted. In the end, though, all that mattered was she was here. And we were going home.

"What are you going to tell Lexie?" I eventually asked. Amber turned a tired glance my way.

"I haven't decided yet. I don't know."

"Well, you better decide soon," I suggested gently, "because she's already up, waiting for me to get back. She'll want to see you." This presented a dilemma for Amber. She straightened in her seat.

"Oh. That's not good," she murmured. "Any ideas?"

"It's your choice, Amber." At this, she gave me a pleading look, searching for guidance. I sighed. "Well, on one hand, Lexie's rather young. She can keep secrets, but it'll be hard for her, and I'm not sure how she'd react to one this big. On the other hand, won't she have to be told eventually?"

Amber gave a sad sigh.

"Why should she have to be told? I don't mean to sound harsh, but it's not like we can be neighbors forever, let alone for more than a month. I'm afraid you, and she, won't always be part of my life."

Well, I was sorta hoping we'd be more than neighbors someday. Alright, I told myself: I am definitely going to have to have a discussion with my brain when I get the chance. It was being brutally honest with me for such a late hour.

"Hey, have a little faith," I encouraged. "You'll be here for more than a month, I'm sure. God's done greater things than bringing down unbeatable enemies in less than a day. He can do it," I insisted.

Amber sighed, looking back out the window.

"Yes, He can," she agreed. "But the question is, will He do it here and now, or later?"

There was a pause. She was right. Turning my full attention back to the road, I nodded slowly.

"I suppose only time will tell."

CHAPTER 46

The Salt Breeze Apartment Complex, Apt. 1307
Friday, November 22, 11:26 A.M.

⸙Amber⸙

Time was running out. I feared Jordan had only convinced me to put off the inevitable. I treasured every moment I could. If I wasn't desperately scouring the endless haystack called Teumessian's database, I was spending time with Chloe, Dylan, Matt, Jordan, and Lexie. I decided not to burden Lexie with my real story. I managed to convince her that my plans to leave were work-related and could be put off a little longer. It wasn't a complete lie, but it wasn't exactly the truth, either. Truth was, it wouldn't be long before I had to flee, because try though I might, I knew it wasn't likely I'd just stumble upon The Four's line.

I needed a miracle.

I've searched through all the sectors; there's no sign of it. But that doesn't mean anything, I suppose. I have to be in the right sector at the right time. The Four might have called in a thousand times and I've missed it because I've been looking in the wrong place! It's all pointless. But I have to keep trying. I can't just give up …

"Oh, cool." My distressing thoughts were put on hold as I looked up from my drawing to glance at Lexie, who was sitting beside me, working on her computer.

"What?" I asked.

"The Smithsonian announced the unveiling of a special exhibit. Some famous painting that was thought to have been destroyed in the Civil War has been found." She paused to scroll down the page and her eyebrows went up. "Says here it's expected to bring in eight hundred fifty-thousand dollars at *minimum*. This was posted just a couple of hours ago, and about sixty tickets have already been preordered. And they're two hundred and fifty dollars!" I leaned over to scan her screen.

"Goodness, that's a lot of people and money," I mused. Lexie chuckled.

"That's what I was thinking. It sounds interesting and all, but I just don't get it. I mean, if I was a blue-blooded bigwig, I don't think I'd pay a ridiculously high fee just to stare at one painting for a couple of hours. I think that money could be better spent on things like charities and concerts. Or maybe paint itself." Lexie stopped to think about this. "I wonder how many brushes you could buy with two hundred and fifty dollars?"

"A lot," I said, laughing. As I casually read down the page, something started nudging the back of my mind, whispering, telling me that among the numbers and stats, something important was hiding. "Hey, Lex. Can I see that for a sec?" I asked hesitantly, gesturing at her laptop.

"Sure," she said, sliding it over to me.

My fingers were flying before my mind could catch up. Digging deeper, I hacked the source of the information. Within seconds, I had found a list of big numbers and important names. I scanned across the data, mind churning to grab and sort everything I was seeing, adding it all together into one big equation: lots of money, plus national publicity, plus high-profile people converging in the same place at the same time. "That's it!" I exclaimed, dashing for the door.

"That's what?" Lexie called after me, puzzled. I came to a screeching stop, backtracked, hurried to her laptop, exited the hack, and then bolted again.

"Thank you, Lexie!"

Granted, it was a long shot. Perhaps I was desperately clinging to an obscure hope. But maybe it was a miracle. Something told me it could very well be the latter. As I had seen countless times before, Teumessian's goal was maximum number of casualties and money acquired. They liked getting attention. The time frame of the announcement was optimal; it had only been a few hours. If they were going to act, they would act now. This was my chance.

Dear Lord, I'm taking a leap of faith. Don't let me fall. Please let this be the miracle I've been waiting for! Please, end this horrid war, this endless, looping, cruel war. Break the paradox that holds me prisoner! I can't win this war on my own. I need you. Please fight for me!

Through the door, to the study room, into my chair, I scrambled to prepare for battle. My headset was my armor, my keyboard my weapon. Syncing my phone, I put a call in to Edge. He didn't answer. I froze for a moment, doubt entering my mind. I didn't know if I could do this alone. I didn't even know where to search. *What exactly am I looking for? How am I supposed to find them? How?!* Then, out of nowhere, a quiet, gentle thought whispered … *Don't worry. Just trust. You're not alone, and you won't be the one leading the charge. Follow His lead.* And with that, I took the leap of faith.

"Cyra, keep calling Edge until he answers … and activate hacking program Laelaps."

>Launch in 3…
>2…
>1…
>Launch complete.

I folded my metaphorical wings and dove into the cyberworld through the hairline crack in Teumessian's firewalls. Just as I was about to begin searching through sector one, my fingers suddenly took over and headed for sector twelve instead. Wondering why I hadn't yet been attacked by enemy A.I.s, I glanced at the stats. I blinked. Interference was at 0%. For a moment, I thought the programs were broken. But then I remembered who was fighting for me. *Thank you, Lord* … I raced on. Just as I slid into sector twelve …

"Hello?"

"Edge!" I exclaimed. "Oh, thank goodness. Listen, I know where Teumessian is going to strike next, and I have reason to believe the line between The Four is open. Sync to my computer and get ready to receive the data."

"Amber, you're hacking solo *again*? What have I told you about this? Do you have a death wish?"

"No. Don't tell me to back out, because I won't. This is it. Teumessian falls today," I insisted.

This caught Edge's attention.

"You know how to find the call?" he asked. Commands came flying to the forefront of my mind, and before I knew it, my A.I. was searching for live feeds limited to four recipients and keyword matches. I smiled.

"I know now." Suddenly, a unique match was found. Laelaps started desperately pawing through the tangled mess of protection code. "Edge, get ready. I think I've found it! Once you have the locations, the FBI will have to strike fast. Success depends on swiftness."

To my surprise, on the other end of the call, I heard the faint noise of keystrokes and an unusual lack of reprimands. Edge was actually taking my word on the matter. I glanced at the stats. Interference was starting to climb. But it didn't alarm me. Suddenly, I broke through. Data poured in. Interference spiked. Hacking as deep as I could into the line, I broke it down to its very source. *This is it. I found The Four!*

"Edge, Edge! This is it!" Grabbing the info, I watched as the progress bar crawled across the screen, desperately trying to beat the clock, which was running down fast.

Then, I noticed a stat report in the corner of my programs; my confidence faltered. There was a *fifth*. An observer was sitting in on the call. Despite being cyber-present, the location was completely invisible. For a moment, it was as if this ghost and Laelaps locked eyes. A sickening feeling stabbed my gut as a sharp shiver raked down my spine. Something was desperately wrong.

The beep of the progress bar snatched my attention.

Download complete.

"Cyra, escape! Get me out!" In a burst of code, it was over. Before the cyber dust had settled, I pushed the unsettling event from my mind, set up a data transfer, and flung the files to Edge. There was a moment of dead silence.

"Oh, my ... " Edge didn't even finish his statement. I heard him leap up, calling for attention and yelling orders, then scrambling off. Slowly, I pushed my chair back and stood. I could still hear the chaos on the other end of the call.

It didn't matter. Sinking to my knees, I wept silently. Edge didn't have to say it for me to know.

It was over. The war was won. *Thank you, God. Oh, thank you ...*

CHAPTER 47

Santa Barbara, West Fellowship Bible Chapel
Wednesday, December 18, 8:12 P.M.

Amber

It was over. The fight was won. The data I had stolen during the hack revealed the exact locations of Teumessian's leaders. The FBI struck fast and all four strongholds fell, along with their members and commanders. Though, mysteriously, there was no trace of the fifth ghost member on the call …

About a week later, Edge showed up at my apartment again. He explained that my contract was null; Teumessian was no longer a threat. Thus, I was no longer obligated to hack. By fighting for the FBI, my past debts were cleared. I was even welcome to remain an honorary agent. But I declined. I had been set free. I didn't ever want to look back.

I pulled Cyra's plug and locked away the Laelaps programs. I would continue to be a white hat hacker, but only at V0RT3X as F1R3ST0RM; never again would I be a war dog. I handed over all Teumessian-related cyber files and burned the paper ones, though I kept my journal and a few other things. My name was reset in the archives: "Alive and normal." A huge war had been fought and won, and even though no one could ever know, I didn't care.

Turning my attention from my past, I looked to the future.

To my amazement, a huge design company offered me a job—a normal, permanent job. Soon I remembered that the purpose of a smile is not to hide secrets or despair, but to show true happiness. And I was happy. I didn't have anything to fear. I was free to be me—to surf with my friends, make new acquaintances, make long-term plans—to live life.

Finally, for the first time since I was born, I knew what it was to be truly at peace.

I stood quietly at the back of the youth group room, watching Samuel chat with Chloe, along with Cassie, Lia, Matt, Dylan, Lexie, and Amber. A few weeks ago, Samuel had finally started talking to Chloe, and his bravery was paying off. Now I wished I had courage like him. I'd been trying to busy myself, but I couldn't help but stop and watch … yet couldn't go over.

I was miserable. I couldn't deny it any longer, even if I only admitted it to myself. I realized that all the feelings and dreams of a life that could never be—the feelings I had captured and bottled up—could be set free. I am head-over-heels, which doesn't make sense to me. When you fall in love, your world is turned upside down, so I felt more like "heels-over-head" would be more accurate.

All I know is I am madly in love with Amber.

Her bright smiles shame the sun. Her gentle, caring demeanor and big, soft heart show no end of compassion. She is quick to forgive faults and easy to trust. She is patient, smart, amazing, affectionate, brave, and beautiful. Whenever I am around her, I can't think straight, yet at the same time have unbelievable clarity. I love her. And it seems she hasn't even noticed yet, which makes me love her even more—even though it is near unbearable.

"Cheer up, Jordan," Dylan said as he came up and lightly elbowed me. "She'll match your feelings eventually." To say that caught me off guard would be a huge understatement.

"What?" I chuckled nervously. "What's that supposed to mean?" Dylan gave me a not-buying-it look. After a moment, I dropped the act and sighed. "You know me too well," I muttered. "Is it really that obvious?"

"Yeah," he admitted, "it's obvious. Well, to me at least. Like you said, I know you too well."

"I wish it was obvious to Amber," I pointed out dejectedly. At this, Dylan chuckled and shook his head.

"Jordan, you hopeless romantic. Stop worrying! I know you're impatient, but give it time. She'll come around."

"But … if I pursue her, will it be the end of us as a group?"

"No, this isn't the end. It's just the beginning of a new dynamic," Dylan assured me. I nodded slowly.

"Do you think I should tell her? Am I ready?" I asked hopefully. Dylan barely hesitated.

"No." For a moment, I felt completely heartbroken, dreams crushed—until I noticed Dylan's grin. He started laughing. "I can't believe you fell for that! The look on your face!"

I gave him a light punch. "That was low!" I scolded. "Your time will come, mark my words." From across the room, Chloe noticed us and waved, encouraging us to rejoin the group. Chuckling, Dylan nudged me.

"Come on, lover boy. Let's go hang with the others before they get suspicious." He started off. I quickly caught up.

"Hey, Dylan," I whispered. "Thanks."

He looked back at me and grinned again. "It's what best friends are for."

CHAPTER 48

The Salt Breeze Apartment Complex
Tuesday, December 31, 7:40 P.M.

Jordan

This is it. You got this. Tonight is the night! Just wait for the right moment and tell her how you feel, just like you've reviewed a thousand times.

I was desperately trying to talk myself into a courageous state of mind. A New Year's party was being held, and Matt, Dylan, Chloe, Amber, and I were all going.

In a moment of bravery, I had volunteered to pick everyone up, guaranteeing I'd have the chance to catch Amber alone at least twice: before we picked up the others and after we took them home at the end. Since Lexie had been invited to a separate event by some old friends, it would just be the two of us. I wasn't sure I'd have enough courage to tell her, let alone the many other things that would lead up to it—but I had to try.

I glanced at my watch for the sixty-first time. Surely Amber would be ready by now. Gathering my last reserves of courage, I started off to pick her up.

I stared at my reflection in the mirror, questioning my decision. Chloe had assured me this was typical attire. I still felt nervous. I hardly ever dressed like this. My hair was down, flowing over my partly bare shoulders, thick and long, a bit more wavy than usual. A section was pinned to one side by an elegant, swirling emerald barrette. My surfer's necklace, which I practically never took off, had been replaced by a small piece of polished amber-stone on the end of a delicate chain. I was wearing the only dress I owned—the lacy green one I had bought when Chloe dragged me off for a makeover—and the only pair of high heels I could handle. They were more like half-a-heel, but I valued my health more than I valued adding height to my stature. I'd even painted my nails a light, shimmery gold.

Honestly, I barely recognized myself. I wasn't sure these monarch butterfly clothes were befitting a plain caterpillar like me. *Maybe I should change into something less fancy,* I decided. *I don't want to seem ridiculous. Yes, better safe than sorry.* Just as I was about to start undoing the clasps at the back of the dress, I heard a knock and Jordan called out a greeting.

"Hey, Amber! Ready?" Hesitantly, I went to let him in. As I opened the door, I was tempted to hide behind it. Jordan opened his mouth to say something, but then saw me and froze. His eyes widened, and whatever words he was going to say were lost forever. I felt myself blushing.

"I ... I think the dress is a little much," I stammered bashfully. "It's rather silly. I was going to change it, but ... Yeah. I should probably change—"

"No!" Jordan's reaction apparently surprised both of us. "No. You're beautiful. It's beautiful! Don't change anything. It's ... you're ... " He seemed to be blushing now. "You're beautiful," he managed to say. I wasn't exactly sure how to handle this compliment, so I tried to return it.

"Thanks, not that much. But you, on the other hand ... you look sharp yourself." Now he was definitely blushing.

"Thanks." There was a slight pause. Jordan tried a little grin. "Ready?" he asked.

I nodded, smiling. "Ready."

Soon, Amber's bashful apprehension melted away and she went back to her usual, comfortable self. Fortunately, she was doing her fair share of talking; I was still recovering my wits. It was hard enough to speak in complete sentences around her as it was, but in that dress, hair down, and that radiant smile ... she was like an angel. I couldn't even think straight, let alone say something sensible, so I kept my attention on driving.

At one point, I felt a new burst of courage and actually got my mouth open to tell her how I felt—and then the courage abandoned me. So I shut it again. Thankfully, she didn't seem to notice. Then, when we were almost to Dylan and Chloe's house, I was about to try one more time, but realized

I shouldn't risk making things awkward right before the others piled into the car.

So, once again, I lost my nerve and kept silent. *This is going to be so hard …*

Before long, we were all together. Chloe too wore a dress, hers peach and sheeny. I felt in good company. I'm not sure who was hosting the evening. Whoever it was certainly knew how to plan a party. There was a decent stretch of open floor to one side and bunches of tables and chairs to the other. There was a long table of snacks and drinks; almost all had caffeine. And admission was free! I decided the event must be some sort of well-kept secret. I saw a lot of familiar faces, among them Samuel, Cassie, Lia, and others from church. I recognized a few artists I'd met and chatted with before, and even Daisy, fellow hacker from V0RT3X. We shared a discrete grin.

Sugar and caffeine carried us through the evening. So many jokes were made. Whether lame or legit, we laughed at them nonetheless. When the initial energy wore off, we talked for hours, about almost everything. We retold our best stories from the past year: our most embarrassing mistakes, deepest disappointments, greatest memories, funniest pranks—the kinds of stories only closest friends would ever believe.

There was music playing in the background all night long: the most popular songs, remixes, and the like. It was the audible energy that helped keep everyone going. Then, just before midnight, it all changed. An upbeat electro-pop song had just ended. There was a lull. It was as if people were holding their breath, waiting for something. Then, a new melody began. A slow one. Cheering erupted. Curious, I turned to Chloe.

"What's going on?" I asked over the slight din, noting that Dylan and Matt had split from the group.

"It's a tradition at these New Year's parties," Chloe explained. "It's the final song, a couples dance, so to speak, ending with one convenient minute to spare, during which everyone scrambles back to their seats for the countdown."

Before I could say anything, I sensed that somebody was standing in front of my chair. Chloe's attention was drawn past me. I turned around to find Jordan. He was extending his hand toward me, a hopeful, kind smile on his face. It took me a moment to realize he was asking me to dance. My mind balked. I was so surprised. Unsure what else to do, hesitantly, I took his hand.

Oh, I was so scared. I'll be honest: I dance to my favorite songs in the far corner of my room when all the doors are shut and locked and no one is around. But my dancing skills are nonexistent, and I know it. And that was dancing alone, with only my own two feet to trip on. Now there were four.

"Jordan," I whispered frantically, "I can't dance. I don't know how to."

Jordan leaned in and whispered, "Neither do I."

He continued pulling me on. Finding a space of unclaimed floor, we both stood, watching the other couples. After a moment, Jordan turned to me. "OK, I think I got it," he said, then took my hand in his and slipped his other behind my back, sending thrilled chills up my spine. Hesitantly, almost trembling—whether from excitement or nerves, or both—I put a hand on his shoulder and … we started dancing.

I caught a glimpse of Chloe, who had been looking on, smiling. Samuel approached her and said something. Slowly, Chloe got up, and he led her onto the floor. Jordan followed my line of sight and smiled.

The dance wasn't the total disaster I was afraid of. It was awkward and clumsy at first, but we got the hang of it before long. Thankfully, Jordan took the lead, his grip firm yet gentle as he guided me back and forth, left and right. I wasn't sure where to look, and eventually my gaze landed on Jordan's face. He was watching me, a tender smile on his lips and a light in his eyes. My heart did some weird flippy thing and sped up; I missed a step and almost stumbled. But I couldn't look away.

I don't know how much time passed, but suddenly the trance was broken as Jordan whispered, "Spin," and twirled me. As I came back around, Jordan leaned, dipping me slightly, then pulled me back up. He was so close, inches away. My heart did that funny thing again; I could hear it in my ears. Distantly, I realized the song was ending. But we didn't move. A few measures of time passed. Then, slowly, without breaking eye contact, Jordan brought my hand up to his lips and lightly kissed it. "Happy New Year's, Amber," he said softly.

Before I could process any of this, there was a great scrambling all around as everyone rushed back to their seats. Caught up in the bustle, we somehow made it back to our table, and within moments, all our other friends had returned as well. Soon, across the room, someone started the chant.

"Twenty! Nineteen! Eighteen! Seventeen! … " We joined in. "… Eight! Seven! Six! Five! Four! Three! Two! One!" Cheers burst out across the room. "Happy New Year!!!"

After sharing resolutions and wishes, we headed for home. The drive was a tired but happy one. All along, I went over what I would say in my head. The memory of dancing with Amber replayed itself again and again; the courage I felt then strengthened me now.

Before I knew it, it was just the two of us. But once again, I couldn't bring myself to say the words that burned in my heart. *I love you. Do you love me?* They just wouldn't come. And time was flying from my grasp. Even though we talked the whole way, I hardly remember parking, or walking in, or the elevator ride to Amber's floor. But then, suddenly, I realized she was pulling out her door key …

… If I don't do this now, I'll lose my nerve!

"Amber, wait," I exclaimed. She turned a slightly inquisitive gaze my way. But when I looked into her eyes, I decided to abandon the plan and just speak from my heart. "I want to thank you. And ask you something."

"Thank me? And ask me what?" Amber asked, letting the door rest against her heels as she turned toward me.

"I wanted to thank you because … until we met, I wasn't very brave. Lots of things scared me, and still sort of do. I was especially afraid of the future. If it weren't for you, I would still live in fear of change, when I never actually had anything to be afraid of! Yet, the thought of what I'm about to say scares me to death, because it could change everything. Life is so good, so full, so complete right now that … there's only one thing I could imagine that could make it better. What I'm trying to say—I want to ask—I mean … " I sighed. *Just do it.* I stopped, took a breath, and let my head clear. "I love you, Amber. I love you very much. So, will you date me?"

There was a terrible, shocked silence, in which Amber stared at me, her eyes getting bigger and bigger. By the look on her face, I could tell she'd not had these feelings toward me. *I just ruined everything. What have I done? I should have kept silent. I shouldn't have told her, I should have—*

"Can I have some time to think?" she asked, slowly, and very, very carefully.

"Of course," I said, nodding.

After a slight hesitation, she turned and promptly slipped through the door.

I stared at it, frozen where I stood. She hadn't said no. That was something, wasn't it? And, I'd gathered the courage to tell her. That was good, right? I wanted to laugh. I wanted to cry. No, wait—I still wanted to die. I couldn't help but feel that I might have just destroyed a dear friendship. Miserably, I trudged downstairs to my apartment. Lexie was already back, but it sounded as if she was asleep. Fine with me. I flopped into bed and gazed up at the ceiling. I wouldn't be able to sleep a wink until I had Amber's answer.

Slowly, I put my back to the door and slid to the floor. My head was swimming. My heart was pounding. My hands were shaking. *"I love you, Amber. I love you very much. So, will you date me?"* The words kept tumbling around in my mind. I couldn't comprehend it. *Jordan ... loves me?*

I sat there for so long, staring ahead, brain-dead. I'd never been in love. I didn't know what it even really meant. What is love? Numb, I rose, distantly realizing I was moving toward the bedroom. Sitting on the edge of the bed, my fingers found my journal and Bible. I flipped through, unsure where to go for guidance. Suddenly, something caught my eye. I stopped and went back a few pages. I could have sworn I saw the word "love" about five times in quick succession. There: First Corinthians chapter thirteen. Yes, I'd read it before. As my eyes scanned the verses, I distantly felt myself pick up my pen and begin to copy them in my journal. When I was done, I read them again, thinking.

Love is patient, love is kind. Love does not envy, love does not boast ... I pondered this for a moment. *Well, I guess I know "what" love is now. But ... how do I use this?* I stared at it, then, slowly, picked up my pen and started writing again. I finished, put it down, and quietly read it out, asking myself if what I had written was true.

"Jordan is patient, Jordan is kind. Jordan does not envy, Jordan does not boast, and he is not proud. Jordan does not dishonor others, is not self-seeking, is not easily angered, and keeps no record of wrongs. Jordan does not delight in evil, but rejoices with the truth. Jordan always protects, always trusts, always hopes, always perseveres ... Love never fails."

And in that moment, I knew. Everything I had just read was spot-on, accurate, true! I realized I did love him. Very much. He was always on my mind, day and night. He'd been there for me from the very start. Whenever I needed advice, I would seek him out. If I was down, he would comfort me, then encourage me to stay strong or make me laugh. He had risked so much for me. He thought me important enough to talk to and seemed to enjoy doing so, and I actually enjoyed listening to him. He cared about me, truly cared. His smile made my heart melt. His embrace chased away my fears. His very gaze was enough to inspire me to be brave and press on.

I owed him my life and soul. Yet now I wanted to give him my heart, also.

My breath caught and tears stung my eyes. *I love Jordan. How have I not seen it till now? I truly, truly love him.*

I jumped up and bolted for the door—then stopped. *If I tell him tonight, he might be so excited he won't sleep. I should wait until morning.* Sadly, miserably, I turned toward bed, even though I knew I wouldn't sleep until I gave him my answer.

CHAPTER 49

The beach across the road from
The Salt Breeze Apartment Complex
Saturday, March 14, 7:24 P.M.

Months passed. I wasn't sure how Chloe, Dylan, and Matt would react to the news that Amber and I were dating. To my surprise, they didn't mind in the least. In fact, they seemed to almost be happy about it. I worried it would make things uncomfortable for all of us, but it didn't.

At first, I was slightly more awkward, bashful, and tongue-tied than usual around Amber, but so was she. It didn't take long for me to lose my fear and simply anticipate each new day. Though every moment may not have been perfect, they were cherished.

As time went on, I discovered more and more about Amber that could have put a rift between us, and she learned those types of things about me, too—and yet, somehow, those things brought us closer. Because I loved her. I loved her with every cell in my body, heart and soul. Nothing would ever change that.

"It's gorgeous," I whispered, gazing at the sky, which was splashed with dark gold, crimson, bright purple, and deep blue. The sea reflected the colors, turning the distant horizon into one big collage of radiant color. Jordan gave my hand a little squeeze.

"Yeah. It is," he agreed. We stood in silence for a few minutes, in awe of the beauty around us. Then, Jordan gave a soft chuckle. "Hey, Amber. Do you ever wonder where you'd be right now if we'd never met? If I'd never run into you that day and made you drop all your groceries?"

I chuckled softly. "To be honest, yes. Once or twice," I admitted.

Jordan grinned. "Do tell," he prompted.

I sighed—a happy little sigh—and thought for a moment.

"Well … I could be across the world right now. Maybe Alaska or New York. Or maybe even Mexico," I said, laughing a bit. "Maybe I'd still be up in my apartment with neither friend nor foe to show for my existence, save for the pizza delivery man. Actually … I'd likely be dead." I shook my head. "Wherever I'd be, it certainly wouldn't be here. I don't really know." Turning to Jordan, I tipped my head. "And you? Where do you think you would be?" At this, Jordan smiled.

"Oh, I know where I'd be." He squeezed my hand again. "I'd be right here, where I've always been, doing the same old stuff I always do." He turned fully to me. "But I wouldn't be anywhere near as happy."

Suddenly, Jordan went down on one knee and pulled out a tiny box, opening it.

"Amber, I've never been as complete as I am when I'm with you. I can't bear the thought of life without you, and I want to spend the rest of mine with you. So, will you spend the rest of yours with me? Will you marry me?"

EPILOGUE

The Journal of
Amber Marie West

June 20, Saturday

This has been, apart from when I got saved, the best day of my entire life. But I can't sleep. I can't stop thinking about today ... I must write it all down, don't want to forget a single detail.

It took all my willpower to make myself go to bed last night. I was so excited, like I was as a child on Christmas Eve. Despite the fact I snapped awake at an unearthly hour this morning, I'd never felt more alive. The sunrise was absolutely breathtaking. Slowly trickling pink and gold scattered over the gradually brightening blue sky, a scene painted from Heaven, I'm sure. I want to always be able to picture it.

Chloe showed up first. I was so excited that I wasn't sure I'd be able to stomach breakfast, but she insisted that today of all days, I would need food. I believe her exact words were, "It is exceedingly important, and quite necessary, that you have a decent breakfast!" And she produced a box of breakfast pastries from among her other things. They were all strawberry flavored. Lexie came next, and the three of us reminisced for about an hour.

It wasn't long before I was surrounded by the best of my female friends. Once we got some excited chatter out of the way, we focused on the task at hand. I never had a "dress-up party" when I was little ... I almost wish I had. I was perfectly clueless! It was one big blur of dresses, shoes, hair, makeup, flowers, jewelry, and everyone asking everyone else's opinion on such things.

Together, along with some more experienced help, we managed just fine. Ultimately, I got into the most exquisite clothes I have ever worn ... the most beautiful dress I've ever seen.

Once that was done, the unbearable waiting ensued. If it weren't for my friends, I would have gone nearly batty. Yet, when it was finally time, I was so thrilled and nervous and scared that I could hardly move. Strawberry butterflies fluttered around in my stomach. The thought occurred to me that perhaps breakfast was a bad idea after all.

Fear, excitement, nervousness, ecstasy, bashfulness, insecurity, anticipation -- I can't list all the things I was feeling as I took those first few steps. But it all faded when I saw Jordan, because nobody and nothing else mattered. Everything was OK.

The next few minutes passed with hardly a thought, and the hours that followed have already blurred in my memory. All I knew was that Jordan was right there with me. To me, only the last few words truly mattered, though every word throughout the day was dear to me.

I had my first kiss ... and my second, third, and thirty-seventh. I danced in the arms of the love of my life -- this time, we knew how.

For once, Jordan and I didn't have to part ways when we said goodnight. He's fast asleep beside me, an arm around my waist. He's such a snuggler. A beautiful ring shines on my finger.

I love today. Today was our wedding day.